"We've Talked Too Much!"

Anger flared in Dane's eyes. Lowering his head, he took her mouth with his, sweetly bruising, holding her against him so that the lean harshness of his body burned against her, crushed her breasts.

She couldn't fight. He was possessing her with his hunger, dominating her completely. It was like being battered and beaten by a storm, but the most dangerous overwhelming crest of that tumult was building within herself.

She gave a little sob as her mouth softened, as her bones gave way and she was helpless in his arms. . . .

Books by Jeanne Williams

Bride of Thunder
Daughter of the Sword
A Lady Bought with Rifles
A Woman Clothed in Sun

Published by POCKET BOOKS

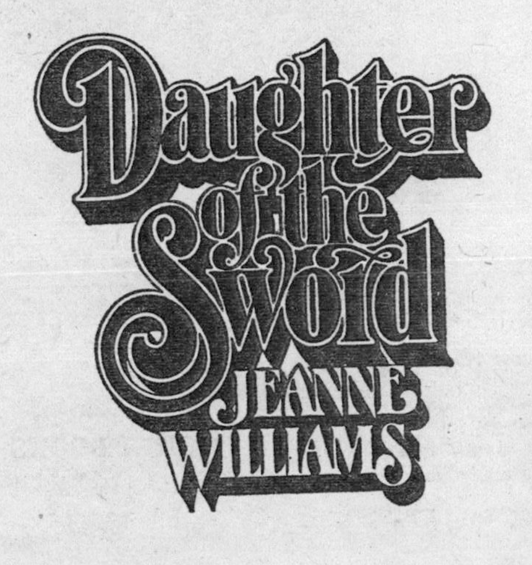

PUBLISHED BY POCKET BOOKS NEW YORK

Another *Original* publication of POCKET BOOKS

POCKET BOOKS, a Simon & Schuster division of
GULF & WESTERN CORPORATION
1230 Avenue of the Americas, New York, N.Y. 10020

ISBN: 0-671-82204-7

First Pocket Books printing February, 1979

10 9 8 7 6 5 4 3 2 1

Printed in the U.S.A.

For My Mother
I do not forget

Daughter of the Sword

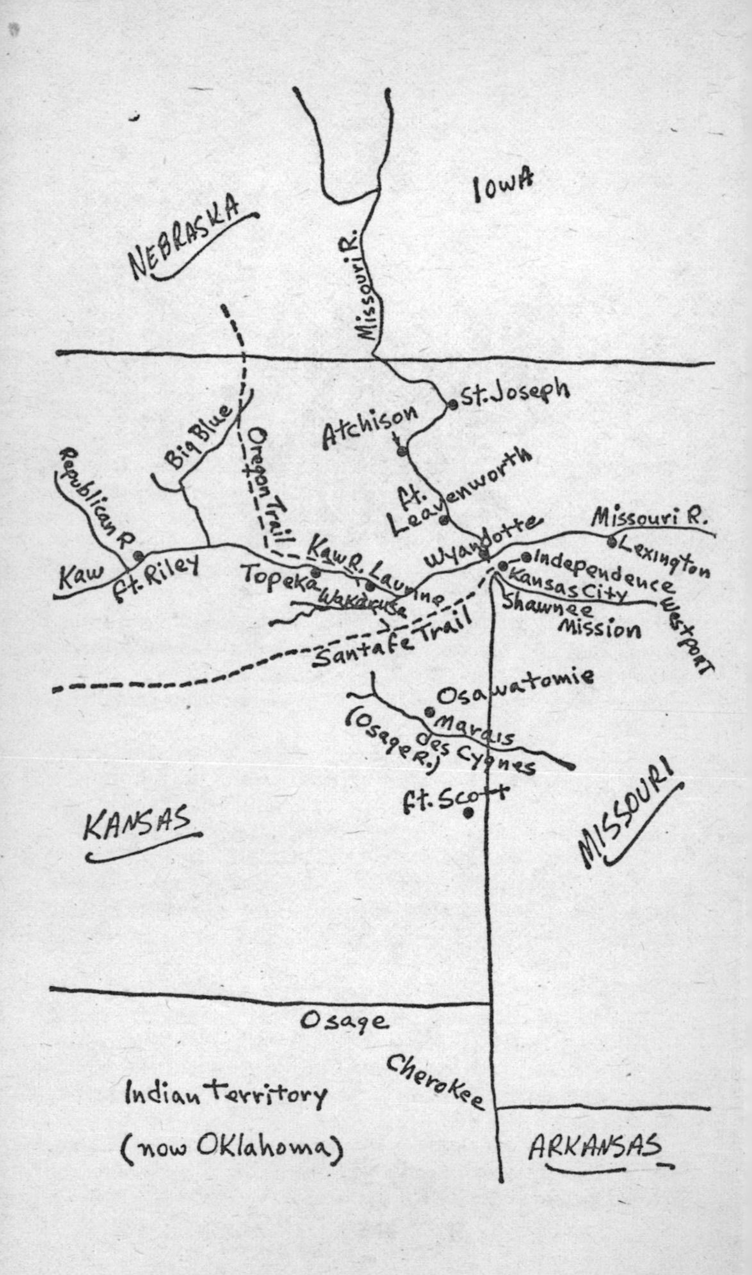
IOWA
NEBRASKA
Missouri R.
St. Joseph
Atchison
Ft. Leavenworth
Big Blue
Oregon Trail
Republican R.
Missouri R.
Lexington
Wyandotte
Independence
Kansas City
Kaw
Ft. Riley
Topeka
Kaw R.
Lawrence
Wakarusa
Shawnee Mission
Westport
Santa Fe Trail
Osawatomie
Marais des Cygnes
(Osage R.)
Ft. Scott
KANSAS
MISSOURI
Osage
Cherokee
Indian Territory
(now Oklahoma)
ARKANSAS

· i ·

Keeping her head back, left foot slightly forward, Deborah Whitlaw tried to parry her twin brother's blade, but he took her knife on his buffalo-hide-armored forearm and feinted beneath it, drawing her Bowie while he lightly traced a crescent that would have ripped her from side to side in the soft vulnerability beneath the ribs, except for the tough hide buckler she wore.

"If I were a Border Ruffian, you'd be dead!" Thos's eyes, usually soft russet, like Deborah's, glowed with a fire-edge of excitement.

Johnny Chaudoin, their teacher, lately a buffalo hunter, though first and always a skilled blacksmith who'd learned his trade from James Black, the maker of Bowie's fabled knife, shook his massive head. "Don't seem right for a lady to learn such tricks," he rumbled.

Deborah flung back her unruly mane of chestnut hair. "Better I know than not be able to protect myself or the people I'm with," she countered. "Since Thos and I are doing the same work, I need to know the same things."

"You shouldn't be into this in the first place," Johnny growled. "Your mother—well, she's a saint, but how she can keep you away from dances and still let you risk your neck with the railroad is more than I can figger. And you're only seventeen."

The Whitlaws and Johnny were conductors on the underground railroad that spirited slaves, mostly from the neighboring state of Missouri, to freedom in the north. Johnny's smithy was a "station," as well as a busy center for shoeing horses, making and repairing tools, harnesses, and wheels.

Much of this rough work was done by Maccabee, a giant Masai. Johnny alone made knives, though, and only for favored persons. He never quite admitted it, but his work was of such superior quality that it seemed certain that Black, his teacher, had given to him alone the secret of the blade that had been cremated with Bowie at the Alamo. When asked if Black had rediscovered the secret of Damascus steel, Johnny merely shrugged his huge shoulders and said he didn't know as to that, but Black had possessed that skill or something just as good.

While Johnny exhorted and excoriated his pupils in French, his grandfather's language, Spanish learned from trading with Comancheros, and the Sioux of his wife's people—never, in Deborah's hearing, had he cursed in English, though he said *"Tatanka espy!"* often enough for her to begin to suspect what it meant, since she knew *Tatanka* was the word for buffalo bull—Maccabee had been hammering out a wedge while Laddie pumped the bellows. Laddie was a warm-skinned, black-eyed youngster of eleven, orphaned younger brother of Sara Field, the Shawnee girl who cooked and kept house for the bachelor stronghold.

She appeared now in the doorway of the log building, which was really three log cabins connected by covered dog-trots. She and her brother lived in one, the large two-room center cabin was for cooking, company, and Johnny, and Maccabee had the flanking structure.

Because of the unusual amount of room, travelers frequently stayed at the smithy, but word had spread among the roughest of rivermen, hunters, and hell-bent Missourians that the comely Indian girl was not to be addressed in any but the most respectful tones. Johnny had sheared off the hand of one man drunk enough to try to handle her.

Sara didn't like knives and she usually timed dinner to interrupt a Bowie lesson. Maccabee signed with his hammer that he'd be along as soon as he finished his present piece of work and Johnny shooed the twins for the cabins.

"Don't ever let your mother know that I'm a-teaching you," he commanded. "I'd rather run the gauntlet than have her look at me stern."

"You may keep her from losing us," Thos reminded. "It's feather-headed to think we can smuggle runaways without being able to defend them." But as he looked at Sara, the fire in his gaze softened, and as soon as he'd washed up at the bench and basin outside the door, he spoke to her softly.

"Reckon we could have a ride after dinner?"

"I'm baking. The bread has to go in the oven after it rises."

"When will that be?" Thos sounded anxious.

He and Deborah had to be home in time to do evening chores. Father and Mother spent most days at the print shop in Lawrence and often didn't return till twilight, so the chores were left to the twins. Thos also helped put together and deliver *The Clarion of Liberty* after its more or less regular weekly publication.

In spite of his ability to sell advertisements and the special printing jobs that kept the press busy when *The Clarion* wasn't being set up, the family relied heavily on the garden Deborah tended, wild grapes, sandhill plums, blackberries, and nuts, eggs from their dozen hens, and milk, butter, and cottage cheese from their cow, Venus, so named by Father because of her generous endowments, the twins suspected, though he said it was because of her melting eyes and long lashes.

Thos brought in jackrabbits, wild turkeys, ducks, and innumerable prairie chickens, providing all their meat except the occasional side of bacon that paid for ads or a printing job, or the buffalo and antelope meat Johnny dropped off every autumn, pretending he had more than he could eat or sell. Deborah couldn't bear to eat what had been a graceful, fleet deer or antelope and was glad that Thos had never killed them.

The frontier was rough. They all did things that would have shocked them when they lived in New Hampshire, not just when conducting runaways, but in the way they lived.

Still, the mud-dabbed log cabin Johnny had helped them build last year was sheer luxury after a soddy, though perhaps the soddy, with its three-foot-thick walls, had been the best place to pass the terrible winter of 1856.

There were no soddies, though, at Johnny's. Stable, smokehouse, and well-house were of shakes, cured before use so as not to shrink much. The root cellar had been the dugout where Johnny lived his first winter in the region, but now it housed only potatoes, onions, and apples, which would keep nearly all winter in the cool, dry darkness.

Sara's garden, too, was much better than the one Deborah had planted, watered, and weeded with so much hopeful care.

In spite of Deborah's admiration for Mr. Fenimore Cooper's Mohicans and a predisposition, inherited from her parents, to find the red man an unspoiled child of nature, she found it humbling to be excelled in "civilized" skills by the Shawnee girl.

Sara could sew finer stitches, too, and was much better at knitting. Deborah sighed, then laughed and shrugged. She'd better become a good Bowie handler! It was her only chance to do something better than Sara.

But she really didn't mind. Sara was really her only friend of the same age. The young ladies of Lawrence bored Deborah, who preferred to spend the little free time she had walking out on the prairie or visiting Sara and Johnny. Of course she'd love to have a horse, but Mother and Father needed Belshazzar to pull the wagon. That left Nebuchadnezzar, who, for all the splendor of his name, was happiest grazing. Father said he took after the Babylonian king's phase when he was being punished by being turned into a beast and eating grass. However that was, he was indignant at being caught up and always eyed the twins with disgusted reproach when Deborah got up behind Thos.

"Go on with your ride," Johnny said now. "Reckon I can put the bread in the oven."

"It's my work," Sara protested, but her eyes lit.

Straight, black shining hair was clasped at the back of her head with a beaded ornament, and fine dark brows arched gently above slightly tilted eyes. Her skin was warm bronze and the primly high-necked and long-sleeved calico dress could not conceal the grace of her slimly curving form. She said now, smiling, "You mustn't spoil me, Johnny. How can you keep your mind on forge and oven at the same time?"

"Tatanka wakan!" growled Johnny. "Holy buffalo bull! If I burn that precious bread or let it run over, I'll make a new batch!"

"But Johnny," teased Sara demurely, "who'd clean up the floor? The last time you made biscuits—"

"Good, wasn't they?"

"Yes, what got in the pan."

Laddie grinned. "My sister say *'Cesli tatanka!'* many times, Shotgun, while she scrubbed the floor and table and cupboards and shelves."

Scowling abashed, for a moment, Johnny quickly recovered. "Your sis, young sprout, better not talk like that!"

"You say it," Laddie pointed out.

Johnny glared. "I ain't no young sweet lady." His outrage faded. *"Cesli tatanka!"* he breathed, stricken. "What all those old heifers said was true! I'm not fitten to have charge of you, Sara, now you're growing up!"

"Johnny! You—you're the most 'fittin' ' person I know!" Sara hugged him, drew back to stroke his grizzled face. "What would have happened to us if you hadn't taken us in? I'd rather have you than any blood parent!"

"No other father!" Laddie said decisively.

"You need a woman, Wastewin. Someone like—well, Mrs. Whitlaw, to teach you gentle speaking and what's proper!" Wastewin was Johnny's pet Sioux word for Sara. It meant "nice, good woman."

Sara's eyes flashed. Turning with dignity, she led the way to the scrubbed plank table with a bowl of wild flowers in the center. "I *am* grown up, Johnny. Isn't your food good? Your home clean? How have I failed you?"

"Now, doggone, don't you go twistin' what I meant into knots!" roared Johnny. "It's not my comfort I'm thinkin' on, though it appears I've let it put me to sleep when I ought to've been paying attention! Mrs. Whitlaw's offered to have you and—"

"Mrs. Whitlaw's a fine lady, but I belong here!" Sara's mouth trembled. "Unless you don't want me anymore!"

Taking his place at one end of the table, Johnny flushed red to the roots of his shaggy, white-streaked black hair. *If he shaved off that beard and sideburns, would he look so old?* What had gotten into him and Sara? It wasn't like either of them to flare up over nothing.

"You go riding." Johnny's tone allowed no argument. "You work too hard, too long." His voice softened, but Deborah, alerted to something unusual, detected pain beneath his words. "Play a little, Wastewin, play and be young. Don't get in a hurry to plumb grow up. All that comes soon enough."

Sara twinkled at him and the strangeness was gone. "Then I will go riding, and, thank you, sir! Take a nice helping of that sheep sorrel; it's good for you. And you, too, Laddie."

Both groaned but did as commanded. Deborah herself enjoyed the tart wild greens, especially after winter's dearth of fresh vegetables and fruit, but there was no excuse for the pickiest eater to go hungry from Sara's table, though Johnny liked to grumble that the blue "delft" stoneware dented the edge of the hunting knife he *would* use at meals. He preferred wooden trenchers.

Marble-sized new potatoes and tender peas in cream

sauce filled the biggest crock. There was hominy flavored with salt pork, stewed prairie chicken, juicily golden pies made from dried apples and peaches, but, most delicious of all, there were biscuits! Of fine wheat flour!

Such flour was used in the Whitlaw household only when a subscriber or advertiser paid with it. The staple for most Kansans was cornmeal.

Cornbread, corn dodgers, pumpkin cornmeal loaf, corn muffins, Indian pudding, griddle cakes, corn gruel—there was no end to the ways resourceful (or desperate) cooks found to use the unbolted meal ground at the mill after a family spent an evening shelling a washtub or barrel full of corn.

Cornmeal mush and hasty pudding, parched corn with milk, hominy, green corn, white pot made with eggs, molasses, and milk—Deborah stopped the all too familiar litany and had another crusty biscuit, closing her eyes to savor it as it fairly melted in her mouth.

Maccabee seemed always silent at meals, perhaps because he didn't fully trust any white besides Johnny, who'd bought him after his master, despairing of ever making him a profitable servant, had beaten him nearly to death.

Incredulous that anyone would buy "dog meat," the owner was glad to make anything off what he'd considered a total loss. But Johnny knew cures from his dead Sioux wife and had found lodging for himself and Maccabee with a kindly farm family till he nursed the great black man back to health.

Suspicious at first, hating all whites, Maccabee couldn't accept Johnny's good faith till the old hunter finally convinced him that he was free to go north, even to find his way back to Africa and the dung-plastered conical huts of his people.

Maccabee refused to go since his owner's lash marks would be forever on him as a sign of his bondage. He learned the smithy work, and when Johnny moved to Kansas Territory, longing to get closer to his old life on the plains, Maccabee came along. It was at his urging that the smithy became a stop on the way to freedom.

Now, his awesome presence loomed even more because of his reserve, but no one, satisfying their first hunger, spoke much.

As Deborah savored the succulent peas and potatoes, she reflected that blacksmithing paid better than journalism. Some customers, journeying west, even paid in cash for the shoeing of their horses or oxen, mended wagons or wheels or harness, though barter was the rule.

The scrupulously exact account book which Sara kept, since Johnny couldn't write and had no interest in such things, showed that he'd been paid in boots, steel, pans, old iron, cord wood, hogs, cloth, flour, corn, quilts, preserves, and game. One entry showed he'd made a new axle for the Whitlaw buggy in return for a subscription to *The Clarion* and some advertising.

These were concessions to Josiah Whitlaw's pride. Johnny couldn't read and he didn't need to advertise. He had more work than he and Maccabee could handle, especially during the summer months, when travelers and freighters bound southwest or for California and Oregon followed the Santa Fe trail south of the Kaw. Those going to the West Coast would cross the Kaw and follow the Big Blue River till they turned west along the Platte, but near Lawrence all westbound wayfarers followed the rutted tracks along the Kaw, which had probably first been buffalo and Indian trails hundreds of years before Coronado came searching for golden Quivira or French trappers and traders met the Comanche, or Zebulon Pike and John Frémont came exploring.

Forty-niners bound for California, troops dispatched to defend the frontier, Mormons seeking a new homeland, and since William Becknell's successful trip from Missouri to Santa Fe in 1821, thousands of wagons of goods for the Santa Fe trade. The headquarters of the freighting business of Russell, Majors, and Waddell was located near Fort Leavenworth. Father had recently run an article praising the firm's policy of fining teamsters who misused animals or swore, whereupon Johnny had muttered that out of the six thousand teamsters the freighters hired, he'd bet the best ones cussed.

Thos was reaching for at least his eighth biscuit. Deborah kicked him under the table. He winced and looked martyred till Sara offered him a quarter of the apple pie.

Real coffee was another luxury of Johnny's. With honey and thick cream, it completed the feast. Deborah suspected that though Sara always set a good table, she made an extra effort when Thos was expected.

Deborah volunteered to do the dishes so that Thos and Sara could be off. Maccabee and Johnny went out to drowse and smoke their pipes under the giant cottonwood that shaded the main cabin. Laddie filled the water buckets and the woodbox near the stove before he grinned at Deborah and settled down with the last piece of pie. He was faithful about work, but when he wasn't needed, he disappeared in the trees along the river.

The four loaves of bread rising beneath the clean dish towel on a shelf by the sunny window gave out a good yeasty smell. Peeking, Deborah was sure they had doubled. She poked up the fire, added a chunk of wood, and was putting the bread in the oven when Johnny came in with that silent, light tread of his.

"So!" He threw back his head and for a moment Deborah thought he was angry. She was glad when he chuckled. "You don't trust me, either, Miss Deborah?"

"I was just finishing up," she said, a bit flustered. "And the bread looked ready."

"And didn't I come in right spang on time?" he asked with great satisfaction. "You be sure and tell Sara so!"

"I'll do that, Johnny." Deborah slipped off Sara's apron and hung it on a peg. "Thanks for the Bowie lesson and dinner. I wish there was something we could do for you."

Johnny made a rude blowing sound through his moustache. "Holy buffalo! You talk like that and you'll rile me into botching that plowshare I have to make! Having you folks for neighbors is the best luck I could have."

"But it's you who's always helping us! You've got everything!"

There was a strange flicker in Johnny's dark eyes beneath the grizzled brows. "Think so?" he asked wryly before he grinned and shrugged. "Man can never have enough real friends. I rest a lot easier knowing that if anything happened to me, you Whitlaws would help Sara and Laddie. Maccabee would do his best, but the pro-slavers would try to get him if I was out of their way and Sara and the place were up for grabs."

"We'd look after Sara and Laddie, of course, but nothing's going to happen to you, Johnny!"

He said grimly, "Now, that's a thing no one can say, sure not in these bad days, Miss Deborah."

She looked at him in surprise. "But, Johnny, the worst must be over, surely? When we first came here, Border Ruffians were crossing from Missouri to steal elections, and pro-slavers burned Lawrence, and John Brown . . ."

She broke off, chilling at the memory. Two of the five pro-slavery slain, cut down by two-edged swords without a chance to defend themselves, had been little more than boys, killed along with their father.

The other two men were bullies, one a member of the pro-slave legislature, but Leticia Whitlaw had prayed a long time and been worn and haggard for days. Father's scathing editorial reported that Brown had, as usual, said the blessing at breakfast with the blood of his victims still staining his hands.

Pushing that dreadful memory away, Deborah said hopefully, "I know it took federal troops from Fort Leavenworth to put an end to all that, but except for wrangling over claims between Free-Staters and pro-slavers, things have seemed fairly calm."

"At least we've finally had a fair election and the legislature's mainly Free-State," Johnny said. "But those proslavers who were elected by Border Ruffians still hope to get Kansas admitted as a state under *their* constitution. President Buchanan's done everything to help them."

Deborah frowned. "Surely that won't happen. There's a bill in Congress to let Kansans vote again on whether to accept the pro-slave Lecompton Constitution. Now that we have a governor who won't let the Missourians steal elections, Free-Staters are bound to reject that pro-slave fraud."

"No use getting into a lather over it. War's certain-sure goin' to come. We're just catching it a little early." Dismissing the grim subject, Johnny squinted solicitously at Deborah. "Want Laddie to catch you up a horse? No reason you shouldn't have a ride, too, even if the love birds didn't ask you."

His tone was gruff, even harsh. Could he regard Sara as more than his ward, his foster daughter?

Impossible! He must be at least forty, and looked more. But men older than he did sometimes take young wives. Deborah stifled the shocking thought.

Johnny had more sense. Besides, Thos and Sara were so in love that it shimmered between them, an almost physical glow, so beautiful, so private, that it made Deborah feel shut off from her twin and best friend, very much without a man of her own, and also afraid for them. To be that happy, that touched with magic, must be tempting fate. And they were so young, only seventeen. *Oh, let them be all right,* Deborah thought.

"I think I'll walk over to the buffalo wallow," she told Johnny. "The wild roses should be thick. Thanks, but it's not far enough to bother with a horse."

"Well, take care you don't step in a prairie dog hole," Johnny teased, for she was continually doing that, gazing into the distance or watching a meadowlark take flight rather than having a care where she stepped.

"Better me than a horse," she countered gaily. For such stumbles could break a horse's leg, whereas she simply bruised her dignity.

She strolled to the forge with Johnny.

A flaxen-haired young man and woman had driven up in a wagon holding various tools and pieces of farm equipment.

"Conrad!" Johnny greeted. "And Miss Ansjie! I see you've brought the lot for me to fix."

"If you'll be so kind." The man's clear blue eyes rested with frank admiration on Deborah. He had a precise, slow way of speaking, and there was an old scar on his left cheek. "Shall we stop tomorrow on our way home from town?"

"I'll do my best," Johnny said. "Miss Ansjie, this is Miss Deborah Whitlaw. Miss Deborah, this is Miss Ansjie Lander and her brother, Conrad. They came here from Prussia!"

"Prussia!" Deborah echoed. "That's so far away!"

"Far," Ansjie agreed, blue eyes wistful before she smiled determinedly. "But this is a very good country—fine, rich soil."

The men unloaded the wagon and the pair drove off, Conrad settling his black hat back on his fair head.

"Nice folk," Johnny grunted. "He's sort of the leader of a group that has a funny religion, but they are mighty good farmers. They have a settlement about fifteen miles west."

"Why did they leave Prussia?"

"Nearest I can figger, Conrad was afraid the Mennonites were going to run into trouble. Thinks it won't be long before the government tries to conscript men into the army, and that's against their faith. He isn't a Mennonite himself, but they lived on his land and he felt responsible for them, I guess."

Johnny hefted a worn plowshare in a way that said he was ready to work, so though she was curious about the handsome young foreigners, especially the striking, authoritative man, Deborah said good-bye and set off on her ramble.

Angling away from the river, she took a dim trail that led to her favorite place, a grassy hollow worn by countless buffalo during the countless years they'd lain down there and rolled to comfort their itching backs. They never came here now, though vast herds still ranged the plains in less settled country.

Deborah had seen a few buffalo, but never great masses like those Johnny spoke of, where the large-headed humped bison stretched like a dark sea farther than the eye could see. From ancient times they had shared this vast open land, these oceans of grass, with Indians who depended heavily on them for meat, hides for robes and tipis, tallow, sinews for sewing, horn for ornaments and utensils. Every part was used, Johnny said, except the heart, which was put back in the earth, an offering to perpetuate the great beasts.

Now the Indians were being gradually compelled to give up their free wandering as towns and settlers edged into the prairies. The strife in Kansas had made eastern investors nervous about backing railroads, but in 1855 the first Territorial Legislature had chartered five railroads and a little track had been laid, some surveying done. When trains began rolling steadily across Kansas, bringing inevitable settlements and fences, the buffalo must vanish.

All their wallows would fill with grass and flowers as this one had. Their shapes seemed to loom and face on the horizon above the rippling buffalo grass, which seemed a new color each time the wind bent it in a different direction, a gently whispering ocean caressed by sun, with red-winged blackbirds taking sudden flight, and meadowlarks singing from their nests in the grass.

Fat black-and-gold bumblebees hummed busily around the pink wild roses that grew in little hollows. There was the clucking of quail and the occasional whir of a prairie chicken taking alarm.

Deborah, like her mother often homesick for the trees of New Hampshire, realized consciously for the first time that she loved the prairie now, its immense stretches where clouds in the sky, intensities of sun, created more changes than did the terrain. Of course, she could still turn from one of the small knolls and gaze back at the distant green line of trees tracing the river. But facing west there was only bluestem and buffalo grass in wave after undulating wave.

Till she came to the bank of the wallow.

The flowered and grassy earthen bowl was perhaps fifty feet long and deep enough so that a man would have to be well over six feet tall to look over the rim. A giant's bathtub, she thought it, and sighed, because she'd hoped there might be enough water to swim.

Splashing about in the sun-warmed water was a rare delight, one that Deborah suspected would be disapproved of by her mother, though Deborah couldn't see why bathing beneath the sky was shameful.

There wasn't enough water to wash in today, though, just a few shallow pools thick with roses. There had been plentiful rains that spring, but water soaked fast into the sandy loam.

She could wade, though, wiggle her toes. Kilting up her full calico skirt, she descended the bank, overgrown with daisies, buttercups, tansy, and black-eyed Susans and the dainty white flowers of wild onion.

Sitting down, she unlaced her shoes, rubbing the red marks left by the high tops. Mother let her go barefoot around home in warm weather. Shoes were expensive and only for Thos, whose feet had grown considerably since he was fifteen, had *Clarion* advertising been bartered for new footwear.

Johnny and Sara had made moccasins for all the Whitlaws, which were used for winter house wear, and Deborah looked forward to the time when these tight, uncomfortable "civilized" shoes wore out and Leticia had to let her go moccasined or barefoot.

Giving the shoes an unloving toss to the side, Deborah thrilled to a distant call and glanced up, shielding her eyes, to follow a lopsided wedge of wild geese flying north. Glinting white and silver-gray, they were tiny specks in the dazzling sky when Deborah wished them a safe journey and, holding up her skirts, stepped into a grassy pool full of buttercups and daisies.

Her feet caressed the grass as she sank ankle-deep. Moving carefully in order not to crush the flowers, she sighed with sensuous pleasure. Free-Staters, pro-slavers, *The Clarion*, the underground railroad, and threat of civil war all seemed far away, like troubled dreams from a humid night of storm and lightning.

This was real. And it was always here, peaceful beneath the sky. It would remain after all these present troubles passed. She must remember it when she got tempery or worn down, quiet and strengthen her spirit with it as Mother did by prayer. Deborah's prayers, except for grace at meals and family worship, were spontaneous thanks for beauties, indignant pleas over injustice, or brief inner cries for help. It wasn't, for her, a means to grace and harmony, though this present communion was, this feeling of being part of the day, part of where she was.

A sound penetrated her bliss. At first she tried not to hear it, but the insistent clamor grew louder. Hounds! She knew hounds were sometimes used to trail runaway slaves, though she'd never seen it. Her heart contracted.

If it were a runaway, what could she do? Ironically, the Bowie she was learning to use was at Johnny's, who insisted the twins be experts with the blades before they could keep them. But she couldn't do *nothing!*

No time to lace up awkward shoes. Deborah ran from the middle of the wallow, splashing heedlessly, pelted up the bank, saw a gray-yellow form streak toward her.

A coyote! It was being coursed by dogs. Deborah had a fondness for coyotes, even though their liking for chickens necessitated shutting the hens up at night.

Amazingly, the animal stopped by her, panting, tongue lolling, exhausted, his golden eyes fixed on her. He couldn't go farther. In his desperate state he seemed to actually be seeking refuge.

How could she give it? No sticks or rocks, no weapon—But her shoes were within reach. She grabbed them by the tops, one in either hand, and let her skirts down to better shield the coyote, which took refuge behind her, pressing into the folds of her dress as he might have taken shelter in a bush. She braced herself as the barking dogs came over the rim.

Four of them, large blue-tick hounds. Deborah, though cautious of strange ones, wasn't fearful of dogs under normal circumstances, but these were excited, striving after quarry. She knew her only hope to save the coyote was to face them boldly, somehow halt and confuse them.

Was their owner close behind, or were they having this sport on their own? Deborah thought she heard a grass-muffled drum of hoofbeats, but it could be blood pounding in her ears. Anyway, help wasn't to be expected from someone who'd set four dogs on one coyote.

"Scat!" she shouted and aimed one shoe at the lead hound.

It struck him on the head. He yipped, then stumbled as the shoe fell between his legs. Another hound tripped over him. There was a tumbling welter of long ears, tails, and legs, but the other hounds came on.

Deborah swung the shoe from its limber top. The hard

leather heel hit the nearest dog on the nose. He yelped and veered to one side while she kicked at the next animal and clouted him with the shoe, once again striking the vulnerable muzzle.

He checked, then launched himself for her arm, but his teeth only slashed the cloth and grazed her flesh. She kicked him in the side so hard that her toes ached, sending him off his feet, but the other hounds were back now, moving in.

They weren't giving up. Aiming kicks and swings of the shoe, Deborah knew she couldn't hold them off much longer. If they all came at once, one or two could drag the coyote from her skirts while she was battling the others.

The biggest hound circled, barking furiously, then attacked on the left. Deborah hit him with the shoe, and as she went off balance, the dogs surged in.

• *ii* •

Screaming, she fought the hounds with hands and feet, trying vainly to ward them off their victim. There was a gray-yellow blur as the coyote ripped at one hound's flank, tore at the throat of another, as they swarmed over him. Sobbing, Deborah hauled one dog off. The coyote was down, bleeding. In a minute they'd have him.

A piercing whistle rang out. The hounds checked, growling, still snapping over their prey. But the man on the blood-bay horse cut at them with his whip, giving that shrill whistle again, and they cringed away.

Deborah dropped by the coyote, but he was up, swaying for a moment. Blood stained his hair in patches and he favored one forefoot, but he made off swiftly, vanishing over the bank of the wallow while the dogs whined and protested, though they settled down to rest after a sharp cut of the whip in their direction.

For just a moment, the horseman watched Deborah from eyes so dark a green they were almost black, the imperious arching of tawny eyebrows easing as he smiled. Springing down from his mount, trailing the reins so the horse would stand, the stranger swept off his hat with mocking courtliness. The rakish, wide-brimmed hats had become very popular because one was worn by Louis Kossuth, the Hungarian patriot.

"You must, madam, have a great fondness for prairie wolves!"

His accent was different from any she had heard. His uncovered hair was dark gold, and from that distance he seemed the tallest man she'd ever met, towering above her, his physical presence so overwhelming that, involuntarily, she stepped back.

"I dislike seeing anything run to earth and torn apart!" Angry to have given ground, Deborah added coldly, "I especially hate such things when they're done for sport."

The jade eyes probed, though a smile touched the edges of a long, well-shaped mouth. She had never seen before a man to call beautiful, but this one was, in a fiercely haughty way, like young Lucifer before his fall.

"Chasing coyotes is thin sport, I agree, compared to encountering such an unexpectedly delightful lady."

Taking her hand, he held it between his large ones for a moment. A curious weakness afflicted Deborah. She had no strength in her legs, was terrified that she might faint or collapse in this man's arms. That she mustn't do! Fighting the dizziness which she told herself was a result of her battle with the hounds, Deborah drew away, but the stranger, laughing slightly, retained her hand. Bowing over it, he kissed her fingers.

"Most lovely lady, I'm Rolf Hunter, lately of Hampshire, in the south of England. Have you a name, or are you a guardian spirit of this grassy dell which is, I believe, known rather unpoetically as a buffalo wallow?"

"I'm Deborah Whitlaw," she said briefly, this time wrenching her hand away. "I suppose I must thank you for calling off your hounds, though I do think it's shameful to use them in such a way. Good-bye, Mr. Hunter."

Catching her arm, he brought her back to face him. She cried out as his fingers gripped the forearm grazed by the hounds. He looked at her torn sleeve, the shallow but bloody trail of fangs.

"You're hurt!"

"It's nothing. A few scratches."

"You look like the losing side in a bout with a tiger! Hold still, Miss Whitlaw, and let me see how much you're hurt!"

"I do assure you—"

"And I assure you that I mean to make certain you've taken no serious harm! It's no wonder the dogs took you for quarry, though. With that pointed chin, red-brown hair, and eyes the color of late autumn leaves, you could be a very winsome little fox."

Somehow, he had maneuvered her into what was perilously near an embrace, pretending great interest in her torn sleeves, gently exposing her arms as he examined them, his sure, hard fingers moving along the weals and scratches in deft caress. Deborah shivered and braced her palms against his chest.

Beneath her hands, she felt the deep, heavy pound of his heart. Once again, a mixture of fear and a new, frightening, yet headily pleasant awareness of him made her feel as if she didn't know herself, as if some unrecognizable and dangerous part of her nature had roused at this man's touch, was responding to it in a way that shocked and terrified her.

"Please!" she said. "Please—"

The golden head brushed lightly against her breasts as he bent to kiss the small wounds on her arms and hands. Against the trapped pulse of her wrist, his mouth lingered.

Whatever this is, I have to stop it!

He was on one knee beside her, cradling her with one arm. Throwing her weight sharply and suddenly against him, she sent him pitching forward, but as she fled, one long arm swept out, brought her down beside him.

"Well, my pretty!" He laughed. "If you lay me down, you must lie with me!"

He might be joking, but Deborah knew the biblical meaning of *lie,* though somewhat hazy on details. She kicked, surprising a curse from him, thrashed desperately as he clamped her down with one knee and leg, catching her head in one hand while the other gripped her wrists.

His mouth still tasted of her blood. Bruising her lips, he stopped her screams. She felt as much as heard the soft, excited laughter deep in his throat, knew herself powerless, yet convulsed in frantic writhing as panic welled up in her, drowning her ability to think or even know.

"Rolf!"

Drifting back to reality, Deborah heard the name like a repeated echo, stirred unbelievingly as the crushing weight above her shifted. She opened her eyes, then dazedly saw another horseman. His gray eyes flicked past her scornfully to rest on the man who was getting to his feet, brushing off his clothes.

"At first I seemed to be intruding on a tender scene." The newcomer's voice slashed like a razor. "But then the lady seemed to change her mind. She has that privilege, Rolf."

Furious at that interpretation, Deborah pushed herself up. "Sir!" she began.

Rolf put a steadying hand beneath her arm, gave her a reassuring smile which made her long to throttle him, and eyed the rider with a quizzical grin. "You do Miss Whitlaw an injustice, brother. You've misjudged the whole thing."

Those cool eyes touched Deborah again. A faint scar marked one prominent cheekbone. Straight black brows were bent in an accusing frown, but he took off his gray hat and bowed ironically.

"Then I must cry your pardon, Miss Whitlaw." His tone dismissed her, hardened as he gazed at the man who kept his hold on Deborah till, angrily aware of it, she pulled away. "Perhaps, Rolf, you'll explain what I've misjudged? I let you out of my sight five minutes and somehow, even on this prairie, you're up to your old tricks!"

"God provides," said Rolf piously. "Besides, honored brother and preceptor, it was more like half an hour than five minutes. Let you get your paints out and you forget everything but whatever weed or clump of grass you're doing."

The man on the steel-gray horse relaxed slightly, but his lean jaw was still set. "I'm waiting to be enlightened."

Rolf's dark green eyes widened for a moment, pupils swelling, before he shrugged. "The hounds ran a coyote into this wallow. He took refuge in Miss Whitlaw's skirts. She fought off the dogs with more valor than discretion, as you can see by the condition of her . . . ah . . . sleeves."

The newcomer's gaze touched her again. His mouth tightened and he sprang from the saddle, tossing the reins in front of his horse. "Are you hurt, Miss Whitlaw?"

He wasn't as tall or broad as his brother, but there was a leashed power about him, a driving but controlled energy that intimidated her, made her cross her arms in a shield, though there was nothing she could do to hide the blush that heated her face.

"I've been scratched worse picking blackberries," she said briskly.

Rolf Hunter lifted an eyebrow. "You see, Dane? I was trying to be sure she wasn't injured, she objected, and the result was what you saw."

"I begin to understand." Dane Hunter's tone was dry. "Miss Whitlaw, my brother and I must be sure you're unharmed and escort you home." He had stepped in front of her as she moved for her shoes. "Please let me see those bites."

"They're nothing!" she insisted. "Thanks for your concern, but I really must hurry or my brother will be worried."

"He might well be with a sister like you," said the older Hunter. "Put out your arms, Miss Whitlaw. I'm no fonder of wasting time than you are."

The cold remoteness in this man's gaze said he thought her a crack-brained nuisance, but he'd do his duty for all that. Reluctantly, she held out her arms.

He examined them carefully, impersonally drawing back torn cloth when it concealed a graze. "You're lucky," he said with a nod of his black head. "Rolf, get some whisky to sluice over those scratches." He glanced at her feet. "Were you bitten anywhere else?"

"No!"

Rolf rummaged in his saddlebag and produced a silver flask. He also had a rifle in a scabbard near the saddlehorn, and a brace of rabbits on the other side. Deborah backed away.

"I—I don't want to smell like a saloon!"

"You'll certainly have to wash and mend the dress," Dane said. "Your parents would rather have you reek temporarily than have you exude the stench of suppurating putrefaction. I've smelled it in field hospitals, my stubborn girl. One welcomes whisky to blot it out."

At that withering derision, Deborah could do nothing but extend her hands and brace herself against the sting of the pungent rinsing. It hurt, but she suspected it was a wise precaution. She thanked Dane Hunter with as much graciousness as she could muster before she collected her shoes.

"You needn't see me home," she said. "I'm meeting

my brother at the blacksmith's near the river, not two miles away."

"Young women shouldn't junket about the prairies alone, as this afternoon's happenings might convince you." Why was Dane's voice so brutal? "Your foolhardiness, thank Providence, is no worry of mine after today, but I'm going to see you home or to your brother. Put on your shoes."

"You've no right to order me about in that offensive tone!"

"Put on those shoes or I'll do it for you." His lip curled. "I had expected American women to be sensible. Instead, you wrestle hounds bare-handed, tussle in the grass with my reprobate brother, refuse well-meant treatment, and now propose to gad off alone across the plains. I can't alter your usual mode of behavior, but circumstances make me responsible for you till you're safely with your people. Then, praised be a merciful God, you're your family's problem!"

Halfway through this flaying, smarting at Dane's unfairness but sure that he'd carry out his threat, Deborah turned her back to the brothers and struggled into her stockings and shoes, concealing her feet and ankles with her skirts. Dane Hunter wouldn't look, or care if he did, but Rolf had a different temperament. Or was it the same one, shaped and altered by different influences, just as Johnny took steel and made from it a knife or a plowshare?

With his scarred cheek, talk of field hospitals, and dominance over his giant younger brother, Dane seemed an outlandish choice for a painter of wildflowers, but perhaps he was one of those English eccentrics like Sir Richard Burton, Lord Byron, or William Blake. It was obvious from their dress, horses, and manner that the Englishmen were well-to-do—which still gave them no right to manhandle and insult people! Rolf may have first simply intended to flirt, but inexperienced as she was, Deborah sensed that the feel of her had ignited passion and her struggles had further aroused him.

What would have happened had Dane not interfered was vague and frightening in Deborah's mind, mixed up with the times she'd seen animals coupling. Leticia had never explained such things to her, but Deborah had gleaned enough from remarks, reading, and observation to know that this hidden thing between men and women was potentially full of happiness or unspeakable shame. And she wondered how, after years of concealing her body and avoiding more than a handshake with men outside the family, she'd be able, even married, to let a man see her.

Well, she didn't want to marry for a long, long time, if ever! As she started to rise, Rolf helped her. The clasp of his hand sent a wave of alarm through her, but with it tingled something keenly sweet, like cider on the turn.

As if he guessed the sensation, Dane jerked his head toward his handsome gray gelding. "Can you ride? Lightning's gentle, but he won't tolerate a heavy hand or sawing bit."

"Thank you, I can walk," said Deborah, though she longed to ride the magnificent animal. Rolf's horse was also beautiful, but so big and given to tossing his head about that she was afraid of him.

Dane shrugged. "You'll ride, either alone or up behind me."

"But my skirt—"

"Oh, the devil with it! Here, you sit modestly in the saddle and I'll hold you on."

Before she could retreat, he'd swept her up and placed her in the saddle sideways, thrust a foot in the stirrup, and swung himself up behind, his arms encircling her as he held the reins.

"Dane, you pirate, I saw her first!" protested Rolf.

"Keep your hounds under control," Dane advised. "Now, Miss Whitlaw, you say the blacksmith's is near the river?"

The short ride was quickly over, yet it seemed very long to Deborah. Sit stiffly erect as she might, the horse's motion brought her in rhythmic contact with Dane Hunter's arms. She gripped the saddlehorn and gazed stonily ahead, but there was no way she could escape his closeness, the faint smell of bay rum and fragrant tobacco. She wanted to steal a look at the face, sometimes touching her hair, but was afraid of detection.

Why did he seem intent on disliking her? Clearly, he thought her hoydenish and rash. Did he think, too, that she'd somehow encouraged Rolf before taking fright?

Deborah lifted her chin, taking comfort in the thought that when this interminable ride was over, she'd never see these arrogant Englishmen again.

Or would she? Jolted into breaking silence, she asked urgently, "You—you're just traveling through?"

"You could say that, though we're taking our time. We have lodgings in Lawrence, but we'll spend most of our time on the plains."

"Dane intends to paint his way across the Territory to the Rocky Mountains," groaned Rolf. "And I had to either come with him or go to India and work for our uncle."

"There's still India," Dane said unfeelingly.

Rolf shook his head. "I'll stay with you," he said cheerfully. "In spite of your trading your sword for a paint-brush, there's a good chance we'll meet some hostile Indians, and there are sure to be buffalo. I'll find something of interest."

"Something to kill?" Dane asked dryly.

Rolf chuckled. "Oh, come now, elder brother! If I hadn't enjoyed other pursuits more than shooting, Father wouldn't have banished me."

"It's a pity you couldn't have been at Balaclava or Sebastopol. There's nothing like real, dirty, unromantic war to tame wild blood."

Rolf sobered. Again, Deborah thought he could have been young, proud Lucifer plotting rebellion. "The damned war ended before I could get sent down permanently from Oxford, but I'll find a war someday, and it won't tame me! I *know* I was made for fighting, Dane, for hunting and wenching and riding the crest of the breakers."

"That Viking nonsense again," Dane snorted.

"The blood runs thin in you, not in me!" Rolf flashed. Hat off, wind tossing his rich golden hair, he could indeed have been one of the warriors so feared by the people of England that the Litany included a plea to be delivered from the fury of the North men. "You tasted war and found it bitter. It will be my wine. You paint Indians. Before this tour is up, I pray for a chance to fight them. When they see my scalp, won't they want it?"

"A few weeks in an army hospital would purge you of this boy's lunacy," Dane said. "It's a shame Mother wouldn't let Father buy you a commission so you could have helped put down the Sepoy Mutiny."

"Isn't it?" agreed Rolf. "I'd love to have taught those niggers a lesson, slaughtering all those British women and children at Cawnpore less than a year ago, rebelling against their officers and Queen!"

"Niggers?" Deborah was startled into asking.

"It's a term bigoted illiterates sometimes use for Indians," Dane explained. "The Sepoys are native Indian troops, some of whom staged a bloody revolt that was put down last year. But I suppose you have read about it."

"Yes, a little," Deborah said apologetically. "We're so beset with our own worries here in the Territory that I'm afraid we don't pay much attention to what's happening in other countries."

Rolf chortled. "When we hear about your problems, we always say you'd have been much better off to have remained a colony. You'd have been saved this slavery row, for one thing, because it was abolished throughout the Dominions in 1840. And think of the advantages of having a government so far away to blame for everything while mostly you could do as you pleased!"

"My forebears were English," Deborah said indignantly. "But they didn't voyage here to submit to tyranny and perpetual interference!"

"That war's over," said Dane, almost jokingly. "Let's not start another one."

No one spoke the rest of the way to the forge.

Thos came forward to meet them and Johnny turned his hammer over to Maccabee, striding to the head of Dane's horse. "You be all right?" he asked Deborah. Only when she nodded did he survey her escort and say, "Howdy, strangers."

Slipping gladly down into Thos's outstretched arms, Deborah introduced the brothers, then briefly explained that she'd tried to protect a coyote Rolf's hounds were after.

"Good way to get mauled," Johnny growled, taking in her torn sleeves and skin. "Lucky these gentlemen came along. Let Sarah have a look at those arms, Miss Deborah—no argufyin', now! Gentlemen, why don't you have a drink now and stay on for supper?"

"Thanks, Mr. Chaudoin," said Dane. "You're most hospitable, but we should be starting for Lawrence."

"Then stop at our place to eat," Thos invited warmly. "It's on the way to Lawrence, and our parents would want to meet anyone who'd helped Deborah."

She bit her lip, longing to say that Rolf had kissed her forcibly and his sarcastic, superior brother had seemed to blame *her* for it, but such accusations could provoke a fight. She wanted neither Johnny nor Thos to endanger themselves. Still, she couldn't bring herself to reinforce Thos's invitation. Turning away, she avoided his puzzled glance as she started for the house.

"You're very kind," Dane said to Thos. "We really should make for town, though. I hear the roads aren't always safe after dark."

"I'll protect you," Rolf teased. "And I shall sup at the Whitlaws', brother, whatever you decide!"

Deborah couldn't hear Dane's response because Sara met her at the door and drew her into the house, wrinkling her nose. "You smell like a brewery! And your dress! What've you been up to, Deborah? Who *are* those men?"

Deborah gave an expurgated account while the Shawnee girl rubbed goose grease into her scratches and added her opinion to the prevailing one that Deborah was fortunate to have escaped serious injury.

"Was I just supposed to let the dogs tear that coyote apart?" Deborah asked hotly.

"No, *meshemah.*" Sara used the Shawnee word for sister. "But you must consider what an action may cost. Your life is worth more than a coyote's."

"Would it be, if I let an animal die like that?"

Sara kissed her. "You're what you are, and my best friend. The strangers are handsome. Do you like them?"

"No! They're patronizing, lordly, and so . . . so English it makes me want to kick them! Why ever did Thos have to invite them to supper?"

"You didn't tell me everything that happened," Sara observed with a slow smile. "But never mind now. Thos has Nebuchadnezzar ready, and you'd better go before he pretends to be lame. Here's a loaf of bread for your mother, and give her my love."

Deborah thanked Sara, who waved good-bye from the door. Thos handed Deborah their dejected-looking mount's reins while he ran back for a few words with Sara. Deborah again faced the problem of what to do with her skirts. Drat Thos! If he hadn't invited the Hunters to supper, she could have ridden with skirts to the knee, and no harm done! As Thos came back and started to climb into the saddle, she said under her breath, "I think you'll have to let me ride in front. My skirts—"

"Your skirts?" he blurted out.

She pinched his arm, then noted that Rolf was quelling laughter, and even Dane's eyes twinkled. Stung past modesty, she put one foot in the stirrup, gathered her skirt, swung her other leg over the saddle into the opposite stirrup, and settled her dress as concealingly as possible.

"Good for you, Miss Deborah," applauded Johnny. "Now you're showing sense!"

Thos gaped, shrugged, and clambered up behind the saddle, holding her around the waist. "See that you don't make us both fall off," he hissed in her ear. "What's got into you?"

"I'm tired of being female!" she hissed back at him. "I'm tired of skirts and not being able to ride astraddle and . . . and lots of things! So you just hold on tight, brother, dear!"

What a shame that Nebuchadnezzar, unmoved and unknowing, couldn't summon up a bit of dash and fire! But he plodded along, dreaming of the corn he got after being ridden, and Deborah gritted her teeth as the Englishmen rode on either side, holding in their horses and answering Thos's eager questions.

Annoyed at his friendliness, Deborah dug her elbow into his chest. "Ouch!" he winced. "Why'd you do that, 'Borah?"

He plunged on, establishing that the brothers had crossed the ocean in ten days in a Cunard iron-clad liner, spent some weeks in the north and south, then traveled by steamboat to Leavenworth and spent a month there, acquiring horses and Rolf's hounds and picking up information about their proposed route while Rolf hunted and Dane sketched. They had only last night arrived in Lawrence and had found, in the home of Mrs. Eden, a widow, lodgings much more comfortable and private than the hotel. Deborah stiffened at that. Melissa Eden acted demure, but she carried herself in a way few men could ignore.

When Rolf disclosed that his brother had fought in the Crimean War, Thos plied Dane with questions and refused to be daunted even when Dane pronounced the Charge of the Light Brigade to be the greatest folly in a war beset with blunders.

"Practically nothing was known about the Crimea—the terrain or conditions," he said. "Lord Raglan, one of our two seventy-year-old field commanders, was so confused that he kept calling the enemy 'the French' even though the French were finally fighting beside us, not against. Half the army was wounded or sick during that first winter, and because the campaign hadn't been intelligently planned or provided for, cold and hunger added to the misery. The only good thing to come out of the wretched mess was the way Florence Nightingale cleaned up the hospitals and saved countless lives. A lot was learned about military medicine and treatment. But so many were wasted, so many young men! And for what? The Turks made some dubious promises safeguarding Christians in their territories, and the Russians agreed to keep their ships out of the Black Sea."

Thos frowned. "But, sir, surely the feat of allied arms was amazing! Invading an unknown region, defeating the enemy on his own ground with far fewer troops and those often ill and poorly equipped!"

"We had the Minié. The Russians didn't." Dane shrugged and the scar along his cheek seemed livid. "They bayoneted us and we blew them apart. Their priests blessed them, our chaplains blessed us, and we became a sacrifice, they protecting Holy Mother Russia, we defending, at bottom, our access to India."

Thos ignored the moral for the unedifying facts. "A Minié, sir? What's that?"

"It's a conical bullet dreamed up by the French, weighing five hundred grains. It shoots harder and straighter, maybe five times as far as the old round ball, and is practically guaranteed to shatter any bone it hits, which the round balls seldom did." Dane's mouth turned down. "Is it progress, Miss Deborah, when weapons become more lethal?"

"You men have always found excuses to slaughter each other. I suppose it doesn't matter whether you do it quickly or at leisure."

" 'Borah!" cried Thos. "How can you say that when you're learning to use a Bowie knife?"

"What?" choked Rolf. He looked at her in astonished delight. "Not the Bowie?"

Dane said nothing, but the startled expression in his gray eyes goaded Deborah far more than Rolf's mischievous glee.

"You don't understand our circumstances," she said austerely.

"I think we do," countered Dane. "Every brigand in Leavenworth had one or two Bowies and several pistols, as did most passengers on the steamboat. But I'll confess I hadn't suspected women, even in Kansas, felt it necessary to go armed."

"We don't," snapped Deborah. "But I could have wished this afternoon, sir, that I'd had the Bowie!" Thos stared at her and she recovered hastily. "But it's well I didn't, since you came in time to haul your hounds off the coyote and me. It would've been a pity to hurt the dogs for obeying their master."

Rolf threw back his head and laughed. "You wouldn't have scrupled to carve on me?"

"No."

"Be warned, brother," said Dane in that intolerably superior way that made Deborah's hackles rise. "These Western women aren't at all what you're used to. You'd best stick to hunting buffalo."

"That's a comely woman at the blacksmith's," said Rolf. "Is she Indian?"

"Shawnee," said Deborah. "My dearest friend."

"I'd like to paint her," Dane mused. "That was an intriguing group: the smith, Indian boy and girl, and that huge black man. Is he a slave?"

"Johnny bought and freed him." Deborah was reluctant to discuss her friends with these overbearing strangers.

"Do you think they'd let me do some studies of them? They could go about their work and I'd just sketch what struck me."

"You'd have to ask Johnny—Mr. Chaudoin, and then see if the others were willing." Deborah gnawed her lip, hating to say still another thing that would add to his conviction that she was an indelicate, unfeminine savage —though why should she care?

She didn't give a fig for Rolf's opinion. Why should Dane's matter? It did, but as to *why,* she was too bewildered and resentful to sort out just now. She only knew that for everyone's sake, she must make Sara's position clear. "Sara Field and her brother are like adopted children to Johnny. It's thought by some whites that all Indian girls are ready game because Indian ideas about marriage and . . . and all that are different from ours. Sara thinks lots of white ways are crazy, but she was educated at Shawnee Mission. The man who wants her will have to get married in church."

"Or that formidable smith or giant blackamoor will get him if you don't first slice him up with your Bowie?" Rolf grinned. He cocked his head at Dane. "Can you imagine Pater's face if either of us came back with an Indian wife? Gad, it's almost worth doing for that alone!"

Thos sounded breathless. "Miss Sara has an understanding!"

"Oh, is that the way of it?" whistled Rolf. At Dane's scowl and Thos's rather wild look, he added good-humoredly, "I'm sure I wish them happy, the Indian maid and her favored swain. But I still think it would be a rare jest, Dane, if our American trophies included a daughter-in-law for Sir Harry."

Dane said nothing, though his face was set. Deborah concluded that Rolf enjoyed baiting his older brother and that it sorely tried Dane to hold his tongue, though argument would merely push Rolf into more reckless assertions and, no doubt, actions.

It was also humiliating to hear them discuss an American bride in the way they'd have spoken of a Hottentot. Deborah took solace in the thought that if the pair did stay for supper, which she heartily hoped they wouldn't, since she wanted nothing more to do with either of them, Mother and Father would demonstrate, even to these prejudiced Englishmen, that Americans could be cultured and gracious even though they worked hard to scrape together a living and lived in a crude cabin.

How, at that moment, she wished ferociously that they were still living in the soddy! That would give these sons of obviously rich *Sir* Harry something to write home about! Especially if a spider or baby field mouse dropped into their plates!

That happy thought improved Deborah's spirits, but as they approached the cabin and sod outbuildings, she looked at them as strangers would, as she had when freshly come from New England, the bark-covered logs of the cabin dabbed with mud, while from the sod and grass roof, wildflowers and weeds grew as thickly as on the ground. The cabin was much easier to keep clean and much lighter than the soddy had been, with four windows instead of two, but snow *did* blow in through the cracks during the heaviest storms.

The soddy had been warmer in winter, cooler in summer, but so dark, and, worst of all, in spite of the cheesecloth fastened to the rafter poles, bits of root and grass and plenty of bugs and spiders dropped regularly from the layer of brush, the layer of prairie grass, and the final covering of more sod.

And when it rained!

Deborah grimaced. If rain was from the north, that

side of the roof soon began to leak and the bed and pallets had to be moved to the south; when south rains came, they were moved north.

And for days after the sun was bright and the outside air was fresh and sunny, the roof dripped sullenly into every bucket, kettle, and pan that could be spared.

After one torrential storm followed by a steady all-day drizzle, the rafters had sunk deep into the walls and the roof sagged till it seemed certain to cave in. Father and Thos had gone to the river and cut several stout posts with which to prop up the overburdened rafter-poles.

Fortunately, it hadn't rained again for a month, so they escaped real disaster, but Mother had given thanks with special fervor when they'd moved out of the soddy, which, rafters propped up by more posts, served now as a stable.

Chickens clucked, making for the coop where they'd be shut up safe for the night, Venus was over by the stable, standing companionably by Belshazzar, who whinnied and ambled forward to meet his pasture mate, who gave an answering and heartfelt response.

Rolf ordered the hounds away from the chickens, enforcing his commands by slashes of the whip, which sent the dogs huddling off behind the house.

Mother and Father, thank goodness, were already home, and the familiar smell of frying jackrabbit and cornbread drifted out.

"I'm afraid we're late," said Deborah, "and we'll have to hurry with our chores, so you'll excuse us for making rather hasty introductions."

Dane frowned. "We'll ride on to Lawrence. Stopping at this hour is presumptuous."

"*You* may go to Lawrence," drawled Rolf, "but I'm invited to supper, and I'm staying."

"But of course you'll both stay!" called Father from the door. "You must be the English brothers everyone in town's talking about! Let's take care of your horses, and then you must meet Mrs. Whitlaw and share our table." He came forward, putting out his hand as the Hunters dismounted. "I'm Josiah Whitlaw."

The brothers introduced themselves and Deborah was glad to see the respect and swiftly hidden surprise in their expressions. Father was in shirtsleeves, his dark trousers were worn shiny, and his fingers were permanently stained from setting type, but he was carefully shaved and his diction was as cultivated as that of his guests.

Leaving them to him with vast relief, Deborah handed her mother Sara's gift of light bread, quickly explained her ruined sleeves, and carried skim milk and cornbread to the subdued hounds, fetching them a pan of water before she fed the chickens and collected five eggs from the hay nests in the coop.

Usually Thos milked Venus, but he'd been rubbing down and watering the horses, lingering over the sleek blood bay and handsome gray as he gave them some corn. He was patting Nebuchadnezzar a trifle guiltily as Deborah passed him with the pail.

"I'll milk," she told him. "You still have to bring in wood and water."

"Thanks, 'Borah." Thos gave her a searching look. "I have to clean those rabbits, too. Young Mr. Hunter gave them to us. Cross your heart?"

It was an old code between them, asking for and promising complete truth, which Deborah at that moment wasn't sure she cared for. "Don't wheedle, Thos! You'd best tend to your chores."

The setting sun reddened his hair as he blocked her way. "Don't *you* get skitterish, my girl! Did either of those fellows say or do anything they shouldn't?"

"It's a fine time to worry about that, isn't it, now you've asked them home and Father's met them?"

Thos flushed. "Quit beating around the bush, or I'll wait for them on the road to Lawrence and see what they have to say about it."

"Oh, for heaven's sake!"

"No. For yours."

She couldn't lie to him; he'd have known it immediately through that extreme sensitivity they'd always had to each other. But neither could she let him fight either of the older, bigger men.

"I was terribly angry at Rolf Hunter for chasing the coyote, and when he tried to look after my scratches, I . . . well, we got into sort of a muddle, which his brother interrupted."

Thos's brows knit. "Did he insult you?"

"Good gracious! Some women might have thought it flattering!" Deborah forced a laugh, giving him a shake. "It's over, nothing's wrong, and though I'd rather not have that conceited pair in our house, they'll be a change for Father and Mother. You, too, from all the questions you were asking."

"I don't see how an officer could give up his commission and start painting posies," shrugged Thos, but, his protective brotherly conscience relieved, he hurried off. He was clearly fascinated by the Englishmen. He'd always loved heroes. Given half a chance, he'd make one of that grim Dane Hunter.

Vexed at the thought, Deborah stripped the last of Venus's milk into the frothing bucket, carried it to the well-house, and poured it into crocks so the cream would settle on the top for skimming. She washed out the pail and set it upside down on the bench, counted the eggs in another crock, saw there were fourteen, enough for Mother to trade at the store.

The cream crock held almost enough for churning butter. Father could trade the new butter because there was still a pound or so left from the last churning. It was only during the past month that they'd felt rich enough to use butter instead of making do with pork drippings and sorghum. There'd be butter on the table tonight, butter and Sara's fresh loaf, as well as cornbread.

Deborah took a deep breath. There was nothing else to do, no other chores, nothing to check on. She had to go in.

And face the strangers.

• *iii* •

Rolf and Dane rose from the round table as she entered. Rolf presented his chair to her so insistently that she let him seat her while he took the other side of Thos's bench.

It hadn't been possible to bring all their furniture from New Hampshire, and what there was, though comfortingly familiar, looked incongruous. The polished legs of Mother's rosewood pianoforte stood on the rough plank floor with the oval-framed portrait of her mother above it and a cut-glass bowl of wild roses on the top beside the thick leather-bound Bible handed down through generations of Father's family.

Father's big roll-top desk was in the print shop, but beneath one window stood a shelf of treasured books with his globe and atlas on top. Over by the fireplace, which was used for cooking, stood the rocker in which Mother had rocked the twins through teething, night frights, and colics, or while she sang or told stories.

A tall china cupboard held delicate porcelain that had been one of Great-Grandmother's wedding gifts, but the stoneware for everyday use sat on homemade shelves. The heirloom silver was used every day. Wear made it more beautiful, Leticia said, and it couldn't break.

There were napkins on the table, too, and tonight Deborah was glad of that, though she hated to iron and loathed wash day above all things. The crude plank table near the fireplace was used for preparing meals, but the dining table was from the east, polished cherrywood with four matching chairs.

In the cabin's other room was the feather-mattressed four-poster where the twins had been born, a bureau, the sewing machine, and a large chest that held bedding and out-of-season clothes. In a curtained-off corner, Deborah slept on a wooden frame criss-crossed with rawhide and covered with a corn-shuck mattress.

Thos had the same kind of bed in the lean-to attached to the south side of the house, though in summer he pitched his mattress in the open. Deborah would have liked to join him and drift off to sleep watching the stars, but her mother flatly refused. One more mark against the odious state of being a female!

Father said the blessing and then passed a platter of rabbit to Dane.

It's not that I mind being a woman, Deborah thought, taking a generous helping of the dandelion greens she had gathered and washed before going to Johnny's. *I just hate being told I can't do this or that and having to wear these cumbersome skirts!* Rolf gave her a side glance and she increased her grievances.

It's wretched, too, that some men are strong enough to treat you any way they please. And I think it's awful that the first man's kiss I ever had tasted of my own blood! I'm going to ask Johnny to let me carry my knife. He will if I tell him someone gave me a fright. And if I have my

Bowie . . . well, then we'll see how enterprising Rolf Hunter is!

At this thought, she smiled so benignly at Rolf that he looked first amazed, then elated. She smiled with equal sweetness into Dane's disapproving eyes and added rabbit, gravy, and a slice of Sara's bread to her plate.

Josiah, bless him, was bragging about Lawrence and how there had been churches and schools almost from the start, in marked contrast to most frontier towns, where a saloon was considered the first necessity.

"The Congregationalists organized Plymouth Church in October of 1854," he said. "We met in a hay tent till it burned down, and then any place we could find till we finally built our good stone church last year. It's a sweet sound on Sunday morning, the church bells in the valley."

"Lawrence does seem a much more substantial and progressive town than most on the frontier," Dane said.

"We have the best buildings in the Territory, the finest hotel, newspapers, and a literary society besides schools and churches." Josiah's dark eyes twinkled and he closed his hand briefly but warmly over his wife's. "Mrs. Whitlaw thinks I'm wearying you. Of course, compared to England, Kansas is a raw, rough place. But we've cast our lot with it, sirs, come here with other like-minded folk to see that Kansas enters the Union as a free state. We hope for this prairie land and we love it."

Rolf was looking bored, but Dane remarked that the people of Lawrence seemed a very different sort from those of Leavenworth.

Mother sniffed, Thos grinned, and Father took a long drink of water. "Leavenworth's full of land speculators, the hangers-on around a military post, and a good many Missourians who keep a foot on both sides of the border, though it's not as bad as it was."

"When we said we were coming to Lawrence," Rolf chuckled, "the mildest thing our landlord said was that it was a nest of doggoned, viperish, Free-State nigger-loving abolitionists."

"Well, Lawrence *is* the Free-State citadel," shrugged Josiah. "We've been under siege twice. In 1855 Sheriff Jones, who was actually a citizen of Missouri, arrested a number of Free-Staters and set fire to the Free-State Hotel after his cannon didn't demolish it. His men wrecked my press and scattered the type before doing the same thing to *The Herald of Freedom*. But the hotel's rebuilt—

the brickyard made 168,000 bricks for it—the presses are running, and our little town prospers."

Dane spoke thoughtfully. "As an editor, Mr. Whitlaw, you must be a special target for pro-slavers. Wouldn't you and your family be safer in town?"

"In New Hampshire the print shop made a comfortable living, but it's another tune here, sir! We must raise as much food as possible. I hope, in time, to have a dairy and devote myself to that and farming when the struggle for the Territory is over, spending only a few days a week at the shop."

Deborah refilled cups with "coffee" made from parched wheat and molasses cooked together till they were almost burned, then cleared away the plates while Leticia took the lid off the cast-iron Dutch oven and cut slices of apple corncake, asking Deborah to bring in a pitcher of cream to pour over it.

When she returned from the well-house, Dane was saying, "I don't perfectly understand, sir, how western land's acquired by settlers. To travelers from a part of the world where all the land's been claimed for centuries, your vast wilderness is mind-boggling!"

Josiah explained the Preemption Act of 1841. Any head of a family, single man over twenty-one, or widow could claim one hundred sixty acres of public land so long as they'd swear they weren't settling on the land in order to sell it, hadn't agreed to turn it over to someone else, didn't own three hundred twenty acres elsewhere, and had never preempted before. Having filed and sworn, the settler could buy the land at the appraised price, which was generally $1.25 an acre.

"Then the land's surveyed first and there are government offices to handle claims?"

"Very often not." Josiah shrugged. "As soon as land's opened, settlers pour in and claim parcels. Land offices don't open till a territory's surveyed. I filed my claim with the office of the United States Surveyor General a year and a half before the Lecompton land office opened two years ago. Then the early claims were put in the regular books."

"The Indians must not look on settlers with much favor," Dane commented dryly. "Don't they consider this prairie theirs?"

Leticia cast her husband a significant glance. Settling on former Indian land had been her sole objection to coming west, and the issue had been fervently debated at the Whitlaw table.

"The Territory's going to be settled," Josiah had argued. "And it won't help Indians or anybody to let pro-slavers have it!"

It was Leticia, deep blue eyes troubled, who answered Dane. "Indians' rights are very muddled in Kansas, Mr. Hunter. To start with, there were the Kansas and Wichita, Pawnee, Osage, and those who came through to hunt, like the Kiowa, Comanche, Arapaho, Cheyenne, and Jicarilla Apache."

"Didn't they fight?" asked Rolf, sitting up eagerly at the name of Comanche.

"They had their raids and battles, because especially to Cheyenne, Comanche, Kiowa, and Pawnee, being a great warrior was the aim of every man, and stealing the horses of another tribe was almost as prestigious as killing its braves."

Rolf laughed and his eyes glowed like foxfire. "They have the Viking spirit. I look forward to meeting them!"

"Most westward travelers pray not to," said Josiah. "What's made a real mess in Kansas has been settling eastern Indians here from as far away as New York to Missouri, at least eighteen different peoples who gave up claims to their eastern lands in return for grants in Kansas."

"Which were to be theirs as long as grass grew," Leticia added.

"You met Sara, who's Shawnee," Deborah put in. "They started moving here from Ohio and Missouri in 1834, built log houses, and began farming very successfully on their reservation, which was over a million and a half acres. They had the first gristmill in the region."

"And back in the Twenties, Daniel Morgan Boone, the old frontiersman's son, was hired by the government to teach the Indians better ways to farm," Thos said. Old Boone was one of his heroes.

"Quaker, Baptist, and Methodist missionaries set up schools and missions," Leticia added, as if taking consolation in that. "One, Reverend Jotham Meeker, published the first Indian-language newspaper, *The Shawnee Sun*."

"That was in 1835." Josiah cast such a longing look at his empty cup that Deborah jumped up to fill it. "Meeker later published the first book done in Kansas, a collection of Ottawa laws."

Dane was frowning, clearly puzzled. "If these tribes have legal claim to much of the land in this Territory, how can it be settled by whites?"

"The government made treaties with the tribes."

"Who had no choice!" interposed Leticia.

Father made a weary gesture. "I know, Letty! Still, legal forms *were* observed. The Indians *were* compensated, given some voice in deciding what was best for their people. The Wyandot, for instance, mostly chose to become U.S. citizens and took individual grants of what had been reservation land. The Shawnee kept two hundred thousand acres bordering Missouri, some taking separate farms of two hundred acres apiece, or holding land in common. They'll get tribal annuities for the rest of their land, paid out over a number of years. And the Osage still have their land."

"They won't as soon as enough settlers want it," persisted Leticia. "They'll be shoved off to some other place that whites don't see a use for, probably to Indian Territory, where Andrew Jackson sent the Cherokee and other Civilized Tribes!"

"Dear lady, you astonish me!" Rolf's lips tucked down in a cynical smile. "What can happen, after all, when superior numbers want something from people not mighty enough to withstand them? Besides, as I understand it, nomadic Indians drift over vast expanses of hunting grounds, though they don't grow crops or have permanent settlements. As a practical matter, can a few thousand savages monopolize land that would provide rich farms for people from your overcrowded sections and the emigration from Europe that is certain to increase? You've already got Swedes, Irish, and Frenchmen. Given a chance for almost free land and a chance of doing well for themselves, you're going to get thousands of settlers from the British Isles alone."

"I know what will happen." Leticia Whitlaw's firmly delicate chin came up. She gazed at Rolf till he colored. "That doesn't mean I think it's right."

"Yet, madam, here you are," he scored.

"Yes."

Dane gave his brother a stern look. "It's clear, Rolf, that Mr. and Mrs. Whitlaw weighed and pondered before deciding to come here, and also clear that the West will be settled."

"Have you changed your oft-voiced opinion, brother, that the Indians are greatly wronged?"

"No. But one might as well defy the ocean as a swelling tide of land-hungry people who see immense tracts going to what they can only consider waste." He smiled at Leticia, and Deborah marveled at the change it made in his lean, scarred face, till now aloof or mocking. "Do you play the pianoforte, Mrs. Whitlaw?"

"It's my great pleasure," she admitted shyly, "though there's seldom time for it."

Deborah glanced at her mother incredulously, at the soft color in her cheeks and unusual glow. A few tendrils had escaped the French knot securing her wavy, light brown hair. Deborah had always taken for granted Mother's gently curved slim figure, but now, watching her as a stranger might, as Dane was, Deborah thought: *Why, she's pretty! Mother's pretty!*

Along with pride came a stab of—was it jealousy? Deborah pushed that horrid thought away. It was only that Dane had rescued Mother, obviously admired her, while he was so bitingly cold and censorious to Deborah.

"It would be my great pleasure to hear you play," he importuned.

"Do, Letty," urged Father. "You haven't played in a coon's age. In fact, I've been wondering if you wished you'd brought the cookstove instead of your pianoforte."

That had been the choice, one she'd never murmured about even on the hottest days, when cooking on the grate placed in the fireplace, or when the Dutch oven baked something black on the bottom and raw inside.

"I'm out of practice," she demurred.

"You'll still sound delightful," Deborah said, rising. "Please, let's hear you, Mother! Thos and I'll do the dishes."

So chairs were moved near the gracious little corner, where the pianoforte, portrait, and flowers made it possible, so long as one didn't notice the mud-chinked logs, to imagine this was their comfortable home in New Hampshire, an illusion quickly banished for Deborah as she measured stringy soft soap into the dishpan, poured in boiling water from the kettle, and tempered it with water from the drinking bucket.

The work went quickly, though, Thos rinsing and drying, while Mother played Mozart and Brahms and Chopin with a sure touch for each composition, be it sprightly or somber. As it grew dark, Josiah lit the brass Phoebe lamp, and in its soft flickering Leticia looked heart-catchingly lovely.

She played Father's beloved "Annie Laurie," "Come Where My Love Lies Dreaming," and she yielded to Thos's entreaties for something gay: "Pop Goes the Weasel" and "Sweet Betsy from Pike." Josiah asked for "The Star-Spangled Banner," and the Whitlaws sang it, standing around the pianoforte. With a quick smile at the Englishmen, Leticia struck up a stately tune Deborah didn't recognize till Dane and Rolf sang "God Save the Queen" in rich baritones.

"Thank you, Mrs. Whitlaw," said Dane, bowing. "One's national anthem always sounds sweetest when in another country. But it grows late. We mustn't infringe longer on your hospitality."

"Just one last song." Josiah rested his hand on his wife's shoulder. "Letty, will you play Mr. Whittier's "Hymn of the Kansas Emigrant?"

Deborah's clear voice rose above her father's and Thos's in this rousing song that had thrilled her since she'd first heard it back in the east.

"We'll seek the rolling prairie,
In regions yet unseen . . ."

They were into the second stanza when a clamor of barking arose, reaching a frenzy as hoofbeats pounded up to the door.

"Come out, Whitlaw!" a hoarse voice yelled into the shocked silence. "Show yourself, you damned abolitionist, or we'll burn you out!"

Mother caught his arm. "Don't Josiah! They may shoot you down!"

"Do you have weapons?" asked Dane beneath his breath.

"Just an old shotgun," whispered Thos.

"Load it," ordered Dane.

Josiah called to the men outside, his voice steady, though his lips seemed bloodless.

"Who are you? What do you want?"

"Never you mind who I am, you blue-bellied Free-Soiler! I want my nigger wench!"

Leticia rose swiftly and went to the door, though her husband tried to stop her. "She's not here, and this is most discourteous of you, brawling up to our home, threatening us! Would you like your own families treated so?"

"By God, ma'am, we don't war on women if they act like women!" growled the leader. "It's your man we want to see!"

"I'll go," Josiah said, but Dane caught his arm.

The intruders sat in their saddles beyond the light from the house, surrounded by the barking hounds. It was impossible to see them, but from the squeak of saddles and shifting hooves, there seemed to be at least four or five.

Rolf muttered, "Keep them talking! I'll climb out a back window and get my rifle from the saddle scabbard. Dane, you'll be ready here?"

"You mustn't risk yourselves," Josiah began, but Dane grinned at his brother.

"I'll be ready."

Josiah put Leticia out of the doorway. "You see me, stranger. Will you step into the light so you can be seen?"

"I'll step into your house is what I'll do, 'cause I think you've got my Judith hid away."

"Look for yourself," said Josiah.

There was the groan of a saddle. "Sit tight, boys, but cut loose with your guns if you see anything funny. We can do for this Yankee like we did for that Free-Soil scum yesterday at Marais des Cygnes."

"Marais des Cygnes?" echoed Josiah, as a tall, raw-boned man with scraggly black hair and beard strode across the patch of light and loomed in the doorway. Dane had stepped into the bedroom with the shotgun. "What've you done?"

"You'll want to print it in your filthy paper, won't you?" The gangling man smelled of whisky. The leather thong around his neck usually meant an Arkansas toothpick hung on the other end. He had a pistol at either side and another knife sheathed at his belt. Thrusting his face close to Father's, he shifted his cud of tobacco and laughed.

"Ain't you the lucky one, gettin' it straight from the horse's mouth?"

"What?"

The stranger was enjoying his game. He cocked his head and gave Deborah a randy look before he grinned at the elder Whitlaws. "You've heard tell of Cap'n Charles Hambleton? Fine gent from Georgia, settled in southeast Kansas and got run out by you damned Free-Soilers."

"I heard Captain Hambleton was charged with horse-stealing," Josiah said grimly.

"You must hear plenty of lies to fill your rag so full of 'em! But those Free-Soilers who drove the Cap'n out of his place ain't laughin' much now!"

"What have you done, man?"

"I just kind of lucked into it," the black-haired intruder said modestly. "Me an' my friends here were chasin' that damned Judith when we met up with the Cap'n and a few dozen other spunky Missouri lads. When they said what they were doin', we just naturally had to throw in."

Josiah's voice slashed like a blade. "What did you do?"

"Why, the Cap'n had a list of the worst Free-Soil rascals. We rounded up eleven, then herded 'em into a gulch that runs into the Marais des Cygnes River. When the Cap'n gave the order, we shot the bastards down."

"You killed eleven unarmed men?"

"Six look like dyin', and five dead," preened the killer. He chuckled at the Whitlaws' horror, adding truculently, "Ain't it exactly five unarmed men your goddamned abolitionist John Brown cutlassed to death at Pottawatomie Creek two years ago?"

"If you read my paper, you'd know what I thought about that!"

The Missourian spat on the floor. "Don't signify what you think, Yankee! Just keep out of my way whilst I look for that high-yaller!"

A glance convinced him no one could hide in this room. He ducked to enter the bedroom, then gave an astounded grunt as a shotgun poked into his belly.

"Have your look," Dane commanded. "I've killed too many men to want another on my soul, even as sorry a one as you. I want you to see for yourself the girl's not here. Then if you *do* come back, I promise that I'll kill you."

The Missourian's jaw dropped. "Who in hell are *you*—some new breed of Yankee? Cain't hardly make out a word you say!"

"Try," Dane said, shifting the barrel slowly around to his captive's back. "Go ahead! Look under the bed and in the chest and behind the curtain. Then you can search the lean-to, the stables, and, if you like, the chicken coop!"

"My boys'll cut you down in your tracks the minute we step outside!"

"Will they?" Dane laughed harshly. "Too bad for you, then, since a shot from them means I blast you wide open."

The night rider seemed to understand *that*. Jumpily glancing over his shoulder at Dane, he bent for a perfunctory glance under the bed. Deborah held the lamp so he could see, then pulled aside the curtain so he could tell there was nothing there but her bed and nothing beneath it.

Dane, receiving a nod of consent from Leticia, lifted the chest lid to reveal tight-packed bedding and clothes.

"Satisfied?" he demanded.

The scraggly man nodded. "Cap'n Hambleton was sure the gal would be brought here if'n she was helped by some gang of nigger-stealers. But maybe she slipped off on her own. She got sweet on my best buck." A leer showed stained, broken teeth. "It was interferin' with her duties, so I sold him off. She took on worse'n a white woman, and a lady, at that! Took a butcher knife to me when I was tryin' to comfort her. I reckoned a whippin' would settle her down. Wouldn't have thought she could move for a couple of days, but she sneaked off that night." He shifted his cud. "Looks like you don't have her, Whitlaw. Me an' the boys'll mosey along."

Dane said to Josiah Whitlaw, "Shouldn't we turn these men in to the law? By this one's own boast, he's done murder."

Leticia laid her hand on Josiah's arm. "You can't let him go; he'll track down that poor woman!"

"What *can* we do?" Josiah said, tormented. "If we turn them over to the militia, they'll be lynched—provided we could capture them to start with! But if they go to trial, with a pro-slave judge sworn to uphold the slave code foisted on us by the Bogus Legislature, they'll be acquitted."

Dane spoke slowly. "You're saying there's no justice in this Territory? No legal way that this man will be tried and punished?"

Josiah shook his head. Deborah knew he was thinking of the dead and wounded at Marais des Cygnes, felt with him a great wave of grief, outrage, the need for vengeance, yet the shrinking from becoming judge and executioner. Deborah knew her father was struggling, praying for guidance. Should he loose this man who killed wantonly, beat women, hunted them as he would animals?

"I'll see to him," Dane said abruptly.

Deborah's breath flowed out in relief.

The man would die. But the deed wouldn't be on Father's head, or his to do. Dane was a soldier; he'd killed before, killed men who were doubtless infinitely better than this wretch. She couldn't have killed him herself unless he were attacking, but thinking of a fugitive colored girl, thinking of eleven men taken from their families and murdered, as Father might have been tonight if the Englishmen hadn't been here, Deborah felt no pity for the Missourian.

"Jed!" came a shout from outside. "What's takin' you so long? If'n you found your gal, you ought to pass her around!"

"Say you'll be out in a minute," Dane grated.

The man obeyed in a hoarse croak. His burned-coal eyes darted wildly from Josiah to the women and Thos. But Leticia was already confronting Dane.

"You mustn't do it," she said, "for your own sake more than his."

"What then, madam?" Dane's eyes were as cold as a winter storm sky.

Something passed between the determined man and the fragile older woman, something of spirit and will, love and courage. "Leave him to God, son."

"God?" cried Thos. "How can you talk of God and this . . . this . . ."

"Enough, Thomas!" Josiah laid a hand on his son's shoulder. It was the first time Deborah could remember hearing her brother called by his proper name within the family. Still, Josiah seemed released from some vision of inevitable apocalyptic terror as he turned to Dane. "My wife is right, Mr. Hunter. Since we can't bring him to man's justice, we must leave him to the judge of us all."

Dane's gaze flicked to Deborah, as if he were trying to read her thoughts. Then, facing the elder Whitlaws, he gave a brief nod. "It's yours to decide. But Rolf and I will escort these men far enough to discourage them from coming back here." He added to the trembling Missourian, "Remember what I promised earlier: if you come back, you die."

"I'm not comin' back!" The man's craggy Adam's apple bobbed up and down. "The law can hunt my nigger like it's supposed to do; I don't aim to get shot by some funny-talkin' furriner!"

Reprieved, he was looking jauntier. Deborah thought she read his mind. "You can't follow this gang, Mr. Hunter!"

she protested. "You're outnumbered. They'll start an uproar in the dark and kill you."

"Not if we have their guns and knives."

He smiled at her without mockery for the first time. An amused tenderness in his eyes and voice that startled Deborah reached into her heart with a thrill of joyful recognition so powerful that it hurt. She knew this man! She knew him in her depths, as if they had been two halves of Plato's sundered being and couldn't be content till reunited.

It was a magical high moment, everything else in suspension, till Dane turned to Thos. "Will you collect their weapons in some kind of sack? We'll deposit them in some deep, muddy stream. These gentlemen will go home with their fangs properly pulled."

"You cain't take our guns!" Jed's Adam's apple seemed about to disappear down his scrawny throat. "After this morning's business, those Free-Soilers'll be riled up like a den of rattlers! If we meet up with them, we'll be helpless as babes!"

"Like the men you killed," said Dane brusquely. And to Thos, he asked, "Are you ready?"

Thos nodded, having found the sack in which cornmeal was brought home from the mill. Mother looked at it with regret, but evidently she decided it couldn't go to better use, as Thos took Jed's knives and pistols and dropped them into it.

"My brother's in the stable with a rifle," Dane told Jed. "So we'll walk out in companionable fashion, you a little in front so this persuasive shotgun won't show, and if your friends regard your life, they'll hand over their arms."

Jed cast him a scared, venomous look but didn't argue. At a prod of the shotgun, he started to go outside. "Keep away from the door and windows," Dane warned the Whitlaws. "Somebody may get off a shot."

Obeying, Deborah stood with her parents to one side of the door, nerves screaming as the men's footsteps faded into the mingled sounds of restless horses and riders.

"Good evening, gentlemen!" Dane's voice was deep and pleasant. "Don't do anything sudden or Jed will have a large hole through his vitals. You won't be hurt if you do as you're told. Put your hands over your heads and keep them there. Rolf, why don't you step out so our guests will know you've a rifle to their backs—a Sharps breech-loader, gentlemen, with which I'm sure you're familiar!"

"One of Beecher's Bibles, compliments of that infernal New England Emigrant Aid Society!" growled one raider.

"Not at all," said Rolf. "I bought this pride and joy with my own money. Picked off a brace of rabbits today at up to five hundred yards."

There were metallic clinkings and muffled curses as the weapons were collected. Deborah began to breathe. It was working! In a moment the Missourians would be on their way.

A shot exploded. Oaths, the sound of plunging horses, two shots blasting almost at once, screams, a cry of agony. Both Whitlaw women started out, but Josiah caught them back, pushing them to the floor.

"Thos—he isn't armed!" Deborah cried.

"He can use something from the bag," Father said grimly. "Stay here! I'll go through the back window."

Casting about for a weapon, he seized the poker and vanished through the bedroom. More shots came from outside, anguished groaning, before the staccato hoofbeats of a galloping horse echoed back, dimming as they reached open prairie.

Lying on the rough planks, mother and daughter stared at each other, then sprang up as Josiah leaned in the door. "Bring the lamp! Young Mr. Hunter's hurt. One of the ruffians got away, but Thos had his guns."

"Thos?" asked Mother, running forward as Deborah brought the lamp.

"He's fine. But I don't think Jed and two of his friends will do any more night riding."

Deborah held the lamp while her parents and Dane examined Rolf, who was leaning against Thos. "Someone had a pistol tucked away and tried to get Rolf because of the Sharps," decided Dane. "You're in luck, my boy. The cartridge went through the fleshy part of your shoulder. I'll plug you up and in a few days you'll be as good as new."

Rolf touched one of the bodies with his foot as Dane and Thos got him to his feet, supporting him between them. "Dead? These three—all dead?"

None of them had moved. Josiah knelt by them, touched and listened as Deborah, raising the lamp, saw one face blown away and gasped with nausea. Controlling herself with great effort, she heard Josiah say, "They're all dead. Here's Jed on the bottom. Got caught in the cross-fire."

Mother took the lamp from Deborah's hand, leading the way to the house. "Come, dear, and get hot water. There's an old sheet in the chest. Tear off some strips. Here, Thos, Mr. Hunter, just bring him along to the bed."

"What about *them?*" Deborah whispered to Josiah, moving her head toward the tumbled heap of what had been living, breathing men.

"We can't help them," Father said. "They'll be seen to later."

He helped ease Rolf's coat off while Deborah hurried for water and washed her hands, then tore strips from the sheet as Mother washed the torn shoulder and stanched the blood with pads. Rolf's face was clammy, but he endured it all stoically.

"Would someone fetch the flask from my saddle bag?" he muttered. A contorted smile flickered at Dane. "For once you can't blame me for wanting a drink!"

"You'll have it." Dane dropped his hand on his brother's good shoulder. "And we'll slosh some over that hole."

He went out and quickly returned with the same flask from which Rolf had drenched Deborah's arms that very afternoon. It seemed an age ago. Mother took the soaked pad away. Dane poured the amber fluid on the wound, then lifted Rolf to reach the back. Rolf said something under his breath. His hand closed tightly on Deborah's, gripping harder as Dane worked the whisky into the mangled flesh. Responding as she would have to anyone's pain, Deborah put her other hand soothingly over Rolf's taut fingers.

Straightening from his task, Dane cast her a strange look before he offered the flash to Rolf. Reluctantly freeing Deborah's hand, Rolf gave her a crooked grin. "Thanks, Miss Whitlaw. Much better than biting on a nail! I hope I didn't crush you."

Green lights reflected from the darkness of his eyes as they rested on her, lingered on her mouth. Was he remembering that kiss, the kiss tasting of her blood? Deborah flushed, but she managed to keep her tone even as she handed strips of sheet to her mother, who had applied fresh pads and was now binding them tightly in place.

"I'm sorry you're hurt. We're very much indebted to both of you."

"That we are," agreed Father. His face was drawn. He seemed to have aged years in the past hour. "Even after three and a half years in this ravaged territory, I have no real weapon but my press—which wouldn't, tonight, have protected my family."

"I'd have used the shotgun," Thos growled.

"No doubt," said Josiah. "We'd have done our best. But I sadly fear it wouldn't have been enough." Shaking his head as if dazed, he spoke in a stronger voice. "I'm forced to believe you, Mr. Hunter. I have no right to expose my wife and daughter to pillagers like those! Letty—"

"We'll speak of it later, Josiah," said Mother briskly. "Mr. Hunter needs something warm and nourishing! I think there's enough meat left for broth, and since rabbit's not so tasty, I'll flavor it with onion."

She busied herself at the fireplace. Deborah tucked the sheet back in the chest, threw out the bloody water, and cleaned up the spots on the floor, thoughts turning irrepressibly to the three dead men near the stable. They had been killers. She trembled inwardly to think of what they would probably have done by now if the Hunters hadn't been visiting. But for three lives to be quenched like that, in a few minutes . . . Tears welled to her eyes and she scrubbed blindly at Rolf's blood on the splintery planks, fighting to hold back hysterical weeping.

"I suppose I should take the bodies into town," Father considered.

"From what you say of the courts, I'd suggest you don't," Dane said quietly. "These men crossed the border looking for trouble. They found it. I hope you'll agree, sir, to letting me bury them decently but obscurely. If it's known where they died, fellow Missourians or pro-slavers might pay you another call, in much heavier numbers."

"It goes against the grain," said Father. "But again, there's sense in what you say."

Dane's lean face relaxed the slightest bit, as if he found Josiah's qualms more endearing than irritating. "After all, Mr. Whitlaw, my brother and I fired the shots, though indeed you were quick off the mark with that poker! The truth might lodge both of us in jail, so I pray you will leave the matter to me."

"I'd be very glad to," said Father candidly. "But you were protecting us. I'll help you dispose of the bodies, Mr. Hunter."

"No, I'll go," insisted Thos.

The two went out. Presently, there was the sound of the wagon creaking along a pause near the stable, and after a few minutes the wagon rumbled off.

Deborah, standing in the bedroom doorway, became aware of Rolf's intent gaze, then hastily started to join her mother.

"Please," Rolf murmured. His head drooped to one side, tawny hair spread on the pillows. "Miss Whitlaw—"

She hurried to him. "The soup will be ready in a moment. Would you like some water?"

He smiled. "Not even whisky. Please, stay here."

So you can look at me?

But he had been wounded for their sakes and he was very pale. Deborah sat on the edge of a stool. He made no move to touch her, but again his eyes touched her face, her throat, moved to her breasts.

A peculiar warmth seemed to melt her spine. A glow traveled through her veins, a sweet weakness. She put up her arms like a shield. How could he make her feel like this when less than an hour ago she'd felt that deep, instantaneous sense of merging with Dane? Was she a light woman—the kind described in Proverbs with lips like a honeycomb, but whose fate was "bitter as wormwood, sharp as a two-edged sword?"

Rolf smiled faintly. His eyes traveled slowly back to hers. By the time Mother brought the soup, he had fallen asleep.

• iv •

Rolf's right shoulder was injured, so Leticia fed him the soup. She and Josiah agreed that Rolf must stay with them till his strength returned and insisted on helping him to Deborah's bed. Thos slept outside much of the summer, anyway, so she could have his place in the lean-to. It gave her a strange feeling to see Rolf's long body stretched out where she slept, though, comically, his feet protruded and Father brought a bench to rest them on.

At least there was small hint it was a woman's retreat. Her two everyday dresses and one Sunday poplin hung on a peg above the beaded moccasins Sara had given her, and a hairbrush lay on a shelf beside the japanned box that held her ribbons, hairpins, and a few pieces of jewelry inherited from her mother's mother, who had been, apparently, more frivolous than her daughter.

Somewhat dubiously, Father placed the flask just beneath the bed. They were bidding Rolf good night, Mother insisting that he call out if he needed anything, when the wagon rumbled into the yard.

Neither Dane nor Thos said anything about where they'd buried the men, and no one asked. Late as it was, and tired as he must be, Dane refused to spend the night.

"It's kind of you to keep my brother," he said, watching Rolf, who seemed scarcely able to keep his eyes open. "But I won't discommode you further. I trust I may call tomorrow and see if he's fit to travel?"

"Come and welcome," said Father. "But surely it's best that your brother stay here till his shoulder's well on the way to healing."

Mother said positively, "He must stay at least the week. Jogging off to Lawrence could start him bleeding or bring on fever."

"But the nursing of him, madam!" Dane frowned. "I hate to burden you—and your daughter." His brow smoothed suddenly. "Our landlady, Mrs. Eden, seems most amiable. Perhaps she'd agree to come out daily and see to Rolf's needs."

Deborah stiffened. Melissa Eden, with her voluptuous body and wide blue eyes, was gently spoken enough, but her full mouth always had a tiny smile, as if she had the joke on everyone else. She attended the same church as the Whitlaws, and several times, during hymns or prayer, Deborah had seen her gaze, no longer sweetly vacant, shift from man to man, impatiently, as if searching.

Once her eyes met Deborah's. There was a moment's shock. Then Mrs. Eden's smile deepened and she gave a slow nod, as if to say: *Don't look censorious, my dear. Your eyes were open, too, not closed in heavenly communion.*

To Deborah's vast relief, though in a tone perfectly gracious, Mother said firmly that she and Deborah could manage very well, though, of course, the elder Mr. Hunter was invited to come sit with his brother whenever he wished.

"Well, if you're sure," Dane yielded, perhaps tardily realizing that the presence of another woman, however amiable, might place more strain on the household than it relieved.

Rolf seemed asleep so the others went to the living part of the cabin, where Mother brought Dane more "coffee." His dark hair was rumpled and he looked bruised under the eyes, but he sat erect, in the way that reminded Deborah that he'd been an officer.

"I've heard that in the West there's less formality in address," he said. "I can see there's a problem with two Mr. Hunters about and two Mr. Whitlaws! Would it be brash of me to hope Rolf and I could be known by our first names and could call young Mr. Whitlaw Thos or Thomas?"

"Highly sensible, Dane," said Father. "Please call me Josiah." He sighed, glancing toward town. "Even without our skirmish being known, Lawrence will be buzzing tomorrow! Just when it seemed that the will of the people was finally going to have to be acknowledged, even by President Buchanan. There'll be raids into Missouri over Marais des Cygnes, and more turmoil in the Territory. It seems there'll never be peace!"

"Oh, peace always comes," said Dane ironically. "If it didn't, people couldn't prepare themselves for another war. And I think you're due for a terrible one in this country, sir. I've traveled north and south, and the way that tempers are running, there seems little chance of compromise."

The Whitlaws regarded each other somberly. "Well, let it be war!" cried Thos, eyes shining. "Look at the way proslavers have bullied and terrorized us since even before the Territory opened! Better have a declared, clean, open war than all this raiding and shooting of defenseless men!"

Dane turned and watched the young man's defiant face. "There's no clean war, Thomas—not ever."

"But you fought in the Crimea!"

"And it was foul and hideous. What happened here tonight was bad and could have been much worse. But in war, Thomas, hundreds die in the same short time, hundreds more are wounded, and they're forgotten in the next carnage."

Thos stared, plainly unable to reconcile this attitude with his budding hero-worship for the older man. "But . . . but some wars have to be fought!"

"Not by me. I'll defend myself or my friends, but I'll not put on a uniform and go off to slaughter men in a different uniform because of trade routes, territorial wrangles, or, worst of all, ideals!" Rising, Dane bowed. His gaze touched Deborah so briefly that she felt snubbed. "Thanks for your hospitality and care of my brother," he said. "I'll be out tomorrow to see how he mends."

Thos and Father went out to the stableyard with him. Deborah stood looking after them, bewildered, half angry. Once, just once, yet unmistakably, their natures had seemed to rush together, fill, at least for her, the void of separateness she had supposed was inevitable as a person grew up. Surely she hadn't imagined that! Why, then, did he virtually ignore her?

"A driven young man," Mother said. "He may not go to war, but he has one inside."

"For one who condemns war, he was ready enough to kill those men tonight." Deborah was shocked at the harshness in her own voice.

"Daughter! He did it to protect us."

That couldn't be argued. But Deborah still felt disturbed and rebellious long after Father and Thos had come back inside and the family had prayed for the relatives of the dead Missourians and their victims of the morning, for the fugitive slave Judith to escape, for peace to come, and for Rolf's speedy recovery.

Lying awake in the lean-to, Deborah turned from side to side on the rustling shuck mattress, unable to rest, though bone-weary.

So much had happened that day that she couldn't take it in: the encounter with Rolf and Dane, the first outsider's kiss she'd ever had, and then the nightmarish visitation of the Missourians fresh from a slaughter that was bound to throw Kansas into renewed conflict! She broke into a cold sweat when she pictured what Jed and his men would have done had the Englishmen not taken a hand. Father and Thos would have fought, certainly; she and Mother would have defended themselves with kitchen knives or whatever they could snatch up. But there was little doubt that, balked of finding and punishing the runaway Judith, the Missourians would have killed the men. It was true that so far even the worst Border Ruffians had seldom attacked women, but Deborah still felt soiled by the raking of Jed's hot glance.

And now Rolf Hunter, who'd at the least exceeded the bounds of rough frolic with her, lay in her bed and she'd have to help nurse him! Indignation at being thus trapped battled with softer feelings roused by the way he'd watched her dreamily that night, seemingly content to have her company. Perhaps he was only high-spirited, wild but not reprehensible. From reading smuggled copies of Samuel Richardson's *Pamela* and *Clarissa Harlowe,* Deborah suspected that the sons of English gentry might consider as fair prey young women beneath them in the social order.

But this was the United States! And she was going to persuade Johnny that she should have her Bowie knife. Then, come night raiders or amorous Britishers, she'd be ready. On that unmaidenly thought, she at last fell asleep.

It was decided the next morning that Mother would stay home. She and Deborah could do the washing while tending to Rolf, and Thos could help Father at the shop.

"Rolf's feverish," Mother said after the men had gone. "I'll try to get some milk and mush down him and dress his wound while you get the water on to boil. Thos has already started the fire under the kettle and dumped in a few buckets to start you off."

Deborah slipped into her moccasins, not wasting time, because it promised to be a hot day, and washing, even in cool weather, was drudgery. Still, she'd rather carry water than cope with that shoulder, let alone the strange sensations Rolf could cause in her.

The trouble with being in the yard, of course, was that when she looked at the stable or wagon, she remembered last night. Pushing it away, she started her task.

She knew Mother wanted to wash her hair soon, so she left the soft rainwater in the barrel and drew up buckets from the well, carrying two at a time to pour into the big black kettle sitting on an iron grate above the fire. Thos had also brought out a bench and put the tub on it. Deborah filled this for rinsing and thrust more corncobs and cow chips under the kettle before adding soft soap.

By the time she went back to the house, Leticia had sorted the washing into dark and white. Deborah carried out the sheets, napkins, and undergarments, put them into the now boiling water, and poked them around with a blunt stick. Mother joined her in time to lift the steaming laundry from the kettle into the dishpan, where spots were rubbed out and more stubborn stains were attacked by laying the article on the bench and beating it with a wooden mallet. The soapy water was, as much as possible, wrung into the dishpan and then returned to the kettle.

"Rolf's shoulder's angry but seems clean enough," Mother said. "He wouldn't eat. After we rinse the white things and get them drying, why don't you see if you can coax him to have a little food?"

There was really no choice. "I'll try," Deborah said and hoped she didn't sound as nervous as she felt.

When the kettle was emptied of whites, Deborah brought the colored things, sighing at the state of Thos's trousers and shirts, though to be fair, the dress she'd worn yesterday had smudges of dirt and blood, which Mother had already rinsed with cold water.

These went into the kettle. Deborah helped rinse the whites and wring them out, dumped the first rinse water, and filled the tub for the second rinse. Colored clothes, thank goodness, got only one rinse! When the sheets and other white wash had been rinsed again and wrung as thoroughly as the women could manage, they were spread over the plum bushes to dry.

"See what you can do with the young man," Mother said. "If he won't have mush or gruel, perhaps he'd like some mashed plums."

Doubting that, for the plums, preserved in water till a sealing scum formed, were sour and not much improved by sorghum, Deborah went reluctantly to the house.

Mother had tied back the curtain to admit the breeze, but it was already warm. Rolf's hair was spread on the pillow like tarnished gold, and his eyelashes lay long and dark against his cheeks. His white linen shirt was open at the front, revealing a strong muscular neck. There were ruffles down the front and at the wrists, making him look, Deborah thought, with a smile at her fancy, like a stricken Cavalier. As she watched him, wondering whether to let him sleep or ask him what of their limited fare he might like to try, his eyes opened, widened at the sight of her, but remained drowsy—as if he continued a very pleasant dream.

Uneasy at his gaze, Deborah asked how he was that morning.

"Much better, now that you've come."

Deborah viewed him wtih suspicion. "You wouldn't eat on purpose!"

"Your mother," he said blandly, "is a charming and estimable woman, but it's seeing you that makes me ready for nourishment."

"That sounds like rubbish, sir!"

"Not a bit! You make me eager to gain back my

strength, Miss Deborah. Not," he added reflectively, "that being ministered to by a lovely woman doesn't have its rewards. But on the whole, I prefer to have two sound arms!"

"I hope you heal quickly, sir, though doubtless the creatures you hunt should be grateful for a respite!"

His eyes traveled to the pulse beating in her throat. "I don't shoot my sweetest quarry. I must admit, in fact, that it sometimes turns and hunts me again."

"Will you have mush, gruel, or preserved plums?"

Rolf chuckled. "And sometimes the object of my hunt pretends it's not pursued. Then, when I catch up to it quickly, it cries foul and swears it was never warned."

"I'm warned!" Deborah turned on her heel. "Now, Mr. Hunter, I've come to wait on you, but Mother needs my help. Will you have some food or wait till she can come to you?"

"Cruel!" he groaned. "I did expect more gratitude."

"I'm grateful. Your aid last night cancels your . . . your rude behavior earlier! But you like to fight, Mr. Hunter. You seized the occasion with gusto. You must pardon me if I feel you acted in accordance with your natural bent."

"Then aren't you glad I happened to be on your side?" he asked jauntily after the merest furrowing of his brow.

"I'd be gladder yet if you didn't seem to glory in a chance at killing."

"You mean I should hate a fight the way Dane does, agonize before and after?" Rolf laughed derisively. "It all came to the same act in the end. Both Dane and I killed last night—protecting you and your family, remember."

"I . . . know."

Remembering the shrieks of pain, the tumble of wrecked bodies, she began to tremble, then turned her face so he couldn't see her tears.

"Deborah."

She blinked and tried to subdue the lump in her throat. "Shall I bring you something to eat?"

His hand closed on her wrist, more compelling in that he lacked the strength to maintain the grip if she resisted. "Sweet Deborah." His voice was a caressing whisper. "Forgive me. I'm a rogue. Bring that mush or gruel or whatever you have and I'll eat it up like a model patient." He brought her hand to his lips, kissed it gently, and let her go.

He ate the bowl of mush and milk, opening his mouth obediently as Deborah fed him. She distrusted his meekness but was too grateful for it to challenge. Avoiding those deep green eyes that never left her face, she concentrated on her task. He didn't try to talk. That made their closeness more intimate. She felt pressed upon by his watching, his silence, and she was glad when the last bite was gone.

"Would you like coffee?" she asked, rising from the stool.

"Whatever you'll give me."

"There are also milk and buttermilk."

"Coffee, please."

She brought him a cup of the makeshift brew and asked if he needed anything else. "Could you fluff a little coolness into the pillows?" he asked.

Deborah took them. They were of the finest down, a luxurious contrast to the shuck mattresses. As she stepped behind Rolf to arrange them, he leaned back suddenly, cheek against her breast.

"The sweetest resting place," he murmured.

His breath warmed her through the cotton, sent a prickling of gooseflesh over her. For a fraction of a second Deborah couldn't move. Then, blushing hotly, she sprang back. But in the instant she'd been transfixed, Dane had entered.

His cool gray eyes touched her; there seemed to be the slightest curl to his lips. Fixing his attention on Rolf, Dane said in a dry tone, "You seem vastly improved, brother."

"Still swimmy in the head."

Rolf was all innocence, though his greenish eyes flickered with merriment as Deborah said to Dane with all the dignity she could command, "Now that you can see to your brother, sir, I'll help my mother. Have you breakfasted?"

"Most adequately, thank you."

With Melissa Eden sitting across from him? Melissa's gowns weren't exactly low-cut, but in a place where everyone but "bad" women wore high-necked ones, her ruffled, tight-fitting bodices were something of a scandal. No doubt, too, the early hour had excused a suggestive disarray of that shining taffy-colored hair. The conjured image put Deborah completely out of temper. Dane was an arrogant, evil-minded man who seemed to blame *her* for what his resourceful younger brother did! But she was anxious over how the town had taken the killings at Marais des Cygnes.

Swallowing her wrath, she asked what was happening in Lawrence. "A messenger rode in with the news during the night," said Dane. "He says James Montgomery's raiding north for vengeance. Jim Lane's rousing the militia around

Lawrence and Topeka and intends to march into West Point, Missouri, to look for Hambleton and his gang."

"I hope they find them all!"

"So does your brother."

"What do you mean?" Deborah's heart chilled.

"I stopped by *The Clarion* and found Thos pointing out to your father that he's seventeen, strong and unencumbered, and that it's his bounden duty to go with the militia and 'Grim Chieftain' Lane."

Deborah's hand went involuntarily to her throat. "Father didn't let him?"

"Between us, we managed to persuade your twin that his first duty was to help protect you and Mrs. Whitlaw in case a real border war breaks out. But he's restive, Miss Whitlaw, restive."

"I—I'll talk to him!" Resentful as she was at Dane, she was still forced to be grateful. "Thank you for persuading Thos, Mr. Hunter." She added with some bitterness, "I'm sure he'd pay much more attention to you than to anyone else!"

He almost smiled. "Call it even for brothers, Miss Whitlaw. I'm sure mine has been a more tractable invalid for you than ever he'd be for another mortal." He gave Rolf a mock-stern glance. "The danger is that he may play sick to enjoy your attentions."

"Oh, he won't do that for long," Deborah assured them both. "If people don't mend when Mother thinks they should, she starts them on a course of castor oil. That always effects a quick cure."

"You shouldn't threaten a wounded man!" said Rolf with a grimace.

Dane laughed. "Well, you young rascal, it sounds as if you're in the right hands!" He began to unwrap the bandage. "Mrs. Whitlaw agreed that since my experience with firearm wounds is greater than hers, it'd be well for me to have a look."

"Will you need anything?" Deborah asked.

"If I do, I'll find it. Failing that, I'll shout for help. Since you prefer that I not hire a nurse, at least I'll see that the whole burden of care doesn't fall on you."

That was like him—too proud to accept favors from colonials! Deborah went out with as much of a swish as her rather limp skirts could manage and was in time to help Leticia with the rinsing and wringing.

One at either end, they twisted the last possible drop of

water from Thos's trousers. "I'd best start dinner," Mother said, pinning up damp tendrils of elusive hair and glancing at the noon sun. "We have the rabbits Rolf gave us yesterday, and Dane brought a mysterious hamper from town." Her almost childlike pleasure at the gift faded. "I'm thankful that Dane talked Thos out of following Jim Lane. I don't like that man and never did—the way he treated his wife and that bloodthirsty rasping way he shouts and stirs people up! He was a pro-slavery Democrat when he was a congressman from Indiana and voted for repealing the Missouri Compromise, which brought on all this trouble, because if that law had remained, there'd be no question of allowing slavery in Kansas, or Nebraska, either!"

There was no way to defend the way he'd forced a divorce on his wife, daughter of General St. Clair, who'd been president of the Continental Congress and governor of the Northwest Territory. It was rumored that Lane had gone through her inherited wealth and come to Kansas, but after the divorce she had married him again!

"Thos thinks he's been converted to the Free-State cause," said Deborah.

Leticia sniffed. "The way he's always getting converted at different Methodist churches? He rides around on that claybank in his moth-eaten sealskin coat, chewing tobacco and telling people how brave he was in the Mexican War. He'd fit better with the Border Ruffians!" She marched for the cabin while Deborah began spreading the colored clothes over the bushes.

So Dane Hunter probably intended to spend most days looking after Rolf? Could it be that besides his wish not to impose, he meant to protect his brother from involvement with a woman he might have to marry if the dalliance went too far? Deborah's cheeks burned at the thought and she shook Thos's trousers till they snapped.

Why was that odious man forever catching her in unexplainable situations? He must surely know his brother's philandering predilections! Still, he behaved as if she'd invited Rolf's amorous nonsense. It wasn't fair!

Smarting, Deborah put out the smoldering fire with soapy water from the kettle and poured the rest on the bare ground. The lye soap would kill plants. Rinse water, however, was precious. Dipping buckets into the tub, she carried this to the garden.

There looked to be enough peas for cooking with new

potatoes. That would be nice for supper and would improve Dane's opinion of their food.

What did she care for his opinion?

She cared. However noxious his manner, there'd been that one heart-stopping moment she could never forget, the sounding of a chord so deep within her she hadn't dreamed it was there. She wouldn't be a fool, sigh after him, or seek his favor, but she'd be lying to herself to pretend that what he thought wasn't devastatingly important. She wouldn't let him guess that, though! Turning the kettle upside down so it wouldn't rust, she put the soft soap back in the well-house and placed the tub where it'd catch any rain water that might fall.

She paused, completely out of chores, hot, thirsty, and hungry, yet reluctant to go in and face those disconcerting gray eyes that convicted her, without trial, of frivolity, wantonness, and perhaps even worse.

"Deborah!" called her mother. "Fetch a fresh bucket of water, please."

Hurrying to the door, she almost collided with Dane, who was carrying the kitchen bucket. He put out a hand to steady her. Its strong warmth shocked through her arm, her blood, her whole body. The touch lasted only a moment but left her weak, as confused as if a whirlwind had swooped her up, spun her dizzingly about, then left her, unsupported by its devilish force, to either stand or fall.

"I beg your pardon." His mouth quirked ironically. "You do rush to your errands! But I'll do this one."

When Deborah, unnerved, said nothing, he halted in mid-stride and scanned her searchingly. "You're flushed, Miss Whitlaw. Are you ill? The sun—"

"I'm used to the sun!" she muttered, eluding that dangerously exciting hand which he stretched toward her. *It's you I'm not used to and never will be!* "I suppose *you* can hardly be expected to understand that washing's a fatiguing task!"

"You'd be most surprised, Miss Whitlaw, at some of the things I *do* understand. I wonder if you can realize, for example, how joyous one can be at the chance to scrub one's clothes when they're caked with filth, blood, and vermin?"

She gazed at him in astonished revulsion, jousting lance splintered by his war-axe. His eyes changed.

"I'm sorry." His tone was full of self-disgust. "You're too young for such talk, and a female besides, for all you cut me up so ferociously." A rueful smile made him seem quite different from his usual overbearing self. "Why, Miss Deborah, must I always be seeking your pardon?"

It was the first time he'd called her that, but she was too disturbed and upset by her chaotic feelings to be friends easily at his first softening. Retreating a pace and looking somewhat past him, she said with frost, "It must be, sir, because you recognize that you offend!"

She passed him, head high, and was mortified to hear him, as he moved toward the well-house, burst into whistling "The Girl I Left Behind Me." That gave no evidence of a contrite and chastised spirit!

As she started setting the table, her mother gave her a chiding look. "Why must you give Dane the rough side of your tongue, daughter? We almost surely owe him for your father's and brother's lives and our safety."

That was undeniable. But all the same . . . There was no way Deborah could explain the contretemps in which Dane was forever finding her without causing her mother consternation—which would manifest itself, Deborah feared, in a sharp curtailment of *her* freedom.

If Mother knew, for instance, that her children were getting Bowie lessons from Johnny! No, Deborah felt her waspishness toward Dane was fully justified, but she couldn't convince her parents of that without revealing things of which she didn't want them to even dream.

"Mr. Hunter's terribly condescending, Mother!"

Leticia's surprised blue gaze was difficult to meet. "Why, to me he's seemed extremely courteous."

"To you, no doubt, he has been, but to me he's—" Deborah struggled, bit her lip. "Oh, never mind! I'll try, Mother, really try to be polite, but he's *so* provoking!"

Mother's puzzled look warmed into a smile of swift comprehension, but all she said was, "Try, my dear. Angels can do no more."

Deborah, with effort, refrained from saying she neither was nor wished to be one of the heavenly host. A fragrant aroma teased her nostrils. She tracked it to the flower-patterned china teapot, taken from the china cupboard for the first time since the move to Kansas.

"Earl Grey tea," said Mother. "And do look in the hamper!" To Dane, who'd returned with the bucket, she sparkled happily, "I don't know how to thank you! We never go hungry, but the fare gets monotonous. These wonderful tins! You must have brought them from England I've never seen such elegant things!"

Lifting tins and jars out of the hamper, she flourished them at Deborah. "Isn't it like Christmas, birthdays, and the Fourth of July all in one?"

Dane grinned at mention of this last holiday and Leticia flushed to the roots of her soft brown hair. "My tongue galloped off with me, Dane, but the Fourth is a great holiday with us and—"

"Madam," he said, grinning more broadly, "I understand perfectly. Of course a nation must celebrate its birth." He selected a can and handed it to her. "I especially recommend this truffled hare pâté, and the truffled woodcock is almost as good."

In spite of resenting Dane's lordliness, Deborah couldn't keep her mouth from watering as she saw the array of delicacies: salmon, oysters, French sardines, mutton stew, marmalade, figs, raisins, a reddish-orange cheese, parcels of sugar and coffee; and a packet which Dane tapped.

"You may want to save this Bombay duck for a journey, which is what it was used for by Indians of the East. It's not duck at all, but dried bummelo fish."

"How peculiar!" Mother looked suddenly stricken. "But Dane, these are provisions for your western excursion! We can't take them."

"We brought far too much," said Dane negligently. "The housekeeper was sure we'd famish 'amongst the savages' and ordered in prodigious supplies from Fortnum's in Piccadilly. We took as little as we dared without causing her apoplexy, but we still have enough to open a shop."

"I wish you'd give away all of that miserable canned Australian beef!" called Rolf from the next room. "Stringy, tasteless stuff! Fresh rabbit's much better."

"Do you feel up to having some for dinner?" Mother asked, crossing to the bedroom door. "I've dredged it in meal and soaked it for a bit in vinegar water to make it tender."

"Any food you or Miss Deborah bring will taste like ambrosia."

Snorting at Rolf's melting reply, Dane went to stand by his hostess. "And what about the food I bring you, my boy? The ladies must perforce give you breakfast and tend to you when I'm not here, but while I am, I'll see to your needs."

Rolf groaned. "And I thought this to be one invalidism I'd enjoy!"

"If you'll give me his plate, Mrs. Whitlaw?" Dane suggested.

"It's mighty ramshackle of you!" grumbled Rolf. And then, craftily he said, "Didn't you engage to go paint that Delaware guide this week—the one who brought back those gold nuggets from the South Platte last year?"

"I've sent my excuses to Fall Leaf. There's plenty of time. Don't fret about my painting, youngling. My first concern is to get you back on your feet."

"You're too good to me by half!" Rolf growled. "But there it is; you've bullied me from the nursery and will probably keep it up till we're in the family vault!"

Dane thanked Leticia for the plate of rabbit and potatoes, then disappeared with it into the bedroom. She followed with a steaming cup of tea and the china sugar bowl, also brought out for this occasion. Returning, she began putting away Dane's offerings, lingering over each small treasure with such delight that Deborah was shaken, glimpsing for the first time what a wrench it had been for Leticia to leave New Hampshire, how valiant she was in cheerfully bearing the grinding everyday drudgeries and harshness of frontier life.

"Real coffee!" she said, sniffing the aroma of fresh-ground beans. "I can hardly wait to see how surprised your father will be when we serve him some of this tonight!" A frown creased her brow, and she paused with a jar of marmalade, glowing rich gold in her hand. "We can't take it all, though. It really is too much."

With short, vengeful jabs, Deborah forked the meat onto a platter and dished up the potatoes, then set the teakettle on to heat. "I'm sure Mr. Hunter was telling the truth, Mother." Her tone was so acid that even she was startled at its sound. "Their housekeeper sent so much of this kind of frippery that we're doing them a favor to lighten their supply load."

"Exactly so." Dane, behind her, put down Rolf's emptied plate and cup. "Apart from that, we can't both of us eat you out of house and home, as we're in the way of doing, without replenishing the larder."

He seated Mother, then Deborah, and sat down facing them—just as if, Deborah thought resentfully, he were the master of the house!

"Will you ask the blessing?" Mother requested.

"I don't believe in God," he said gently. "But I'm glad you do, Mrs. Whitlaw. It will bless me to hear you pray."

After a horrified stare that dimmed to sadness, Mother bowed her head. So did Dane. Deborah scarcely heard her mother's soft voice.

Dane was kind and considerate of Leticia even when admitting atheism, an almost unimaginable thing. Why, then, was he so ready to mock her—Deborah? And why, oh, why, did he have to appear when some outrage of Rolf's had put her in an unexplainable position?

She resolved to ignore him. But the tea, which Mother poured out after grace, was so delicious, especially sweetened with real sugar, that Deborah was compelled to express appreciation.

"Your pleasure is doubly mine," Dane said. His gray eyes touched her in a way that made her heart leap.

Wildly, in a tumult of conflicting desires, she thought that his kiss would never have the taste of blood, that he could sear away that branding of Rolf's.

If he would . . .

• V •

A battalion of Free Staters had invaded Missouri and searched West Point for Hambleton and his men, who were not found, but James Montgomery, the black-bearded Campbellite preacher from Ohio who'd made a log fortress of his home in southeastern Kansas and who was that region's acknowledged Free State leader, had raided north, within fifteen miles of Lecompton, the pro-slavery capital.

Free Staters, especially neighbors of the murdered men, wanted blood for that spilled May 19 at Marais des Cygnes. That part of the Territory seethed, and so did Thos, eager to get into the fray. Deborah feared that at the next crisis, he couldn't be held back, a fear shared by Sara, though Johnny seemed to think it was inevitable.

"There's war coming," he told them after Deborah and Thos had survived their first knife lesson since the day they'd met the Hunters and Rolf had been wounded by the night riders. "It's been fated since the first slave was brought to these shores; that was the wind we planted and the whirlwind we'll reap."

Rolf's eyes shone. He'd been moved to Melissa Eden's house a few days ago in the buggy, but this was his first horseback outing and a bandage was still bulked beneath his fine linen shirt. He and Dane had been invited by Thos to meet the twins at the blacksmith's so that Dane could ask permission to sketch, and, of course, the English brothers had been asked to stay for dinner.

Johnny seemed to trust Dane, but his smoky eyes went hard when he looked at Rolf, probably because Rolf's gaze rested familiarly on Sara, as if she'd been a mare he was thinking of buying. He laughed now and said, "A real war? I envy you!"

"I don't." Dane's quiet tone was taut with controlled anger and something else—horror? Pity?

"Maybe this excitement over gold in the Rockies will drain off the worst hotheads," said Deborah hopefully.

"Cesli tatanka!" scoffed Johnny.

"Unfortunately," said Dane, "the mostly young men who'll do the fighting won't be the ones to declare war. The split between agricultural and industrial interests, deepened by the hatchets of abolitionists and pro-slavers, are bound to crack this nation apart. The only question is: Will the South be allowed to separate, or will the North fight to hold it?"

"Going to be war soon or late." Johnny scowled as he cut off a bite of tough beef and the edge of his hunting knife grated on the delft plate. *"Tatanka wakan,* even if the North let the South go, which it won't, there'd be a fuss over the western lands just opening up, and slaves would be running away north whilst the abolitionists would be helping them. The whole border'd be the way Kansas is right now. No, this boil's coming to a head! Cain't be no real peace till it's lanced and the poison's drained and the wound can heal clean instead of growin' a thin scab over a putrefying abscess."

Violently, Sara pushed back her chair. "No matter which side wins, it won't help my people!" Her eyes gleamed and in that moment she was hostile to them all, even Thos. "If only Tecumseh had been able to get the other tribes to join those of the Northwest who fought on the British side in 1812! He journeyed south and west, telling chiefs the white tide would soon be lapping against them, but they didn't believe! Tucumseh fell in battle, and with him died the spirit of the Shawnee."

"I've heard of him," Dane said. "The British commissioned him a brigadier general. He was a military genius."

"Which the British commander wasn't," rejoined Sara, though obviously surprised and pleased that the great leader of her tribe had been heard of in England.

"But would it have made a difference to the Indians if the British had won?" Deborah asked.

"Who knows? In return for Tecumseh's help against the Americans, the British were ready to promise that they'd prohibit further taking of Indian lands. The point is that if, right then, the Indians east of the Rockies had united, they might have had some chance of holding their lands, which instead have been nibbled away as the tide crumbles the sand."

Springing up, she began clearing away the dishes. Deborah helped, wishing to comfort her friend but not knowing what she could truthfully say.

It hadn't been only settlement from the East, but the time of the free-ranging Indian had been numbered from when Coronado, seeking for golden Quivira, had written to the king of Spain that though he found no gold, the soil was "rich and black . . . well watered by arroyos, springs, and rivers . . . the most suitable that has been found for growing all the products of Spain."

He spoke of the plums, nuts, sweet grapes, and mulberries, doubtless in an effort to assuage the disappointment of his gold-hungry sovereign. Spain never colonized Quivira but though she'd had to surrender her claim, first to Mexico, then to the United States, to the region north of the Rio Grande and her settlements in Texas, California, and that vast area in between, those lands were lost to the Indians as surely as was New England and the East Coast. Here on the plains in the heart of the country, proud Comanche, Kiowa, Cheyenne, and Sioux would challenge the white man for a little while, but they were few and scattered.

Thos said in a strained voice, "I guess you'd be glad, Sara, if all of us whites killed each other off!"

She turned on him in a swirl of yellow skirts. "How could I want you or your family dead? Or Johnny?"

"Whoa!" Johnny, too, rose and stretched, went over to tilt up Sara's flower face, gaze down at her in stern tenderness. "Listen, honey! Weren't the Shawnee driven from Ohio by the Iroquois and later from the Cumberland Valley by the Cherokee and Chickasaw? Did they pay you for the land or help you settle elsewhere?"

She gave him a mutinous stare, lovely and small in his gnarled brown hands. "If one must be robbed, better by one of the same color!"

"Maybe. But the Lakotah who now watch the Holy Road, the Overland Trail, and see thousands of wagons use up the game and grass and firewood, ruin the hunting and wintering grounds so that Nebraska comes from "Nablaska"—trampled flat—those Lakotah whipped Mandans and Arikara on the Missouri and got their lands, took the Black Hills from the Kiowa, fought Crow and Cheyenne for their hunting grounds. Red, white, yellow, or black, when human's *can* take, they generally do. Ain't right, ain't fair, ain't good, maybe. But it's so."

Sara stood still beneath his touch, but resistance was clear in every line of her body. "Why do you say these things, Johnny? They're true, but this can't make me glad that the whites devour land like prairie fire."

"Not glad," Johnny said carefully. "Not ever glad. But not so bitter that your food's poisoned on your tongue and your soul withers. Then for sure would you be destroyed, little Sara. You can defeat the whites in this, not letting them ruin your joy in the sun."

He let her go then and went out to the forge, flanked by Laddie and Maccabee. Dane followed. He had permission to draw and paint to his heart's content; in fact, to Deborah's chagrin, he'd made swift impressions of her and Thos as they dueled. Probably he'd show them to his highborn friends, who'd conclude that Americans were so barbarous that even their women fought!

Rolf lounged against the wall, dark green eyes as contemplative as a cat's, but Thos looked so miserable that Deborah caught his hand, closed it over Sara's, and gave them a shove.

"Isn't there enough war without you two starting one?" she demanded. "Go for a walk and don't come back till you've made friends with one another!"

"But the dishes—" protested Sara, hanging back.

"I'll do them. Just get along with you! We'll have to start home soon."

Thos linked his arm with Sara's, drew her toward the door, shooting his twin a grateful look. Deborah, too late aware that she'd left herself alone with Rolf, attacked the delft soaking in the pan.

Why was it that his caressing gaze made a strange, half-sweet, half-frightening warmth tingle through her? Thanks to Dane's nursing of him, Deborah had seldom been alone with Rolf during the week he spent at the Whitlaws', and then, warned by his previous tricks, she'd kept out of reach, though his lifted eyebrows and aggravating smile said that he noticed her avoidance but could wait.

Now he strolled across the room and took the dish towel off a peg. "I don't have my full strength back, Miss Deborah, but I think I can wipe up for you."

"Thanks."

"What a stiff and starchy tone!" he chided. "Why so unkind, Miss Deborah? I vow I can feel your artillery swinging toward me the instant I approach!"

"You very well know why!"

"I was only trying to treat the bites you'd gotten from my hounds."

"Indeed!" She clanged down a soapy kettle, giving it such a vigorous swish in the rinse water that he was well besprinkled. "I wasn't bitten on the mouth, sir!"

Why had she blurted that out, let him know how well she remembered? He laughed softly, so close beside her that she moved away. "Have you no charity at all, my sweet, for a poor, bedeviled man? How wild you were in my arms! I dream of it still—your writhing that pressed you against me till I swear on any martyr's bones you please that only a statue could have kept from doing as I did!"

Made weak by his urgent voice recreating that afternoon, Deborah swallowed hard and grimly told herself this must be how he'd laid successful siege to many women. If he thought it'd work with her, he was due for a surprise.

"Mr. Hunter," she said icily, "while you were an invalid, I could understand, if not appreciate, your attempts to . . . to inject a bit of interest into your monotonous days. But now you're in town, able to fare about and seek diversion. Seek it elsewhere!"

"You're not forbidding me your house?"

"Not so long as you behave yourself."

He worked silently a moment. "How can I convince you that I'm not just seeking 'diversion'?"

"Respectful behavior would be a start."

"That's so dull," he said with such scapegrace mournfulness that she had to force back a smile. "What if I proposed to you?"

"Your proposals could earn you a knife in the ribs! Johnny's making one especially for me that I'll carry when I leave the house." She gave her head an emphatic nod. "Next time you or your dogs come at me, Mr. Hunter, you'd best beware!"

He chuckled. "Don't I already go in awe and dread of you, Artemis?"

"I'm not a huntress. If you'll remember, that was precisely the reason of our first . . . difference of opinion."

"Prim prunes and petunias! Is that what you call it—you in my arms, soft hair in my eyes, your blood on my mouth as I found yours? Difference of opinion? Deborah—"

He shook with laughter, winced as his shoulder pained him, sobered abruptly as she turned her back on him, close to mortified tears, as she wiped out the big cast-iron skillet.

"The kind of proposal I had in mind is made from bended knee," he said. "But I don't want to get into that absurd posture, Deborah unless you give me some encouragement."

Astounded, she whirled on him. "Your words are more absurd than any posture, sir!"

"I must agree with you." Dane stood in the doorway. His tone had a lash-like sting. "I'm glad, Miss Whitlaw, that you put no credence in my brother's impetuous statements. If he married without Father's approval, I doubt that either he or his bride would have much joy of it."

"That's an insulting remark!" Deborah flamed. "If my feelings for your brother, sir, were such that I'd marry him, then I do assure you that a cut-off of your father's money wouldn't matter a bit!"

"Perhaps not to you," said Dane, unruffled. "But it would to Rolf."

"Now plague take you, Dane. I—"

"Seem to be running a fever which has impaired your judgment." Dane turned from his brother. "I came to tell you, Miss Whitlaw, that Mr. Chaudoin says your knife is ready. Rolf, we should be starting for town."

"Go when you're ready, and so will I." Rolf set his back to Dane, but the gesture was lost. Dane was already disappearing. "Absurd or no, Deborah, I'll ask my question another time." Rolf dried the last pan and hung up the towel, good humor returning. "How will you carry your Bowie, love? In a sheath at your belt? Around your neck on a thong, strapped above your knee?" Sunlight made his eyes like green glass. "To glimpse its hiding place would be worth a stabbing!"

"You may get one if you keep on like that," Deborah retorted, but she was too excited about finally having her own knife to be really annoyed. She hung up the dishpan and hurried out to the forge.

Maccabee was shaping what looked to be a hinge, and Johnny sat on a stump, whittling away at a block of wood with a Bowie Deborah thought to be her own.

"Oh, you'll blunt it!" she cried.

"That's what I'm trying to do."

"But, Johnny—"

"My gal, if Black couldn't whittle on hickory for an hour and still shave the hair off his arm, he wouldn't sell the knife. I've whittled the hour, so now let's see."

Lifting his brawny arm, he smoothed the gleaming blade along it, leaving a bare swath beside an earlier testing patch.

"So here you are."

Rising, Johnny twanged the tip of the knife with his thumb. It gave out a bell-like crystalline sound. While it was still singing, Johnny put it into her hands.

Sun dazzled off the ten-inch-long blade, razor-honed on both sides of the last two inches, where the tip curved wickedly. The broad back of the blade had a brass guard for parrying. The crossguard at the hilt was almost three inches long.

From the curve, beginning as roots and following the back of the blade, where it tendriled into leaves and fruit at the hilt, was worked a grapevine of gold and silver, a pattern repeated in the seasoned black walnut handle through which the shank of the blade ran, ending in a knob.

It was a rare knife, beautiful, awesome—terrible because of the purpose for which it was so perfectly crafted.

"I—I can't take it, Johnny!" Deborah held it out to him. "The gold and silver, all the work! You could get a hundred dollars for it!"

"I made it for you and you alone," said Johnny. "It's a lady's Bowie, if there can be such a thing, shorter and lighter than most, but tempered to last through fire, flood, and battle."

A chill prickled the nape of her neck, then traveled down her spine. While she and Thos had practiced, using the Bowies had been a game, a test of skill. Holding this knife, her own, forged especially, made her realize that accepting it ended the game. If she took the blade, she might die by it. She might have to kill.

Could she do that?

Then she remembered the night the Missourians came. How glad she would have been of this knife! And she knew she would have used it, if forced, to defend herself and her family. The runaway Judith hadn't been there that night, but those like her had been sheltered at the Whitlaws' before and surely would be again.

With a sighing breath, Deborah closed her fingers around the grip. "Thank you, Johnny."

"He should really tap you on the shoulder with it and say, 'Be thou a good knight!' " Rolf's voice held lighthearted mockery, but his gaze rested avidly on the blade. "Isn't Thos to have one of these?"

Thos, who'd been standing by Sara, pulled a buckhorn-handled, longer, larger knife out of a brass-tipped sheath. "Mine's different. Fourteen inches long, wider, and broader. We hope Deborah never has to use hers, but I'm bound to use mine."

Rolf whistled. "May I see it?"

Once it was in his hand, he hefted it, admired the blade, then tested it on the fine golden hairs of one knuckle. "What a weapon!"

"It is," said Johnny. "When Jim Bowie got back to Texas after collecting the great-granddaddy of this knife from James Black, three men who'd been hired to kill jumped on him from out of the brush. Bowie leaned over his horse's neck and with one swoop took off the head of the one who'd grabbed his bridle. Meanwhile, Bowie got stabbed in the leg, but he swung out of the saddle, cut upward, and spilled the guts of the man who'd knifed him." Johnny chuckled. "The third figured to make tracks, but Bowie caught up with him and split his skull right into his shoulders. In 1830 that was, and after that nearly everyone who came to Black for a knife wanted one like Bowie's."

"I want one of this size and weight with a design of gold," said Rolf. "When could you have it done?"

"Wagons'll be rolling west for the next month or so," said Johnny. "They have to make it across the mountains before the passes snow up. So I'll be shoeing oxen and fixin' wheels and yokes. Can't take on any special jobs."

"I'll pay whatever you ask, half in advance."

"Cain't do it. Sorry."

Johnny sounded not at all sorry, nor was he all that dedicated to speeding westward travelers smoothly on their way. When broken-down wagons had camped near the forge for days or a week while Johnny made or fixed whatever was broken, or shod uncooperative oxen, a job he loathed, Deborah had heard him tell complaining travelers that if they didn't like his gait, they could learn smithing themselves.

A frown drew Rolf's tawny eyebrows together. "You'll surely make more from my knife than from weeks of regular work!"

"Ain't the point. I'm a smith. Folks count on me to make a new kingpin or axle or shoe their horses and oxen. This time of summer, I have to tend to necessaries."

Rolf flushed and swallowed. He clearly wasn't used to pleading with craftsmen to accept his custom. "Mr. Chaudoin, I'm willing to wait till you have the time."

Johnny didn't answer. "Well?" pressed Rolf.

"Won't be no time," said Johnny.

With an outraged gasp, Rolf tightened his grasp on the knife. "You're saying you won't make me a knife, any time at any price."

"That's the size of it." Johnny looked relieved. Subtlety wasn't his forte, but he clearly hadn't wanted to offend the Whitlaws' friend with a straight refusal.

"May I ask why?" Rolf's eyes had gone near black and his tone was silky.

Johnny considered, massive head to one side. "I'll shoe your horse or fix your buggy, make you a stirrup or mend your saddle. But I don't make knives for everybody."

Showing his teeth in an unpleasant smile, Rolf said, "Yet you made one for a woman."

Ignoring him, Johnny picked up a sheath from the bench where he kept his tools and supplies for repairing wagon woodwork. The sheath, like Thos's, was reinforced at the bottom with brass, and it was fitted to a soft leather belt.

"Sara and I did some experimentin' about the best way for a lady to carry that big a knife. You *could* wear it under your arm, but it'd always be bumpin' and would show unless you had on a coat or shawl. You could wear it in the top of your boot, but you don't have any. It'd show if you wore it around your waist, and while that's fine for men, it don't look . . . well, hell, ladylike!"

Laughing, Sara took the sheath from him and gave it to

Deborah. "You may find a better way, but I thought you could wear it *under* your skirts, and have a side slit like a pocket so that you could reach for it quickly."

"Isn't that a bit . . . underskirted?" Rolf, diverted by the rather piquant discussion, laughed at his own joke.

"If Deborah has to use the knife, she'll need the advantage of surprise." Sara wasn't amused.

Holding a cooled hinge in the forge to heat again to working temperature, Maccabee chuckled. "You just hide that knife, Miss 'Borah, and when one of them pro-slavers bothers you, carve him up and do it good! He'll have a Bowie and pistols, an' your first try may be the onliest one you get."

With a last look at the wonderful blade, Deborah sheathed it. She felt chilled and burning at once, as if on this warm, fine day she'd caught a fever. "I hope it can stay under my mattress most of the time," she said. "But when we're conducting—" She broke off, remembering that Dane and Rolf didn't know about the underground railroad. "When I'm away from the house, I'll wear it the way you suggest, Sara."

"Thought you folks'd be moving to town," Johnny said, pointing his chin in that direction.

"Father wanted to. But Mother, though she wants to send me to town, won't go herself."

Once again, Deborah repressed a mention of the railroad. In several near arguments, Mother had insisted that it was important for the underground to have a station outside Lawrence.

"Not many come this way," Father had urged. "Perhaps a dozen in the three and a half years we've been here."

"Each one, now, is safe and free." Mother's eyes shone with a deep feeling. "Why did we come to this Territory, Josiah?"

Now, studying Deborah, Johnny look relieved. "Whoa! So you'll be moving into Lawrence. I'm right glad of that, lass. Not many Border Ruffians would raise a finger to your ma, but you—" He shook his grizzled head. "You might be more than some hot young devil could keep his hands off of."

"But I'm not moving to Lawrence, Johnny." There was an edge in Deborah's voice. Just as Mother had resisted Father's wish to settle his women in town, so had Deborah resisted her mother's attempts to deposit her there.

Scanning her face, Johnny looked worried but proud. "You Whitlaws are all alike—stubborn."

Both Sara and Deborah burst out laughing. He glanced from one to the other like a buffalo pestered by hummingbirds, then growled self-righteously, "I'm just determined." He squinted anxiously at the twins. "You keep them rib-ticklers out of sight of your ma, now! I don't want her usin' one to lift my hair."

"We'll be careful," Deborah promised. Yielding to impulse, she dropped a kiss on his weathered cheek near the tightly curling gray sideburn. "Thank you, Johnny! For the knives, and for teaching us."

"No one's ever learned it all," warned Johnny with pleased embarrassment, placing his sinewy hand over the spot her lips had brushed. "Keep in practice, mind, and when you can, come over and let me make sure you're rememberin' what I told you. Head back, knife low. Don't ever lift it so high you leave yourself bare. Throat to hips, that's your target, and a good uppercut—"

Deborah felt slightly sick. This was making the possibilities much too real! As if guessing her discomfort, Sara interrupted: "Johnny! If you don't let them go, they'll be late, Mrs. Whitlaw will see the knives, and I think you'd rather face the whole Sioux nation than an angry Mrs. Whitlaw!"

"*Tatanka wakan*, yes!" Johnny shot a harassed glance at the sun. They had eaten late that day and it was mid-afternoon. "Get along home, then! But remember, there's part of me in the knives. Be careful how you use 'em."

They nodded solemnly. Thos went to fetch Nebuchadnezzar. Johnny was striding toward the forge when Rolf stepped in his way. "Mr. Chaudoin, about a knife—"

Dane caught his brother's arm. "Let it be!" he said. He smiled and bowed to Sara. "Thank you for dinner. It was excellent."

From the pile of things waiting to be repaired, Johnny selected a plowshare. Since plowshares were made of expensive, malleable chilled steel, Johnny was constantly welding extra steel to the old point and shaping it to cut a furrow. Shares only slightly worn down could be heated cherry-red and hammered out, though this made them thinner. With a final nod, Johnny turned to his work.

As Thos halted Nebuchadnezzar near the stump so Deborah could get up behind him, Rolf gave her a hand up. "What a lucky thing I was here today," he murmured in her ear. "Now I'll know where that formidable weapon is hidden."

"If I had to draw it, you might not find that such a great advantage," she said a trifle breathlessly, putting her arms around Thos.

Rolf's hand, concealed by her skirt, gave her ankle a lingering brush. "I wonder," he said. "To find it might be worth a slashing."

She pretended not to hear, as calling their thanks and waving good-byes, she and Thos moved off on their unenthusiastic steed.

Thos was so elated with his knife that he spent most of the way home invoking gory and glorious fact and legend of the Bowie. In the 1855 elections, when Claib Jackson had led across hundreds of Missourians to vote pro-slavers into office, hadn't they bragged they could each go eight rounds without reloading and would go the ninth with the Bowie knife? Hadn't Unitarian minister Theodore Parker married a black couple and then placed a Bible and a Bowie knife in the husband's hands to show he must defend both body and soul?

Deborah responded automatically. What did Dane think of her having the Bowie? His cool gray eyes had been impenetrable. There was no doubt, certainly, of what he thought about her marrying into his blue-blooded family! Not that there was any danger of that! But Rolf must want her badly to make such a suggestion, even in half-earnestness. She sighed.

Why, why, was Dane so politely guarded? He couldn't think her a coquette. She'd never flirted with him for a second, and, furthermore, she never would!

"Thos," she said, interrupting his excited flow, "did you make up with Sara?"

"Oh, sure. She wasn't mad at me, you know—just at blue-eyes in general. I wonder, 'Borah! Did they really burn Bowie's knife on that funeral pyre at the Alamo, or did some Mexican hook it? That knife *could* be rattling around this minute down in Texas or Mexico!"

"I can't see that it matters, since Bowie's dead and it was his use of the knife that made it fabulous."

" 'Borah!"

"Well, I don't see any use in idolizing *things*. But just think of poor James Black living on, blind all these twenty years, not able to do anything with the secrets he has locked in his mind and hands!"

"His father-in-law was a mean old cuss, all right," Thos agreed. "Think of waiting till his daughter was dead and then sneaking up on Black when he was sick, beating him, and leaving him for dead. Somehow managed to sell Black's property, and beggar as well as blind him."

"I guess the father-in-law never forgave Black, his former apprentice, for marrying his daughter. But it was such a cruel thing, and the old man left his own grandchildren the same as orphaned. Neighbors took them in."

"And Black still lives in Washington, Arkansas, with that Jones family which took him in after Dr. Jones tried to cure his blindness." Thos shook his head. "Funny that strangers should be so kind when a father-in-law was that wicked."

"Johnny stayed with Black till he was settled, didn't he, and then came west?"

Thos nodded. "Trapped for a while and then settled down with his Sioux wife till she died. Funny he's never married again."

"Not really."

Thos twisted his head around. "What do you mean?"

Deborah hesitated. What good would it do to tell her twin that she was sure Johnny loved Sara as a woman? It might make him angry or guilty, or he might speak of it to Sara, which could cause all sorts of trouble.

No, it was Johnny's secret. Having guessed it, she should help him keep it. But what a shame it was! Only a tenderly loving, big-hearted man could have watched his beloved forever stroll off with the man *she* loved and manage to smile on them both.

"I mean Johnny's busy with the forge and he has sort of a family." Deborah's evasion sounded lame and she bolstered it by demanding, "What woman would be able to fit into that household? Maccabee, Laddie, Sara, and Johnny. They don't need anyone."

Over his shoulder, Thos gave his sister the pityingly superior glance of one who knows about love to one who doesn't. "Johnny's not *that* old. Of course, most ways it may be fine as long as Sara's there, but she won't be much longer."

Now it was Deborah's turn to ask, "What do you mean?"

"Sara thinks you know."

"That you're both head over heels? Anyone with eyes must see that. But you're so young, Thos!"

"Fellows younger than I am get married every day, and girls a sight younger." He grinned annoyingly. "You're the one who better look out, or you'll be an old maid!"

"That's better than having a baby a year so that you die worn out at thirty and your husband has time to marry and bury two or three more poor women!"

"You sound like Dan Anthony's sister Susan," laughed Thos.

Young Dan Anthony had come out from Boston with the very first New England Emigrant Aid Company settlers. He and his outspoken sister were the children of a wealthy Quaker who'd been suspended for marrying out of meeting and expelled for letting his children dance at home. Dan ran a paper at Leavenworth, and his friend, John Doy, was active in the underground railroad. Deborah admired what she'd heard about Susan Anthony, who'd stayed in New England and taught school till she organized a woman's temperance society in 1852. Four years later she'd become New York State's agent in the American Anti-Slavery Society, but she was agitating more and more for women's rights.

"Women are almost as defenseless as slaves when they marry!" Deborah said, giving Thos a pinch for the sins of his sex. "We can't vote, and we have about the same rights as children, lunatics, and criminals!"

"Oh, Lordy!" choked Thos. "Can't we free the slaves first?"

"Yes, but I'm not anxious to become one myself! Seriously, Thos, have you and Sara talked about getting married?"

"Well, sure, we have. But Sara's nervous about marrying white, and even though you and I know it's rubbish, she's scared Mother and Father won't like it."

"You can talk her out of that notion, or I will, if you like."

Thos shrugged. Suddenly he wasn't the twin with whom she'd shared all her life, but a young male with his thoughts on battle. "There's not much use in getting into that yet. There's war coming, I'm going to be in it, and I don't want to leave a widow."

"Silly, you aren't going to die! There may not even be war!"

"There will."

That dark, ever-menacing shadow! Wouldn't it ever go away? Deborah said impatiently to conquer the fear chilling her heart, "I think Sara would rather be married to you for a little while than never at all! I would if . . . if I loved someone."

Her tone faltered. For some reason, Dane flashed before her, watching her with those wintry eyes which she so longed to see turn warm and interested.

"Maybe that's how a girl feels." Again, Thos sounded so patronizing that she was between wanting to kick him or giggle. "But I won't marry Sara till I can take care of her and until I can feel pretty sure I won't be going off to fight in a few months."

"You're going against nature," Deborah teased. "Father says sudden marriages and . . . and attachments always multiply during wars. Instinct drives young men to reproduce themselves in case they die in battle."

Thos said disgustedly, "If that's your notion of romance, maybe you'd better stay single! And ladies don't talk about reproduction!"

"Sara does," Deborah reminded him tranquilly, "because Johnny's raised her not to be ridiculous about plain, everyday facts."

"It's different for Sara."

"Why?"

Thos's jaw thrust out stubbornly. "You said yourself she was raised another way."

"All the same, she doesn't talk like a lady, but *you* want to marry *her* instead of some mealy mouthed female who faints at plain language."

They had ridden up to the stable and Thos slid out of the saddle before he helped Deborah down. "I pity the man you marry—if you ever do," he groused. "He'll never win an argument, that's certain!"

"Maybe he won't argue when he knows I'm right!" Deborah retorted.

Thos groaned. "Lord have mercy!"

Deborah wrinkled her nose at him, sobered as she looked at the Bowie she'd fastened around her waist for the ride home. "I suppose we'll have to hide these under our mattresses; that's about the only place Mother won't run across them. I hate deceiving her, Thos. Don't you?"

Would there never be an end today of his acting male and lordly? After all, he was her twin—born five minutes later, in fact! "There are lots of things Father and I don't tell you and Mother," he said. "Father says a man shouldn't worry his womenfolk unless it's necessary for their safety.

So," he concluded virtuously, "it may be different for you, but not telling her doesn't worry me a particle."

"Hah!" said Deborah. "You're not telling her because you know she'd take it away. But I suppose we'll have to hide them if we want them—and after the way those Missourians rode up on us, we need all the defense we can get!"

"Now blessed be God!" came a strange deep voice from the cabin. "I'm almighty glad to hear you talk that way."

Brother and sister whirled, both reaching for their knives. "Good!" The tall, gaunt graybeard in the doorway nodded. His blue-gray eyes burned into them. In his belt he wore a short sword and pistol.

Even before he spoke, Deborah knew him. "I'm John Brown," he said.

• *vi* •

Brown of Osawatomie, descended from Plymouth Pilgrims, who with four of his tall sons had, during the brief Wakarusa "war," driven to the defense of Lawrence in a lumber wagon with fixed bayonets attached to it; Brown, who hated slavery with such fervor that he felt he did God's will to cut down five helpless men at Pottawatomie Creek; Brown, who'd stumped New England raising money to battle pro-slavers and help slaves flee their masters. What had Thoreau, who'd met him in Concord, thought of him? Or he of Thoreau, for that matter?

Madman, monster, devil-saint?

Deborah didn't know how to treat him, but Thos hurried forward, clasping his hand. "This is an honor, sir! What can we do for you? We're Tom and Deborah Whitlaw. Our folks should be home in about an hour."

"I've seen them," said Brown. He was called Old Brown, though he was only in his late fifties. Age wasn't a word to apply to him. His bony frame looked as indestructible as granite. Lined face relaxing in what seemed to be a smile, he said, "Put up your horse, boy. I won't vanish till your sister gives me something to eat, if she'll be so obliging."

His cutlass winked in the sunlight. Controlling a shudder, Deborah wondered if it was the one he'd used on the Pottawatomie. Father had written a blazing condemnation of that; yet, when it came to the underground railroad, Brown was the heart and soul of it here, and for that they respected him.

He was too obsessed, too bloody, for man to judge. God must do that. God or the devil.

"Of course I'll give you a meal, Mr. Brown." Deborah stepped across the threshold. "But can't you stay and have supper with my parents?"

"No. I must be down near Fort Scott tomorrow. But your good parents will have company." He raised his voice, but a gentleness was in it. "Judith!"

The name stirred an echo. Wasn't that the name of Jed's "nigger wench"? From out of the bedroom moved a tall, slim woman. Her flesh was the color of dark honey and her hair leonine, almost yellow, cut short enough to mold her head like a curly, luxuriant helmet. She had uptilted hazel eyes, a full red mouth, and her broad nose increased the resemblance to a splendid tawny cat.

"Judith is on her way north," said Brown. "Your parents said you'll keep Judith and help her on her journey."

"Yes. Of course we will. But, Judith, was your owner named Jed?"

Judith's white teeth showed, but she only nodded. "Praise the Lord!" said Brown. "Your father told me what befell those scoundrels, Miss Whitlaw. A pity one escaped. God's will be done, I say! God's will be done!"

Strange words, terrible words, from the mouth of one who'd killed as many men himself. Brown's God was Jehovah of the thunders, God of Battles, Lord of hosts, who slew the first-born of Egypt, drowned Pharaoh's chariots, and rejected Saul because, though he obeyed God in slaughtering the Amalekites, "man and woman, infant and suckling," he kept the fattest cattle and sheep.

"I'll get you something to eat," Deborah said, trying to conceal her horror of the man.

She tucked the Bowie under her mattress and hurried to build up the banked coals, putting on real coffee. Whatever she thought of Brown, Father would want him to have their best.

"I'll help." Judith's voice was soft, slurring, fitting her graceful movements.

She was quite thin, with a fragility that made Deborah shudder to remember that Jed's big hairy hands had been able to do as they pleased with this woman. How could anyone think that was right? Infuriated with laws that made women the legal plaything and drudge of men, Deborah banged down a can of truffled woodcock, then apologized at Judith's nervous start.

"I'm sorry," Deborah said, smiling quickly. "Will you eat with Mr. Brown or join my family later?"

"Never aten with white folk, missy."

"Please call me Deborah." Reaching for the other woman's hand, Deborah held it till Judith's eyes widened and she gave a little smile.

"Never run away before, neither. Reckon I have to get used to lots of new things. And I'm hungered. I could maybe eat with Mr. Brown?"

"Fine." Thos came in and Deborah introduced him to Judith before he went out to grain and water Brown's horses.

On the table Judith put marmalade, white bread baked from flour that had been one of Dane's almost daily gifts, glasses of buttermilk and butter, which Deborah fetched from the well-house, warmed-over greens, fried mush and sorghum, and the woodcock. Brown and Judith started in voraciously.

"You keep some luxury here." Brown's craggy brow furrowed as he glanced from the truffled delicacy to the sugar and coffee Deborah had brought on a tray. His manner left no doubt of his opinion of such fripperies when their exorbitant cost might go toward operating the underground railroad. It took money to smuggle slaves into Canada and provide subsistence till they found homes and jobs.

"The luxuries are gifts from the English gentlemen who helped fight off Jed and his Missourians," Deborah said. "I hope you'll take a packet of food with you."

Brown grunted assent and partook of the woodcock, as if to prevent mortals of lesser integrity from wallowing in such corporeal delights. Thos brought in fresh water and sat down eagerly across from Brown.

"Are you bringing many 'trains' in, sir?"

"Why do you care?"

Thos flushed. "Why, I—I'd like to do more than I am. I was wondering if—what—"

"I can use bold men." Brown's stormy eyes swept him with the force of a strong wind. "I'm going to run a hundred thousand dollars' worth of slaves through this Territory before I'm done! But you're useful here, young man. I won't use you across the border without your parents' consent. Get that and then seek me out."

"Thos!" Deborah cried, but his eyes were shining.

Across the table he reached for John Brown's bony hand. When he shook it, Deborah's scalp crawled. For a moment, the hand her brother gripped seemed skeletal, stained with drying blood.

"I'll come," vowed Thos. "It may take a while to convince my parents, but I'll come to you as soon as I can."

Deborah's fingers shook as she put sardines, white bread, figs, raisins, and a cut of Gloucester cheese into an aged pillowcase. Why did the dreadful old firebrand have to turn up and kindle Thos's already nearly uncontrollable yearning for action? Yet, though she blamed Brown, she knew in her heart that Thos, since the Missourians' night raid, had been like a spirited young horse plunging against restraints. He was bound to break loose soon.

But not with Brown—please, not with Brown! Who knew what midnight slaughters and massacres the grim old wretch might carry out?

Distressed though she was, Deborah offered him more coffee. He refused, rising and rearming himself before he closed his veined hands over Judith's. "Do as the Whitlaws tell you, and may you get safe to Canada," he said.

"Can't thank you enough." The hazel eyes glittered with held-back tears. "I'll pray for you every day of my life, Mr. Brown."

"Bless you for that," he said gravely. "Men say I've committed crimes, but I prayed long and hard before—and after—every enterprise. I believe God is with me."

No, thought Deborah as he nodded to her and took the food. *The shadow of death is with you. Or you are the shadow.* He seemed to tower, gray, angular, an Old Testament prophet of wrath and desolation. She closed her eyes in a kind of panic. When she looked again, he was gone.

Mother and Father greeted Judith kindly when they came home that night, but they had shocking news. A smoldering quarrel over a boundary between Jim Lane and Gaius Jenkins, also a Free State man, had ended with Lane shooting Jenkins dead.

Ex-sheriff Jones, pro-slaver and leader of the 1856 sack of Lawrence, walked through the gathering crowd, urging them to lynch his old enemy, Lane, but the present sheriff, Sam Walker, warned Jones that if the crowd hanged anyone, they'd probably begin with their old scourge, Jones himself.

Sheriff Walker brought a carriage and took Lane to jail. Since Lane had been fired on first, it was unlikely that he'd be indicted. "But," said Father, much distressed, "it's frightful that Free State men should kill each other. The New Englanders have tended to back Jenkins, while the Midwesterners have believed all of Lane's stories about Jenkins being taken into Lecompton by a 'nigger'—pardon me, Judith, but that's how he put it. And Lane swore that Jenkins had plowed over his daughter's grave."

"I don't trust Jim Lane," said Mother. "And I think his wife's a ninny to have married him again. I don't know why he wants a farm. Precious little plowing *he* gets done trying to live up to that absurd name. Grim Chieftain! Chief of what?" When Thos, stricken at this assessment of his hero, started to protest, Mother shushed him. "Let the grand jury deal with him and let's have our dinner! Judith, my dear, you've had an ordeal, but we're glad to have you and we'll do our best to make you comfortable and safe."

"Thank you, ma'am," Judith murmured. From beneath her downcast dark lashes, she appeared to be carefully studying the elder Whitlaws, on whom her freedom and, perhaps life depended.

For her part, Leticia looked with sympathy at the younger woman's stained, torn calico dress, mute testimony to her flight through the brush of Missouri and southeastern Kansas. "We'll heat you some bath water, and I have a good salve if you have any deep scratches. Could you bring any other clothes?"

"Only had one other dress, ma'am, and I had to leave it 'cause when I got a chance to run away from that devil, Mr. Jed, I never stopped or looked back till I was on the Kansas side of them border mounds."

Government surveyors had, beginning in 1854, surveyed the Territory into townships, sections, and quarter-sections, marked by stones wherever available, and when not, by posts set in deposits of charcoal with a mound heaped around the marker. Markers denoting state lines were often mounds two feet high a mile apart. Every sixth mound was four feet high, and sometimes tree seeds were planted at these conical heaps of earth.

A fortified stone wall, of course, wouldn't have turned back Border Ruffians hot on the trail of an escaping slave. Judith must know that better than anyone. But to be on free—if disputed—ground, rather than in absolute slave territory must have greatly lifted her spirits.

"I think one of my dresses will fit you better than Deborah's," decided Mother, who was a few inches the taller. She took Judith's hands and kissed her. "Welcome, with all our hearts! Is dinner ready, Deborah? I declare, I'm famished!"

Judith refused to take Deborah's bed, but Thos persuaded her that he preferred sleeping outdoors, so she agreed to use the lean-to. She was shy of Father and Thos—small wonder after her experience of Jed—but she became passionately attached to Leticia and tried so insistently to please her that Deborah began to feel a bit displaced, a trifle jealous.

She scolded herself harshly. Wasn't Judith entitled to kindness and sympathy after what she'd endured? And it was still a long, hazardous way to Canada. Still, between bad conscience over hiding the Bowie, fear that Thos would join Brown, and Judith's absorbing considerable amounts of her parents' attention, Deborah was filled with unease.

Thos thought her restlessness had a different root. "Why're you always looking toward town?" he said and grinned the day when, with Judith helping, the twins started harvesting their acres of wheat.

This had been sowed by hand after the plowed field had been harrowed by a large dead plum bush, which had been dragged by Nebuchadnezzar to cover the seed. The grain stood six feet high, hadn't been beaten down by rain, and the Whitlaws, this year, should have their own good flour.

Deborah and Judith followed Thos, gathering the loose wheat and binding it with its own straw into bundles that they heaped into shocks. The cradle, wooden fingers fastened to a scythe, left the grain in swaths with heads in one direction, but it was hot, laborious labor, and Deborah, in no mood for her brother's teasing, scowled as he continued.

"Shall I tell Rolf you miss him?"

"I don't!" Deborah snapped, straightening to ease her aching back. "I'm glad he's gone!"

She was, certainly, yet there was no denying that his presence had made life interesting. She didn't want him to make love to her; but it was flattering to know he wanted to, and highly exciting. Perhaps she *had* begun to enjoy eluding him.

Vanity and wickedness, sure enough, but no woman could be completely indifferent to Rolf when he was on his best, most charming, behavior.

"If it's not Rolf you miss, it must be Dane," persisted Thos. "Best not pin your heart on him, twin! I hear he escorted Mrs. Eden to the literary society the other night."

Deborah's heart plunged. Could Dane be enamored of that *fast* widow? Was that why he never stopped by?

Thos said hastily, "He's been painting Dry Leaf and some other Shawnee, too. Been gone a lot." Deborah scarcely heard this would-be comfort. She hadn't seen Dane since more than a week ago, when Johnny had given her the Bowie, though Rolf had stopped off once with the livery stable's smartest carriage. Deborah had refused to go driving with him, he'd left in a huff, and he hadn't been back, either!

Deborah gave an exasperated sigh. The chaff itched maddeningly between her breasts and wherever it had lodged on her sweaty skin. Judith and Thos must be just as miserable. How she wished the buffalo wallow were full of clear, cool water and they could go there and swim, float lazily, and watch the roses, buttercups, and Johnny Jump-ups along the banks!

Might as well wish for ice cream or a lake right here in the field. Thos stopped to get a drink from the water jug they'd brought along. Deborah wiped her face and held the neck of her dress open to the faint breeze.

"You don't have to help us all the time, Judith," she told the older young woman. "You're company, you know."

"Work to be done," said Judith. "I eat and I can work."

"But Judith," Deborah floundered, "it—well, it doesn't seem right that you should run away from Jed and then work just as hard for us."

Judith's chin lifted stubbornly on her slender throat. "I know you people in danger for me. No way I can pay that. But I can leastways earn my food."

Thos finished drinking and was picking up the cradle

when suddenly he shaded his eyes and pointed. A rider with a led horse. " 'Borah! Is that Dane's gray?"

Peering at the figures silhouetted against the broad, bright sky, Deborah's heart pounded, mingling with the hoofbeats now dimly reaching them. "I think it is," she said. "But why does he have the other horse?"

"We'll soon know. Judith, till we're sure it's someone we can trust, you'd better scoot into the lean-to."

She was already gone, soundless. The fewer people who knew where she was, the safer. Johnny knew, and so did Sara and Maccabee, for the smithy was an alternate station, and Judith might possibly need help from them. The Hunters didn't know. The day Rolf had stopped by with the carriage, the young women had been doing the washing and Judith had hidden in the well-house.

Standing in the field, the twins watched the horseman. Even before Deborah could see his face, she knew by the set of his head and shoulders that it was Dane—coming when he didn't have to; when there was no invalid brother to visit; when he knew the senior Whitlaws were at the shop. Deborah's hands, tightly clenched, were perspiring. Her stomach curled into a tight little knot.

What should she say to him? How should she act? How could she bring back that moment when their gazes had met, recognized, united, on the night the Missourians came?

Don't be a fool. He hasn't come near you in a week. You may have imagined how he looked at you that night of the raid. You were frightened enough to mistake anything.

Anything. Except the way *she'd* felt.

He had been escorting Melissa Eden. Deborah couldn't believe it was strictly because of his interest in things literary. So she swallowed to bring her voice under control, and as he reined in the horse called Lightning, halted the saddled, bridled, honey-colored mare, Deborah greeted him with cool politeness, though Thos strode up to shake his hand and invite him to dinner.

"We're ready to quit and eat." Thos mopped his dripping forehead. "Hot work, but we'll finish up tomorrow." He added proudly, "We ought to make thirty bushels to the acre, so we'll have some to sell on top of all the flour and grain we need ourselves."

"Do you have an extra scythe or sickle?" asked Dane, stroking the neck of the restive little mare.

She was about the prettiest creature Deborah had ever seen, groomed to shining, her mane as flaxen as a Dutch girl's, the golden muzzle silky and neat. Her saddle blanket was vivid blue and the saddle was trimmed with silver conchos.

A mount for a princess, Deborah thought wistfully. Even Sara's spotted pony wasn't this handsome. Dane must be taking her to Johnny's for shoeing. And then—oh, grief and horrors! Was the mare for Melissa Eden, chosen because it matched her hair, and with a blanket the color of her eyes?

If so, Dane was besotted, indeed, and she, Deborah, had been dreaming, hoping—more than she'd realized until now. Feeling acutely sick, Deborah muttered that she'd better start setting dinner out, and she made for the cabin, hearing Thos, in puzzlement, say there was a sickle, and Dane, dismounting, say, "Good. After dinner, I'll help."

You help? Deborah thought incredulously. He wouldn't know how to hold a scythe, would blister those painter's hands in minutes! She stopped at the well-house for buttermilk, butter, cottage cheese, and a few eggs to fry with left-over potatoes. Thos and Dane were unsaddling and rubbing down the horses, so Dane must intend to help with the harvest. A fine sight he'd be with his fine tailored broadcloth all covered with chaff and straw! Perhaps he could wear Thos's other trousers. Dane was much broader through the shoulders, but not, she judged, through waist and thighs, an immodest but undeniably interesting thought.

Entering the cabin, Deborah put down her burden, stirred up the fire, and put on potatoes mixed with eggs and chopped green onions before she went to the lean-to and conferred with Judith.

"Mr. Hunter's English and doesn't want any part of our quarrels. He means to help with the harvest, so unless you'd rather stay hidden all afternoon, it might be as well for you to come out now."

"He a growed-up man you can trust?" demanded Judith. "Tongue won't get carried away?"

"He's a grown-up man." Deborah realized, with grudging, that she had to admit that. "And I think he always thinks before he speaks, which makes for dull conversation—or none at all! But I'm sure, Judith, that he won't say anything about you."

Judith nodded, rising from the pallet. "Comin' in, then.

I want to help with the wheat. Ruther do anything than stay hid like a fox in its den!"

Dane, of course, had brought a gift: hickory-smoked ham. Deborah introduced him to Judith, adding that it was highly important that he not mention her to anyone.

He nodded and spoke pleasantly, as if he met runaways every day. Judith smiled. Tension went out of her, and she helped Deborah set out the meal, including generous slices of ham.

"That's a good man," she told Deborah under her breath while Thos and Dane were discussing the gold rush that was bound to follow the return of some prospectors with considerable "dust." "He's not the kind would ever bed a woman who didn't want him." As Deborah gasped at this plain speaking, Judith laughed, a rich, throaty chuckling. "That don' mean he has to do without! He your beau?"

"No," said Deborah shortly, dishing out the potatoes.

She set them down with something of a bang. Dane shot her a questioning, amused look, then rose quickly to seat her while Thos did the same for Judith. Such courtesies had embarrassed Judith at first, but Leticia had pointed out that Judith was entitled to the treatment due a woman and should grow accustomed to accepting such gestures gracefully.

It was taken for granted by now that Dane would never accept the visitor's honor, saying grace, so Thos did, sounding especially sincere when he said they'd be most grateful and glad when the bountiful harvest was over, *and* the threshing *and* the flailing and winnowing.

"Dane's through with Fall Leaf's portrait," Thos said. "And Fall Leaf liked it so much that he wants one for himself."

"And of his favorite horse," Dane added. "He declined to pay in gold nuggets like those he brought back from the South Platte, so we did some horse-trading. Do you think I was cheated, Miss Deborah? Two large oils for that cream-gold mare?"

"I've never seen your work except for sketches," Deborah said. "But if I had them, I'd trade two Rembrandts for that horse and still feel I had the best of the swap."

Dane looked appalled before he chuckled. "I'm overwhelmed at your valuation of art! But I suppose a horse *is* more useful in this country."

"Yes," Deborah said rather shortly.

Dane looked at her quizzically. "I'd hoped you'd go riding with me this afternoon, Miss Deborah, to let me see if the mare's suitable for a lady, but it looks like today and tomorrow morning must go to harvesting. May I hope that tomorrow afternoon you'd favor me with your company?"

Deborah stared at him, swept by conflict. To ride that fairy-tale animal one whole afternoon with Dane, to have that time wtih him, no matter what followed—

Yes! She'd have that, at least. He didn't need to know how it was for her, how much and what.

"If we get in the harvest, sir, and if my parents consent, I'd be delighted to try the mare for you—though you must understand most of my riding's been a matter of hanging onto Thos while Nebuchadnezzar plods along."

"You're exactly right for what I need to ascertain," he assured her. "And your parents have already agreed to trust you to me."

When? Startled, Deborah glanced up at him and encountered a strange light deep in his eyes, like the blue nimbus bordering candle flame. It pierced into her like a white-hot blade. Fighting a slow inner trembling, she tore her eyes away while she still had some shreds of composure left.

What was the matter with her? How could she respond in this frightening, mind-dizzying way to a man who'd kept his cold, careful distance and was courting a sensuous, experienced woman who must know how to match and please him as no girl possibly could—at least not one brought up and trained by Leticia Whitlaw!

Eagerly turning the subject to the gold at Pike's Peak, Thos said that Father was printing a book by one of the returned prospectors, and that a number of other guides were being published by various printers. Merchants were ordering in wagonloads and çargoes of supplies to outfit the swarms of gold-seekers who were already leaving, hoping to get a head start on the flood of easterners certain to come west with the spring weather.

"They've already platted a town named Denver right at the foot of the mountains," Thos said.

"And that's still in Kansas Territory?" marveled Dane.

"Sure," said Thos airily. "This is a big country." His russet eyes sparkled. "I'd sure like to try my luck. Just imagine, finding gold!"

"Why don't you?" asked Dane with an indulgent grin. "Rolf would probably go with you; he's on fire to do anything, so long as it's not boring and ordinary.

Boyish enthusiasm changed abruptly into a man's set purpose. "John Brown's back in Kansas."

"So I'd heard." Dane shrugged. "I don't know why he and Montgomery and the rest of those men in southeast Kansas don't just let the inevitable happen."

Thos scowled at this criticism of the men he longed to follow. "What do you mean?"

"Days are past when Missourians could cross by the hundreds and vote. The pro-slave Lecompton constitution's bound to be voted down this summer. The Free Staters have won. It'll simply need time to make it all legal."

"You say that when it's less than a month ago that those men were murdered on the Marais des Cygnes!" cried Thos. "How can you remember that and wonder at their friends wanting vengeance?"

"As one who got more war than he wanted, I confess to bafflement over why each side seems intent on having the last massacre."

Much on his dignity, Thos said, "Maybe you don't understand, sir, being a foreigner, but Brown won't rest while there's a slave in the country. And I think he's right!"

"I believe he even advocates kidnapping them out of slave states," remarked Dane.

"He does. And I'm going to help him."

"Thos!" Deborah turned on her twin, made savage by fear. "Don't go with that horrible old man!"

"Why, 'Borah!" Thos stared at her, eyes growing larger and larger. "I don't like what happened at Pottawatomie, either, but this is the same as war! Brown—well, you know Father says he's a torch to burn down the whole house of slavery."

"He may be that." There was a bitter taste in Deborah's mouth. "He may be God's sword. But he's terrible." She caught her twin's gaze and held it. "I mean this, Thos." She spoke slowly, measuring her words. "I'd rather see you dead than dragging unarmed men out to slaughter. I'd rather see you dead."

White to the lips, Thos seemed dazed. With a dull shake of his head, he pushed back the bench and reached for his hat.

"I'll get out the sickle for you," he said to Dane.

Judith grabbed Deborah's arm and gave her a hard shake. "What you mean, sayin' such a crazy thing? That's your brother—your twin! Almost you! You go after him right now, an' say you don' mean it!"

"But I do!" Deborah sprang up and began clearing the table, fighting tears that stung her eyelids.

"That's a funny thing to say when you've got a Bowie under your mattress!" Judith scorned.

"Fighting's one thing," Deborah flashed, scrubbing at the tears that *would* fall. Had she bungled, only managed to set Thos more stubbornly in his wish? "If there's a war, I'd go if I could, and I'm sure Thos will. It's this cold-blooded slaughtering I can't bear!"

Dane had risen. She didn't know how it happened, but he was holding her. "Your brother won't kill like that," he soothed, stroking her hair as she wept against his shoulder. "I've been a soldier, Deborah. I know the ice-cold natural assassins. Thos isn't one. But cry. Get all the fear and worry out."

His voice was gentle. He comforted her with it and his hands till the wrenching sobs eased. What a baby he must think her! Or a hysterical woman, which was worse. Freeing herself, Deborah choked out an apology and hurried to help Judith with the dishes.

Dane watched her, hesitating a moment. Then he took off his coat and tie, rolled up the sleeves of his snowy linen shirt, and went out. Apparently he was serious about helping.

Judith ignored Deborah as they did the dishes, though several times Deborah caught hazel eyes regarding her with puzzlement that verged on hostility, and several times Judith gave a vexed shake of her lioness's head. It was clear there was much she wanted to say about John Brown, which was natural since he'd helped her, but Deborah didn't want to hear his tactics defended.

Maybe a man like that was necessary in times like these, or like Robespierre in the French Revolution, or Oliver Cromwell, but she shrank from such men in a revulsion multiplied by their self-righteousness. She prayed with all her might that Thos would keep free of the hypnotic power Brown exercised over his sons and those who followed him.

When the women went out to the field, Dane was swinging the sickle in a smooth, controlled way that made Deborah positive he'd done it before, grasping a handful of grain, shearing it off, and leaving it in a little pile. This was more laborious and slower than the cradle, but Dane had a bit of a start and managed to hold most of it as she collected the heaps and bounded them.

She was afraid that he'd blister his hands on the sickle and soon ran back to the house to locate Josiah's winter gauntlets.

Dane looked at her quizzically as she called to him and proffered the gloves. "You must think me tender, indeed." He smiled, but he did put them on. "My best friend, much to my father's dismay, was the gamekeeper's son. We often helped in the harvest, in fields far from where my father might spy us. Rob and I knew the river and woods better than any poacher. While I was off at school, I never met among the gentry's sons anyone I liked as well as Rob."

"Is he still at your home?" Deborah tried to conjure up an image of what Dane's country was like, but she only saw thatched cottages and gray turreted castles.

"No." Dane's face closed. "He came into the army with me. He died at Balaclava."

Turning abruptly, he swung the sickle, as if cutting at some old enemy. The waving wheat blurred in front of Deborah. It was a moment before she could see well enough to bundle up the grain.

• *vii* •

Chores next morning, breakfast, family worship, with Judith taking part by now as if she'd been born to it. Dane rode up as the older Whitlaws were leaving, and the others were in the field while morning cool lessened the itch of chaff on their skin.

Meadlowlarks sang from the surrounding grass and prairie chickens whirred when the harvesters came near enough to alarm them. Mockingbirds, crows, and red-winged blackbirds greedily devoured grain fallen from the reaping. They were welcome to that but were shooed away from the shocks.

After the wheat was thoroughly cured and dry, it would

be thrashed and then the horses and Venus would be turned in to feed on the nutritious stubble. Now they were barred by the prickly Osage orange hedge grown high enough to be protective in the three years since the Whitlaws had planted the sproutings given them by Johnny.

"I don't like fences," he growled, "but you've got to have 'em if you're going to grow crops." He'd spat prodigiously. "One damned thing follows the other. Plains Indians move around, gather berries, nuts, roots, and such like wild foods. They eat a lot of those without getting tied down to a patch of land and a crop they have to stay with."

"But Mr. Chaudoin," Mother had protested, "white people don't roam around like that. By farming and raising domestic animals, many people can be fed off comparatively little land."

"And that's good?" scoffed Johnny. "The whites multiplied till they filled up Europe and started spillin' over here. Now they've crowded up the land east of the Mississippi, they're gobblin' up the plains, pourin' into California and Utah and Oregon. Where they'll go then only Wakan Tanka knows, but if they keep on litterin' worse'n jackrabbits, they'll have to farm the ocean or find a way to plow the stars!"

At fifteen, Deborah hadn't learned to suppress impertinent questions. Frowning, she'd asked, "But Mr. Chaudoin, if you like Indians ways so much, why didn't you stay wtih the Sioux?"

"Deborah!" rebuked Mother, but Johnny grinned crookedly, tweaking one of Deborah's plaits.

"Didn't belong after Sweet Grass died. Truth to tell, I never belonged all that much. The Lakotah believe they're Wakan Tanka's only true children, and their word for stranger also means enemy. My father-in-law never stopped calling me 'dog face' and 'flop-ears' behind my back, and my brothers-in-law were glad their sister had no children from a 'crooked foot.' "

Thos, also uninhibited, asked with wide eyes, "But didn't you call them gut-eaters?"

"Thos!" thundered Josiah.

Bursting into a roar of laughter, Johnny hugged Thos and patted him on the shoulder with the force of a playful bear. *"Cesli Tatanka!* They *were* gut-eaters, and so was I! Nothin' better than 'boudins' wrapped around a stick and roasted crisp! Next time I get a buffalo, you'll have to try 'em!"

Thos and Father had, pronouncing them excellent, but the Whitlaw women had left the small intestines for smoked fat from the back bone and rich steaks from the hump.

And the Osage orange, set out in furrows and watered painstakingly from the well till they had a good start, now protected the wheat, planted last fall for the first time.

Corn had been the first crop, quick-growing, easy to plant and harvest. That field was fenced with rails from trees cut along the Kaw. The Whitlaws were still enjoying roasting ears, but before the blades started yellowing, it'd be time to strip them from the ears and dry them for fodder, leaving the stalks supporting the naked ears to wait till autumn for harvesting.

In spite of the heat, stooping and tying that made her back and shoulders ache, Deborah got great satisfaction out of the harvest, as she had earlier from planting. Whatever Johnny said about crops, she felt it was a miracle for hard, dead-seeming grain to spend a season under earth and come up, radiantly green, to grow into food by the grace of sun and rain.

It was Demeter restoring the fields when her daughter came back to her from death, Attis, Adonis, Osiris, Tammuz, those who died and lived again. Josiah Whitlaw was a student and lover of mythology. Along with fairy tales, fables, and Bible stories, the twins had grown up with the Trojan War and Ulysses's wanderings, gleanings from Herodotus, Plutarch, Pausanias, and Strabo, and the Norse legends upon which Mr. Richard Wagner was building a great operatic cycle after his earlier success with *Lohengrin* and *Tannhäuser*.

Leticia had always been somewhat troubled by Josiah's filling her children's minds with what she called "heathenish false gods and idols," to which Josiah countered that since false gods were forever being mentioned in the Bible, he thought people should know something about them.

Though Father faithfully attended services and was a good friend of Reverend Cordley, an English-born graduate of Andover Theological Seminary and the University of Michigan, who had come to pastor the Plymouth Congregational Church in Lawrence last year, Deborah secretly believed he had no religion at all, or a very broad one, depending on how one looked at it. He liked the Sioux name for God, Wakan Tanka, or Great Holy, and had said more than once, even to Reverend Cordley, that if Unitarians weren't so contentious and proud of their brains, he'd have joined them.

Adding another bundle to a shock, Deborah smiled. How her thoughts had ranged, from Babylonia to Greece! But it wasn't surprising that the harvest took one back: to Ruth, gleaning in an alien field and finding a husband; even to Cain, who killed his brother because God had preferred Abel's flesh offering to Cain's fruit and grain. There was something ancient and enduring, a binding of generations, in gathering a harvest.

Father said machinery was sure to be invented for planting, cutting, binding, and threshing, but so far methods hadn't changed drastically since some man or woman first poked holes in the earth with a sharp stick and covered the seed with his or her heel.

Machines would make it easier and faster, of course, just as the one for sewing invented by Mr. Howe and developed by Mr. Singer had made a tremendous difference in making clothes. Deborah was certainly glad the family had one, and she wished mightily that someone would invent a washing machine. She truly hated the whole hot, monotonous, tiring chore, which had to be done week after week. In winter, it wasn't quite so bad, though then one's hands got numb and chapped.

But harvest was once a year, an earth magic that promised food through the cold months, and handling the grain, smelling it, seeing the growing number of shocks dot the field—all these made the work a sort of ritual, a ceremony. She'd never dare say that to Thos, of course, who felt about any kind of farmwork the way she felt about laundry—even if he weren't so stiffly angry at her for what she'd said yesterday. That memory made her eyes sting and she pushed it away. Thos *had* to understand. He'd get over his hurt.

She wouldn't tell him, either, what an odd contentment filled her when she watched Dane's broad shoulders swing the sickle, or how she tried to pick up the wheat where she fancied his hand had gripped it. And she was going riding with him—all afternoon!—on the honey-cream mare that had spent the night at the Whitlaws', so that last night, after the chores were done, Deborah had been able to walk up to the beautiful creature and feed her part of one of the green apples Father had garnered that day as pay for advertising.

It had been some help for the ache at her twin's continuing coldness to caress the soft, sensitive muzzle that nudged her palm for more goodies, to murmur praises to the alertly tilted ears.

"I can hardly wait to ride you, Beauty," Deborah whispered. *And be with Dane . . . though what good would that do?*

The field, now, was almost cut. Thos and Dane finished at opposite ends and stood grinning at each other a moment before Dane looked at Deborah.

His smile faded. As if caught irresistibly, his gaze dwelled on her unbuttoned throat, the worn calico clinging moistly to her breasts.

A man and woman had shared harvest, working in rhythm, honoring the strength of each other. Now they shared something else. Dane's eyes came back to her face.

"Why don't you ladies wash up and start dinner?" he asked. "Thos and I can finish binding."

Deborah shook chaff and straw from her, and with Judith she started to the house. Had she imagined the way his gaze had lingered? Had it been, wretched thought, an uncontrollable male reaction that had nothing to do, really, with her? What she hadn't imagined was the way she'd felt. As she and Judith washed at the bench by the door, her flesh seemed to be burning—not from the sun, but from his eyes.

They were nearly through the meal when horses nickered and hooves sounded down the lane. Motioning the others to sit still, Dane crossed to the door, stiffened, and gave a small shrug.

"Well, Rolf, I thought you were hunting today."

Judith rose and hurried to the bedroom. From there she could make a quick escape to the lean-to. Deborah took her plate and fork and hid them in the dishpan.

"And I thought you were painting." Rolf's mocking voice approached the house. "Now what can be the magnet that draws us from our usual pursuits and passions?"

"I had a mind to help with the harvest." Dane, reluctantly, it seemed, let his brother enter.

"Oh, yes, you've always acted like a throwback to some yeoman in our family." Rolf's eyes rested on Deborah. "Even to my uneducated view, the wheat seemed all cut and shocked. No boiling kettles and washtubs fill the yard. Am I so lucky, Miss Deborah, as to find you at leisure?"

"Let me set you a place," she offered. "You must be hungry."

"So I am." He took the side of the bench just vacated by Judith. "Thanks for your charming concern for my outer man. But you haven't answered my question."

"Miss Deborah's riding with me," said Dane. His level gaze met and held his brother's. "She's consented to try the mare Fall Leaf traded me."

Rolf paused, fork halfway to his mouth. "So that's what happened to that fantastic beast! The fair Melissa simpered to me that the blue blanket exactly matched her eyes."

"Mrs. Eden has an unnerving way of leaping to conclusions and forcing—or trying to force—others to jump, too." Dane's tone was dry.

"How tactfully you put it." Rolf grinned. "Discourage her gently, will you? If she decides she can't have you, she may start in on me."

Did he mean—were they saying—? Deborah's heart gave a strange little skip. Dane didn't *sound* in love with Melissa Eden. But perhaps they'd just had one of those lovers' quarrels, which, when made up, whetted and doubled desires. She poured buttermilk for Rolf, then drew back as he straightened in a way that brought his head against her shoulder.

"I can accompany you, brother," he said to Dane. "You might be glad of my pistols if you encounter roving desperadoes, be they Free State or pro-slave."

"Thanks, but I'm able to look after Miss Deborah."

Again, Deborah's heart tripped and began to pound. If Dane's whole concern was in testing the mare for a lady's mount, he woundn't care if Rolf came along, would he? But probably he thought Rolf's harum-scarum riding style would make the mare, or Deborah, fidgety.

Rolf's mouth hardened. He stared at Dane for a long moment, eyes seeming almost black. Deborah didn't know how tense she was till he chuckled and she relaxed.

"It seems I must hope for another day. But it's not too soon to invite you all to a celebration July 4."

"July 4?" echoed Thos and grinned. "What kind of celebration? A shooting match?"

"No jollities like that," Rolf promised. "But I'm told it's a great holiday. Rather than skulk about the fringes like the defeated enemy, I decided to be quick off the mark and host some festivities myself."

With a slow, admiring whistle, Thos said, "That must be what you British call 'cheek.' What a dandy notion! It'll be the talk of the Territory."

Rolf said modestly, "Well, I doubt if it'll crowd out politics or the gold rush, but I'll do my best. I've engaged the Free State Hotel and they'll prepare the food, though I've promised to bring in the game. Want to help, Thos? Four or five of us are going out on the prairie a few days early to try to bring back a wagonload of buffalo meat."

"I'd like to go." Thos flushed with excitement. "Depends on what work there is here."

"I hope," said Dane blightingly, "that one from this group's been buffalo hunting before!"

"They all have," retorted Rolf. Pointedly turning his back on Dane, he looked eagerly at Deborah, sure of her approval. "I talked to your father this morning, Miss Deborah. He's agreed to arrange the program so it'll be a proper Fourth, even if an Englishman's putting it on."

If Father helped, involving the older, more settled community, it should go off beautifully. Though Lawrence had celebrated in 1855 with an ice-cream supper, festivities often were boisterous, attracting people from miles away, including Indians. Youngbloods and drifters would always flock to free food and gaiety, but an Englishman's appropriation of the holiday might have been taken amiss by Lawrence's New Englanders, who had a fresher memory of the origins of the Fourth than did native Midwesterners.

"You become a diplomat!" Dane marveled. "Sir Harry would admire your tactics, if not the cause on which you mean to lavish his money."

"Why don't you contribute, too, elder brother, so that if we run short of funds and have to tell why, *pater* can be angry with us both?"

"I'm living off commissions I carried out before I left England, and an advance from my publisher," Dane said. "I haven't spent a penny of Sir Harry's remittances."

"All the more for me!" Rolf laughed. He sobered, pushing back his raw-gold hair. "Come now, Dane, you know I've lost more than this fête will cost in one night's gambling! And you can't deny I've mended my ways. I haven't been up all night since we left Leavenworth!"

The twins had to smile at his idea of virtue, but Dane balled his fist and rubbed it affectionately against his brother's jaw. "You've done rather well, youngling. Not bosky above a half-dozen times in a whole month! But we needn't fear, just at present, that your sprouting wings will waft you beyond our ken!"

"But you want me to ride beyond it," Rolf said with remarkable good nature. "I suppose you deserve a reward for helping with the harvest, but I'm hereby bespeaking Miss Deborah's company for the Fourth of July."

"She can answer that later, you rapscallion!"

"All right, I'm going." Rolf cast down his eyelids and said in a comically sultry tone, "Melissa's invited us to tea this afternoon. I'll have to comfort her for your absence."

"With you there, she'll have no time to think about me," Dane chuckled. If he were jealous, he didn't show it. "Now go, or unsaddle your horse. It's not right to leave him standing like that for hours."

Rolf pulled his forelock exaggeratedly across one eye. "Right, sir! This instant, Captain Hunter! I was just about to do it, sir—"

He dodged his brother's forceful hand and went out, whistling jauntily. Dane's breath came out in a sigh.

"That's a relief. Never know with that young cub!"

"What do you mean?" asked Deborah after she'd called to Judith that it was safe to come out.

Rolf left at a canter. Dane frowned as if debating how much to say. "For less than thwarting him in the way I did this afternoon, he's pulled a pistol on me. He's like some tricky explosive, sometimes igniting at a feather touch, other times taking mortal insult as a joke."

"That must be difficult for you."

Dane shrugged. "Father's despaired of him. He looked on this journey as kill-or-cure. Of late I've dared to hope it's cure. Rolf has, for him, been well behaved."

Deborah had started doing the dishes, but Thos firmly walked her out of the kitchen space. "Judith and I'll do these, 'Borah. You two get on with your ride."

"But—" she protested. He shook a chiding finger. They hadn't really spoken since her outburst yesterday, and she was joyous to see the old tenderness back in his warm brown eyes.

"If it hadn't been for Dane, we'd still be in the field."

"Go along," Judith commanded, taking over the dishpan.

Thus evicted, Deborah changed from her dusty dress

to her best one, except for Sunday's dark green poplin. This gown showed the wear of use and washing, but it was her favorite, a soft gray-green cotton with gathered sleeves, ruffles at the throat.

She'd washed her hair the day before the harvest. In spite of perspiration and chaff, a vigorous brushing brought it to lustrousness and she tied it back with a matching ribbon. Staring in the small mirror at eyes dancing with eagerness, she thought she looked at least pretty till she remembered Melissa. Then she felt young, sunburned, awkward, and plain, with a too-large mouth, too-firm jaw, and eyes so big that they gave a waifish look to her thin, almost triangular face.

Confidence waning, she glanced at her brown, stubble-scratched hands, with blunted fingernails and work-toughened palms. Not hands a man would long to press to his face or lips! And her dress was faded, her hair wild and curly—not at all like Melissa's smoothly sculptured coif.

Oh, oh—damn!

Shocked at the profanity, Deborah gritted her teeth, then glared at the trembling-lipped mirror image. *Stop it!* she told herself. *You work and you look like it. You're a frontier woman, not an aristocrat or even a townswoman like Melissa, with little to do but tend to her face and body. It's a battle, here, even to keep clean. Anyway, Dane Hunter's known countless handsome, cultured women, dressed and styled in the latest Paris modes. You'd only be ridiculous in trying to ape them. Be what you are. At least you can show him all women aren't the same!*

Aren't they? mocked an amused, cynical inner voice. *Doesn't every woman want to seem beautiful to the man she loves?*

Quelling this treacherous inquisitor, Deborah marched into the main cabin, told Judith and Thos good-bye, and stalked past Dane, head defiantly high.

She thought irefully that she detected the slightest tug at the corner of his long mouth, but he said nothing as they approached the horses he'd saddled and bridled while she was dressing.

The gray, clean-limbed and mettlesome, stood two and a half hands higher than the mare. Curried to shining, flowing manes combed, they made a breathtaking pair. Deborah caressed the horse's neck and muzzle, the broad space between the liquid eyes where a little star-like whorl of white grew in all directions.

"Pretty, pretty thing!" she crooned. "What's your name?"

"What would you suggest?" asked Dane. "Fall Leaf got her from Californios. They called her Chica, or Chiquita, which means 'little girl.' "

"Chica. Chiquita." Deborah tasted the words.

Endearing but not splendid. Something like Glory or Beauty came closer, but might be grandiloquent for every day.

"It's nice to have a Spanish name for a Spanish horse," Deborah said. "Chica's easy and sounds happy."

Dark eyebrows quirked. "Now, how does a name sound *happy?*"

She thought, couldn't explain, and said helplessly, "Some just do."

"Is Deborah a happy name?" he persisted, smiling in that teasing, tender male way that utterly weakened and confounded her.

"No." She sighed. "It sounds stern and righteous and Old Testament—but I hate 'Debby,' and ' 'Borah' isn't much better!"

Dane chuckled. "Deborah's clean and honest. Strong. Musical, too, if one gives the syllables full value. But I'm sure your lover will find you a sweet, soft name."

Could he have any notion of how his eyes, gentled to a misty gray-blue like autumn haze along the Kaw, managed to overwhelm and engulf her? Drowned in their depths, she tried to speak several times before she blurted out, "I—don't have a lover!"

"No?" Again the cocked eyebrow, the smile that deepened the cleft in his chin, tempered the formidable hardness of his jaw. "That's bound to be soon remedied. I couldn't get a sidessaddle, so I hope that, for safety, you'll sit astride."

She hesitated, torn between propriety and comfort, but he swung her up as if there were no question, then held the reins while, in blushing confusion, she tugged and wrestled with her skirts. Arranging these as best she could, she was mortified to see that moccasined feet and legs were exposed almost to the knee.

Merriment lurked in his eyes, the curve of his mouth, but to scold would only amuse him further. He'd certainly seen a good deal more of some women than a glimpse of leg; she mustn't let him disconcert her even more. She took the reins from him. Their fingers brushed, and in spite of all her self-lectures and chidings, flame shot through her, seared deep into secret parts never reached before.

What *could* she do about this? It was surely too wild, too desperate and wanton, to be in love, the kind uniting her parents. Sara and Thos might feel something like this, but that was different. They loved each other; each held the quenching, the peace, for the other's fire and storm.

Deborah knew enough of men to think that perhaps if she told Dane how she felt, he would kiss her, make free with her, ease this fever in her blood. But she wanted more than that, more than temporary quieting of what she was sure the Bible would condemn as lust. She wanted his tenderness, his smile, to hear his voice, to feel his touch. She wanted him to be with her their whole lives long.

"Where would you like to go?" he asked, swinging lightly into his saddle with an authority that reminded her he'd been an officer.

With you—just with you. Where there'd be no Melissa, pro-slavers, or John Brown—and no ugly, forbidden "lust," either, only this shattering, heart-catching way I want to be in your arms, feel your hands, so strong and sure on the reins, touch me instead. . . .

Drawing back to reality, she laughed with disbelieving pleasure at the freedom she had this one afternoon, the range of choice, even without letting her dreams sweep her away. Being mounted like this was so different from perching on Nebuchadnezzar, hanging precariously to Thos, so different going the five miles to the smithy or the river between chore time, and chore time was the most they could reasonably do without exhausting the old horse, and she wasn't allowed to ride alone.

But today—oh, they could ride along the Kaw, or into Lawrence, or west across open prairies where the only shade was cast by clouds passing before the sun! They could visit Johnny and Sara, or go south to the Wakarusa and maybe find blackberries there.

She drew a deep breath of exhilaration. "Why, it—it's wonderful!" she sighed. "On Chica I can go anywhere!"

He laughed and she remembered how small even her widest world must seem to him. "Perhaps not *anywhere,*" he said. "But most places you could wisely consider."

She'd better make the most of her chance! "Could we

ride to the river?" she asked. "And then come back by the buffalo wallow?"

"Whatever you say," he nodded. "Chica has a tender mouth, so you don't need much pressure, just a light, firm touch."

The mare was a joy, responding to the lightest touch of reins against her neck. High-strung but gentle, she mouthed the bit a little, hinting she'd enjoy a faster pace.

"Shall we let them out?" Dane asked when Deborah began to feel fairly sure of herself and Chica.

Deborah nodded, leaned forward, and gave the mare her head. Lightning was the rangier, bigger horse, but Chica's rocking, exhilarating lope kept her even with him till Dane began to slow the gray horse, and Deborah, hair flying, gasping with excited laughter, patted Chica's neck and carefully drew in the reins.

"Like flying!" she cried. "Oh, Dane, she's perfect!"

He scanned them judiciously. "I believe you're a good weight for her. She could carry you all day without tiring."

They left the trail leading to the smithy and rode through unmarked prairie, sending jackrabbits bounding and sending meadowlarks into warning song. Several times prairie chickens rose up from under Chica's feet and she started, but she never panicked or reared.

"How do you mark your boundaries?" Dane asked.

"There are charred posts at the corners, and we'll fence someday if we get neighbors with livestock. They might help us put in and tend an Osage orange hedge. If everybody cut and hauled posts made from river trees, it'd be terrible, because there's not much wood."

She looked across the vast, shimmering ocean of grass, rippling in the breeze, changing color like velvet according to which way it was touched: now rose, now russet, now green. "I love it like this," she said, "open and free. The claims next to us are owned by people who live in town and do just enough to keep the claims in force. But when the troubles quiet down they'll start farming or sell to someone who will. And I suppose there'll be some kind of cheap, easily raised fence before too long, now that settlers are coming out where there's neither stone nor wood."

"The plains Indians are going to hate that," said Dane. "Their men, at least, have lived a life most whites would regard as leisure—hunting, fighting more in the spirit of winning tournament honors than to wipe out an enemy."

He gave a wry laugh. "When whites call Indians lazy, I suspect they're jealous."

"Indian women aren't lazy, however you look at it," retorted Deborah. "They gather wild foods, prepare game, tan hides, and make tipis and clothing."

"Yes, most of what whites call work is beneath a warrior's dignity," teased Dane. "Excellent system, for males. But now the white man's trying to saddle the warrior with his own humdrum workaday habits like a little boy who doesn't want his friends to play if he can't."

The comparison was apt, but Deborah didn't smile. She feared it would be a long time, and much blood would be shed, before white and red man lived peacefully, longer, probably, than it would take for the North and the South to settle their quarrels.

"You were happy a few minutes ago," Dane said, riding closer, "happier than I've ever seen you. What's made you sad?"

She made a helpless gesture. "I wish the prairie would never be fenced, yet I helped plant the hedge around our wheat. I wish the Indians could keep their hunting grounds and ways, but I don't want to get scalped. We've had border war in Kansas ever since the Territory opened, and everyone seems to think the whole country's going to explode. Thos may go off with that horrible old John Brown!" She swallowed hard and blinked. "With all this, I'm ashamed to be happy!"

They were nearing the Kaw, the fringe of cottonwood, walnut, oak, and willow making a green promise twisting through the grasslands. Dane said nothing but looked straight ahead. Was he angry? Put off because she was worried about the storms threatening her world?

He couldn't understand. He was an Englishman, here to paint and travel. But somehow it was important that he *did* know how she felt. It hurt to feel separated from him, cut off. They reached some massive cottonwoods, their trunks pale, leaves rustling, their silvery undersides contrasting with the fresh shine of the tops. Dane swung down, looped his reins over a limb, and strode up to Deborah.

"Get down." He raised his arms and lifted her to the soft, leaf-mulched earth, kept hold of her wrist while he tied the mare. "Now," he said grimly, walking Deborah into the murmuring shade, "you just said a despicable thing—that you're ashamed to be happy!"

"Despicable?"

"Yes. That sort of talk's for long-faced, self-flagellating people who taint the joy and strength of the stream of life because of its whirlpools and rapids, its terrors and griefs. There'll be times enough that you must weep, be sad, be angry. But as surely, you must be happy when you can, keep a high heart."

"But—"

"Not to delight in good things is to despair, Deborah." He took both her hands, turning her to face him. "Even as poor a Christian as I am knows that despair is a sin."

Weak at the pulsing flame traveling from his hands through her, Deborah tried to draw away, but he held her with tender strength, shifting one hand to tilt up her face so that his eyes captured her as relentlessly as his grasp.

"I was in despair when we met, Deborah—deep in sin. You gave me joy and hope. Can you give me more? Can you give me love?"

"Love?" Her mind whirled. "But I—I thought you—Melissa—"

"Mrs. Eden?" He looked startled, then laughed. "Because she trapped me into taking her to the literary society? You funny darling!"

"But—Chica! The blue saddle blanket!"

"What strange fancies you get!" He was now astonished. "You didn't know Chica was yours?"

"How should I?" she said crossly, still disbelieving. She must be dreaming or in a fever or—no, he wouldn't play this cruel a joke! "You never came after Rolf was well enough to go back to Lawrence, and even when you were visiting, you never paid any attention to me!"

His eyes danced like sunlight on deep water. "That's all you know about it! I paid attention to very little else! But you never looked at me if you could help it. You treated me, in fact, as if I had the plague!"

She could only stare at him, speechless. His long fingers caressed her face. "Rolf was—is—much taken with you. At twenty-two, he's much nearer your age. I'm twenty-eight and feel twice that. If you were going to care for him, I didn't want to compete."

"That was mouse-spirited!"

"But practical." He smiled ruefully. "I was all but betrothed to a young lady before I was posted to the Crimea. Rolf gallantly kept her company during my absence, and the upshot was that she fell in love with him. Rolf was genuinely dismayed, but he claimed he'd done nothing to make him obligated to offer to marry her after she broke off with me. The lesson I learned was to be sure any woman I was serious about first had a generous exposure to my dashing younger brother."

"I've had it." *More than you know!* "Rolf is—disturbing. But I couldn't love him in a thousand years. I think you should court where you're minded, not hold back for him!"

Dane's face turned somber. "I've no wish to kill my brother. Yet if you were mine and he tried to win you, I know I would. So I gave him his chance first, for all our sakes."

Deborah stiffened, remembering. "You told him your father would stop his money if he married me."

"So he would. I thought you, as well as Rolf, should know that."

Insulted, Deborah tried to wrench free; she kicked at Dane's shins. "You think I'd care about that if I loved him?" She choked, struggling in fury.

"I had to be sure."

Sudden realization chilled her. She stopped fighting and stared at him in a way that brought puzzled concern to his face. "You can't marry me, either," she said. "So what are you asking beneath all the fine words? That I should be your—" She hunted for a word, then remembered it from the Bible. "Your harlot—is that what you want?"

He winced as if she'd stabbed him. Anger flared in his eyes. "We've talked too much!"

Lowering his head, he took her mouth with his, hard, sweetly bruising, holding her against him so that the lean harshness of his body burned against her, crushed her breasts. She couldn't fight; he was possessing her with his hunger, dominating her completely. She had no strength at all. It was like being battered and beaten by a storm, but the most dangerous overwhelming crest of that tumult was building within herself. She gave a little sob as her mouth softened, as her bones gave way, and she was helpless in his arms.

His lips were still urgent, but now they moved caressingly along her throat and eyelids, then came again to her mouth, which received him tremblingly.

"Oh, my love!" he said against the pulse of her throat. "My dear darling! Harlot, indeed! Where'd you learn such a word?"

"It's in the Bible," she said indignantly, striving too late to regain her balance and dignity. "A great many times! Rahab and—"

"Never mind." He smothered her words with a kiss, then drew back to smooth the line of her jaw and chin with his fingers. "I really don't care about those ancient ladies of ill repute! When can we be married?"

"Married?" she echoed. "But—you told Rolf—your father won't like it!"

"He will when he meets you. Besides, I'm not dependent on him. If he disowns me, I can't offer you the manor and luxury, but from my mother I've a house in Cornwall where we could live quite comfortably on what my paintings and books bring in."

"Cornwall?" she said blankly.

"If you don't like it there, we can find a tenant or sell that place. I think you'd love Devon or Wales." At her sound of protest, he laid his fingers lightly on her mouth. "Now don't think I'm proposing without your parents' blessing! I called on them yesterday at the shop and asked if I might give you the mare and ask you to be my wife."

"Wife?" Could it be true?

He laughed softly, punctuating his words with kisses. "Wife! What an ugly, stout, nonsensical word for what you'll be to me! Darling, love, sweetheart, dearest—all very well, but not enough!" His tone roughened. "You're those to me, Deborah, and more. You're my woman."

He would have kissed her again, but she put her hand against his chest. "I love you, Dane. But I can't go to Cornwall—or Devon or Wales."

"You'd prefer London?" He sounded a little disappointed but shrugged it away. "We can manage, though I'd hope you'd have enough of it in a few years." He bent towards her again.

Averting her face, she spoke quickly before his arms and mouth could rob her of control and reason. "I can't leave my country, Dane!"

He frowned, then smiled compassionately. "Well, I can see that leaving your family, going to a strange land, would be alarming. Maybe you'd like to go back to New Hampshire?"

She shook her head. Why was it taking so long for him to understand? Why was he offering every accommodation except what was, for her, necessity? Surely, if he'd let her wishes govern so much, he'd honor the important one. It seemed reasonable enough, yet the muscles of her throat were taut, harshening her voice.

"I have to stay in Kansas, Dane—till the border wrangling's over and people like Judith don't need our help."

His fingers gripped like steel. "Don't be foolish, Deborah. Your going won't make any real difference, except to us. Your parents were relieved to think I'd be taking you away. When they came here, they never envisioned how long the struggle would last or what dangers you'd be exposed to. They won't blame you for going."

"I'd blame myself. I'd be worried about them all the time. I'd feel like a coward—a—a deserter!"

His lips twitched. "My love, you're not in the army!"

"I'm doing something I believe in. I have to see it through."

He dropped her hands, stepping back, a nerve in his lean cheek twitching. "That's more important than marrying me?"

"Oh, Dane! Not more important! But it's something I have to do before I can think about myself."

He didn't answer, but his eyes were incredulous. The distance between them after their closeness seemed very great. Using her courage and love to make her bold, she stretched out her hands. "Dane, couldn't you live here? It shouldn't be years and years. And if you will, then when things are all right, I promise I'll live with you in Cornwall or anywhere!"

He took her hands and kissed them, held them to his face, clearly fighting an inward battle. At last he straightened up, releasing her. "Deborah, it'd be so easy to say yes. But I want to get you out of this, away from bushwackers and men like Jed, away from where you'll need that Bowie! You can't imagine how I hate the idea of you with that border ruffian's weapon! I know this place and these times have forced you to it. But do you think I'd let my wife expose herself like that—escort runaways, defy men who love looting and murder?"

"Maybe you're afraid you'd have to fight again!" It wasn't fair, but his disgust at her Bowie, the hint that he found her unwomanly, stung deeply. The stricken look on his face pierced to her heart, made her say contritely, "Dane! Dane, please! I didn't mean that!"

"But you would, my dear." He smiled crookedly. "You're full of martial zeal. I'm convinced no war is worth its carnage." He considered her carefully. "Do you mean that if I married you and we stayed in Kansas, you'd insist on continuing with the underground? Oh, yes—I know your farm's a station. Judith's not the first fugitive you've hidden."

Deborah's chin trembled, but she lifted it. "Of course I would! What use would there be in my staying, otherwise?"

He nodded as if all the parts and pieces had come together. "Very well, my darling. It seems you know your mind."

He led her back to the horses, then was starting to lift her to the saddle when his arms tightened and he brought her against him and kissed her mouth till she could only cling to him, drawing him closer, opening to him like a flower ravished by the sun's warmth. He groaned. Looking up at him, she saw his eyes were blazing. Sweeping her up in his arms, he carried her a small distance and sank down with her on a grassy bank, crushing wild blossoms. "I'll have this much of you!" he said thickly, and he took her lips again.

She didn't know what was happening; she didn't care. She only wanted more—all of him, the touch and taste and feel. When his tongue touched hers, she thrust back, welcomed his probing, pressed savagely against him, willing him to somehow soothe the building, tormenting flame flickering through her.

He undid the buttons of her dress, then fondled her breasts. She caught in her breath, moaning. His mouth brushed the straining rigid nipples, closed on first one, then the other, drawing out some of the pain, softening her urgency so that the fire became a honey melting, a soft, deep yearning which he'd satisfy. He knew how. She had to have him—this one time. It was a sin, but they loved each other; he'd wanted to marry her. . . .

Abruptly, he sat up. "Goddamn it to hell!"

She opened startled eyes and pushed up on one elbow. "Dane—"

"No!" Roughly, he buttoned her dress, then pulled her to her feet. "Not till I know we can marry! Damn it, I love you! Your parents trust me!"

This time he almost flung her into the saddle.

• viii •

She had never been happier than when riding toward the river with Dane, and never more disappointed, ragingly frustrated, than when riding back. She wanted to weep, strike out at something, cry that it wasn't fair, that it was too cruel, too wretched to be offered the man she loved but to be compelled to deny him and herself because of his rigidity.

And her own. Even in her furious grief, she had to admit there was some validity to his view. Hopelessly trapped between her love, the ecstasy of being Dane's cherished, protected, passionately loved and fulfilled woman, and the sure knowledge it would all sour if she left her duty, abandoned her family, Deborah writhed inwardly.

How could he be so stubborn?

She ground her teeth. He hadn't even made love to her while they could both plead being carried away! He thought her a puritan, but when it came to self-righteousness, he had to be second only to butchering old John Brown!

Feeling slashed and raw, Deborah saw the waving grass through a haze of tears, fought desperately to keep her back straight and not snuffle. How did *he* feel? His broad shoulders were erect and his face was stonily impassive: stiff, upper-lipped British officer.

Oh, *damn* him! Why had he let her know he loved her if he was going to make impossible conditions? Forlornly, she knew that many women would've been glad to get away from Kansas, the drudgery of a farm, the ever-present threat of violence. No use in blaming him for thinking she'd jump at the chance to leave.

Through a blur of tears, she saw his dear, dark head; she longed to cradle it against her and whisper that nothing mattered except their love. . . .

Only it did.

"Shall we go by the buffalo wallow?" he asked in an expressionless tone.

Unable to speak, she shook her head. She wanted only to be home, to give way to the storm of weeping building within her.

They rode for a long time in silence. At last he said, "I'm going to paint my way west, probably spend the winter in California. By the time I come back in the spring, things may have changed. Unless you forbid me, Deborah, I'll ask you again to come with me."

Her heart sank at the thought of his leaving but rose because at least he wasn't definitely, positively putting her out of his life—though it might be better for them both if he did.

"Things may change by spring," she said tersely, "but it'll probably be for the worse."

He gave her an almost humorous glance. "And I thought Americans were optimistic!"

"In the long run, yes, but I don't see how anyone can expect anything but trouble for the next few years."

His gaze touched her, lingered. The longing between them was almost palpable. How could he go away? Life would be all one color without him, the dry, sere, yellow-brown of the prairie in autumn, the frigid white of winter. But if he came in the spring, oh, then she would live again! For that little while. It was something to hold on to, however doomed. Something *might* happen. Peace might be nearer.

Or—she scarcely dared think it even to herself, yet she couldn't keep from it—Dane might decide to live in the Territory.

"Whatever happens," he promised, "I'll see you in the spring."

Her scalp prickled at that. To make such a vow seemed an almost sacrilegious daring of fate. He was making a long, hazardous journey; she lived in a wild land in wild times. "Don't promise," she said hastily, as if trying to avert a curse. "Just come if you can—if you still want to—"

"Oh, my love," he said, "if I were in my grave, I'd still want to!"

As they rode up to the stable, Thos came out and offered to see to the horses, but Dane said he was riding on to Lawrence. "You can take care of your sister's horse, though," he said, swinging down and lifting Deborah lightly to the ground.

"I can't keep her!" Deborah protested.

"What else can I do with a lady's horse?" shrugged Dane. "Would you want it on your very tender conscience that I sold her to someone who might not be as good to her as you'd be?" He chuckled, hands still on her waist. "Think of Chica, not your pride."

"But the saddle—"

"The livery stable owner traded it to me for a pair of boots. He won't want to trade back."

She moved away from his hands. The feel of him was an indelible brand. Whatever happened, she was his—even if they never possessed each other; even if they never met again.

"You make it hard to say no." Her voice was tremulous and she thought her face must be as naked.

His mouth curved down. "You say no with great facility, sweetheart. But since it's you I love, *you* with all your stubborn resolves and absurdities, I suppose I can't cavil with fate for surrounding my special rose with extremely spiky thorns."

He bent his head and kissed her. She answered with total yielding, melting into him, trying to be part of him. Shaken, he put her from him. Obsessed by her own yearning, she still thrilled triumphantly at the trembling that ran through his tall, strong body.

"Little witch," he murmured as Thos came out of the stable, "you flow against me like that when there's nothing I can do about it but ache and dream of you! But you're so young! If any other man can woo you from me, better he does it now."

He shook hands with a surprised Thos, then adjured him to take care of his twin, and going to the cabin, he made an expeditious farewell to Leticia and Josiah. He refused dinner. The whole family waved him off. Deborah was half-glad, half-sorry that he couldn't kiss her again.

Thank goodness, though they must be full of questions, the family didn't ask them right then, but went about their evening work and let her watch the big gray horse and its rider vanish into the distance.

Her heart felt wrenched from her body. She had to wrestle with all her strength against the wish to saddle Chica and ride after him—beg him to stay, or, if that failed, go away with him. Her family would approve. They wouldn't blame her; they'd even be relieved.

In a conflict like that of this border, which was only an exaggerated concentration of the hatred and mistrust growing between the North and the South, slave and free states, what did one person matter, one young woman?

Very little, probably. Except to herself. But that, really, was the essential thing, the core of her being. *Good-bye, my love,* she said silently. *Good-bye, my darling. Be safe and well and happy.*

He was out of sight now. Tears streamed from her eyes as she stared into that emptiness. It seemed an eternity till spring.

The family was clearly perplexed, and as supper neared an end, Deborah found it impossible to bear their tactful, worried glances. Might as well say it straight out to all of them at once rather than have to go through it with each of them separately.

"Dane asked me to marry him," she said, trying to keep her tone steady. "He won't stay in Kansas, so I told him no."

Thos stared at her in shock. "Well, for heaven's sake, 'Borah, why should he stay in Kansas?"

"He doesn't have to, but I do."

Father cleared his throat. "Daughter, your mother and I talked about this after your young man called on us yesterday. We agreed it would be best for you to be in a safer place. Don't feel you must stay because of us."

Why was Judith watching her so enigmatically? Unable to speak for a moment, Deborah shook her head. "Why won't anyone believe I care about what happens here? It's not just because you're here. I belong, too! I can't go off and forget it!"

"But—" Thos began.

Leticia put her hand over Deborah's and pressed it. "That'll do, Thos. So long as Deborah's not staying because of the family, it's her decision."

"She looks mighty unhappy about it!" Thos snorted.

"Things more important than bein' happy," Judith said unexpectedly. Her tawny eyes regarded Deborah with approval instead of with their usual guarded skepticism.

"He's coming back in the spring," Mother said. "By then things may be better."

Deborah nodded mutely. Rising, she began to clear away the table.

Judith, helping her, murmured consolingly, "He be back, Deborah. He be back."

But what good would that do if nothing had changed?

Deborah supposed that Rolf would go with Dane. A few days after the parting, she was grooming Chica, a task she enjoyed both because she loved the little mare and because Chica was Dane's gift. Chica's ears pricked up and she whinnied as a rider came into view on the rutted trail to town.

A bay horse. And from his arrogant posture and massive shoulders, Deborah recognized him long before she could make out his features. Rolf. The wrong brother.

Alarm shot through her. Thos was in town delivering the paper. Rolf had been circumspect of late, but there hadn't been much choice, they hadn't been alone. Now, to all purposes they would be, since Judith must be warned to keep out of sight.

Going to the cabin in a casual manner, Deborah stepped inside and warned Judith. "Don't come out even if you hear us quarreling," she said. "There's something about Rolf I don't trust."

Judith's teeth showed. "Don't fret your mind, Deborah! If it sound like I need to come out, I do it so he won' know what hit him!"

She made for the lean-to while Deborah, reassured by Judith's promise, went outside and pretended surprise as Rolf trotted up the lane. "I thought you'd gone to California," she said as he sprang down and looped his reins around a post.

He smiled at her, green eyes watchful. "I was—invited. But Dane couldn't lasso and drag me all the way."

"You—you're staying here till he comes back?"

"That distresses you?"

She shrugged, carefully working the tangles out of Chica's mane. "I should think California and the way there would be much more interesting than Lawrence."

"Ah, but you see," he said and laughed, "with Dane gone, things become extremely interesting."

He'd moved to stand across from her; now he ran his hands over the mare in a proprietary way that made Deborah go stiff.

Challenging his amused gaze across Chica's withers, she said coldly, "You won't find me interesting, Mr. Hunter. My feelings haven't changed."

"*Mr.* Hunter?" he mocked good-naturedly. "Come now, we know each other better than that!" She said nothing, concentrating on Chica. "My feelings haven't changed, either," Rolf said slowly. "And you *do* interest me; in fact, you're the only woman who's ever done so for more than a fortnight."

"Even Dane's almost-fiancée?" Deborah couldn't resist asking.

Rolf lifted one shoulder. He was strikingly handsome today in a fringed doeskin vest over his full-sleeved, open-throated white shirt. He was holding his black slouch hat, and his golden hair shone bright in the sun. "So he told you about that? Mighty dull young lady. If he hadn't chosen her, I'd never have looked at her. I spared him years of boredom."

"Is that what you're trying to do now?"

"Lord, no!" The pupils of his eyes contracted to tiny points, and in the harsh light, the usually dark jade irises glowed with almost a sulfurish cast. "You're the only woman I've ever wanted enough to marry."

"That's unfortunate. I don't wish to marry you."

His mouth hardened. She was glad Chica was between them. Then, again, he began to caress the mare, his hands sensitive and sure. The way he'd touch a woman? Deborah pushed the unwelcome thought away, startled and revolted at the awareness of him that shot through her, though she didn't like him, didn't trust him.

Was that what Dane's lovemaking had done? Awakened her senses, brought her to ripening when he wasn't there for the harvest? She must be winter, then, the sleeping, frozen earth, until he came back.

As if guessing the treachery of her quickened blood, Rolf laughed. "I'm not sure that what you want counts all that much in what you do. You wanted to marry Dane, I'll be bound, but you didn't."

"If you know that much, you know why."

"My noble brother sees it as his duty to take you away from here. I wouldn't." Rolf gestured expansively. "Have me, Deborah, and I'll join Lane and scourge the pro-slavers or jog along with old Brown on slave-stealing—anything to help your cause."

"Anything for a fight," she said wonderingly. "You don't care at all who wins Kansas—whether we come in as a slave state or free!"

"Not a particle," he said cheerfully. "But if we were

married, I'd serve your cause." He slanted her a teasing look. "As keen an abolitionist as you are, that should persuade you to take me."

She made a sound of revulsion. "It's terrible that you'd be willing to kill over something you don't believe!"

"Believing's what makes it holy?" He chuckled derisively, but there was jealousy in his voice. "If Dane had made the same offer, you'd have thought him a hero!"

"He wouldn't fight unless he believed. Besides, I don't think Englishmen should get mixed up in our troubles."

"Afraid we'd recolonize you?"

Deborah didn't answer. She was appalled at Rolf's lighthearted proposition. He might have been asking her to dance. Why hadn't Dane taken him away? Was this more of his waiting to see if she resisted Rolf before venturing himself? Didn't he realize how jealous his younger brother was? She believed that his obsession with her sprang mostly from her being the woman Dane wanted. As if realizing that he was antagonizing her, Rolf shrugged and stopped stroking the mare.

"Aren't you going to ask me in?"

"No. Thos is in town, as I suspect you perfectly well know!"

"I'm thirsty."

"Would you like buttermilk, water, or coffee? I'll bring it to you." He colored to the roots of his waving hair.

"I want to come in your house and sit down, damn it! It's not as if I hadn't often been a guest."

"When Thos or my parents were here. If you want to wait outside till they come home, you're very welcome to."

He stared at her so angrily that she decided to try vaulting onto Chica and making a bareback dash if he tried to touch her. He crossed his arms resolutely and she thought he'd schooled himself to be patient.

"All right. I'll call when your family's home, sweet Deborah." Stepping around Chica's head, he took Deborah's free hand and brought it to his lips. "Give me some credit for doing this instead of what I want to," he said huskily. He almost flung her hand from him, then turned abruptly to his horse.

Mounted, he watched her broodingly. "You'll be mine. I want you to want it, to choose me over Dane, so I'll play your game. But don't doubt the end."

Spinning the big bay around, he was off, raising dust. Deborah's breath escaped in a rush. Thank goodness, he was gone! She shivered in spite of the heat. That he hadn't used force, that he'd thought her alone, yet respected her, was more troubling in a way than if he'd pulled her to him as he had that first time they met. He must love her.

That could be dangerous. She remembered his kiss, touched with her own blood. Was there no way to be rid of him? Deborah pressed her face to Chica's shoulder. Why had Dane left her?

The winter would be so long.

The next day was Sunday. Rolf, impeccably turned out in a black suit, sat behind the Whitlaws, perturbing Deborah so much that she scarcely heard a thing Reverend Cordley said. He accompanied them to the buggy and eagerly accepted when Mother invited him to come out for dinner, promising to catch up as soon as he got his horse from the livery stable.

"I do wish you wouldn't ask him to our house," Deborah said as Josiah started the horses.

"I'm sure your mother feels that with his brother gone, he needs to feel at home somewhere," Father said, casting her a surprised, slightly reproving look. Leticia was watching her, too. Without revealing the way Rolf had treated her the day they met, Deborah couldn't object further, so she bit the inside of her lip and wondered, with a mixture of dismay and half-guilty anticipation, if Rolf was going to be a frequent visitor.

At least with her parents and Thos around, Rolf couldn't say or do much.

But he could look.

While he listened attentively and in apparent agreement to what Leticia and Josiah had to say about the coming vote on whether or not to accept the Lecompton constitution, while he talked with them about English politics and his impressions of the United States, often, when no one else could notice, his eyes rested on Deborah, the flame within them touching off a smouldering restlessness that had nothing to do with her distrust of him or her love for Dane.

She must never be alone with Rolf. That much was sure. Meanwhile, his visits broke the sameness of the days. It was flattering to be tacitly courted by the handsome, rich young English aristocrat who had all feminine Lawrence in a flutter, and if Dane *would* go off and leave his brother, he could hardly expect the Whitlaws to forbid him the house.

Rolf exerted himself to mesmerize Thos, letting him use his rifle and the Colt revolver he had, interestingly, bought in London.

"Your Mr. Colt had opened a factory in Britain and wanted to exhibit his pistol at the Great Exhibition, or World's Fair, of 1851, when under Prince Albert's patronage a fantastic array of inventions, wonders, and follies were displayed at Hyde Park. British gun-makers were afraid of Colt's mass production, but Robert Adams accepted Colt's challenge and the two showed off their guns."

"I remember something about that," mused Father. "The results were never formally announced, were they?"

Rolf shook his head. "Though Colt made an excellent showing, Adams put out the story that the Colt misfired ten times while his own revolver, which cocked and fired each time the trigger was pulled, instead of needing to be thumb-cocked like the Colt, didn't, according to him, misfire once."

"Did it?" asked Thos eagerly.

"You don't expect me to accuse a fellow countryman," chuckled Rolf. "But Sam Colt was clever. He began giving his Colts to men of influence—Prince Albert, the Prince of Wales—and before long his pistols were being used in Africa against the Kaffirs. After that, his revolver became so respected that the *Times* said the Light Brigade might have carried their charge at Balaclava if they'd been armed with Colts."

Thos shook his head, admiring the big weapon with its nine-inch barrel. "So it's not just Texas Rangers and westerners who use these!" he said. "It's a beautiful thing."

"Not to me, it isn't!"

Deborah spoke sharply. Her twin was growing more restless all the time, bored with farm chores and *The Clarion*. She was terribly afraid that if John Brown or Jim Lane called him for some border exploit, he'd go. Rolf's white teeth flashed as he smiled at her.

"Ah, Miss Deborah, I remember that you admire knives, which can be deadly, too."

Would he give away the secret of her possession of a Bowie? She said grimly, "Blades are beautiful and can be used for other things. Revolvers are strictly for killing."

"True enough." Rolf shrugged. "Though I doubt if many civilized people eat with their Bowie knives like your squaw-man friend. I wonder if he has time now to make a Bowie for me."

"I doubt it. With all these people rushing for Pike's Peak, he has lots of horses to shoe and wagons to mend."

"Now you're being diplomatic." Rolf's eyes were very dark, like heavily tarnished copper. "Chaudoin will never have time to craft me that knife, but I'll have one, anyway."

Dissolving the tension, Father remarked that countless Bowies had been made in England, and the conversation shifted to trade and the dependence of English mills on Southern cotton, which might conceivably lead Britain to support the South if war came.

"But I don't think we will, sir," Rolf assured Josiah. "The Crimean War was costly, the Sepoy Mutiny shook the army, and I can't believe that anyone but the cloth manufacturers would favor mixing into your internal affairs."

"I hope not," Josiah said. "I certainly hope not. The South has few factories, but if it could get its needed manufactured supplies from England, a war, if it comes, could drag on much longer."

Covering a yawn, Rolf got to his feet. "I think my country's learned its lesson about transporting troops and maintaining them on your shores! We'll be celebrating that next week, in fact! You'll be my special guests, and I'm counting on Thos and Miss Deborah to come in early and be sure everything's properly arranged."

"I don't—" began Deborah, but Thos squeezed her arm.

"We'll be glad to," he said. "May I bring Sara?"

"Bring the blackamoor if you want," said Rolf. "I'll get a surrey, stop for you, and then we can collect Miss Field."

The glow on Thos's face kept Deborah from protesting again. He so clearly longed to squire Sara in public, show that she was his sweetheart and that he was proud of her. Not even Rolf could do much with her brother in the same carriage. It was a bit like riding with a muzzled lion, but at least that would be one evening when she wouldn't sigh and cry over Dane and wonder why he'd left her!

Early on the Fourth, Rolf drove up in the livery stable's grandest surrey drawn by a matched pair of chestnuts. Big rosettes of red, white, and blue adorned the top of the equipage, and the horses had multicolored cockades fastened to their reins.

The elder Whitlaws came out to admire the rig. They'd

drive directly to town, taking the blackberry pies Judith and Deborah had made yesterday. Thos whistled joyfully. "Sara's going to love this!" he cried. "She didn't much want to come—said this was no celebration for *her* people, but she just has to like this!"

"Do you like it?" Rolf asked softly, helping Deborah up to the leather-cushioned seat.

"Very nice."

"Careful, the sun might melt your words!"

His jaw corded for a second before he went around to tell Josiah and Leticia that they'd all meet later in town. Thos climbed in back, Rolf gathered up the reins, and they were off past the shocked wheat and the corn that would soon be ready for pulling fodder.

It would be hot later, but the morning breeze was still fresh and swept the grass in undulating shimmers, first pale green, then rosy-russet. The horses trotted briskly, but the surrey was much more comfortable than the Whitlaw buggy, and riding in it, open to air and scenery but shielded by a canopy from the sun, was luxuriously delightful.

Too, Deborah had worn the green dress that brought out the auburn of her hair and deepened the warm amber of her eyes. It even made her sun-browned skin look richly golden, almost the color of Judith's.

It was too bad that Judith couldn't go to the Fourth celebration, but at least she no longer spent Sunday, after church, hiding in the lean-to. Well before Rolf came, she took Chica and rode to Johnny's for the day. Strangers didn't come by the smithy much on Sunday since Johnny said even God needed a day off after working all week, so it was a fairly safe outing.

"Why so pensive?" Rolf's voice was amused. "You were sparkling like champagne when we started, but you've heaved three sighs in as many minutes."

"I—I'm sorry. I was just thinking."

"Think about me," he teased, "or I'll speed up the horses till you'll have to hang on to me to stay in the surrey!"

Deborah laughed in spite of herself. "Father says people don't know what to make of your putting on this celebration."

"Infernal gall or good sportsmanship?" He grinned, handling the reins with practiced skill. He had large, well-kept hands with blunt fingers. Shocked at the sudden, charged memory of how they'd held her so inexorably within a few minutes of when they'd met, Deborah's blood

quickened. She didn't like him, didn't trust him, but—
"You can tell your friends it's gall," he said cheerfully. "I'm a damned poor loser."

"Then you'd better learn more grace," she retorted.

"Why? I don't intend to lose."

"Everyone does sometimes."

His eyes raked over her, burned her mouth and throat and breasts. "I won't." In spite of her conviction that she'd never love or yield to him, such determination was unnerving. "How can you say that?"

His dark green gaze flicked her lightly, rousing once again that treacherous, hateful, but potent awareness. "I gamble high for what I want, Miss Deborah. If I stake my life and lose it, I won't know that I've lost—not long enough to matter, anyway."

"That's how I feel," said Thos enthusiastically. "If something's worth trying for, it's worth all you have!"

"And it's a form of winning, anyhow," mused Rolf, abruptly thoughtful, "to throw oneself completely into risk. I'd rather do that than figure odds, collect my careful winnings, and live a hundred years." He laughed back at Thos. "There'll be a turkey shoot today. Want to use my Sharps?"

"Oh, can I?" cried Thos.

Deborah scowled. "You're not really going to shoot at the turkeys?" For sometimes in the popular shooting matches, this was done, and the winner had to at least draw blood.

"I knew you wouldn't like that," Rolf said. "No, there'll be a target. The other hunters and I have brought in enough buffalo meat and venison to feed the Territory, but there'll be barbecued oxen and pigs, too." He chuckled. "I think my biggest triumph was in persuading your rather puritanical city fathers that a ball wouldn't ruin anyone who wasn't! Your father helped there!"

Deborah nodded, remembering a few vigorous dinner-time discussions. Mother didn't approve of dancing, mostly because of the drinking and fighting that often went with such galas, but Father had placated her by pointing out that the ball would be exceedingly well chaperoned, at least several respectable married ladies for every single girl, and liquor wouldn't be sold on the premises or any-place where the ladies' Temperance Vigilance Committee had a say.

Deborah had never been to a dance, and her mother's grudging acceptance of this one didn't make much difference. Since she couldn't dance, she'd help with tending babies for young matrons who *could,* and with serving the food.

"I've got the best fiddlers in the Territory," Rolf boasted. "They're set to start with four strings and wind up with two, and Jem Tucker can even saw out a waltz!"

"A waltz!" breathed Deborah. It sounded deliciously wicked, conjuring up bare-shouldered jeweled beauties whirling seductively in the arms of uniformed hussars or noblemen in Paris and Vienna and London.

"And you shall dance it with me," Rolf promised.

Deborah shook her head. "I can't dance at all—and certainly not that!"

"If you can't dance, you might as well start with the waltz." He laughed.

"But—it's scandalous!"

He threw back his head and roared. Sobering, he eyed her with indulgent wonder. "That's what dowagers said when it was brought to England in 1791. But no one would dare accuse Queen Victoria of license, and it's probably been the leading dance ever since the Regency period! Would I lie to you?"

"Yes!"

"Sara and I'll dance it," Thos predicted. "Come on, 'Borah, don't be starchy!"

She would've danced with Dane—oh, so gladly! To be close in his arms, swirling to music in the air and the slower, deeper, steadily increasing tempo of their blood . . . But he was halfway to Santa Fe by now. It would be months, if ever, before they danced, and why?

He hadn't needed to go off like that, proposing one day and leaving the next, giving her no time to be his acknowledged love, to savor the sweetness. Not a bit of it! When she wouldn't give up her principles, he'd been gone as soon as he could manage it, and no doubt when and if he came back next spring, she'd be treated to more of the same—an imperative question followed by abrupt departure when she gave the answer she'd almost surely have to give.

Why couldn't he have stayed at least a little while? Why couldn't they have had some time of loving, even if they couldn't agree, even if it came to parting in the end?

In her heart she knew, with a thrill of female power, the answer to that. He didn't trust himself not to take her, and if he did, with his stubborn honor, he'd feel he had to marry her. For a moment, gripped by a rush of savage sweetness, she closed her eyes and gave herself up to the memory of his hard, tender mouth and caressing hands.

Rolf's voice invaded her yearning. "Have you left the earth, Deborah? You can't escape me that way, you know! When you look so dreamy, I want to wake you up."

"I'm awake." Straightening, she saw the ribbon of trees along the Kaw, the buildings around the smithy. Frustrated longing was oppressive within her, a heaviness she felt she must throw off or be crushed by. *Dane, Dane, why did you leave me?*

Lifting her chin, she said, "I'll dance the waltz!"

• ix •

Lawrence was teeming with several times its normal population as Rolf drew up by the imposing three-storied Free State Hotel on Massachusetts Street. A boy ran to hold the team and Rolf gave him a coin, coming around to help Deborah down while Thos did the same for Sara.

"Thos, if you'll see to the ladies, I'll drop the surrey at the livery and be back in a hurry," Rolf said. He bowed over Deborah's hand, gave her a roguish look, and left them to survey the jostling crowd.

Gold-seekers on their way west; former New Englanders in their dark suits; frontiersmen in red shirts, laden with pistols and Bowies; Indians in a mixture of native and white-man clothing. Every woman creature from toddler to grandmother wore her best, and though bright-hued calico dominated, there were lawns, muslins, jaconets, tarlatans, and some silk gowns.

"Look at *her!*" whispered Sara.

Melissa Eden was moving toward them, followed by admiring male stares and envious feminine ones. Her blue silk dress billowed out in three flounces, embroidered with darker blue roses, and a white crepe bonnet fetchingly trimmed with a crimson rose set off her pale blonde hair.

"Good morning, my dears!" she cried gaily, catching Deborah's hands in a grip that was surprisingly strong, then twinkling up at Thos, who colored and shifted his feet. "How charming you look—so fresh and young you need no artifice!"

Another way of saying they looked rustic, Deborah thought, though Sara's yellow muslin deserved no condescension. Perfectly simple and hoopless, the dress molded Sara's slender frame but softly emphasized the sweet curving of her high, small breasts, and the color, picked by Johnny, made her look like a bright-petaled dark flower.

Firmly, Sara detached her hand from Melissa's. To cover the fleeting awkwardness, Deborah complimented the older woman on her gown and remarked that this promised to be the biggest celebration ever held in Lawrence.

"To be sure," agreed Melissa, laughter tinkling in a way that gave men an excuse to eye her appreciatively. "Lawrence isn't all that steeped in age and festivities, of course, though this certainly is more to my taste than that ice-cream-and-cake Fourth we had a few years ago."

"But that November there was a ball for the Kansas Rifles here at the Free State Hotel," Deborah reminded her. "Five hundred people came to that and danced till three in the morning."

"I was there," Melissa said, smiling, "but you, I believe, were not."

Deborah flushed. "Mother doesn't really approve of dancing, and I was only fourteen then."

"How nice," commented Melissa, "that my handsome young boarder has apparently been able to overcome your estimable mother's rather strict views on this occasion." Her eyes fixed on Deborah and there was no smile in them, just naked hunger. "Have you heard from Dane Hunter?"

It was as if a knife plunged into Deborah and ripped upward. "Not since he left." Her voice sounded normal, though her lips were stiff. He hadn't said he'd write, and she didn't expect it, but of course she hoped he'd try to send a message on the mail stage, or by some east-bound traveler or freighter.

For a moment Melissa's face looked gaunt, a foreshadowing of how the years would deal with her, before she shrugged. "Then it seems we must make do with his brother," she said brightly. "But if you hear, I should appreciate knowing how he gets on. He was going to do my portrait before he so suddenly decided he had to get west before snow blocks the passes. Oh, there's Captain Harrington, down from Fort Leavenworth! How splendid to see him!" And she rushed off to a tall officer of the 1st Cavalry, which, along with St. George Cooke's 2nd Dragoons had, under presidential orders, tried to keep the peace during the reign of the pro-slavers, thus earning the hatred of Free Staters. Now, though, with Territorial Governor Denver striving for justice and the national Congress aroused and determined that actual Kansas settlers should determine their laws, the final defeat of slave power, through the coming vote on the Lecompton constitution, seemed assured, and soldiers who'd chosen this celebration over that in Leavenworth mixed freely in the crowd.

The Independent Order of Good Templars had organized the parade. Led by the marshal and his aides, the band struck up and led the procession from New Hampshire Street to Vermont Street and back to Massachusetts Street to the river, followed by other officials of the day, including the chaplain, Reverend Nute of the Unitarian Church, members of various lodges, the Lawrence Glee Club, children, and then all the people who were crossing to North Lawrence for the celebration. Rolf whisked Deborah into the procession.

There was no charge for the ferry that day, but it took a while for everyone to cross over.

Once in the shade of the walnut grove, the flag was hoisted and the guard fired salutes, including one for the United States and one for "Kansas, soon to be the thirty-fourth state!"

A Mr. Branscomb read the Declaration of Independence, and one oration followed another as men who had almost despaired of the Territory's becoming a free state strode forward and proclaimed that the spirit of liberty invoked in the Declaration had survived its bloody trial in Kansas and would survive whatever lay ahead.

"For we're free men!" cried one graybeard. "And we'll have no slavery here! Hurrah for John Brown and Jim Lane!"

He got his cheers, but several New Englanders pushed to the front and shouted that Lane had murdered Gaius Jenkins, a better man than he was and not a come-lately to the cause, either. A general fight was brewing when Reverend Nute called for silence and prayed in a way that calmed hot tempers and reminded everyone that they were celebrating their country's birthday.

The band struck up the "Hymn of the Kansas Emigrant," "Song of Montgomery's Men," "Yankee Doodle," "Old Hundred," "Auld Lang Syne," and finished with "The Star-Spangled Banner" and thundering applause. Before the crowd could drift away, the mayor stepped up by the flagpole and raised his arms for attention.

"There'll be a turkey shoot next, folks, and then a barbecue in the grove for those who prefer it and a feast at the hotel, courtesy of a most generous guest from England who figured since his country couldn't whip us, he might as well join us! Mr. Hunter, would you like to say a few words?"

Smiling down at Deborah, Rolf squeezed her hand and moved with swift grace to the mayor. "Thank you, sir." He bowed, shaking hands. "I must confess it gave me a strange feeling to know my countrymen were that 'foe's haughty host in dread silence reposing,' but I'm glad we war no more." His eyes danced, resting on Deborah in a way that made people turn to look. "I've found much to admire and love in your Territory, and I'm honored to join with you in this joyous and solemn anniversary. Ladies and gentlemen! Had I wine in my hand, I'd toast to you this great Kansas, the heart of the United States!"

The cheers echoed and reechoed. For all his accent and fine tailoring, the handsome young Englishman had captured them, and when he moved back to Deborah, it was like a conqueror.

There must have been fifty contestants in the shooting match, firing at a target painted on a stump from a standing position without steadying their pistols.

Thos, using Rolf's Colt, was lucky enough to hit the mark, but lost in the second round when only Rolf and two rough-looking professional hunters were left.

To the crowd's astonishment, Rolf hit the center on the third try, while his rivals, perhaps the worse for drink, badly missed. There was silence for a moment after the mayor announced the winner, but then cheering burst out.

More to this English lord than met the eye! Be a proper man yet if he stayed in this country! One of his opponents, though, was less forgiving. Spitting a brown mess of tobacco near Rolf's feet, he squinted and growled, "I'm used to movin' targets, stranger. Movin' targets. Bet you wouldn't show so fine at that kind of real shootin'?"

Rolf's body went so still that it seemed he didn't breathe.

"Why don't we both move?" he suggested. "Walk away from each other and fire when we're ready?"

"By God, you're a sport!" The hunter eagerly began to walk backward, but the mayor dropped a hand on his arm.

"None of that!" he commanded. "Come along. Can't you smell that barbecue?"

Rolf stared after them a moment, shoulders hunched as if to attack. Then he saw Deborah. Tension eased from him and he smiled, coming back to her and giving her his arm. "Now you have a turkey," he said.

Deborah looked at the big caged bird. She could have eaten him with appreciation had he appeared well cooked on the table, but, as always, seeing the creature alive first ruined her appetite for its flesh.

"Do you suppose we could just . . . let him go in the woods?"

Thos gave an indignant whoop. " 'Borah! Think how good he'd be for Thanksgiving! Don't be a ninny!"

"Oh, doubtless another turkey can be found for that." Rolf shrugged. "I'll bring one out and you can kill it before your sister lays eyes on it and starves us out of mercy! This one can be a live offering for your national holiday. A shame it's not an eagle, but I believe your Benjamin Franklin thought the turkey should have been your country's symbol." He laughed down at Deborah. "Shall we turn him out now?"

She nodded, grateful to him for not deriding her. In spite of his disgust, Thos came along, as did Sara, and after the willow cage was opened, the four of them shooed the bewildered bird deeper into the trees till its bare blue head and irridescent bronze, green, and blue body blended into the bushes.

"Doggone foolishness!" growled Thos, but Sara stopped his grumbles with slim brown fingers on his mouth and drew him on ahead.

Rolf stopped Deborah behind a large cottonwood. "Since I gave up my reward, do I get another?"

Useless to pretend ignorance of the current that ran between them, though it was heavily charged on her side with hostility and fear. She couldn't endure the burning of his gaze; she looked down at the dead leaves underfoot.

"I—I've aready said I'd dance with you."

His hands tightened. "Deborah, I'll swear I was the first man to kiss you. I still remember the taste of your blood, the sweetness of your mouth. . . ."

"Dane should have been the first!" she said fiercely.

"Dane's gone and I'm here." Rolf's tone was husky. Shifting her wrists to the grasp of one hand, with his free one he caressed her face, her frightened eyes, the side of her throat. Liquid fire trembled through her.

"No!" she whispered. "No!"

With a strangled sound, he put her away from him, almost dragged her after Thos and Sara. "I could kiss you, Deborah, and you'd like it, though you'd swear you didn't. But I want more than a kiss—I want you."

"I love Dane."

"Who's gone kiting out to California and may never come back? Who won't marry you unless you'll leave your people?"

Tears filled Deborah's eyes. She couldn't answer. After a few minutes, during which he was plainly struggling with himself, Rolf spoke roughly.

"Do you know the story of Boreas, Deborah?"

Surprised, she searched her memory. "He was god of the North Wind, wasn't he?"

"Yes, and long and long he loved a princess of Athens and wooed her with soft words and singing, trying his best to be gentle, though it wasn't his nature. After some seasons, he despaired of winning her and swept her up, carried her to a rocky shore surrounded by dark clouds, and ravished her. Once it was done, once he behaved according to his true self, she became his wife and bore him twin sons who became Argonauts."

"An interesting myth."

"And lesson."

"It wouldn't have worked if the woman had loved someone else."

"Who knows? The sure thing is he had her."

"I'd hate a man who used me that way!"

"Hate's very close to love." Rolf's breath came faster. "In an embrace, Deborah, a struggle can be as rapture-making as returned desire."

Thwarted need twisted through her. "Don't talk to me like this!"

Rolf chuckled. "Will you tell your brother? A shame if I had to hurt him! I don't think your father's ever shot a gun in his life! Now don't berate me, darling! I won't do anything—yet—to imperil my honored guest status in your home!"

Thos and Sara had waited for them, and all together,

they flowed with the crowd back across on the ferry and to the hotel.

The considerable portion of celebrants who preferred to wash down their meat with whisky were feasting in the grove, punctuating their meal with whoops, song, and occasional shots, but the women and more settled and substantial citizens flocked into the hotel to partake of venison, buffalo, roast pork, and turkey less fortunate than the one Deborah had loosed.

The women of Lawrence had added their dishes and silverware to the hotel's supply, and they joined with the staff to prepare and set out food that loaded the tables. There were tubs of roasting ears of corn, crocks of butter, willow wash baskets heaped with cornbread, great kettles of boiled potatoes and wild greens, hominy, green beans flavored with side meat, constantly renewed skillets of gravy, and innumerable pies—molasses-sweetened sorrel, blackberry, rhubarb, dried apple, and peach. There were even a few cakes, breathtaking extravagance, and big bowls of custard and pudding. A basket of green apples was kept replenished for the children, and most people left the cake and fresh strawberries for the elderly, but there was no lack of succulent red slices of watermelon. There were pitchers of buttermilk and sweet milk, steaming pots of "coffee," a little of it real, and an assortment of pickles and relishes that would have been prize-winners at a county fair.

When table seating ran out, the remaining throng filled plates, platters, or pie pans and sat on the stairs, the porch, and any available perch, or stood while plying forks, or, in some cases, Bowies.

Off and on during the day, Deborah had glimpsed her parents, and now she was glad to see them settled on a couch with the Cordleys. After Sara and Deborah preceded their escorts through the line, Rolf suggested they all go sit on Melissa Eden's porch, just off Massachusetts Street, where they'd be less crowded.

The prospect of comparative peace was inviting. Carefully balancing filled plates and cups, the four maneuvered out of the hotel and down the street, then got to one side as a wagon creaked past.

"Miss Lander!" Sara cried. "Mr. Lander!" And then, as the wagon stopped and she recognized the shaggy-haired, broad-torsoed man supported in Conrad Lander's arms, she ran to the wagon. "Johnny! Johnny, what's wrong with you?"

"Mmm," grunted Johnny, trying to sit up. He failed and slid back.

"Is he hurt?" pleaded Sara. "Oh, what—"

Ansjie Lander flushed painfully. Her brother said, "Mr. Chaudoin's not . . . well."

"He's drunk," Rolf cut in brutally. "Stupid drunk. But what's that blood on his face?"

"Blood?" Sara tried to clamber up, but Thos put her back and climbed up himself.

Ansjie Lander said carefully, "Only a scratch. Mr. Chaudoin had out his knife, but Conrad persuaded him to come with us."

A few more questions forced the main facts from the reluctant young Prussians. Unaware of the holiday, they'd stopped that morning at the smithy to find Johnny in a belligerent mood, though they hadn't realized that he'd been drinking. He had insisted that they all go to Lawrence to celebrate, scolding the Landers for not trying to honor their adopted country. Between bullying and coaxing, he'd gotten them to come while he rode horseback beside them.

Arriving in the middle of the speeches, the Landers had lost track of Johnny till the barbecue was under way. He had jumped up by the flagpole and challenged any and all to a fight. Another equally drunk riverman had accepted. Johnny had wrestled him down and was pounding his head on the ground when Conrad intervened. Only his sister's presence had kept him from being mobbed for halting the sport. The scar stood out whitely on his tanned cheek. From the erect way he carried himself, Deborah was sure that he, like Dane, had been an officer. His blue eyes rested on her in a way that made her feel terribly young and yet very much a woman.

Sara's eyes were full of unshed tears and her mouth quivered. "He never gets drunk," she muttered. "He told me he had lots of work today, that he couldn't come—" Shaking her head, as if to clear it, she turned to Thos. "I must go home, take care of him."

"Maccabee's there," Thos protested. "Good Lord, Sara, men get drunk every day, and if I know Johnny, he wouldn't want you around watching him!"

"I know him better than you do," she said coldly, then handed him her plate and kilted up her skirt to climb into the wagon.

"Oh, damnation!" Thos cast a hunted look about. "Sara, I'll go with you!" He tried to foist the cups and plates on Deborah, but she retreated.

"Sara, you both need to eat," she reasoned. "It'll only take a minute."

"I'm not hungry!" Sara half-wept.

"Yes, you are," chided Thos. He handed her one plate and a cup of buttermilk, took a hasty bite of venison, and admonished her rather thickly to eat up and not delay the Landers.

In less than ten minutes the wagon creaked on its way, Thos beside it on Johnny's paint horse, which had been hitched to the tailgate. Deborah, who'd been battling flies away from her now thoroughly cooled plate, looked at it and said, "I'm not hungry."

Rolf somehow lodged his cup on his plate and took her arm. "As Thos told Sara, 'Yes, you are,' " he said. "Don't let that old savage's going on a toot ruin your day. It's just his way of celebrating."

"No. Johnny likes his whisky, but I've never heard of him having too much before."

Rolf shrugged. "Well, it's scarcely a tragedy. There'll be hundreds of people in his condition tonight and who will share his headache tomorrow."

Melissa Eden's white frame house had hollyhocks around it and was shaded by a big black walnut tree. Mechanically taking the wicker chair Rolf placed for her on the vine-shaded porch, Deborah gazed unseeingly down the tree-shaded streets with their well-built houses. Lawrence, because of its comparatively well-educated and better-equipped founders, was a much more prosperous and attractive town than most thrown-together, happenstance frontier settlements, whose main attraction was generally liquor. Lawrence had had schools and churches from the start, plus enough professional men to give it advantages seldom found on the prairie.

"It's not like Johnny. He—he despises men who get drunk and start bragging and brawling. It must be that even though he wants Thos and Sara to be happy, he can't stand the way they're getting closer."

Rolf's tawny eyebrows climbed. "That old rip loves the Indian wench? Then surely he's had her!"

"He has not!" Deborah stared in outrage. "Johnny was friends with her family. When her parents died six years ago, he brought her and Laddie to live with him. She's been like a daughter."

"Bit old and pretty for that now," said Rolf clearly skeptical.

"You don't believe a man can want a woman who's in his power, yet deny himself because he thinks he's not right for her?"

Rolf lifted one shoulder, then let it fall unargumentatively. "A man might try. But sooner or later, Deborah, restraints snap." In a more sympathetic voice, he added, "Maybe Chaudoin had to get drunk or take the girl next chance he had. Do Thos and Sara know how he feels?"

Deborah shook her head. "I couldn't believe it myself when it first struck me this spring, but today makes me sure it's true."

"It may work out," Rolf suggested. "Chaudoin married one Indian. He could marry this one, too, after Thos has his fun."

"Fun!" Deborah choked at the crudity. "Fun's not what Sara and my brother want! He wants to marry her, when they're older, when the country settles down."

"What will your parents think?"

"They love Sara!" Detesting the cool cynicism of Rolf's bland expression, Deborah felt driven to explain further. "Sara's proud of her people and sees marrying white as a sort of rejection of her blood, I think. She'll get over that. I'll be glad to have her for a sister-in-law."

Studying her for a moment, Rolf's full mouth curved down. "Strange if I get a red Indian for a sister-in-law by marriage," he pondered. "But since Sir Harry's got to swallow a camel, a gnat won't hurt him."

"I'm not going to marry you, Rolf. And it doesn't seem likely that I'll marry Dane."

"You won't marry Dane," Rolf said calmly. "I think you'll want to marry me by the time we're finished, but if you don't, no matter. You'll still be my woman."

She spaced the words out evenly, though blood pounded in her ears and she didn't know if she was more aroused than angry. *"I will not."*

He only smiled, watching her in such a disconcerting way that Deborah gave him a final look of defiance and concentrated on her food. They ate in silence. Deborah brooded over Johnny, longed for Dane, and came near hating him for leaving her alone, exposed to his brother.

"I want to go home," she said as they started toward the

hotel. Fiddlers were tuning up amidst a hubbub of laughter and talk while more boisterous sounds of merrymaking floated from the grove.

"Why, the sun's not down yet! The party's just beginning!"

"I don't feel like dancing or hearing music—or any of that!" Suddenly she thought of what should have occurred to her long ago. "I've got to find my parents and go home with them! I can't drive with you now that Sara and Thos are gone."

The look in Rolf's eyes told her he hadn't overlooked the situation. His square jaw hardened but he clamped his lips shut on whatever he'd started to say and moved her along the street, then up the steps of the hotel.

Taking their plates, he brushed aside Deborah's insistence that she should help with the dishwashing. "I've paid the hotel to hire people for that and the clean-up," he said. "Dane left me enough to pay for everything. Said it was cheaper than my gambling. Wait here and then we'll find your parents and decide how I can have that waltz you promised!"

While he was gone, Deborah vainly scanned the crowd for the elder Whitlaws and was thoroughly nervous by the time Rolf, besieged by handshakes, smiles, and congratulations, made his way back to her.

"I'm afraid they're gone," she said.

"So Reverend Cordley just told me," Rolf agreed. "Your father said since Thos and you wouldn't be home in time for chores, he'd have to see to the milking and such."

"Then we'll have to leave right now to get there before dark!"

"Deborah, Deborah! I've seen enough of Kansas customs to know it won't hurt your reputation to drive home alone with me! Couples do it all the time!"

"But I don't want to be alone with you!"

"Ah." His eyes went obsidian-black, with only the faintest tinge of green. After a moment he smiled. "But *I* want to be alone with you, and though I was resigned to putting up with your brother and his Indian maiden, it seems the fates have rewarded my patience." He smiled cajolingly. "If you're destined to drive with me, what does it matter, daylight or dark?"

"It matters!"

"Are you afraid of the dark? Or of me?"

He mustn't know that to her in some ways he *was* the

dark, unknown, tempting, fearful, yet exciting. When she looked into his eyes, she was staring into midnight. And she caught there an image of herself that frightened and shamed her, recognition of restless, building need, the craving Dane had awakened but refused to satisfy.

She was afraid of the dark and Rolf, but more, she feared herself. As she tore her eyes from his triumphant ones, she swallowed and said harshly, "I want to go now, Rolf. If you won't take me, I'll start walking."

"Little fool!"

She whirled away, moving blindly for the entrance. His fingers closed on her wrist, turning her around. "Deborah!" he scolded. "You'd try the patience of a saint!" They stood in silent conflict for a moment, but when Deborah tried to pull free, he sighed and covered her hand with both of his. "I can't believe the things you make me do! If I find a chaperone for the drive home, won't you keep your promise and give me the waltz?"

She had promised, and rushing home would in no way help Johnny or Thos or Sara. The way that Rolf subjugated his haughty will to her wishes made her feel under obligation to him, at least for this occasion.

"I don't want to be silly," she said in a halting voice. "If you find someone to go with us, I'll stay for some of the dancing. But you have to understand that I'm worried about Johnny and the others and can't feel particularly gay."

"I understand that I picked the most difficult woman in creation to court," he said feelingly. "But never mind. Come have some punch and I'll find a chaperone—even if I have to appeal to Reverend Cordley!"

When he returned with the news that Melissa Eden would accompany them, Deborah groaned inwardly but felt she could scarcely protest when she was insisting on a third person. It did cross her mind that the lovely widow would probably save him from too frustrated an evening, but that was none of her business. She shouldn't even think of it.

The big room had been cleared as much as possible. Older people and women sat on the chairs and benches pushed against the walls. Mothers were trying to get their babies to sleep in upstairs rooms loaned by the management, and though a few young children still sat in their parents' laps or darted around squealing, most of them were napping on upstairs pallets, which mothers took turns at overseeing.

The three fiddlers on a small wood platform bowed into an uproarious version of "Golden Slippers," had the crowd whistling and clapping, then saluted each other, and the flanking musicians stepped back to join in the dancing till the present player tired.

He was Tarry Wagoner, Deborah learned from comments around her, the Territory's best fiddler and renowned for his calling.

He soon had the floor full of couples, four to a set, and chanted in time to the sawing of his bow and tapping foot.

"Salute your partners!" he called. "Join hands and circle left!"

He played and sang them through swinging and circlings and promenades, winding up with: "Grab your honeys, don't let 'em fall! Shake your feet and balance all! Ring-tail coons in the trees at play, grab your partners and all run away!"

Loud applause greeted the end of the number and Tarry shouted that as many as could get on the floor would do "Jolly Is the Miller Boy." This was more singing game than dance, and when Rolf took her hand, Deborah stepped into the circling wheel of partners. There were three men to each woman, so young girls and grandmothers skipped briskly along as the miller boy tried with each switching of partners to steal a girl and leave another man in the middle.

It was impossible to stay pensive in the midst of the scrambling and laughter, or to care that she didn't know the steps. All she had to do was *be* there and let the eager men whirl her around or sweep her forward.

During the "Virginia Reel," Captain Harrington whispered in Deborah's ear that she was charming, and one bewhiskered, rather ferocious-looking gentleman, during their first brief partnership, told her he was a widower, and on the second meeting he said that he had a mighty good claim, a yoke of oxen, ten cows—and would she marry him? A dashing young scout for the cavalry asked if he could come calling, and shyer men gazed in their admiration. It was heady and exhilarating, especially since it had never happened before.

"I've got the belle of the ball," laughed Rolf as he claimed her for a cotillion. "Don't say you're not enjoying it! Your eyes are like amber stars!"

"I've been offered a yoke of oxen and ten cows," she teased. "And that cavalry scout is handsome!"

"I'll give you a field of oxen and cows, and I'm much better looking than that!"

A riverman swept her away. At the end of that dance, Tarry Wagoner rubbed off the sweat that was glistening on his red sideburns and went over to the punch bowl while a slight, black-moustached fiddler took the platform.

Just to let the assembly have no doubt he could bow country style with the best, he played "Possum Up a Stump" and then announced a waltz. A few ladies insisted on returning to their seats, but most were coaxed into more or less gingerly permitting their partners to clasp their waists and, as a bull-whacker within earshot of Deborah phrased it, "makin' a lunge at that crazy kind of hugged-up tune!"

Rolf's hand on her back and his pronounced, graceful lead soon dispelled her awkwardness. She loved the gliding dip, the way the dreamy music directed their motions. Perhaps it did place her body too close to Rolf, but she avoided his eyes by closing hers, and his arms became Dane's, his touch was her lover's, for this magic time she was with him again; she wished the dance could last forever.

But it ended. Reluctantly, she opened her eyes. Rolf's were blazing. He became very much himself. What a fool she was, going soft in his embrace like that, drunk on music and excitement! She put up warding hands and stepped away.

"It—it's late. I have to go home."

He turned her hand over and kissed her palm, lips searing the exposed flesh. His voice was a rustling sigh. "You danced with me."

She tried to laugh. "And with dozens of others."

"You didn't give yourself to them."

She made an inarticulate sound of regret and dismay. He'd noticed then, sensed her yielding to the fantasy of Dane. Rolf couldn't be allowed to think that softness had been for him.

"Rolf, I'm sorry!" He stared at her and she said miserably, "The music—it was so lovely I got lost in it. I know it was wrong but I . . . made believe you were Dane."

She flinched at the shock that paled his face, then put out a hand he ignored as, recovering, he gave a hard laugh. "It might be interesting to see how long and under what circumstances you could maintain that illusion! But I'm warned now, and you had best be: from now on I'll take care that you know whom you're with!" Turning, he called over his shoulder that he'd be back shortly with the surrey.

Refusing the men who eagerly begged her to dance, Deborah felt overheated and strangling for fresh air. Making her way to the door, she was joined by Melissa Eden, who was explaining to a disappoined Captain Harrington that she really must help these delightful young people be together in spite of Miss Whitlaw's quaint prudery. And splendid as it would be to have the captain's escort, he had duty next day and would never be in time for it if he spent the night jaunting about the prairies. She'd never forgive herself if he were court-martialed, but assuredly they'd have other times. Perhaps he could call next week?

Deborah was sure Melissa meant to spend a good portion of what was left of the night in her young boarder's arms. Fevered, yet shamed at the thought, Deborah wondered if the older woman pretended, too, and if she knew what Dane's ardor was like, the better to reproduce it with his brother.

Such imaginings were wicked, a dark quicksand that inexorably drew one into a lewd morass. Dane couldn't love or respect her if he knew the wanton way she'd relaxed in Rolf's embrace—unless, wretched notion, he was doing the same thing with other women!

When the hurt of that subsided, she accepted that he probably was, and more, that he wouldn't stop at dreaming. Men, she suspected, usually didn't if they had a means of gratification. Nor did women like Melissa.

So while Melissa and Rolf eased each other, while Dane might very possibly be spending himself with some distant woman, Deborah would sleep alone.

This night had shown her the folly of dreaming. It was a long drive home.

Rolf had taken himself in hand and he and Melissa bantered most of the way to the Whitlaws', an undercurrent of male-female anticipation so strong between them that Deborah, contrarily enough, felt shoved aside, woefully young and inexperienced. When Rolf walked her to the door, he thanked her for dancing and said he'd visit soon, but he didn't linger. And as he went back to the surrey, Melissa's knowing, sensuous laughter welcomed him.

Deborah stood in the dark cabin for a few minutes after

the surrey wheeled off. Chica was near the stable, so Thos was home. Deborah thought of waking him up to learn about Johnny, but she decided that could wait till morning. If anything had gone too wrong, Thos would've stayed at the smithy. Let him sleep.

But Deborah, through a stifling, restless night, could not sleep at all. She was worried for Johnny, her brother, and Sara, confused and ashamed at her mixed reactions to Rolf, and achingly needful of Dane. It was so long till spring!

And even if it came, and Dane with it, what chance would there be that his resolves or hers could be different? Turning repeatedly on the shuck mattress, she wept for her love.

• X •

Summer wore on. Johnny seemed none the worse for his spree, but Thos grew more and more fidgety. "Can't go to the gold because all this slavery business is coming to a head," he grumbled as they pulled fodder, helped by Judith, stripping leaves downward from the ears of tall corn and putting bunches of them to dry in the crotches between stalks. "Can't get married; wouldn't be fair to Sara if I have to go off to war!"

Deborah paused, scrubbing away chaff and perspiration. "Don't talk that way, Thos! We *could* have a war just because everyone seems to think we will!"

Thos shook his head gloomily. "More than that to it, 'Borah. Seems like everything's about to bust wide open, and I wish it would so we could have it over with and get on with living!"

Though she might chide her twin, Deborah felt much the same way. She laughed ruefully. "Well, Thos, it's lucky we've got work to do!"

He gave some leaves a particularly vicious jerk. "Seems

mighty tame and all-fired dull when this part of the Territory's got gold fever and that miserable old pro-slave Judge Williams in southeast Kansas is still handing down decisions Free State men can't swallow! Doggone it, 'Borah, this isn't a time when a man belongs in a corn patch!"

"We have to eat. The horses and Venus will need this fodder come winter. I think a corn patch is a pretty useful place to be!"

"That's right," said Judith unexpectedly. "Got to eat and sleep no matter what. No one tend the crops, everybody go hungry!"

"You're women!" scorned Thos.

"Good thing, if that mean we got some sense," retorted Judith. "Best lay up the harvest and leave blatherskitin' to crazies like Jim Lane!"

Lane, after a grand jury failed to indict him for killing Gaius Jenkins, was trying to regain his popularity with law-abiding folk by getting religion at several different Methodist churches, and though one tavern keeper had been heard to say he didn't want his horses watered below where Jim Lane had been baptized, the Grim Chieftain's shrill-voiced spell was working.

He sold his old claybank horse and gave the money to women who were starting a public library. And he was fond of saying that the only time he'd ever used profane language was in the Mexican War when his "Midwestern farm boys" were up against fancily tasseled lancers and he'd exhorted his troops to "Charge on 'em, God damn em! Charge on 'em!" His ambition was to represent Kansas in the Senate once it became a state, and Father resignedly said that would probably happen.

Rolf continued to meet the Whitlaws at church and go home wtih them for Sunday dinner. Deborah found it like being watched by a large cat, having no notion of when it might spring.

August 2 came and the Lecompton constitution was soundly rejected, which broke the last clutching of what had once been the pro-slavery death grip. True, Kansas would now have to wait for admission till its population reached that required for a congressional district, but Free Staters were in control, and when Kansas became a state, it would be free.

After years of struggle for this goal, there was more weariness than triumph in the Whitlaw home, which reflected the mood in Lawrence and around the Territory. It wasn't a question of Kansas now, but a matter of whether and how the nation itself would survive. There was thankfulness in the Whitlaws' prayers, but little joy and much anxiety.

The fodder had long ago been stacked in a corner of the stable and the naked stalks stood in the field, supporting the hardening ears. The wheat which Dane had helped reap was ready now for threshing in the circular spot the twins had raked down to the hard clay, banking up the topsoil in a diameter of about twenty feet.

Father stayed home to help with the actual threshing, placing bundles of wheat with grainy heads pointing to the center of the ring, while an overlapping row was turned with its stalks to the center and its heads on top of the first row's. Judith and the twins took turns leading Nebuchadnezzar and Belshazzar around the ring till the straw was crushed. It was stacked behind the center of the ring and new bundles were placed.

It was hot, tedious work, followed by winnowing. Fortunately, there was a breeze, which blew away the chaff as the workers poured the wheat from buckets onto a sheet. Failing a natural wind, one would have had to be laboriously created by stretching a big cloth tight and fanning it.

Still, at the end of the sweaty, tiresome labor, along with aching backs and muscles, the family had a hundred bushels of wheat stored in big covered bins at the side of the stable that served as a granary.

Since getting to any mill and waiting one's turn meant a number of days, Father decided to take Mother with him to the mill at Topeka and visit friends. Thos rode Chica to *The Clarion* office and tended to business there in the elder Whitlaw's absence, while Deborah and Judith caught up on laundry, cleaned house, and washed each other's hair.

Father and Mother returned with bags of real flour, and for a while the Whitlaws indulged in an orgy of biscuits, "light" bread, and even a cake made with sugar from one of the collections of small luxuries Rolf brought from time to time.

September passed with sowing wheat and shucking corn, and Father brought home that month's *Atlantic Monthly*, purchased at the City Drug Store, which also carried *Harper's*, *Knickerbocker*, and *Godey*. That night, while the family was gathered for dinner, he read them Whittier's poem "Le Marais du Cygne."

"Free homes and free altars
Free prairie and flood—
The reeds of the Swan's Marsh
Whose bloom is of blood!"

It was long and Father's voice broke several times before he finished. "Now the whole country will be stirred up about the massacre," he said, putting the pages down. But Deborah, though she felt sick to remember Jed and his night-riding Missourians, thought that much the same poem could have been written about John Brown's slaughter at Pottawatomie. When would "Bleeding Kansas's" wounds be stanched?

Along the river, maple leaves were flaming, and goldenrod and purple asters stood knee-high, while wild geese honked over, going south. Deborah, Thos, Sarah, and Laddie gathered hickory nuts and hazelnuts, walnuts, pecans, and small, tangy wild grapes. Thos and Sara laughed together, feeding each other the choicest grapes, so that Deborah was almost glad when Rolf, as if by accident, joined them on their third expedition.

He behaved so well that even Sara thawed toward him, and by the time autumn moved into winter, the four young people, in the rented surrey, were frequently together—at taffy pulls, pie suppers, the literary society, church, or simply out driving, sometimes with a picnic lunch.

Deborah wasn't sure how it happened. Rolf never directly asked to take her somewhere, but he would mention some plan to Thos, who was delighted at the chance to squire Sara around without having to borrow his parents' buggy and horses.

When Deborah told herself that she should stop seeing Rolf, she shrank from spoiling her twin's happy times with Sara, and she was moreover compelled to admit that the autumnal days would be drab without the almost weekly outing.

Rolf didn't try to get her alone or kiss her, even hold her hand. The only physical contact they had was when he helped her in and out of the surrey or steadied her on rough footing. Now and then there was tingling shock as their eyes met, but she avoided gazing at him and rarely glanced up to find him watching her.

Grateful at his changed manner, she puzzled over it for a while, and though she found no satisfactory explanation, she decided that she, Thos, and Sara made pleasant company for him.

It was too late now to go on to Pike's Peak; he'd have to wait for spring. While it was rather surprising that he didn't winter in Kansas City or St. Louis, he had good hunting and drinking companions among the wilder youngbloods headquartering at Lawrence and was snugly ensconced in Melissa Eden's house.

He wouldn't be the first man to spend a season somewhere because of pleasures found in a woman's arms. Deborah's cheeks grew hot when she wondered about them, and she quickly banished such forbidden speculations, but these did return, and she had to confess to a certain unreasonable pique that Rolf had apparently been able to divert his passion for her into the delights he must share with Melissa.

The first snows fell and winter began in earnest. When Deborah rode Chica, cakes of slippery ice collected in the shoes, dropping off after a time, but making the footing treacherous while the snow lasted. Rolf brought a bobsled now instead of the surrey, when snow was on the ground, and they traveled to the jingle of sleigh bells, with robes tucked over their feet and legs.

Christmas was nearing. There'd been no word from Dane, and even Rolf began to worry. Then, on the same day, within the same hour, Father brought home a large oilskin-wrapped parcel and Rolf rode out with a letter, both sent from Santa Fe with a trader who was going to winter in St. Louis. At Rolf's voice, Judith pulled on a coat and went through the rear window to the lean-to.

With shaking fingers, Deborah untied rawhide thongs laced around the oilskin, then unwrapped a tight-woven gray and brown blanket to reveal a sketch pad bound in leather. On the first page, he had written in a bold, slanting script:

> So you share my journey, sweetheart—you have been with me every day, in everything I do.

"One hopes not quite *everything*." Rolf's voice was strained. He'd been reading over her shoulder.

Flushing, Deborah gave him a rebuking glance and took the pad over to her mother, near the lamp. With Father, Thos, and Rolf peering over her shoulder, Deborah turned the pages she'd later treasure and study, so tremulously elated that she kept fumbling.

The first sketch was of the buffalo wallow. "Where we met," was penciled in the corner. Next was the smithy, with Johnny and Maccabee. There were Mother and Father in the office of *The Clarion*, but the rest were drawings of the journey west—buffalo, Conestoga wagons, antelope, geese flying overhead, prairie dogs at their burrows, meadowlarks and mockingbirds, hawks and owls, a cavalry patrol, freighters, bull-whackers, tall Osage Indians, handsome Cheyenne, stocky Comanche, Bent's old fort, and then the New Mexican mountains and the plaza of Santa Fe, the inn, La Fonda, the cathedral, and a sampling of the town's Indians, *señoritas, caballeros*, trappers, and scouts.

All of the pages had a phrase or sentence, speaking to Deborah, inviting her to see what he had. She was so happy she was near crying. These days and weeks and months during which she'd felt abandoned, locked away from his thoughts—he'd made these memories for her!

"He has a gift for catching the spirit of people and creatures with a few lines," Father said. "No wonder he finds it possible to live from his work."

"Oh, I dare say Sir Harry's name helps a bit," interjected Rolf. "Some smaller parcels dropped out, Miss Deborah. Aren't you going to see what they are?"

Deborah left the sketch pad in her mother's hands and returned to the bundle. Father's name was attached to a pencil box inlaid with an etched silver map of the New World. For Thos there was a magnificent buckskin hunting shirt, fringed and beaded, trimmed with triangles of black velvet. A fringed blue shawl for Mother made her give a soft cry of pleasure while Thos was jubilantly pulling the shirt on, holding out his arm and giving it a shake so the fringes would dance.

Another shawl, golden brown, had "JUDITH" tagged to it. Mother quickly took it and put it on the pianoforte with hers.

Last, for Deborah, was an exquisite lace head covering of black with a carved tortoiseshell comb. As she unfolded the whispering cobweb, a small silver medallion fell out of a bit of tissue.

Lifting it with its delicate chain, Deborah smoothed out

its wrapping, and once again Dane's forceful writing spoke to her:

> St. Rita's the succorer of lost causes. Perhaps she'll pray for ours. I should be in California by the time you get this, but I'll be with you as soon as the snow melts from the passes.

"Has my agnostic brother turned papist?" demanded Rolf, scowling at the sweet face of the saint.

"With 'Borah so stubborn, he probably figures he needs all the help he can get," said Thos irreverently, preening himself. He added condescendingly, "That Spanish head thing's all very well, 'Borah, but wouldn't you rather have a shirt like mine?"

"It'd look funny over my dresses." She laughed. "Mother, how do you think the comb goes?"

"One of the sketches shows a lady with a mantilla."

Mother searched through the pages till she found the drawing. The girl peered coquettishly over her fan, with lace framing a triangular face not unlike Deborah's own in contour.

How well had Dane known his subject? Deborah thought jealously, and she was glad he'd gone on to California, though heaven knew where there were women at all, savage or civilized, many of them would look at him with more than subtle invitation. She was a fool to torture herself with that.

She was a fool.

As if sensing how her daughter felt, Leticia's hands were comforting as she swept up enough of Deborah's hair to hold the comb in place at the back of her crown. Over this, she arranged the graceful fall of lace and then gazed at her daughter with a startled expression, then glanced at the picture.

"Why, Deborah! Except that her hair and eyes are black, this lady could be you!"

"It could," agreed Father bemusedly. "Same mouth, same tilting up of the eyebrows."

Rolf scanned both drawing and Deborah, then grinned sardonically. "It would seem my brother has an eye for your kind of woman, Miss Deborah. But no *señorita* could look as ravishing as you, with that lace setting off the copper in your hair."

How like Rolf to wound and flatter at the same time!

Refusing to meet his eyes, Deborah longed to see how she looked. "Take the lamp to the mirror, child," Leticia suggested with a smile. "And then we'd better have dinner! Build up the fire, Thos, and I'll make the biscuits."

Holding the lamp to reflect her face in the small mirror, Deborah saw a curving mouth, large, dark-lashed, wine-amber eyes, flawless skin—a face that echoed the enchanting one in Dane's sketch. *I—I'm beautiful!* she thought. She quickly added: *It's the mantilla and the lamplight.* But she wished that Dane could see her so.

Putting down the lamp, she fastened the medallion around her neck and slipped it between her breasts, where the cool metal swiftly warmed.

He hadn't forgotten her! He'd thought of her as he drew people and animals and scenes of his journey; he'd sent her a way to see with his eyes, mysterious beauty for her hair, a saint to lie near her heart as a constant remembrance.

It made her sad that there was no way to send a gift back, but perhaps if she prayed very hard, he'd feel that and know how she loved him.

Rolf read his letter during the meal, including Dane's wish that he share it with the Whitlaws. It could have been the story of thousands of west-bound travelers. For safety, he'd joined a trade caravan, its wagons groaning under loads of iron and tools, mirrors, gewgaws, powder and lead, ribbons, stroudings, woolen goods, and all manner of cloth from cotton to bombazines, velvets and silks.

He'd met and painted half a dozen kinds of Indians, traveled along the Arkansas River, Sand Creek, Cimarron, the Rio Colorado, camped at Council Grove, Pawnee Fork, Point of Rocks, Rio Gallinas, and more than a score of other places, including the crumbling adobe ruins of Bent's Fort, blown up by William Bent when the War Department refused to buy it from him in 1852, five years after his brother Charles, governor of New Mexico, was murdered in the Taos rebellion of Indians and Mexicans against the new power of the conquering United States.

A group of Texans had tried to annex New Mexico during the time when Texas had been a republic, but though the people of Santa Fe had been glad to see the *gringos* marched off to prison in Mexico, Santa Fe had come to depend on trade with the United States, first by pack-train and then by wagon, beginning in 1821, when

William Becknell took his first wagons over the trail. Merchants and women were glad to see the caravans, and if some of the men weren't, bloodier brawls could be seen in any frontier town.

Dane ended by saying that Rolf couldn't consider his western tour complete without going over the trail and on to the coast. Why didn't he start early next spring?

"Will you?" Thos asked longingly as Rolf, tight-lipped, folded the letter and thrust it into his pocket.

"Who knows?" Rolf looked around at the Whitlaws in a way that gave Deborah an uneasy feeling, as if a hawk had nested among quail or a wolf had curled up by its prey. His mouth lost its grim set, curving in a smile. "California, Pike's Peak, Oregon—lots of places to go in your country! I want to see them all." His eyes fixed on Deborah. "Still, for me this will always be the center of your world."

Father sighed. "It's certainly the eye of the hurricane!"

By now all the Whitlaws must have been as aware as was Deborah that Judith was huddling under her blankets in the dark lean-to, growing hungrier with every minute Rolf lingered. Rising, Deborah began to clear the table, and Mother joined her.

"We've already had Christmas!" said Leticia. "What wonderful presents, and so kind of Dane! Perhaps it's as well we opened them now so we won't be distracted by them on the Lord's birthday."

Rolf's chair grated as he pushed it back. "It's not time to declare the holiday over yet," he said, and he looked as if he wanted to say more on the subject but caught himself. "Some people from the literary society are putting on *Macbeth* this Saturday at the hotel. Shall we see how they manage?"

"Oh, let's!" cried Thos. "Sara's never seen a play!"

So once again, though with Dane's presence renewed by his gifts, Deborah felt more troubled than ever about it, Rolf had engaged another evening.

He told the family good night. Thos went out with him to the stable, and Mother got Judith's shawl from beneath hers. "I'll call Judith now. This pretty thing should help make up for her discomfort. It was kind of Dane to remember her."

"Mother!" Deborah glanced up from the dishes. "Do you realize that we're still hiding Judith from Rolf?"

Father and Mother exchanged startled glances. "I—suppose we are," Mother said wonderingly.

"He's been here half a dozen times to every visit of Dane's," Deborah went on. "Yet during the harvest, Judith wasn't nervous about his seeing her. It seemed perfectly safe."

Josiah nodded. "It seemed natural to trust Dane." His brow furrowed as he pondered over this curious fact that none of them had really noticed before. "Maybe it's because Rolf's young and impetuous, a boy in many ways for all his sophistication. Dane's a man. From the moment one meets him, there's no doubt of that."

"That must be it." Sounding relieved, for she was fond of Rolf, Mother hurried off to call Judith.

"You're scowling, daughter," Josiah observed. "You must know Rolf better than any of us. It's clear he's much attracted to you, which has worried your mother and me, because we knew you cared for Dane. Have you reason to mistrust Rolf?"

He likes excitement," Deborah said evasively. "He needs to prove himself as much a man as Dane. I'm afraid he might do that, on a whim, in ways that could be . . . well, pretty terrible."

But Judith was back, delighted with the shawl, which she stroked as if it had been a soft animal. And after the dishes were done, the family had to look at Dane's sketch pad again before they went to bed.

So did Rolf when he brought the bobsled that Saturday and had early supper with the family before he drove the twins to collect Sara. While Thos ran up to the cabin for her, Rolf turned to Deborah. The bobsled had bracketed lamps, but the moon was so bright they weren't lit, bright enough for Deborah to feel apprehensive at Rolf's expression, or lack of it.

In the pale white luminance, his face was a mask. "You must be flattered, Deborah."

"Why?"

"Haven't you studied the women in Dane's sketch pad?"

She had, often. There were old women, lined faces reflecting all their seasons and griefs and joys, women of years, proud or submissive, trusting or suspicious. Deborah was sure all these were chosen for character, the challenge to capture the essence of a human being. But the younger women—something about them troubled Deborah, haunted her more than could be explained by tormenting doubts about how well he'd known them.

"I've looked at all the drawings many times," she told Rolf coolly.

"I'll bet you have! Especially the handsome wenches!" Rolf's lips peeled back from strong, perfect teeth, a rarity in the frontier men, where tobacco-stained stumps were often seen in fairly young people. He laughed harshly. "I thought it the night you opened the pad, and I had a chance to make sure of it after supper tonight. Every young woman in those sketches—Cheyenne, Osage, Comanche, or Mexican—is really you!"

"But—" Her protest died as she remembered the various faces, some gay, some moody, looking from the pages, framed by plaits, mantilla, or blanket, hair blowing free in the wind.

That was what had nagged and eluded her. Costumed and changed to fit the parts, she'd appeared to Dane all along his journey! Had he done it on purpose?

"Now you'll wonder," continued Rolf, deftly reading her mind, "if he did more than paint those images of you, if he made love to you along the trail in the bodies of other women—"

She covered her ears. "Stop it!"

Regretfully, he shook his head. "I can't. This shows me more than anything else possibly could how deeply you're set in my brother's soul. He's always taken pride, when drawing from life, in rendering exactly what's before him. Now, either as a tribute or because he couldn't help it, he's painted you into every likely female between here and Santa Fe!"

Deborah didn't know how to answer. A fated sadness in Rolf's tone made the nape of her neck prickle. She was glad that Thos and Sara came out of the cabin at that moment and hurried to the bobsled.

Melissa Eden as Lady Macbeth had a chance to prowl daringly in a white silk nightgown that exposed her arms and ankles and would have, under any other circumstances short of a fire in her chamber, made her an exile from decent society. Mr. Montmorency, a lawyer, played Macbeth with much flourishing of a cutlass, which made Deborah think involuntarily of John Brown's merciless use of his sword at Pottawatomie Creek. Macbeth's feet were pointed to the audience so that his death struggles provoked more laughter than horror, but this was compensated for by the most ingenious contrivance of the evening when Macbeth's gory head appeared, reeking with blood, held aloft by the hair. This illusion was created by having Montmorency stand behind the other actors, who hid his body.

Deborah shrieked along with most of the women, then clapped wildly as the gratified thespians took their bows, Mr. Montmorency still gruesomely bloody.

Rolf invited the performers to a late meal, which he'd arranged for ahead of time. Melissa, sitting on one side of him, prettily returned his champagne toasts, though Deborah, Thos, and Sara drank milk.

"I hear you received a most fascinating sketch pad from the other Mr. Hunter," Melissa said to Deborah. A shawl draped loosely around her did nothing to conceal the molding of her legs beneath the silk. "Do please bring it by, my dear. I'd like to see what he discovered on the way to Santa Fe." She gave a limpid sigh, smiling at Mr. Montmorency, now scrubbed till his freckles shone, and obviously entranced by her. "Such intriguing men, artists, but highly undependable, I fear."

Rolf snorted. "Undependable? Dear madam, you don't know my brother! All discipline, control, and duty! He should have stayed in the army and would to God that he had! I could have made this trip then without his shadow over me even when he's in California!"

"Dear Rolf! Is it so hard to be a younger son?"

"I don't mind that. What hurts is being a younger brother!"

Melissa laughed softly. "To someone like Dane, I can see that it might." Her wide blue eyes slipped to Deborah. "But he *is* gone, and you seem to be most adequately filling his place."

"That's right," toasted Mr. Montmorency. "Here's to constant lovers!"

"It's late." Deborah pushed back her chair and rose. In that moment she almost hated Melissa, with her sweetly mocking innuendos.

Rolf glanced at his ornate gold watch. "We *had* better be going. I told the boy at the livery stable to have the sled out front at eleven o'clock sharp." Rising, he made a careless gesture to the waiter. "Please see that these ladies and gentlemen have everything they want, and I'll settle with you tomorrow."

"Everything?" queried the waiter, glancing at the champagne.

"Everything," Rolf said carelessly. He bowed to the performers. "My compliments once more for a most spirited entertainment!"

He escorted Deborah out to a chorus of thanks and good wishes. The horses were waiting, jingling their bells. Rolf gave the boy a coin and helped Deborah in while Thos assisted Sara.

"You've got style!" Thos said with an admiring wistfulness that grated on Deborah. "You do everything smooth and gracious as a lord!"

"Money helps," Deborah couldn't keep from saying.

Sara sputtered into her lap robe.

Thos said, " 'Borah!"

But Rolf laughed. "Why, Miss Deborah, I'm glad to hear you say that. It betokens the first faint emergence of realism I've detected in you! If it thrives, who knows what may happen?"

Snow crunched under the horses' hooves. The moon possessed the silver rolling prairie stretching to where it melted into the crystal night. If only Dane were here. . . .

Rolf cast her a grimly merry look. Disconcertingly, he said, "He's not here, my sweet. But I am. And I have for you the most elegant present you can imagine."

"I'd prefer that you didn't give me presents."

"But I prefer to."

"If it's too fine or costly, I can't accept it."

"It cost almost nothing. You might say it was a labor of love."

Deborah gave up the joust. She stiffened as Thos leaned forward and said eagerly, "Did you hear what some people were saying at intermission? Fiddling Williams, that rascally pro-slave judge, sent two Free State men to jail in Fort Scott. Montgomery got together a rescue force. John Brown turned up and was for burning down Fort Scott, but Montgomery just wanted the prisoners loose—and he got 'em! Captured Fort Scott and broke out the Free Staters."

"Then it's all over," said Deborah, relieved.

Thos shook his head. "Not by a long shot! Brown's going to invade Missouri!"

"What?" she demanded.

"Well, he's getting men together—going into Missouri to bring out slaves, maybe horses."

"Helping slaves get away's one thing; taking horses is plain stealing!"

"Doggone it, 'Borah! Brown'll sell the horses to help escaping slaves get north and on their feet!"

"It's still stealing."

Thos gave a grunt of exasperation. "That's like saying killing in war's murder!"

"Some people say it is, though I think it may have to be done." Deborah thought of the Bowie knife under her mattress, the frightening responsibility she'd undertaken when accepting it. She clenched her hands as she tried to reach the twin she loved and feared for. "Thos, you may have to do something awful because of what would happen otherwise, but you don't have to pretty it up and pretend it's good or heroic or anything but plain, ugly have-to!"

"You just don't understand!"

"I do. Thiefing's thiefing, killing's killing, and why they're done doesn't make them glorious."

"That's right," confirmed Sara. "Men are always thinking honor, big name, fighting. Women think about an empty bed, children without fathers, winters with no food, no one to care for the aged."

"Seems to me women like uniforms," thrust Thos. "They flirt and fall in love with soldiers even if they do an about-face, weep and wail, and don't want them to go to war!" He made a sound of disgust. "Women want it both ways! A strong fighting man who'll stay home for their sakes and plow or have a business!"

Even Deborah and Sara had to laugh at that, but when Rolf spoke, his tone was scathingly serious. "Most women may be like that, Thos, but your sister isn't! She's a stern judge, like her Old Testament namesake, and has no patience with hot blood. According to her lights, El Cid was a brigand, Roland a fool, Siegfried a bully, Julius Caesar a disaster, and knights errant a plague of grasshoppers consuming the labor of honest peasants! No use in waving pennants or banners at her—she'd use them for babies' diapers or scrubbing cloths!"

That stung, though perhaps because there was truth in it. Deborah remembered the flag waving high and free on the Fourth of July and her eyes misted. To her, in spite of everything, it stood for liberty, for faith in man, for justice. For these, she'd given up her love; for these she'd taken the knife; for these she'd die.

"I might wrap a baby in the flag if there were nothing

else," she said, "or use it to bind up wounds. But it means as much to me as it does to any man." She turned on her brother. "And I still say, Thos, that—"

"Thiefing's thiefing!" he groaned. "All right! Maybe I won't take horses."

"Thos, you won't join those raids across the border! That's what we hated the Missourians for!"

He turned provokingly gay. "If Sara won't marry me soon, I may do a lot of things!"

"Hush!" blurted Sara. There was a laughing scuffle. At the end of it, she said desperately, fondly, "What can we do, Deborah? One week Thos says we can't marry because he'll probably have to go to war. I want to marry him then. The next week he wants to marry, but I say no, your parents won't like it. And besides, how can I marry white, desert my people? We turn like those new machines, those windmills!"

Deborah reached back and squeezed her friend's small, capable hand. "It's a time of shifting winds, but it won't always be this way." Pray that it won't. "And you know we'll all welcome you into the family. Mother and Father know you and Thos have been keeping company for months. Most couples would've been married long ago!"

"Really?" murmured Rolf. "Surely, Miss Deborah, you and I've been publicly together for the same length of time. Am I to take it that your reputation will be compromised if we don't marry?"

Aghast, Deborah stared at him. Because he'd never directly asked her out, because she went so Sara and Thos could, she'd never, incredibly enough, realized that people would assume Rolf was courting her.

Keeping company for pure amusement's sake was frowned upon. When a couple started being seen together frequently, it was expected to lead to marriage. People could and did change their minds, of course, but a young man who had a succession of attachments became known as wild and was banned by the parents of respectable girls, while a woman who repeatedly gave her swains "the mitten" acquired a reputation as a jilting Jezebel.

All this shot through Deborah's head, but she was more annoyed than dismayed once she faced the undeniable fact that, in community eyes, she most certainly was being courted. "I'm not that worried about my reputation," she said fiercely. "The only man I want to marry is Dane. He'd understand perfectly how this has been!"

"I wonder if you do," mused Rolf.

Deborah ignored that. "Don't hurry," she advised Sara. "But don't wait all your life, either, because you're afraid you might be wrong. If you make a mistake, you can usually recover. But if you never try, what can you do?"

They were drawing up at the smithy. Eyes shining in the moonlight, Sara hugged Deborah. "You—you'd want me for a sister-in-law?"

"You are like family, whether you marry my harum-scarum brother or not!"

"Oh, stop talking like a matriarch of the tribe!" growled Thos. "You're exactly two minutes older than me!"

He took Sara to the cabin. While he was gone, Rolf watched Deborah, but she, feeling his gaze, afraid to meet it, stared over the dazzling blue and silver snow and at the ghostly trees along the river.

"Have you heard about the Medary Ball in Lecompton on Christmas Eve?" he asked. "It's a cotillion party at the American House to honor the new governor. May I take you?"

It was his first direct invitation. She took it as a kind of testing. "Thank you, no," she said.

"Why not?"

"I—I never realized before what people would be thinking."

He said roughly, "Are you afraid of that—or that it might come true?"

Thos came back before she could answer.

• *xi* •

Thos brought in a wild turkey, which was, the day before Christmas, basted over a pan to catch the drippings while mincemeat and pumpkin pies took turns baking in the Dutch oven. When the turkey was nearly done, Thos maneuvered it off the spit into the pan, and before it finished cooking on the grate, Deborah stuffed it with cornbread seasoned with drippings and onions.

Mother had stayed home that day to help with the cooking and have her hair washed. She leaned over the tub placed on a bench while Judith soaped her thick, soft brown hair and Deborah poured slightly heated rain water over it till it squeaked and shined.

Judith rubbed it as dry as possible and worked out the tangles with painstaking care, a task that had always been Deborah's. Mother's hair was fine, hung to her hips, and she was so tender-scalped that getting all the snarls out was time-consuming; still, Deborah felt a bit excluded and just a tinge jealous, feelings that she sternly rebuked. If Judith remembered her own mother, she never mentioned her. It was likely they'd been parted long ago. Terrible for human beings to be treated like stock animals!

"Shall I wash your hair?" Deborah asked Judith. "There's plenty of soft water. We'd best use it up before it gets messy from sitting in the barrel."

When Judith smiled, which was seldom, her face changed from taut, tigerish beauty to glowing, hesitant sweetness. "That be good, Deborah. Got to wash your hair, too, so we'll all look nice."

"Good grief!" cried Thos, reaching for his sheepskin vest. "Soap, vinegar, *three* women prinking! I'm going out to chop wood!"

But that night after supper—the festive meal would be dinner after tomorrow morning's church service—when the family gathered around the pianoforte to sing carols, Thos seemed to be watching his mother and sister with unusual attention, as if he were really seeing them, not taking them for granted. The women had tied up their fluffily unruly hair with ribbon: Mother's blue, Judith's green, Deborah's yellow.

"You all look so pretty tonight," he said as the notes of "Joy to the World" lingered. "I'll remember this forever."

"Cross your heart?" Deborah teased in their old twin fashion.

"Cross my heart." He smiled, but there was a seriousness about him that troubled Deborah. "If Sara were here, it'd be absolutely perfect."

Mother rounded on him with surprising energy. "Well, why isn't she here?" You know she's welcome! She could share Deborah's bed, go to church with us tomorrow, and spend the day!"

"She could?" Thos sucked in his breath. "I'm going to the smithy tomorrow, but if I'd known—"

"You might have asked." Mother's tone had an unusual edge, and her gaze was reproving. She glanced at Josiah, who cleared his throat.

"Your mother and I have been wondering, Thos, why you don't ask Sara to be your wife. We'd be grievously disappointed if it's because she's Indian."

Thos jumped, as if branded, going first red, then pale. "Father, how could you think that?" he demanded in a high, strained voice. "I *have* asked her, even though I know it's not fair because of the way it looks like war."

Deborah put her hand protectively over Thos's wrist. She said with a chuckle, "Besides, Sara's not terribly eager to mix her Shawnee blood with white!"

That rocked the elder Whitlaws. Judith struggled with but couldn't repress what would have been a giggle in anyone else. Josiah and Leticia looked at each other and exchanged rather shamefaced smiles. "We're sorry, Thos," said Mother, reaching up to touch his cheek. "You *are* young and perhaps you should wait, but do bring Sara over tomorrow and let us start getting better acquainted."

"I—well, that's something else I've got to tell you!" Thos shoved back his auburn fleece and swallowed hard. "I have to leave tomorrow, go straight on from seeing Sara."

"Leave?" cried Deborah.

Mother and Father seemed too shocked to speak for a moment. Then Father spoke carefully. "What do you mean, son?"

Thos looked miserable but determined. "When John Brown brought Judith here, I told him I'd come if he sent for me. He has. Several of us are starting out tomorrow."

"But I heard just today that he'd crossed the border on the twentieth," said Josiah. "He's probably back by now and heading north with any slaves he managed to get away with."

"And any horses and valuables he could steal," added Deborah. "Oh, Thos—"

"I won't steal anything," he said, "unless that's what you call helping slaves escape! Yes, Father, Brown should be back, but he wants another band of us to cross into Missouri; in fact, he plans to keep up such raids till abolition comes or till we've smuggled every slave who wants freedom out of the South!"

"Son—" began Josiah grimly.

Mother sighed and got to her feet, moving like a suddenly old woman. "Thos, you help with the railroad here. And you're so young! Brown may be an instrument of God, but if so, he's a terrible one. As much as for your body, if you follow him, I fear for your soul!"

Thos bowed his bright head, took his mother's hands, and held them. "I won't kill if I can help it. I won't steal. I'll try to act, Mother, as if you—and Father and 'Borah—could see me. But I said I'd go, and I have to."

She put her arms around him and wept. Judith glared at Thos and made an accusing murmuring, but when Leticia had command of herself, she stepped away. "Your father and I have raised you to follow your conscience. We can't oppose this if you've thought it through and feel you must go."

Face glowing, Thos said thankfully, "I prayed you'd understand. I can't explain it, but the day Brown came, I knew I had to do what he asked, when he asked. Maybe that's why I haven't coaxed Sara more; it didn't seem right to marry and leave her."

"We'll feel that she's our daughter," Josiah promised.

Mother took Thos's hand and Deborah's, kneeling down. Father and Judith joined them. Instead of reading Mr. Dickens's *A Christmas Carol,* as was their Christmas Eve custom, they prayed: for Thos's safety and guidance; the freedom of slaves; peace with liberty throughout the land.

Thos was so relieved that he was happy in his good nights, but Deborah, keeping her cheek against his warm one for a moment, glanced around at her family with a chill of apprehension.

Where would they all be this time next year? Would they ever, on this earth, keep Christmas again?

She tried to comfort herself by touching Dane's medallion, but he was far away, he might even be dead, and even if he came back, unless something changed mightily, it would only be to leave her again. The busy cheerfulness of the day, the quiet happiness of the carol singing, seemed bright joys that were slipping away, being engulfed by the rising storm. Thos was going into danger, and for the first time in their lives, she wouldn't be with him.

He left the next morning after family prayers, the muffler that Deborah and Mother had knitted for Christmas warm around his neck, saying he'd be back as soon as he could. He'd take Sara the jewelry box he'd carved for her from seasoned black walnut, with Deborah's gift of earrings, given her by a rather frivolous great-aunt. Though she never wore them, Deborah enjoyed looking at them, but she wanted to give Sara something nice.

Deborah and her parents drove off to the Christmas service in town. A sense of loss saddened what should have been a time of grateful upliftedness, and when Rolf sat where Thos should have been, Deborah was furious with him, even though, through gestures, he'd asked and received her mother's assent.

After the service, he was, of course, invited for dinner, and he accepted with particular enthusiasm. When, riding Sangre, he caught up with them, he had a bulky pack tied behind the saddle.

"Where's Thos?" he asked.

Father was prepared. "He went to see Sara before leaving for Missouri. If he uses his eyes and ears, he should be able to do a good article for *The Clarion*."

"Isn't that risky? For the son of a Free State editor to be roaming around Missouri?"

"No one has to know he's my son."

"That's so. Wish he'd waited till after today; I'd have gone with him. But I hoped you'd ask me to dinner, and, besides, I had presents to deliver!"

"Oh, you mustn't!" protested Mother. "Not after Dane sent such lovely things!"

"More than ever because of that!" Rolf's jaw hardened. "I should hope I know you better than Dane did! After all, he was just in the countryside precious little more than a month!"

Distressed, Leticia said under her breath to Deborah, "I'm glad I worked his initial on a few good linen handkerchiefs your father's never used. But there was no money for gifts. It was sweet of you, daughter, to let me make Judith a dress from that cambric the storekeeper traded your father for advertisements."

"She needs it more than I do," Deborah said.

Judith, that morning, had been ecstatic with the gown—the first new one, she said, that she'd ever had. For Mother, she and Deborah had quilted a cushion for the rocking chair, filling it with garnered feathers, and had made a winter bouquet of gentian, cattails, thistles, and grasses arranged in a leached root tangle. Mother had knitted socks for Father, and Judith and Deborah had knitted him a scarf, tucking into it book marks of thin, inner cottonwood bark on which Deborah printed some of Josiah's favorite quotations.

From her parents, Deborah got cotton stockings and a new comb. Judith and Sara and Thos had collaborated on a fringed soft leather belt—she knew it was designed to support the Bowie beneath her skirts—and beaded, fringed leather gauntlets, quite beautiful.

For a moment now, Deborah couldn't help but think how wonderful it would be to have a tithe of the money Rolf squandered to spend on her family and friends, get them some elegant and useful things.

A warm new cloak for Mother and a blue wool dress, some bonbons from the drugstore, a suit to replace Father's shiny one, boots and a rakish Kossuth hat for Thos, shoes for Judith, who, at least, thanks to Sara, had moccasins. Her long, narrow feet wouldn't fit in any of the Whitlaws' footwear, so she wore one pair of moccasins outside when there was rain and snow and changed to a dry pair indoors. A red vest for Johnny, a lace shawl for Sara, wool shirts for Laddie and Maccabee. *And I'd like an absolutely stunning dress, misty, gray-green or the color of russet leaves, velvet, with taffeta petticoats and a hoop under a wide, wide skirt, and matching French kid slippers; it's worldly and vain, but just once in my life I'd love something gorgeous!*

She was immediately ashamed to be covering frivolities when her brother was riding off into danger of body and soul. And now, because of Rolf, Judith would have to take shelter in the lean-to instead of sharing the Christmas meal. Deborah sighed. The wrong brother had gone west. If Dane were here, Judith could sit at the table and they'd have such a happy time; he'd even say sensible, comforting things about Thos. But here was Rolf with his bulging pack, clearly set on outdoing Dane.

He was going to be angry when he learned that now that Thos was gone, she'd no longer go anywhere with him, though he should have guessed that when she wouldn't go to the Medary Ball.

Judith, who'd come to expect Rolf after church, had evidently seen him and gone to the lean-to. Rolf and Josiah took care of the horses while Leticia and Deborah put on the turkey, dried green beans that had been simmering with side meat, light bread and butter, stewed dry rhubarb, and mincemeat and pumpkin pies, with a bowl of thick whipped cream.

Rolf placed his pack by the door and ate quickly, though he complimented the women on the food. His mind was clearly set on distributing his largesse. Deborah would have loitered except for Judith's exile. Surely he wouldn't stay overlong at what was a family celebration.

Father prevailed on Mother to play carols while he helped Deborah with the dishes, and Rolf leaned on the pianoforte and sang in a rich tenor. Mother joined in, laughing with pleasure, for none of her family had more than passable singing voices.

Because he'd lightened her mother's spirits, Deborah felt somewhat less resentful of Rolf. When the dishes were done, Mother rose from the pianoforte and excused herself, returning in a moment with the handkerchiefs she initialed for Rolf, gave them to him, and wished him a merry Christmas.

"A small gift," she told him. "But it comes with much goodwill."

He admired the embroidery, then tucked the linen squares into an inner coat pocket. "I'll treasure them always."

"Handkerchiefs were made to be used," Deborah said.

If he must, why didn't he play Lord Bountiful and take himself off so Judith could come out, so they could talk freely about Thos, share their anxieties and reassurances?

Casting her a droll look, not at all out of temper, Rolf opened his pack. "Ladies first," he said, handing to Mother an exquisite box of silver and enamel. When she raised the lid, part of a Brahms sonata tinkled out. The velvet-lined interior held lavender satin sachets.

A perfect choice for Mother, who put down the lid and gazed at the jewel-bright enameled flowers and birds between delight and dismay. "It's too much, Rolf. I can't accept such a rare, costly thing."

"It was made for you, ordered out of St. Louis. If you don't want it, I suppose I could give it to Mrs. Eden."

"Keep it, my dear," Father advised, patting her hand. He smiled at Rolf. "Even had we the money, conscience wouldn't let us buy such beautiful luxuries while there are so many in need. But a gift—perhaps I'm twisting principle, but I can't think it wrong for my wife to keep and enjoy what you went to much thought and trouble to get for her."

Rolf glanced at Mother, whose face was glowing. She

looked so beautiful and young that Deborah realized with a pang that Mother was only thirty-seven but aging early because of frontier hardships and makeshifts. If they'd stayed in New Hampshire, in their comfortable home, there was little doubt that Leticia would have looked less worn, had more time to rest and care for her appearance. Or even if they'd settled in Lawrence instead of taking this farm, where they could serve as a station for the underground railroad.

Even though Deborah often felt that life without Dane was joyless, she could face the consequence of refusing his terms with much better grace than she could watch her mother's quiet, daily sacrifices. Father had given up comforts, too, and a safe income, but the main burden of change had fallen on Leticia: the laborious struggle to make a home, and feed and clothe the family from the little that was available.

Of course things were better. They had the cabin now, not that miserable dark soddy. The garden had given a bountiful yield, and there were stores of dried pumpkin, rhubarb, green beans, corn, and berries. Potatoes and turnips were buried under straw in the storage part of the stable, and in the well-house were barrels of brine-preserved tomatoes and wild plums kept by covering them with plain water. As well as plenty of cornmeal, there was wheat, both ground and to eat as cereal. But the rigorous years had taken a toll on Leticia that Deborah hadn't fully noticed till that brief transfiguration caused by Rolf's gift.

If it hurt Deborah that Leticia's finest gifts came from the Hunters, it must surely be a sort of reproach to father, but he gave no sign of this; he only seemed happy that his wife was.

Next Rolf handed Father a leather-bound volume. "I've heard you say you admire Walt Whitman," he said. "And he does seem to make more sense than most poet fellows."

Leaves of Grass had been published several years ago. Not being able to afford the books of authors he admired, which were temptingly displayed at Wilmarth's store, was one of Father's privations, and he thanked Rolf with no attempt to hide his almost childlike pleasure. During the long winter evenings he'd read the poems aloud to the family, pausing at the end of each for discussion and appreciation. Again, Deborah grudgingly admitted that Rolf couldn't have chosen better.

Now he drew out something glossy and darkly shining,

gathering it caressingly into his arms. He placed it in Deborah's lap, first holding it so the Whitlaws could see the satin-lined fur cape.

"Seventy mink in that," Rolf boasted. "I trapped them on the river, then hired a couple of Indian women to treat the skins and stitch them." He stroked the lustrous fur. "Fit for a queen! But I didn't spend money on it, Miss Deborah—at least not much." He smiled at her, eyes a lighter green than usual. "I spent my time, hours of my life."

Deborah had seen mink a few times, weasel-like, graceful creatures with white breast patches. Seventy of them? She stared at the cape and saw not the silken fur but animals writhing in traps, trying to gnaw themselves free, lacerated, freezing. She couldn't be overly squeamish. Using the hides of meat animals prevented waste; the beasts would be killed, anyway. But she became sickened at the thought of killing something in order to wear its coat. She thrust the cape into Rolf's hands.

"I—I can't keep it!"

He stared at her, uncomprehending. "It wasn't costly, not in money." He glanced at the elder Whitlaws. "You don't object? I know the rules about gifts of clothing, but surely this is different!"

"Deborah must do what she feels is right," Mother said. "It's not, I think, a question of expense."

"Then *what?*" Rolf demanded, swinging back to Deborah.

"I hate traps!" The furs even seemed to her to bear the smell of blood and retain some essence of the animal's pain. Nauseated, she shook her head, trying not to cry. "It's horrible that you killed these little creatures for me! I could never touch that cape!"

Her voice broke. Rolf stared at her, eyes dilated to blackness, his face pale. "You mean it," he said at last, so stricken that she would've felt sorry for him, except for the deaths of the minks whose skins he held. "You hate what I thought you'd love to warm yourself in!"

"If I'd known—" began Deborah.

"Then it wouldn't have been a surprise, would it?" He laughed savagely. "A surprise for both of us! Now what shall I do with this sumptuous, if despised, garment? Mrs. Whitlaw, do you share your daughter's qualms?"

"I agree with her," said Leticia gently, "though I'm sorry for your disappointment."

He stuffed it into the pack. "No doubt I can dispose of it to some merchant, or live rent-free at Mrs. Eden's for far longer than I expect to." When he rose and faced them again, he'd regained control and even had a faint smile. "So, Miss Deborah, I must still find you a suitable gift. This becomes a true challenge! It may take some time, especially now that my confidence is so badly shaken. Could you restore me by agreeing to go to a concert Saturday night?"

Deborah wasn't expecting to be invited in her parents' presence. Though appalled at his gift, she shrank at rejecting him a second time in a matter of minutes, but to make her refusal consistent, she must stick to it.

Dreading his gaze, she forced herself to meet it. "Thank you, Mr. Hunter, but I've considered myself a—a sort of chaperone for Sara and Thos. Now that he's gone, it would be improper for me to go with you to merrymakings, kind as it is of you to ask."

"Kind!" He sucked in his breath, obviously choking down a torrent of bitter words. Controlling himself, he said lightly, "I found a chaperone for the Fourth, and I am sure I can do it again."

At bay, Deborah flushed, unhappily conscious of her parents' embarrassment. It wasn't fair for him to press her like this right after he'd given them such perfect gifts, right after she'd had to refuse the one he'd thought would charm her.

"Forgive me. I should have explained long ago, but I thought—oh, never mind! I consider myself pledged to your brother."

"Pledged?" Rolf's tone rose incredulously. "You couldn't agree! And don't think Dane may change his mind. He never will!"

Lifting her chin, Deborah said firmly, "He's still the only man I'll marry. I *am* pledged."

Rolf set his hands behind him and turned away for a few seconds. When he faced them, it was with a smile that had the chill dazzle of ice. "I'm a great sinner. I covet most what is my brother's. But don't worry that I'll plague you further. Thank you, Mr. and Mrs. Whitlaw, for making me welcome. I doubt that we'll meet again, so let me wish you good fortune, and an end, soon, to the turbulences that shake this Territory."

Much distressed, Leticia said, "Are you going away? The passes to the west will be high with snow till spring."

He shrugged. "I'll find some excitement till the way's open to Pike's Peak. Leavenworth had attractions for me, though Dane abhorred them, and it's not far to Kansas City."

Reaching into his coat, Rolf extracted a Bowie from an ingenious sewed-in, brass-tipped sheath. "Chaudoin wouldn't make one for me," he told Deborah. "But I bought one in town. I've learned to use it. Anyone who takes me for a greenhorn will find himself well gored." He bowed with the grace he might have used at court. "Good-bye. Now you can call in that mulatto. I've known since the harvest that she was here; I saw her working in the field with Dane. Apparently you trusted *him*."

He started for the door. Deborah blocked his way "You —you won't tell?"

He watched her, his mouth curving down. This was no longer a man hoping to please her, but a mocking, outraged stranger. "You wouldn't believe me, would you, my dear, whatever I might say?"

To Leticia, wordlessly offering back the music box and book, he shook his golden head. "Indeed, madam, acquaintance with you and Mr. Whitlaw has been a rare experience for me, one I'll treasure. If there were more people like you—but how can there be? With all my heart, I wish you well." He spoke to her parents, not to Deborah.

Josiah went out with him, then returned looking grave. "A reckless youngster, for the moment, at least, bound on going to the devil. I wish his brother were here."

Judith, called out of hiding, smoothed her new dress and gave a sniff. "Devil been waitin' for that one since he was born! Wouldn't have stayed clear this long except for Mr. Dane."

Helpless and resentful, Deborah said, "If he gets into trouble, I'll feel partly to blame. I should never have stepped out the door with him." *But I was lonesome, he was flattering and fun, and I could pretend I went for Thos's and Sara's sake. If only no one else has to pay for my folly!*

"He knows about Judith," she said. "Do you think he might tell?"

"Daughter," rebuked Leticia, "he's not a monster. Why should he give her away?"

Father frowned. "I don't believe he'd do it on purpose, but if he got to roistering among Border Ruffians, he might let drop much more than he would deliberately." He turned to Judith. "Winter's a hard time to go north, child, but perhaps you should."

The dark-lashed amber eyes seemed to grow huge. "I like it here with you."

The Whitlaws exchanged glances. No one pointed out that Judith's presence, revealed, might provoke another raid from Missouri. One of Jed's gang had escaped. It could well be that only the distance of the Whitlaw farm from the border had kept him from rallying other brigands and retaliating. If such men knew an escaped slave was hiding at the Whitlaws', it'd be like a crusade for them to take her back, punish her protectors.

Leticia smiled. "You've become one of our family, Judith. It'll be a sad day for us when you do move on. Of course, you may stay as long as you choose."

"Maybe I better go to Mr. Chaudoin's," proposed Judith. "Not so many travelers stoppin' how it's winter. I don't trust that Mr. Rolf one mingy bit. Never forgive myself if I bring trouble on you, but I hate to go north. Rather find a way to stay hereabouts if that can be."

"We'll hate to lose you," said Father, considering. "But it might be best. It would be Johnny or Maccabee who would take you on the next part of your trip, anyway, if you do have to go farther."

Judith's mouth trembled and her eyes brimmed. "Should I leave now?"

The early winter twilight would be falling soon. "Wait till morning," Josiah said. "Deborah will want to go with you, and I don't want her out alone after dark. This is blizzard season."

Indeed, it was. One struck during the night. Deborah and Judith, who'd been sleeping in Deborah's tiny "room" since the weather turned cold, awoke to find a powdering of snow on their bedding and the floor, forced through cracks by the scourging wind.

Going anywhere was unthinkable, but the stock had to be seen to. From the window, tiny wind-driven particles of ice completely hid the soddy, the chicken coop, and the well-house. "I hope this isn't going to be a winter like the first one we spent in Kansas," Josiah said, bundling up. "And I hope Venus and the horses all got to the stable. Stay inside, Deborah." In spite of his worry, he tried to joke. "I won't be much uglier if I get frostbite, but it wouldn't help your nose!"

"If Chica's not there, I've got to find her."

"She was in the stable when Rolf left," Josiah said. "Maybe she felt this coming." He gave a small cough.

"Let me go," said Deborah quickly.

He shook his head. "I'm fine. You do too much rough work as it is."

"You'd better stretch a rope from the cabin to the stable," Leticia said, already tying together lengths of rawhide. "You know how people can get lost and freeze just outside their own doors."

Father used the rawhide and was back in half an hour with a half-bucket of milk and news as good as it could be under the circumstances. Chica was still in the stable, and Nebuchadnezzar, Belshazzar, and Venus had come in during the night. The soddy, built as a dwelling, was a good shelter; the body heat of four large animals was considerable, and unless the temperature fell below zero and stayed there for a time, the animals should be fine. He'd filled the mangers and there was enough snow drifted around the door for them to eat it for moisture. Also, he'd tossed grain in for the chickens, which similarly found their haven.

Since no one could go anywhere and nothing could be done outside, Mother made pancakes for breakfast, served with homemade blackberry syrup. After the dishes were scraped and put in water to wait till more accumulated, and after worship, Father read aloud from Mr. Whitman's poems while the women mended or knitted, though this was difficult. Their fingers were stiff with cold, though the fire was kept built up and they sat as near it as was safe, wearing their coats and wrapping quilts or blankets around their legs. Several days' supply of wood, corncobs, and cow chips was stacked in the kitchen, and the main lot was piled near the door. The water buckets had been filled last night, and if it proved too hard to get to the wellhouse, they could shovel out enough ice-snow to melt for their needs.

With the animals secure, the storm should pass with no real hardships. *Should.* That terrible winter of '55–'56, they'd had to bring the horses and Venus into the soddy, for that had been all the Whitlaws had had time to build before the earth froze. Temperatures stayed twenty and thirty degrees below zero for one stretch of days. Water froze in the buckets and food froze brick-hard. Father had written his news items with his inkwell on the hearth, because when he tried to work at the table, ink froze on the pen.

The Whitlaws had been used to the New Hampshire cold, but there they'd had no livestock to care for. Nor were they prepared for what no one could get used to—blizzards. These furious winds could come up even on a sunny day and send snow and ice whipping against man, beast, and shelter like myriad stinging tiny razors.

"I hope that Rolf won't have gotten caught in this," Leticia said once, gazing out at the impenetrable whining gale.

"He can't have," Josiah assured her. "He couldn't pack and leave Lawrence last night, surely, and the storm was going full blast before dawn."

"I hope Thos isn't in it," Deborah worried, prowling about from sheer restlessness.

Father sighed. "Daughter, we must pray for Thos, but we can know nothing of where he is. It boots nothing to fret."

And I don't know where Dane is, either. Why do men have to go off to places where you can't know how they are or what they're doing?

"Deborah," said Mother, "why don't you make a big kettle of potato soup? Put in dill for flavoring and remember not to add the sour cream till it's nearly done."

It was a task calculated to stop her pacing. Twinkling ruefully at her mother, Deborah attacked the potatoes.

Father's voice had hoarsened and he began to cough. The slight cold he'd had seemed to be rooting itself in his lungs. Mother gave him a soothing syrup of boiled onions, and Deborah and Judith placed the benches by his chair, arranging pillows so that he had a sort of couch near the warmth.

"A lot of fuss," he grumbled.

"You've no excuse not to take care of yourself since you can't get out to do anything else," Mother said practically. "If you rest now, maybe the cough will be gone by the time we can drive to town."

Thus obliquely reminded of the cold he'd neglected last year that had left him coughing for months, Josiah subsided and began working on an editorial.

"Slave-catchers have been working the river towns lately," he said, glancing up from what he was writing. "They've kidnapped free Negroes and sold them as slaves.

This kind of outrage makes it easy for hotheads or youngsters like Thos to feel justified in almost anything they do across the Missouri line. But it shames me to see Free State leaders like Jim Lane and Montgomery and, yes, John Brown, be rightfully called horse thieves and plunderers."

Was there ever a cause whose defenders had all been honest and decent? John Brown was more madman or thunderbolt of Jehovah than mortal, but there was no dodging the fact that Free Staters had pillaged in the name of liberty and that the best horses seemed to belong to proslavers, whom it was righteous to rob.

If Thos could keep clear of such disgraces!

The soup was bubbling, giving off an appetizing smell of onions and dill. Deborah moved it to the side of the grate and began to make biscuits. Her movements were clumsy because of her bulky coat and chilled fingers. Her nose was cold, too, and so were her feet, in spite of several pairs of Thos's wool socks.

Would the wind never stop? Now that Father was ailing, the outside chores were up to her. Cutting out biscuits with a floured glass, Deborah arranged them in the Dutch oven and added sour cream to the thick soup.

If the storm abated, she'd bring in the extra stores of cream and butter from the well-house. There was no worry now that they'd get too warm in the house! Eggs had better be kept inside, too, and the frozen ones should be used up. But it was more pleasant to find room for food in the cabin than to make space for horses and a cow and chickens, much better to find ways to use up frozen food than to have none.

They ate heartily of richly flavorsome soup and biscuits dripping with butter. Short on cash, as they always were, Mother insisted that the family have all the eggs and products of Venus's bounty that they could use before selling any.

"As long as we're not in debt to anyone, we'll eat as well as we can," she had said early in their Kansas days. "It keeps us strong and cheerful. We need to be both." But she often gave butter or cottage cheese or eggs to people in need.

Josiah's grace at meals often strayed to politics and seemed long, especially when one was hungry. Leticia's was always the same, but blessedly short. *"Bless this food to its intended use. Help us to pay our honest debts and lead us in Thy ways."*

"This soup's just what I need," Father said, propped up on his makeshift lounge. "And I must admit that now that I've decided to let you ladies make an invalid of me, I'm enjoying it! I may never go back to work." This speech brought on a fit of coughing, echoed by a small, suppressed cough from Judith, which she hastily said was just a crumb lodging in her throat.

It was an interminable day, punctuated by Father's coughing. By four o'clock Deborah had resolved to see how the animals were faring and milk Venus, even if she had to battle the ferocious wind and find her way by using the rawhide Father had left in place. She was bundling into her coat when the wind died.

To ears now accustomed to the howling, it seemed deafeningly still. The skies even looked a little brighter, as if far above the gray overcast the sun was trying to reach the earth.

"Maybe it's over," Judith said hopefully. Coming from the milder climate of hilly, tree-sheltered southern Missouri, she felt the cold more than the Whitlaws, though she never complained. "Shall I help you, Deborah?"

"Thanks, but there's no use in both of us tracking in snow. There's not that much to do."

Though it had tamed remarkably, the wind still gusted ice powder that cut Deborah's face where the scarf left her eyes uncovered, and it stung up and under her skirts so that she gasped and made all the haste she could to the soddy.

It seemed heavenly warm there, redolent with the clean fragrance of hay. Speaking to the animals, she stroked them all and gave Chica a special hug. "Think about spring," she murmured into a twitching silken ear. "There'll be green grass, sweetheart, and Dane will be back. It won't be winter forever."

She shoveled out the manure, tossing it on the snow-covered heap that would be used for fertilizer next spring, refilled the mangers, washed her hands in the snow, and milked Venus. She left the milk in a protected corner while she fed the chickens and collected five eggs.

Nesting these judiciously inside her coat, she took the milk to the house, unloaded the eggs, gratefully drank a cup of hot "coffee" Judith fetched her that warmed her hands as well as her center, and then, grasping the shovel, she picked her way to the well-house.

It was badly drifted up, but like all the buildings, the door faced south and it didn't take long to shovel the entrance free. Right now the snow had an icy crust that would probably even support the weight of Venus or the horses. It wasn't too difficult to walk on, and she decided against shoveling paths to the well-house and stable, though she did clear a space around the cabin door and she knocked the frigid covering off part of the woodpile. After she brought perishables from the well-house and filled the water buckets, she put some wood just inside the cabin to dry.

The storm *might* be lifting, but there was no way of being sure, and she meant to put this reprieve to its fullest use. The well-house yielded twenty frozen eggs, congealed butter, and frozen pans of cream. The plums were now preserved in ice, and the brine on the tomatoes was sludgy, but Deborah felt that neither could be made more inedible than it already was.

Mother took charge of the salvaged food and Judith opened and shut the door while Deborah lugged in wood and corncobs. She preferred that the cow chips dry thoroughly again outside.

Father's cough seemed worse as night came on, but he was now using this rare, enforced leisure to go through recent *Clarion*s and bill advertisers, scribbling busily between firelight and the flickering lamp.

"Wonderful how the town's grown," he said, pointing to the pages announcing for sale Goodyear India rubber boots and coats, hydraulic cement, made-to-order tweeds, tin roofing, coffins in the latest styles, copper-toed children's shoes, Faber's lead pencils, wallpaper, and paper window shades, which could be had gold-bordered or oil-painted.

Deborah loved to read the advertisements, especially Dalton's exciting description of new ladies' clothes, but she was always surprised to see percussion caps and revolvers mentioned along with jewelry and clocks by Frazer's in the Eldridge House, or note that Ridenour and Baker sold gunpowder as well as groceries.

For supper, Mother had peeled eggs and put them in the skillet with butter, scrambling them as they thawed, adding frozen cream.

Dishwater heated as they ate, and after the meal Deborah and Judith did the day's dishes while Mother read aloud, more of *Leaves of Grass*.

The washed skillet was heating on the grate to be tucked in at Father's feet. The girls would get the top and bottom of the Dutch oven. Wrapped in towels, cast iron would hold comforting warmth till bodies could begin to warm the frigid bedding. Deborah banked the fire well, fervently hoping the storm was over and that Father wasn't going to be really sick.

If only Thos were here—or Dane! Thrusting the covered Dutch oven lid at the foot of her bed, Deborah told Judith good night and sternly told herself not to worry. She would just have to do the best she could, ease Mother's load as much as possible.

It seemed a year since Rolf had left them, longer since Thos had. Yet that was all only yesterday.

• *xii* •

She awoke the next morning to Father's coughing. He wasn't better and it was still snowing outside. No blizzard, thank goodness, no piercing swirl of pulverized ice, but big, feathery flakes that, though beautiful, layered relentlessly on the previous fall.

Deborah, shivering, pulled on her clothes and hurried to build up the fire, then put on the coffee brew. Strange how new concerns could override others. With the thick, blanketing snow outside, the roads and trails drifted and impassable, they seemed in a white, muffled, isolated world of their own. Judith couldn't get to the smithy, but neither could any slave-catchers reach them. What preoccupied Deborah now was Father's cough and keeping the family and animals warm and fed.

She realized she was making more of it than probabilities warranted. If Josiah had been well or had Thos been there, she would scarcely have worried. The stock was in a good shelter with plenty of hay and fodder, the chickens were safe, there was plenty of food, and fuel was right outside the door. She was being a proper goose!

Self-scolded into adopting a brisk, confident manner, Deborah asked Josiah how he was. "Cough's a nuisance," he grumbled, rubbing his sideburns. "But I'll see to the stock, daughter."

"You won't," said Leticia firmly. "And you can just stay under the covers till the other room warms up."

"You took care of things during the blizzard," Deborah reminded her father, dropping a kiss on his forehead, where the dark hair was receding. "It's warmer today and the wind's died down."

"We won't get the paper out this week." He fidgeted. "And provided it didn't snow in town the way it did here, the legislature's probably meeting there right now."

"Won't they have to meet at Lecompton?" asked Leticia.

"Yes, but they hate that place for being the pro-slave capital. Bet they do just what they did last year—meet at Lecompton and adjourn to Lawrence." He chuckled, eyes lighting up. "And this session, I hear, they're going to repeal the bogus laws the Bogus Legislature adopted from Missouri, except for the slavery code, which wasn't harsh enough. Going to throw it out from start to finish! That'll be real news!"

"You can make next week's issue extra large," Leticia suggested.

Father nodded. "That's so. I've got time to work on several articles I've held aside till I had a chance to do them satisfactorily." He looked pleadingly at his wife. "Are you *sure* I can't get up yet?"

"Breakfast will be soon enough," she said. "Judith, will you start the biscuits while I scramble the rest of those eggs?"

Deborah put on her coat and scarf, took the milk bucket, and stepped out into the steady, gentle, inexorable fall of snow.

All that day it snowed off and on, the skies never lightening, dusk closing in as softly as the big flakes. In spite of the syrup, Josiah's cough was deep and wracking, but he vowed that apart from that, he felt perfectly all right and he expected he'd improve if the women would let him get up.

The next day was much the same, though it snowed

less and the skies seemed a little brighter to Deborah's straining eyes, though it could be so long since she'd seen the sun that these heavy leaden clouds were beginning to seem normal.

During the snow lulls, Venus and the horses ventured out, hooves caking with ice, but finding no forage, they soon returned to the soddy. Deborah brought in more wood and corncobs to dry.

By now she was weary of being cooped up and welcomed the outside chores in spite of the biting cold. In the cabin, she found herself waiting for and tensing at Josiah's spasms of coughing. Surely it was only a bad cold! Yet pneumonia behaved like a cold at the start.

Mother was worried, too, yet she read to him, studied what he'd written, and made suggestions, all the time maintaining a calm and sweetness that was balm to Deborah's frayed nerves and seemed to have a like effect on Judith.

Always quiet, the young woman had been almost silent all day. Perhaps the decision to shift hiding places was making her agonize about whether to go north or wait, hoping she could live in this more familiar region rather than try to make a life in another part of the country.

Bringing in the eggs and milk, Deborah wished her twin were home. More than to help with the work, she needed someone to joke with or grumble at. As she took off her coat, Judith began to cough. This time she didn't try to say it was something stuck in her throat.

Deborah awoke the next morning to find that Judith wasn't in their partitioned cubby, though she remembered half-waking up in the night to her coughing. It turned out that Judith had moved her pallet near the fireplace in order not to disturb Deborah. She was feverish, and Josiah, who insisted he was *much* better, ceded the benches so her bedding could be raised from the floor.

He seemed to be coughing less, so it was likely that he, and now Judith, only had troublesome colds. Deborah and Leticia looked at each other with an unspoken mutual worry: What if one or both of them fell sick before the others had recovered?

I can't get sick, thought Deborah. *I won't!* And she dressed to do the chores.

That day and the next two were overcast and freezing, but mercifully there was no more snow or strong wind.

The animals ventured out, walking gingerly, but didn't stray far from the stable and food.

Judith stayed feverish, coughing till the sputum was bloody, but said colds always took her this way and she'd be better soon. Fortunately, Josiah was. On the sixth day, though he still had a nagging little cough, he shoveled a path to the stable and well-house.

"This won't stay frozen hard enough to walk on forever," he said. "And when it thaws, we'll have mess enough without floundering in wet snow and soaking ourselves above the knee!"

His effort was just in time. The sun was out the next day, sparkling with blinding brilliance over the unbroken white vastness, drifted here and there into dunes or crests.

The roof, punished by the weight of accumulating snow, now began to leak hesitating muddy drops in spite of the cheesecloth. Deborah and Mother placed buckets or pots beneath the dribbles, and Father and Deborah took shovels and, standing on the woodpile and benches, scooped off as much snow as they could. They couldn't reach the center, but Josiah got out his fishing pole and whacked at the snow till some fell within reach, and the rest was thinned to where it should melt off fairly soon.

Venus and the horses soon trampled the space around the stable into dark muck, but they fared out in the field now and hooved or nosed the snow aside to reach stubble or grass. The chickens pecked and scratched. All living creatures seemed freed by the sun, stirring again, loosed from wintry prisons.

Deborah's shoes were soaked and mud-caked after each sally into the yard. She cherished hope that such abuse would ruin them so that this spring Mother'd have to let her go barefoot or moccasined. And by winter, perhaps she could have a pair of men's boots, which could be oiled to protect against the weather, or even rubber ones.

The brightness seemed good medicine for Judith. Her fever was gone and she ate with appetite. The cough was less frequent, though it still wracked her when it came. By noon she refused absolutely to keep to her pallet, washed carefully, and helped shift and empty the leak-catching receptacles.

It was time now, while the roof wept and the snow almost visibly shrank and melted, to be part of the world again; to wonder when the way to Lawrence wouldn't be a quagmire; to wonder when Thos might be coming and what he'd have to tell them; to wonder when Judith would be well enough and the path clear enough to go to Johnny's.

"Maybe in a few days, if it keeps thawing," Father surmised to that last question. "Won't hurt to take care of that cold, child."

The sun shone next day and the next. Thawing continued, though the snow and run-off froze at night. Judith said she was well enough to go to the smithy, and Father was impatient to get to *The Clarion,* to hear what the legislature was doing, and start setting up the big double issue.

So, on the tenth morning after their marooning by snow, after breakfast and family worship, Deborah and Judith started off. Judith's other dress and the few things Deborah and Mother had been able to give her were tied in a bundle behind Chica's saddle. Judith, afraid of horses, had finally been coaxed into riding the sweet-tempered mare, so Deborah rode Belshazzar. She'd belted the Bowie beneath her skirts. She was out of practice. If Johnny had time, he might give her a lesson.

Josiah and Leticia would be starting for Lawrence soon, but Neubuchadnezzar had been out in the field and Father had to go after him. He and Leticia embraced Judith and wished her good luck with her wayfaring, though if she did go north, they wanted to get over to Johnny's and see her a last time.

"No way to thank you," she whispered. "Every day of my life, I'll pray God have a care for you."

"And we'll pray for you," Leticia promised. She kissed Deborah, too, though ordinarily they didn't do that on parting. "Be careful, dear. You may visit, if Sara's not too busy, but start home right away if it starts looking stormy."

Deborah promised. And with a final wave, they started off toward the smithy.

It was slushy underfoot. Chica stepped daintily, annoyed at the splattering, but Belshazzar plunked down his big hooves as if resigned to all that bedeviled honest horses, including girls who should have the sense to stay home. It was cold but at least not freezing, and the sun made it seem warmer than it was.

"I'm goin' to miss your folks," said Judith. "Specially your mama. My mama died havin' a baby when I was real little. About all I can remember is how she screamed and screamed."

"Did the baby live?"

"No. It was yellow, scrawny as a plucked old rooster. Must've belonged to Mr. Jed's pa, or maybe even Mr. Jed. He was about twenty then and down in the quarters most every night." Judith gasped in belated recollection. "Your mama wouldn't like me tellin' you such things, Deborah."

"She'd be sorry they happened. I'm really going to miss you, Judith."

Judith hadn't talked a lot, but she'd joined into whatever needed doing, and once she'd come to trust Deborah, she had often smiled or shot her glances of understanding. They were close to the same age, though Judith didn't know hers exactly. Still, in some ways, she seemed much older.

With Thos gone, too, it was going to be lonely. Deborah forced cheerfulness into her voice. "Sara's going to be glad to have another woman at bachelors' hall."

"I can help her, that's sure! The mending alone she has for those three men critters! Never get to the end of it 'cause into the basket they keep tossin' socks, shirts, and trousers." Judith illustrated the careless motions of the male part of the household so disgustedly that Deborah burst out laughing.

Judith frowned. "That Maccabee—ought to get a woman, stop loadin' Sara down."

"He can't just kidnap someone off a wagon train, and he doesn't like to go to town."

"Takin' the easy way," said Judith. "Let him wash, mend, and cook for himself and see how fast he finds a wife!"

"I hope you're not going to scold the poor man."

"Sayin' what's true's not scoldin'." Judith grinned and Deborah laughed back, glad to see a spark of devilment in the usually subdued young woman.

They could see the distant fringe of trees along the river now, the sprawl of the smithy like tiny toy structures set down in the remaining snow. By tomorrow the prairie should be fairly clear except for drifts along the slopes.

Johnny, Maccabee, and Laddie were at work and saluted briefly, shouting a welcome as Sara came to the door. Quickly mastering her outward disappointment that there was no word from Thos, she helped the girls stable the horses and, when Judith's decision was told, made her feel warmly at home.

"I don't want any more menfolk around, but a woman —well, I'm glad to have you!" she said.

They had milk and fresh-baked cinnamon rolls, sharing their snowbound experiences.

An old bachelor from upriver who'd brought his team to be shod had been forced to stay longer than the night he'd counted on, and a courting couple on their way home from a late party had come hammering for shelter as the blizzard began. They had gone their ways yesterday. "And I suppose the courting couple will have to get married to avoid scandalization," ended Sara with a chuckle.

Since Johnny was behind in his work, Deborah felt she couldn't ask for a Bowie lesson, and Sara must have plenty to catch up on. Shortly before noon Deborah said her good-byes and started home, leading Belshazzar.

In just these few hours, more snow had dissolved. This would be a good time to thoroughly clean out the stable and chicken coop, put down new straw. It might not hurt, either, to scatter straw along the mucky path from the house to the stable. And she could start another kettle of potato soup.

It was going to be quiet without Judith or Thos, especially after the cabin's being crowded since Christmas. Deborah intended to stay very busy, preferably outside.

She was about halfway home when she noticed something whitish rising above the snow, tinging the sky like a low cloud.

Smoke!

Deborah made a choking sound. Could a coal have rolled from the fireplace? Father was always so careful!

Deborah tried to urge Belshazzar to hurry, but a grudging trot was all he'd do. Frantically, she dismounted and fastened his bridle around a scraggly plum bush. She'd get him later.

The ride seemed to take forever, though Chica plunged gallantly through the slippery mush. Gradually, the shape of the cabin and stable rose above the white horizon. Smoke rose sluggishly from the roofs. If a fire had started from the fireplace, without wind to carry it, how could it reach the stable? She couldn't see anyone moving about, though surely the blaze must have started before or very shortly after her parents left. It was a strange time for fire, with the sod and brush roofs so recently saturated with melting snow.

And no one moving. . . .

Fear at something uncanny, something worse than fire, clutched Deborah. She urged on the reluctant horse with voice and heels. Now she could smell the acrid odor of damp wood, grass, brush, and sod. She saw the overturned, broken, smoldering buggy, the carcass of a cow—her mind refused to say it was Venus—lying in blood that stained the trampled snow.

There were other broken things near the buggy.

Chica shied from the smoke, refusing to come closer. Numbly sliding from her back, Deborah made her wooden-feeling legs carry her forward. It—it couldn't be!

Mother. Father.

But maybe they weren't dead. Maybe— Swooping toward them, she groaned as she lifted her mother from Josiah's body, and she had to let her drop to cover what had been done. From throat to abdomen he was hacked and slashed, as if by cutlasses or knives. One arm lay severed, the one beneath Leticia, as if he'd tried to protect her.

The only wound Deborah could find on her mother was the contused lump on the side of her head which matted the soft brown hair with blood. Perhaps they—who were *they?*—hadn't meant to kill her but had struck too hard when she tried to save her husband. Quick hope flared in Deborah. It wasn't such a bad wound!

"Mother!" she pleaded, raising her, touching her face, listening for a heartbeat. "Mother! Don't! Come back—"

No warmth, no breath, not the faintest motion. Deborah knelt in the bloody snow and couldn't believe it. Oh, John Brown had cutlassed five men at Pottawatomie, Hamilton had slaughtered five and wounded more at Marais des Cygnes, and there were the countless murders of one settler here, a few others there, raids and counter-raids.

In May three Missourians had died almost in this same spot. It hadn't seemed quite real; it had happened in the night and she'd never seen the bodies, didn't know where they were buried.

This was real. Daylight and sun, Venus with her throat gaping, the chickens tossed here and there, necks wrung.

Why? Who? Almost certainly pro-slavers, most likely from Missouri. Had they been pursuing Thos or another runaway?

Rising stiffly, Deborah moved toward the cabin, mechanically thinking she should try to put out the fire. The roof near the fireplace had caved in and burned, but the rest of the pole-supported sod and brush emitted only sulky yellow smoke. Nearing the door, eyes stinging from the thick vapors, she saw that the fireplace had evidently been heaped with wood, and the furniture had been dragged close.

Charring parts of the benches, tables, the four-poster, the rocking chair, sewing machine, and, yes, the pianoforte thrust out of the blackened remains of clothes, shuck mattresses, and her parents' featherbed. Books were sprawled everywhere, some ripped from their jackets, blackened and torn.

Entering, she stood among the wreckage, the smashed china, wantonly scattered food, then wandered into the bedroom. The chest had been too cumbersome to move, or they'd been in a hurry, but Mother's music box was gone from on top and the drawers had been rifled. The shawl Dane had sent Leticia and Deborah's mantilla were gone.

Like a wound-up clockwork toy, she moved back to the main room. The silver was gone. Evidently the looters had taken what they could, small treasures, Nebuchadnezzar, and destroyed everything else, even poor Venus, who couldn't have kept up with men in a hurry to get far from the place they'd pillaged.

At the edge of the cindery heap of furnishings, she saw Dane's sketch pad, some of the pages torn or burned. She picked it up, along with the Bible some religious or superstitious raider had left on the chest, then hunted till she found a comb and clean cloths.

She wanted to wash the blood off her parents, compose their bodies. That seemed very important. The vandals must have been gone for hours, must have struck this morning when Father was hitching up the buggy. Little chance of catching them.

Should she go to Johnny's, her first impulse, or to Lawrence? Lawrence, it had better be, so that Reverend Cordley could see to the burial and the militia could try to find the men who'd done this.

Yes. Then she'd go to Johnny's; then she could cry. For now she must wash her mother and father. She couldn't bear to leave them like this.

Putting the Bible and Dane's sketch pad on the smashed

buggy along with the cloths and comb, she loosened Chica's cinch and dragged some unburned hay out of the stable. The smoking roof had caved in over the mangers, but, as with the house, the damp sod had prevented a consuming blaze. Deborah didn't care. She'd never live here again and was sure that Thos wouldn't, either.

Later, because utensils, tools, and such were expensive, she'd get someone to come with her to sort out what was usable from the ruins, just as Johnny would salvage what he could from the buggy.

Someone had tossed a few strangled chickens down the well and knocked over the barrels of tomatoes and plums. Deborah threw out the bucket where the birds had lodged and wiped it with snow, lowered it, and untied the rope, carrying the bucket over to her parents.

Except for what streaked her hair, it was Father's blood on Mother. Deborah cleansed the head wound, smoothed the hair to hide the lump, washed Leticia's face and hands, scarcely realizing that the whimpering sounds were coming from herself.

Father— Father, do you forgive them? I never shall.

Father. How can I wash away the blood and see the wounds? How many? Eight. A dozen. More. And your arm. If I put it like this, it looks almost natural. But your shirt is bloody, your vest and coat. If I fix them like this, your hurts are covered. Oh, my father, what have they done to you?

Fighting off the convulsive sobbing that wrenched her inwardly, Deborah rose. She'd left Belshazzar halfway to Chaudoin's, but the plum bush wouldn't hold him if he got hungry. He wouldn't die. She'd better ride for Lawrence as fast as she could.

But her parents' bodies! If she left them here, with night coming on, coyotes or wolves might be drawn to them. It was a wonder they'd gone unmolested for as long as they had, especially with Venus also giving off a blood scent. The door was torn off the hinges of the house and the stable was open.

The well-house. She'd have to leave her parents there. She hated to drag their bodies, but better she than scavenging beasts. Kneeling by her mother, she was trying to work the dead arms over her neck so she could take most of the weight on her back when she heard the sound of hooves.

The murderers? More despairingly glad than frightened,

she felt the Bowie against her thigh and promised there'd be new blood mixed with her parents'. But it was only one rider on a big bay horse.

Rolf.

"Oh, my God!"

In an instant, he was down on his knees beside her. His big hand touched Mother's bruised head, Father's hand. He recoiled, shuddering, when the severed arm moved. "I'll kill them!" he said beneath his breath. "Every damned one!"

"Who?" Deborah stared at him. "You know . . . ?"

"I was hunting. Saw some riders. They said they were after a thief. I joined in." She flinched. He said roughly, "Hell, Deborah, don't look at me that way! I've never hunted a man before, and I felt like doing *something* after the way you slammed the door in my face!"

"You—didn't come here?"

"No!" Seizing her shoulders, he gave her a shake. "I cared more for your parents than I ever did for my father! It's partly for them that I've been so tame."

"Then what did you do?"

"The party split, looking for a sign. I stayed with the group that was on the Wakarusa. The other bunch, eight or nine of them, must've done this."

"You were riding with pro-slavers."

Rolf didn't answer.

"You must have known it!"

"What do you expect?" His tone was sullen. "You wouldn't have me, I was hell-bent, and these men happened to come along. I'd have ridden with John Brown just as fast if I'd run into him."

"That's what makes it hideous! You don't care!" Moving her head and body in dazed anger and pain, Deborah had a sudden flash of terrible certainty. "The *thief*. Did they—you—find him?"

"They trapped him in the snowdrifts by the riverbank." Wetting his lips, Rolf looked past her.

"Was it Thos?"

He nodded. She moaned, struck out at him, clawing her fingers, then remembered, too late, the Bowie. Capturing her wrists, he held her in a steel grip till she stopped struggling.

"Deborah, they shot him before I came up! I didn't know it was Thos until I saw him dead."

"But you knew they were after someone."

"A thief, they said!"

"And you knew that's what they call someone who gets a slave away from them!"

"Deborah, if I'd been there in time, I'd have fought for Thos! Don't you believe that?"

She looked into the fathomless dark green eyes, then glanced quickly away. "I don't know."

"Damn it, if I hadn't defended you last May, your men would've died right then!"

"Now they're dead, and Mother, too," Deborah said tonelessly. "Everyone but me." She collected her fragmented thoughts, battling for sanity. "Thos's body?"

"When the others started back—they'd agreed to rendezvous with the second party at the border—it was natural for me to drop out. I rode off toward Lawrence, but when the gang was out of sight, I went back and buried Thos. The ground was frozen but I found a hollow where a big tree had been uprooted and put him there, covered him with earth and branches, and worked the big tree over him."

So the coyotes and wolves wouldn't tear him apart.

"Why did you come here?"

"To tell you what had happened. A few miles back, I ran into the second party's trail. Since then, I've ridden as fast as I could." Rising, he pulled Deborah to her feet. "Let me give you some whisky. It'll make you feel better."

She choked back a flood of wild, furious words. "Please, you go to Lawrence and send out Reverend Cordley. You can tell the sheriff or militia what the pro-slavers looked like."

"I won't leave you here!"

"Someone has to watch the bodies."

"Where's that mulatto wench?"

"She left this morning. I went partway with her. That's why I wasn't here when this happened."

Rolf pondered a moment. "I'll bury your parents—not permanently, just to protect them till a carriage can come out from town. Thos's body can be fetched, too, and they can have proper burial. I'll describe the Missourians, damn them—I'll go after them myself! I swear to you that I'll avenge your family. But you must come with me now." He tried to make her sit down on the ruined buggy, but she pulled away.

"Let me find something to put over them so they won't freeze or get dirty."

The ground in the stable wasn't frozen, though it was packed so hard that Rolf had to use a pick-axe till he reached softer earth. Deborah found several half-burned quilts, the patchwork cushion she and Judith had made for the rocking chair, and part of the featherbed, which had stopped burning when the roof fell on it.

When the shallow grave was ready, she lined it with a quilt, placed the cushion for her parents' heads, and in spite of his protests, helped Rolf carry the bodies to the stable, arranged them gently, then covered them with the other quilts and the featherbed.

Rolf spaded on the soil, then upended the tubs and iron kettle on top for protection. There'd be prayers later, the minister's words, a decent burial. But for now Josiah and Leticia were washed, decently covered, and together. And the whereabouts of Thos's grave was known; he could be buried with them.

God, my God, why did you let it happen? How could you? If you have power and didn't stop this, you're evil! If you re weak, why do you ask for worship and want to be obeyed?

"Come," said Rolf.

He tightened the cinch and helped her up, then put the reins in her hands. When she asked for the Bible and sketch pad, he put them in his pack, then brought out his silver flask, holding it to her lips. "Just a swallow," he coaxed. "If you collapse, it'll take longer to take care of everything."

She choked at the fiery liquid, gasped at the taste, but it did leave a warm streak from her throat to her vitals. She let him give her a second drink. Then he mounted Sangre, who'd been sharing hay with Chica, and they started for town. There seemed to be nothing else to do. She despised Rolf for joining the brigands, but she believed his story. After all, he could have lied. And she needed help.

Darkness fell and the slush grew crunchier as it began to freeze. Deborah had been stricken with uncontrollable shivering shortly after leaving the farm. Rolf had tied a blanket from his bedroll around her and several times insisted that she drink from the flask. This helped temporarily, but she finally refused.

"I—I'm getting dizzy." Her tongue was clumsy. "Rolf, I must be—" Even after all that had happened, she couldn't say the word.

"Drunk?" He turned to stare at her. "My poor darling, I didn't think! On an empty stomach and you not used to it at all, yes, you could be a little bosky. Not much," he added soothingly. "But I could get a fire going, make you some coffee, and open a tin of meat."

"No. Even now there's not much chance of those devils getting caught."

Rolf said flatly, "Every man jack of those who raided your farm is going to die."

Deborah's heart leaped at that, though her beliefs and long training made her say, "More killing won't help."

"Oh, don't mouth such stuff, Deborah! If those men were before you now, wouldn't you kill them if you could?"

The coldness inside her warmed as it had to the whisky, then faded as she thought of her parents. "I would, except for what Mother and Father would think about it. They'd rather be murdered twenty times than have me kill once."

"They won't know."

"But I would."

Rolf turned his head in the night. She could feel him watching her, though she couldn't see it. He sighed, baffled. "Dane was right. You don't belong here."

"Oh, yes, I do!" Outrage and the anguished need to honor her family by carrying on their battle made her voice shake. "I'll never leave till Kansas is free, and I won't rest while there are slaves!"

Rolf didn't answer for a few minutes. When he did, he still sounded aghast. "You're too upset to decide such things." Pausing, he took a long breath. "Your family's gone, Deborah. You need someone to take care of you—a husband. Marry me."

So distraught and shocked that she couldn't speak at first, Deborah dropped one word like a stone. "No."

"I'll track down the men who killed your family. I told you before I'd join the Free Staters if you wanted that. I will. I'll steal out slaves, help them north. Anything you say. Use me, Deborah. I'll be a sword in your hand."

"I love Dane."

"But he won't let you live here if you marry him."

"Then I won't marry him."

Rolf made a gutturally obscene noise. "You can't stay single! However you pretend, you're not made of ice. The frontier's full of woman-hungry men."

"So I must pick one to protect me from the pack?" Deborah's scorn brought a growling protest from Rolf, but the spurt of anger faded in her grief.

She couldn't believe that her parents were dead, though images of them hunted her. And Thos, her twin, born with her into this world: How could he leave it without her, leave with so many years unlived? What would Sara do?

Appearing to accept tardily that this wasn't the time to urge his suit, Rolf, to Deborah's relief, fell silent.

Sheer exhaustion plus the unaccustomed whisky made her feel separated from her body, floating above and contemptuous of its weariness, its hunger, the way it craved sleep.

That weak flesh might rest; but this true-seeing part of her never would. It was the difference in a piece of raw metal and one heated for the anvil, shaped and hammered to a cutting edge, to a purpose. She didn't need Rolf or any man to be her sword; she would be her own.

But first this body, this burden, must sleep, must eat and drink. She would care for it as one did for an animal, but it must not rule.

Yet ultimately, by its weakness, it did. She was half-asleep when roused by Chica's halting, and before she knew where or even who she was, she was lifted from the saddle and cradled in strong arms that smothered her awakening struggles.

"It's all right, Deborah." Rolf's voice in her ear. "Melissa'll bring you something warm to eat and you can sleep. I'll tell Reverend Cordley what's happened, and then I'll start after those raiders with all the men I can collect."

"I don't want to stay at Mrs. Eden's!"

"You have to stay someplace, and her home's more comfortable than the hotels or the good minister's house."

"But—"

"At least have some food and a hot drink. Then we'll decide what to do."

A lamp shone through filmy curtains and he knocked, calling, putting Deborah on her feet but supporting her weight even though she tried to stand alone. "Melissa," he said as the door opened cautiously, "if some of the chocolate's left, please make some hot. Miss Whitlaw's had a severe shock and needs rest and food. Is there soup, something nourishing that can be heated quickly?"

Melissa wore a quilted blue velvet robe, furred at the collar and cuffs. Her blonde hair, loosened for the night, waved about her face. "The poor child does look done in," she said, as if Deborah couldn't hear. "The rear bedroom's empty and the sheets are fresh. Shall I put her to bed and take in the tray when it's ready?"

"I can eat at the table." Deborah was indeed hungry and knew she must restore herself physically for what lay ahead, for the work of her family now passed to her.

Melissa's blue eyes sharpened, though her voice was gently sympathetic. "Come to the kitchen, then, dear; it's cozier. I close off the dining room after supper and it's like the North Pole in there now."

Sweeping ahead, she indicated an armchair at the side of the table nearest the stove, poked up the coals in the comfortingly warm stove, and put in small kindling for a quick, hot fire. The teakettle was already on, and, taking down a saucepan, she stepped into the pantry. Rolf joined her for a moment, speaking softly, evidently explaining what had happened.

As Deborah sat down, Rolf came back, helped her off with her coat, scarf, and gauntlets, then wrapped her in an afghan he took down from a peg.

"Let's get off those moccasins," he said, propping her feet up on a padded round stool. Embarrassed at his handling, Deborah tried to pull away, but he stripped off the soggy footwear, swore as his fingers touched her. "Good Lord! If it weren't for these double wool socks, you'd probably have frozen feet! Why didn't you say something?"

"I didn't notice."

She felt cold all over, cold to the heart. His hands hurt as they chafed heat back into her toes, feet, and ankles. Melissa had set the pan on the stove. Seeing what Rolf was doing, she went out and was swiftly back with a pair of heavy knitted bedsocks, quite different from the blue velvet slippers that peeped from beneath her robe. She would have slipped them on, but Deborah, thanking her, did that.

With a small shrug, Melissa shaved chocolate into a mug, melted it with boiling water, and added milk from a pitcher. "Here," she said, giving it a stir as she brought it to Deborah. "This will do you good."

Chocolate was a rare treat. Deborah was ashamed to find it delicious; it seemed wrong to enjoy such a thing, but it gave heat without the sting of whisky.

Rolf had helped himself, both to the coffee on the stove and to his silver flask. "You should eat before you go to Reverend Cordley," Deborah said.

Rolf frowned, then said to Melissa, "I'll have a bowl of that soup, please, if there's enough."

"I always have enough for favorite boarders, even when they grow irregular in their comings and goings," Melissa said.

"I pay what you ask and rather more," said Rolf.

She brought two large bowls of the creamy soup, then lightly caressed Rolf's dark gold hair. "You do," she agreed good-humoredly. And she put out spoons, light bread, a crock of butter, and knives.

"I'll just be sure your room's all right," she said to Deborah, and she disappeared in a graceful sweep of velvet.

• *xiii* •

It was an effort to take the first few mouthfuls of soup, but it went down smoothly, warmly, and tasted so good that Deborah finished the bowl, though she had no appetite for the bread. Rolf, chewing a crust hungrily, nodded approval.

"That's it. You'll feel worlds better tomorrow."

Tomorrow. A sickness gripped her, dread, a horrifying sense of unreality. If only she were at Johnny's, with Sara and Judith. She'd go there as soon as she could. But tomorrow she'd wake up beneath Melissa's roof, have to face pitying, curious people. And sometime, though not tomorrow, she'd have to decide what to do about *The Clarion* and the farm.

But tonight she'd sleep. She was drowsy, very drowsy,

in a warm room for the first time since . . . morning. Rolf's voice pierced the haze thickening about her.

"After I see Cordley, I'm starting after those bushwhackers. I may be gone a week or more. Shouldn't take too long. From the way they talked, they're all from around Westport."

"Rolf—"

His jaw set. "I'm going to do it, Deborah. You may not feel better, but I sure as hell will."

"If you don't get shot."

"I won't. I've got you to come back to."

Startled from her sleepiness, she stared at him. Wouldn't he ever understand? Before she could shape words, he leaned forward, taking her hands.

"I've been thinking. This is how it's going to be. And you don't need to argue, darling. I've been your good little boy, and all it got me was the door. I'm going to be your man."

She tried to jerk away from him, but his grip was inexorable. "Listen, Deborah, you and I were betrothed on Christmas Day. When I went to see you today, I found—what I found. You are naturally grief-stricken, even a trifle unbalanced, and must be closely protected till you regain your health. To hasten that, I'm taking you away. A happy marriage and new surroundings should cure you. I have no intention of abandoning the woman I love, demented though she is by the loss of her family."

"No one would believe such rubbish! I'll go to Reverend Cordley and—"

"My dear, you won't. No doubt he'll come to see you, but he'll be prepared for anything you might say, grievous delusions. Everyone knows we've been keeping company since the summer. Our betrothal's expected. And it gives me, in the absence of close relatives, almost a husband's rights."

Reverend Cordley was Father's friend; he didn't, perhaps, know her well enough to attack a plausible story. But Johnny would believe her!

As if he read her mind, Rolf said, "If your blacksmith squaw-man hears where you are, for his sake, you'd better let him think what the town will. Because if he does interfere with my plans, try to take you away, I'll kill him."

The Bowie pressed against her leg. Its touch reminded her that she wasn't defenseless. But she must pick the right time. She didn't want to kill him, only to hold him off till she could escape or wound him enough to make him harmless. If she got to Cordley first, she thought he'd believe her.

Drooping, she said, "I can't fight you now, Rolf. I—I'm so tired! I just want to sleep."

"So you shall, love. Come along."

Melissa was outside the kitchen. Perhaps she'd been listening. "I put out a nightgown and robe," she told Deborah. "Shall I help you get ready for bed?"

"Thank you, no," said Deborah.

"Good night, then. Do call me, dear, if you need anything in the night. My room's across the hall from yours."

"Thank you," Deborah said again.

No use appealing to Melissa, who was paid by Rolf, who'd be pleased to have Deborah out of the way when Dane came in the spring. Rolf opened the door of the last room on the right.

An oil lamp burned on a mirrored dresser. The covers were turned back from snowy sheets and eyelet-trimmed pillowcases. A ruffled flannel nightgown was spread across the bed next to an emerald-green velvet robe. A flowered china washbowl and filled pitcher were on the washstand next to perfumed soap and a pile of clean towels.

This would have seemed like heaven if it hadn't actually been a jail. "Here you are, darling. I'll leave money with Melissa to get you some clothes, whatever you need." His gaze fixed longingly on her mouth, but he only took her hand instead, bringing it to his lips, pressing it to his face.

Her right hand was positioned to draw the Bowie from the secret slit in her skirt. In a moment he'd be gone. But if, with her left hand, she could pull the belt around—

Holding her breath, she succeeded. Now a quick reach beneath her skirt and she'd be armed! He was still kissing her open palm.

Bending swiftly, she reached up. As her hand closed on the knife, Rolf's fingers closed over hers, outside the skirt, but gripping till she couldn't move.

"Don't you remember? I was there when Chaudoin gave you this knife, when you decided how best to wear it." He laughed softly, eyes blazing green-gold in the lamplight. "I'll put it in safe-keeping for you. Someday it may be an intriguing souvenir."

His free hand found the skirt slit, reached behind her to untie the leather belt, then slip the knife out of her desperate grasp. He tossed it, still sheathed, on the bed. "Sweetheart," he said huskily, "you owe me something for that."

He brought her to him, taking her mouth, arms and hands, smothering her resistance, crushing her against him as if he burned to imprint her on the hard length of his body. She felt consumed, stifled, was close to fainting when he wrenched from the kiss, groaning.

"Did you mean to kill me?"

She stared into those strange jade eyes. "I meant to do whatever I had to in order to get away."

"If I took you now, you might, being the puritan that you are, feel bound to marry me." His hand touched her breast, then fell as she gave him a look of hatred. "No, Deborah, I won't dishonor you. Before I hold you naked in my arms, before I do everything I dream about, I'll marry you."

"You won't. That would be my dishonor."

He flushed before he went pale. "Don't provoke me," he said between his teeth.

Releasing her, he swept up the belted knife. "I'll be back as soon as I can. When you think it over, I believe you'll know my plan is the best for you. At any rate, it's inevitable. If you won't marry me in a week or a month, you'll be glad to when our child's on the way." Pausing in the door, his tone softened. "Give us a chance, darling. If you let me, I'll make you the best husband in the world."

She could have been sorry for him if she hadn't been so besieged and fearful. "You'll never be my husband. I'd rather die."

His mouth went taut. He took a stride forward, then checked himself. "I doubt that. In spite of your prudishness, you have in you a fountain, sweet like wine, dizzying. I had a sip of it one day. Soon I'll drink my fill. Your fountain will never go dry, Deborah. It'll well up, replenishing you, making you—and me—drunk with delight."

Weakend by fatigue and outrage, Deborah gripped the bedstead. Her legs were swaying. Rolf wavered before her, outlined by a nimbus of light.

"Sleep, love," he said. "Sleep now."

The door closed. There was the sound of a key, a sharp click. Moving her head to clear it, Deborah walked shakily to the one window and pulled back the flounced chintz curtains. The glass had been broken out and Melissa had apparently decided that boards were cheaper and less fragile. The opening was tightly nailed shut.

It was a prison.

But Melissa would have to open the door to feed her. Rolf would be gone a week or more. Cordley would come, surely, and he *might* be convinced that her brain wasn't turned. She might persuade him to at least talk to Sara, who'd swear Rolf wasn't her fiancé. Her gaze fixed on the lamp.

She'd hate to do something that might endanger others, but if nothing else worked, she'd dash the lamp in the corner and set the house on fire. That'd give Melissa more to worry about than keeping a prisoner.

Deborah was absolutely sure she wouldn't be in the room when Rolf came back. What she must do now was sleep, recover. She was going to need all her will, all her strength.

For the first time in her life, she went to bed without praying. What could she say about the grave in the stable, that other one on the Wakarusa, marked by a fallen tree? The flesh of her flesh lay underground, her parents, her twin; she felt naked and alone in a wind as flaying and icy as a blizzard.

To sink before it, to freeze to the warmth of eternal slumber, to join those she loved . . . Dane, she loved, but he'd left her. She saw no way, even if he came back, that he'd fit into the life before her. And she had to live. She was the only one to carry on her family's work, to remember and honor and vindicate them.

The weeping was all inside her now. Slipping out of her damp stained clothes, she washed, blew out the lamp, and got into bed. It seemed shameful to be naked and it was cold, but she couldn't bring herself to put on Melissa's gown.

She dreamed, seeing her parents or Thos in the distance, calling and running to them. Sometimes they faded from her vision. Sometimes they turned and were dead and she saw their wounds.

She jerked erect at the sound of the door closing. The room was dusky, but it must be day since slivers of light knifed through the boarded window and outlined the door.

A tray sat on the floor. Melissa's voice came through the keyhole. "If you need anything, there's a bell. Reverend Cordley's gone out with half a dozen men to bring in your parents and brother."

"He—he didn't stop by to see me?"

"He did, but I told him you were sleeping. He's very glad, dear, that you have a fiancé to look after you in this awful time."

Deborah started to spring out of bed, then remembered her nakedness and drew the covers close around her. "You know Rolf isn't my fiancé! You know—"

"I know he brought you here in an understandably distraught condition. The shocks you've had would turn any mind. Rest and quiet will make you well faster than anything. I shall see that you get them."

Did Melissa believe what she was saying? Or was she inflicting subtle torment while pretending to sympathize? No use accusing or railing at her. Deborah choked back scalding words. "My brother was engaged to Sara Field at Chaudoin's smithy. Could word be sent to her?"

"She'll probably hear it from some traveler."

"She has a right to come to the funeral."

"As your fiancé, Rolf must make decisions like that."

"But he'll be gone for days!"

"And meanwhile he's holding me accountable for you." Melissa's tone sharpened. "I'm sorry for you, child. I'll do what I can to make you comfortable, fetch you anything within reason. I've already washed your clothes, and I'm going to look for shoes and stockings. All the books I have are on the tray along with the Bible and sketch pad Rolf had in his pack. I'll borrow some more fôr you since I know you like to read."

"But you won't help me get away! You *know* it's Dane I love!"

"I know." Melissa's tone was steely for a moment before it grew caressing. "But he left you, didn't he? It's Rolf who's helping you, a strong, rich, handsome young man who's mad for you, who'll take you to a city and give you everything." Melissa's words were full of envy. "You're extremely fortunate, and if you don't know it, your brain *is* fevered!"

No use talking to the woman.

After waiting a moment, her steps receded down the hall. The room was cold and Deborah reluctantly pulled on the green robe before she moved across the carpet to the tray. Dane's sketch pad and the Whitlaw Bible were beneath Sir Walter Scott's *The Talisman,* Charlotte Brontë's

Jane Eyre, and Hawthorne's *The Scarlet Letter*. All three novels were well worn, apparently often used to escape this small, raw settlement on the fringes of civilization. Melissa must have dreamed that Dane, or perhaps even Rolf, would offer her a wider, more romantic life.

Deborah put the novels on the table by the one cushioned chair, placed the Bible on the dresser, and put the sketch pad on the bed. Her clothes were gone. Melissa must have collected them soundlessly before closing the door. A dark gray poplin dress lay across a bench along with the daintiest lace-trimmed chemise, drawers, and petticoat Deborah had ever seen.

Unless she stayed in bed or wrapped herself up in the covers, she had to wear something of Melissa's. Her feet were icy now and she was shivering, so she carried the tray to the bedside stand, lit the lamp, piled the pillows high, got in bed, pulled the coverings up to her waist, and put the tray on her lap.

There was a glazed pot of real coffee and real sugar in a silver bowl. In one covered dish was cooked wheat, and the other held slices of ham and buttered toast. There was a pitcher of cream, and the marmalade was surely a gift from Rolf or Dane.

The good smells teased Deborah's appetite. She thought she'd have some toast and coffee. That roused her hunger and she finished everything.

Much restored by the hot food and coffee, she dressed, put on the house slippers, and brushed her hair. The chill soon made her add the robe to her clothing. She made the bed, then tried vainly to peer through the cracks in the window boards.

They were too narrow. It was like being sealed in a box. Deborah had always hated small closed spaces, confinement. Even had nothing been wrong, this imprisonment in a dimly lit room would have maddened her.

She couldn't stay here all day and night and the next and the next till Rolf came back, if he ever did! She couldn't! There must be some way to get out of here!

The other boarders!

Melissa must have another two or three. If only Deborah could make one of them understand, get one to believe her, let her out, or at least carry word to Johnny! Trembling at this sudden hope, Deborah pressed her hands to her forehead and tried to think.

If Melissa had gone out to buy stockings and shoes, this

might be the best time to try to attract help. Deborah took the silver hand bell from the tray and rang it, listened, then rang it again.

No sound of response. Melissa must have gone shopping. Taking a deep breath, Deborah doubled her fists and pounded on the door, calling as loudly as she could for help.

There was confusion in the hall, a man's puzzled voice, Melissa's answer, accompanying footsteps hurrying to the door. "Such a pity, Mr. Townsend—the poor girl's on the verge of insanity, and no wonder! Mr. Hunter could calm her if he were here, but he felt, of course, that he must go after those Border Ruffians." Just outside the door, her voice dropped. "Actually, it's a good thing you're here, though I wouldn't have disturbed you. I need to put these stockings and shoes inside and take out the poor child's breakfast tray. But you'll understand that I need some help in coping with her in this hysterical mood."

"Indeed, ma'am," came a gruff, hearty voice. "I'll do what I can to help with the young lady."

"I knew you would, Mr. Townsend." The key clicked. "I hope it won't be necessary to restrain her, but if she flies at me or tries to dodge past, I'll rely on you to stop her as gently as possible."

"Be easy, Mrs. Eden. I had a sister who took fits. Many's the time I kept her from doing herself or others a mischief."

"How fortunate that you're here!" Melissa breathed in a way that would have inflated any male chest.

The doorknob turned.

Mr. Townsend proved to be a broad, beefy man with ruddy cheeks and brown hair and brown eyes. He stood planted in the doorway, filling it. Trying to get past him could only mean a humiliating scuffle. Melissa opened her shopping bag and took out an attractive pair of black kid shoes and several pairs of stockings.

"Would you like to see if these suit you?" she asked.

Deborah ignored her. Trying to look sane and reasonable, though she was beginning to think perhaps she really was going mad, Deborah looked straight into the man's eyes. "I'm not out of my mind," she said carefully, keeping her voice level. "I'm not engaged to Rolf Hunter. Please, whether you believe me or not, send word to Johnny Chaudoin—"

The man's face closed. "I never saw anyone as drunk

as that blacksmith was the Fourth of July. Forget about that heathen, Miss, and let Mrs. Eden and Mr. Hunter take care of you."

"But—"

He shook his head bullishly. Melissa, picking up the tray, smiled and shot Deborah a glance of amused triumph. That touched off an explosion, searing white fire igniting in Deborah's brain. She screamed wordlessly and sprang at Melissa, reaching for her white, slender throat, knowing only that she burned to change that mocking smile to fear.

The tray clattered to the floor, with dishes shattering and rolling. Deborah's fingers grasped for Melissa's throat, missing as she was dragged backward, pinioned so close to the burly man that she sickened at the smell of sweat and tobacco.

"There, Miss Whitlaw," he soothed. "It's all right, just calm down—"

Sobbing, she writhed in his grip, kicking and hitting at him, though one part of her mind knew this made her case worse. "You—you fool!" she choked. "If you'd tell Johnny—"

Townsend shook his head regretfully. "Plumb daft," he muttered. "Is it safe to let her loose, ma'am?"

Melissa sighed. "I hate to tie her up but it may be the only way to keep her from hurting herself. Will you hold her, sir, while I find something that'll confine her without chafing the skin?"

The thought of being tied, left helpless in the room with torturing memories and fears, paralyzed Deborah for a moment, then sent her into a frantic struggle, desperately gasping when she tried to speak and couldn't.

"Can you keep her jaws apart so I can give her these drops?" said Melissa from what seemed far away. "It'll help her sleep."

"Had to do it for my poor sister."

The man's thumb and finger pressed her jaws, forcing them open. She tasted bitterness disguised as sweet. She felt strangled, then involuntarily swallowed the water poured down her throat.

"If you'll put her on the bed, Mr. Townsend, I suppose I'd better tie her, much as I hate it."

"It's the best way to keep her from doing herself a mischief," he consoled. "She'll thank you later. Why, maybe after a good sleep or two, she'll start coming around."

"You're comforting as well as mightily helpful," Melissa said.

Shocked into quiet, Deborah lay still, eyes closed, as broad pieces of cloth were fastened around her wrists and her ankles. The quilts were brought up beneath her chin.

"There!" Melissa's satisfaction should have stung like salt on a new wound, but Deborah was exhausted past caring. "She can't get into any trouble now."

"She's so—quiet." Townsend's rough voice was troubled. "Sure she's all right? Maybe I should get the doctor."

"He's out east of town delivering a baby," said Melissa. "Rest is the medicine for what ails this girl."

"That's right, ma'am. Rest and good care, which you'll surely give her." They were moving to the door. "You call me if I can help at all."

The door shut on Melissa's gratitude. The key grated, as if turning in Deborah's head. She had to control herself or her nerves would snap. Her futile outburst had confirmed the story that she was unbalanced; Townsend would spread his account. Even if, for appearances' sake, Melissa called the doctor, he knew Deborah only by sight and would probably concur that her mind was unhinged. It was simpler, after all, to let rich, popular Rolf Hunter take care of his fiancée.

Johnny would help, or Sara—or Judith, if she could. But by the time they learned of her imprisonment, Rolf might have somehow smuggled her away. Besides, she feared what Rolf might do if Johnny interfered.

In a frenzy of impotence, Deborah wrung her wrists, trying to loosen the cotton strips, but her efforts only tightened the knots and forced the strips into more constricting bands. If her feet weren't tied, she could have walked around, at least, gone over to the lamp and knocked it over. She probably still could roll off the bed and worm her way to the chest, then struggle up and break the lamp. But she didn't want to burn to death, and, with her feet encumbered, that could certainly happen.

Her mind was hazing. Images formed and vanished against her closed eyelids, swelled and darkened like giant waves. These toppled, closer each time. They closed over her.

She must have awakened at the sound of the opening of the door. By the time she was drowsily aware of where she was in spite of a dull oppressive ache that increased to throbbing as she opened her eyes, Melissa was gazing down at her.

Placing a tray on the stand, she pulled up the chair. "It's evening, dear. Time passed quickly, didn't it?" I've brought some nice chicken soup."

"I don't want it."

"You have to eat."

Deborah said nothing and closed her eyes. Melissa's voice took on an edge. "Mr. Townsend came in a little while ago. Shall I call him?"

The memory of his hairy-tufted knuckles and strong odor made Deborah sit up reluctantly and accept the spooned, creamy liquid.

"That's better," approved Melissa. "It'll taste good if you'll let it."

It did warm Deborah. "Is Reverend Cordley back?" she asked.

"Yes. Everything's being taken care of."

"The—the funeral?'"

"It'll be tomorrow. Rolf's paying for the best black walnut coffins, all covered with black alpaca. Naturally, disturbed as you are, no one expects you to come."

"But I have to!"

"And start your raving hysterics?" Melissa shook her head, full mouth tightening. "Indeed, you won't. Rolf entrusted you to me. Apparently the only way to be sure you don't run off or cause trouble is to keep you in this room. That's what I'm going to do."

Black and crimson swirled before Deborah, coalescing into shapes: her parents' bodies, blood and fire, a dead tree on the river. But worse, what she felt she could not bear, were the crowding ordinary flashes: Thos's eyes merry as he said, "Cross your heart?"; the way he'd cut the wheat, or gazed tenderly at Sara; her mother at the pianoforte or in the kitchen; Father saying grace or reading aloud some passage he wanted them all to hear. . . .

Never to happen again? Never, any of them, to breathe or smile or move? How could it be? Deborah felt as if great parts had been ripped from her body and she was bleeding to death, but it was so cold that she bled slowly.

"I can't stay here like this," she said through numb lips. "It will really drive me mad."

"What can I do?" Melissa demanded angrily. "It's your own fault you're tied up. I'm sorry about it, but I can't have you throttling me every time I bring you food."

Battling to keep from begging or crying, Deborah finally got command of herself enough to say, "The Bible—it ought to be buried with my parents."

"I'll give it to Reverend Cordley," Melissa said eagerly, glad to find one point of conciliation. "I'll read to you, or talk if you'd rather. Truly, Deborah, I'm trying to help. When Rolf gets back—"

Deborah averted her face. "I'll appreciate your taking the Bible to the minister. And I want to talk to him, though you and Rolf probably have him thinking me insane."

"Take some more of these soothing drops," said Melissa, pouring them into a spoon.

"I've slept enough. All that's left are nightmares."

"Shall I fetch Townsend?"

Deborah opened her mouth and swallowed the drops and the milk Melissa offered.

"Shall I read till you sleep?" Melissa asked.

"No."

"Suit yourself," said Melissa. Flouncing over to the chest, she picked up the Bible, then hesitated a moment. "I don't like to leave you in the dark, but crazy as you're acting, you might manage to set things afire. I'll put the bell here on the stand where you can reach it."

"Aren't you going to ask Reverend Cordley to come?"

"Yes, of course, but if you're asleep he won't want to disturb you."

Deborah laughed mirthlessly. "What'll you do, Mrs. Eden, when these drops don't work anymore?"

"Long before that, Rolf'll be back," said Melissa with feeling. "And I'll be glad to give you over to him! I'm doing my best, but you haven't a speck of gratitude or sense, either!"

She blew out the light. Quick steps, door opening, closing. Deborah was sure Melissa would keep the minister away as long as possible, keep her tied and drugged.

Her parents and twin were in their coffins and would be buried in the morning before the unembalmed bodies began to disintegrate. She really didn't want to see them buried, but she clung to being near what was left of them as long as she could. In an agony of loss, she beat at the pillow with her bound hands, then gave way to wrenching sobs. If only Dane were here! But no, damn him, he'd gone away and left his brother!

Of course, the Missourians Rolf meant to kill might get

him, instead. If he didn't come back in a few weeks, Melissa couldn't keep up this deception. She'd have to let Deborah go and insist that she'd believed Rolf's story and carried out his orders in good faith.

But tonight there were bonds and darkness, tormenting familiar images of Father, Mother, and Thos as they would never be again. Like a treadmill, Deborah's thoughts kept grinding, grooving deeper into her spirit with each monotonous circling.

If what had happened was God's will, she couldn't trust or worship Him. If it wasn't God's will, then what was God? The whirlwind's answers to Job didn't ease her. She didn't care who'd laid the foundations of earth, shut up the seas, commanded the morning, or divided the watercourses. She only knew the heavenly Father she'd been taught to revere had let her earthly father perish terribly.

Cruel as it was, she could accept Thos's death. By breaking man-made law, he'd done what he knew could bring killing. It was a volunteer's risk. But her parents had died in their own yard. They'd sheltered runaways, helped them escape northward, but they hadn't used or believed in violence.

No. She couldn't believe, ever again, that good was stronger than evil. She couldn't pray. She rebelled against her family's death as she did against her bonds, uselessly, hurting only herself. But the laudanum was misting her senses. At last she slept.

She awoke to a firm hand across her mouth, an arm cradling her head. "Deborah, it's Sara!" came the soft whisper. "Are you all right? Do you remember me?"

"I haven't lost my mind," answered Deborah as Sara's palm relaxed. She sat up and resisted the instant throbbing in her temples as Sara untied her. "Let's get out of here!" Questions could wait.

Deborah's head felt swollen with pounding blood, but she located the new shoes and stockings and fumbled them on. Faint light came through the window, from which the lower boards had been removed. She groped and got her coat and scarf from a peg, then picked up the sketch pad from the bottom of the bed. Her gauntlets were in her coat pocket. Rolf had her Bowie. She wished she could have traded Melissa's good clothes for her old ones, but they hadn't been returned.

Sara waited, a shadow in deeper shadows. Did she know

about Thos? She must. Wordlessly, Deborah put her arms around her friend, but Sara gave her a strong push toward the window.

Scooping up her skirts, Deborah cautiously put a leg over the sill, found hard earth, then climbed all the way out. Sara had joined her in an instant, then was tugging her toward some trees not far from the street. No lights burned in the town and the sky was dark except for stars.

"Chica must be in the livery," Deborah whispered.

"She was. Judith's got her down by the river. Don't talk now, *meshemah*. We don't want dogs barking."

They circled out of town and back to the river well beyond the ferry, Sara leading, Deborah just behind. Soon she heard the faint creaking of saddle leather, the shifting of restive horses.

"Judith?" whispered Sara.

"You find Deborah?" came the low-pitched response.

"Wouldn't be back if I hadn't."

A hand searched, closed on Deborah's arm, found her hand, and squeezed fiercely. "You ain't crazy? Ain't marryin' that Rolf like they say?"

"No and no!"

They hugged each other and this time Sara was in the embrace, though she quickly broke it. "Come on, let's get out of here!" she urged.

Deborah hung back. "The funeral—it's tomorrow."

"So? Will it help your family to leave Rolf a clear trail to follow?" Sara thrust Chica's reins into Deborah's fingers. "These Lawrence people think you're mad. You can't take shelter with them."

"But if I stay at the smithy, Rolf's already threatened to make trouble!"

"You won't be at the smithy," Sara replied. "Hurry! We can talk once we're well away."

• xiv •

They picked up the road along the Kaw, and when they were far enough away for talking, Sara and Judith explained.

Belshazzar, still saddled and bridled, had wandered to the smithy yesterday morning. Probably he'd gone home first, smelled blood and smoke, and retreated to the nearest place of which he had good memories. Johnny and Maccabee were gone, summoned early from their beds to help a wagon that had mired at a ford some miles upriver and broken a wheel.

Alarmed, Judith had wanted to ride with Sara to the Whitlaws', but Sara pointed out that the Whitlaws had risked much to help Judith to freedom, and if she got caught now it would undo their efforts. Promising to come back as soon as she could, Sara rode fast to the farm and encountered Reverend Cordley and his party as they carried out their grim task of exhuming the bodies.

Cordley had told the horrified Sara Rolf's version of the raid and about Thos's death, along with the news that Deborah, at least temporarily out of her mind with shock and grief, was under Melissa Eden's protective care.

"I told Reverend Cordley that you weren't engaged to Rolf and that I didn't believe, either, that you'd gone mad." Sara's tone was bitter. "But he doesn't really know me, and I suppose, having just heard about Thos, that I sounded crazy myself. Anyway, when he went on being pityingly kind, I told him he was a fool and rode back to the smithy. Johnny and Maccabee still weren't home. After we talked it over, Judith and I decided it might be best if she and I got you out."

In the gray light, Judith's nod was emphatic. "Johnny, he'd storm in and fight anyone gave him trouble, maybe get himself hurt or killed or do damage to nice folks who think *they're* protectin' you. Even if he get you away, Rolf goin' to know where to look."

"So we told Laddie to take care of things and to tell Johnny and Maccabee only that we'd gone to see you and not to worry."

"Johnny doesn't know about—about my family?"

Sara's voice trembled. "Not unless he's happened on to someone who told him. Judith and I left the smithy in the middle of the afternoon, but we stopped a few miles out of town and waited in a ravine till all the lights were out and everything was quiet. I wasn't expecting your window to be nailed shut, though. Johnny's going to swear when he sees what I did to one of his knives by prying the boards loose."

"You—you must have wanted to go to Thos, Sara."

"Why?" asked the Indian girl harshly. "If he had been left to me, yes, if I could wash and prepare him. But another group had gone for him. I wasn't his wife. Had I tried to touch him, mourn as I wished, it would only create scandal. No. I'll remember him as he was."

Judith said in a tight, aching voice, "Rather would've died than bring all this! Your folks were so good to me, Deborah. They died on my account."

"No," cut in Deborah strongly. "I don't know what tale Rolf's put out, but he told me he fell in with the gang for excitement. He says he didn't know they were chasing Thos till he was shot. The raiders had split up. It was just bad luck that part of them hit our farm. Any Free Staters would have done as well. Don't blame yourself, Judith. If there was any real reason for my parents' death, it was John Brown's slave-stealing trip to Missouri."

She wasn't quite as sure as she sounded that some member of the band hadn't heard about Jed's death at the Whitlaws' while hunting his runaway, but there was no use in Judith's carrying a burden of guilt. Leticia and Josiah wouldn't have wanted that. When it came right down to it, they had faced and accepted the chance of death when they decided, after Jed's raid, to stay on the farm.

They'd been slaughtered, but they weren't victims. Like soldiers, they'd decided not to abandon a post and had lost their lives for it. That pride was the first balm for Deborah; not much, but a slight easing.

She told her friends then of how, after leaving them at the smithy, she'd seen smoke coming from the direction of her home.

Only the day before yesterday! It seemed years. Two full days ago, her parents had still been alive. Now they were dead forever; there could be no change in that. And Thos! She thought of John Brown with hatred. If he'd never come to their house, if Thos had never looked into those spellbinding fanatic's eyes! If—

As a bleak, rising sun tried to pierce through high, wintry clouds, she muffled her face in her scarf and gave way to silent weeping.

Two shapes appeared on the sere rim of the horizon, from which all snow had melted, assuming size and gradual identity, first as horsemen, then as a very large man and a shorter one, black and white or Indian, and at last, Maccabee and Johnny.

Meeting on the open prairie, the five stopped. *"Cesli tatanka!"* growled Johnny, sliding from his spotted horse and striding up to Sara. His old horsehide jacket was buttoned up to the last bone toggle. "I ought to skin you, Sara! I see you have Deborah, but what if you'd gotten yourselves shot or jumped on by some bunch of cutthroats?"

"We've got Deborah, and without a fuss, Johnny." Sara divided a withering glance between him and Maccabee, who was watching Judith with his heart in his eyes. "You two had come thundering into town and there'd have been trouble. Folks there believe she's crazy and engaged to Rolf Hunter—"

"Same thing!" Johnny grunted. Scowling, he moved awkwardly over to Deborah. "You all right, lass?"

She couldn't speak. Shaking his grizzled head, Johnny gave her hand a rough pat. "Nothin' helps right now. I know, honey. But your folks was the finest I ever knew. Thos was the son I wish I'd had. *Hopo!* Let's get going!"

He rode ahead with Sara, from the rise and fall of his gruff tones alternately scolding, questioning, praising. Judith kept to one side of Deborah, with Maccabee on the other. He said that he and Johnny had gotten back after dark last night along with the broken wheel from the mired wagon. Johnny hadn't believed Laddie's story, though the boy stuck doggedly to it, and after a hurried meal, Johnny had ridden off to the Whitlaws'.

Even in the night, he'd been able to guess most of what had happened. Cabins might burn, but that doesn't rearrange furnishings, smash up a buggy, or cut a cow's throat and wring chickens' necks. He'd gone back to the smithy and this time had convinced Laddie that for Sara's sake, the boy should tell what he knew. Maccabee had awakened during that and insisted on coming along.

"Guess we wasted our time," he said in his deep, pleasant voice; giving an admiring glance to Judith. "But land alive, woman, what you mean pokin' 'round town—an' you a runaway?"

"Deborah needed me."

"Maybe someone else needs you!" he reproached.

"We don' talk on that yet."

"If you're goin' to be up to tricks like this," he rumbled, "the sooner we talk, the better."

Judith tossed her head. "You don' like my tricks, now's the best time to find out! After all the Whitlaws did for me, you reckon I'll hide when trouble strike them?"

"That's what you need a man for."

"Ha! Sara and me did as good as you and Johnny could've! Didn't get into any scrapes, either!"

"That's the Lord's mercy!"

"Oh, our thinkin' it out real careful had somethin' to do with it," retorted Judith airily. "You ever get in trouble, we'll do the same for you!"

Maccabee's reluctant laughter rumbled. "Full of sass! Wonder you didn't get it whipped out of you!"

"You're not the meekest man I ever saw!" Judith's tone was wry but not angry.

It was clear that Maccabee loved her. Impossible to guess how she felt. She'd never spoken of the man Jed had said she fancied. Thinking of Dane, Deborah wondered how long a woman should let herself be bound by a memory, then repeated the question as she watched Johnny up ahead next to Sara.

With her young love gone, could the girl come to think of Johnny as a man rather than a foster father? Deborah hoped so. It would help if some happiness followed all the wreckage and misery.

Johnny stopped abruptly, reining his horse around, ignoring Sara, who caught at his arm. "Deborah, do you want to go to your folks' burying?" he demanded. "If you do, I'll take you! And I'll notch the ears of anyone who makes a move to shut you away!"

"Johnny!" Sara wailed and looked imploringly at Deborah.

It wasn't necessary. Deborah had washed her parents,

then helped put them to rest the first time in earth near their home. And she'd rather keep Thos in her mind as she'd seen him last, riding away, intent on adventure. This way, he would never seem quite dead; it would lack the brutal finality of seeing him coffined and in the grave.

Strange. Horrible as it was, she could not have believed her parents dead without seeing them so, would have remained joined to them. This way, cruel as it was, she'd have to come to terms with and finally accept their deaths. Even in her grief, she dimly sensed that remembering Thos as alive and simply gone was no serious threat to her sense of reality.

He was her twin, as nearly herself as any human could ever be. In a physical sense he would survive in her, and that was comforting. But she'd never depended on Thos as she had on the man and woman who had made her with love and bodies, shaped her with their minds and hearts. She must manage now without them. To do that, she had to *know* she could no longer turn to them.

"Thank you, Johnny," she said now. "But I've buried them once. I don't want to do it again, in front of a lot of people."

Searching her face, Johnny's frown cleared. He gave his massive head a nod and turned his paint.

Laddie had coffee ready and the household was soon settled around the table. To her surprise, Deborah was hungry. For the first time since the disaster, food smelled good, not disgusting. She had a fried egg and mush with milk and honey. She still wasn't up to the crisped side meat everyone else devoured with relish, except for Sara, who had only a little mush.

Now that there was a chance to study her friend, Deborah was worried. Sara's usually warm, high color was dulled. Her eyes were deeply shadowed and her thin face, always angular, now looked bony. Of course, she'd only yesterday learned about Thos.

A marvel that she'd been able to make plans, carry them out. *We must watch out for her,* Deborah thought. *Push her to eat in a few days if her appetite doesn't pick up.*

Johnny, too, was watching Sara, heavy brows knit. At last, as if discarding several things he wanted to say, he sighed and pushed back from the table. "Got to get at that busted wagon wheel," he said. "We're not goin' to need dinner, so why don't you gals have a rest? Tonight we'll talk over what Deborah wants to do. I've got one idea that I think is pretty good."

He went out with Maccabee and Laddie. The three young women began clearing the table. "Why don't you stay here and keep out of sight like I do?" asked Judith.

"If Rolf comes back, this'll be the first place he looks," Deborah said. "He's already warned me, and he has money to hire bushwackers. I can't bring that down on you."

Sarah put her arms around Deborah and laid her cheek against hers. "What I have, from food to life, is yours. But I think we needn't worry. If Johnny says his thought is good, it is."

Certainly it was unexpected. As they ate supper that night, stew with hot biscuits, in the kitchen warmed by the fireplace as well as the cookstove, Johnny passed his big bowl to Sara for another helping and looked across the table at Deborah. "Lass, you have a place under my roof. You know that."

Deborah nodded. "But Rolf—"

"Reckon I can clean that young whelp's plow any time he tries settin' it down in my territory," snorted Johnny. "I'll be kiln-dried if I see how a man like Dane got a brother like that, but I guess it started with Cain!" He took a bite of stew so hot it burned his tongue, yelled, *"Cesli tatanka!,"* and then apologized. "Good stew," he told Sara. "Rich and strong with onions and buffalo meat. But I better let it cool a mite."

His charcoal-colored eyes turned to Deborah and probed deep. "I want you to know you can come here any time. When I can't defend my place against the likes of that gold-haired fooforraw, I'll douse my forge and throw my hammer into the Kaw! I know you gals think a lot of one another, and that's a consolation at times like this. But I've studied it hard, and it seems to me you'd do best for a while in a new place with new people, somewhere that you wouldn't hear pro-slave or Free Soil every other word."

Deborah stiffened. "I won't go back to New Hampshire."

"No, lass, for sure, not unless you want to."

"I have to stay in Kansas. There's no place to get away from what's going on."

"Yes, there is." Johnny grinned like an amiable bear at the puzzled stares centered on him. "The Landers' settlement."

"But they—they don't understand what's going on in the Territory," Sara objected.

"Ain't that exactly what we need?" demanded Johnny. "They don't have no part in our quarrels and don't want any. Conrad was tellin' me how he got so sick of all those European wrangles that he decided to start fresh in a new country. He bought land for the colonists he brought with him, and they have a vote equal to his in runnin' things."

"The men, maybe. I'll bet the women don't," Sara guessed.

From the way her eyes were swollen, she'd done more crying than sleeping that afternoon in spite of being up all night. Deborah, head still dully aching, hadn't tried to nap but had minded the stew and darned socks out of the perpetually replenished basket by Sara's chair.

Her dry eyes felt pierced by thorns that held them open. She couldn't cry anymore. Hollow, empty, she felt detached from her own body. She was grateful to sit in her friends' home, do ordinary work that accumulated no matter what the griefs of a household. She had mourned to exhaustion, but Sara, refusing to give way till Deborah was rescued, must now go through disbelief, horror, rebellion, with sorrow flowing always under peaking, changing wild emotions like a sea powering waves that tower high, then crash back and vanish into the waiting depths.

With her pert remark to Johnny, Sara wordlessly announced that though she would go with the swelling crests rather than be swept off her feet by trying to stand against them, she wanted to smile when she could, live each moment as it happened, rather than decreeing a week, a month, six months of mourning.

Johnny gave her a relieved scowl. "Why do you want an equal vote, Wastewin, when around here you run the whole shebang?"

"Sound good to me," said Judith, casting Maccabee a provocative glance. "If women can't vote and their husbands can boss 'em around, that's close to bein' slaves."

"That so?" retorted Maccabee. "Who totes the water and wood? Who takes off their shoes so's your floor don' get tracked up? Who—"

"Thing is," pursued Johnny, "Conrad's not mixed up in our troubles, his sister, Ansjie, is about Deborah's age, and Friedental's a busy, happy place. Lives up to its name, Valley of Peace, except it isn't much of a valley."

"Maybe they won't want strangers," Deborah suggested.

"They'll want you!" said Johnny heartily. "Why, that day you met here at the forge, Conrad asked about you, and again after the Fourth of July when they kept me from making a complete tarnation fool of myself. Guess they get lonesome. They're well educated and would've been more at home in some big city if they hadn't believed they should try living from the work of their hands." Johnny shook his head. "Comes from readin' too many books, frettin' about what's not fair. But you could talk to them. Main thing is, what with everyone in Friedental bein' Proosian, it's like another world, but you're really only twenty miles southwest of here."

Sara put her hand over Deborah's. "I'd love to have you here, *meshemah,* but I like the Landers very much. Their company would be good for you now. You can come back to us when you feel like it."

Instinctively wishing to stay with her friends, Deborah knew she mustn't be at the smithy when Rolf came looking for her. If he found no trace of her, after a while he'd surely give up, leave Lawrence. But she insisted that the Landers be told about him and her whole situation before deciding whether to offer her shelter. He was unlikely to look for her in a small Prussian Utopia, but they had to know it was possible. So it was agreed that the next morning Laddie would ride to Friedental with a letter written by Sara.

While Judith and Deborah did the dishes, Sara painstakingly composed the message, using a page from the account book she kept so accurately for Johnny.

"There," she said, leaning back, as if her strength were gone. And surely it must be.

Johnny's eyes rested on Sara, whom he loved but couldn't comfort. "Just have to get through it. But I tell you what I'm goin' to give all you women—a slug of good whisky in hot apple cider."

Rising, he got the cider jug from a bottom shelf and poured a generous amount into a kettle. "Comes to that," he said heavily, "I can use a snort myself."

Deborah never knew when Judith joined her and Sara in the room Sara usually shared with Laddie, who was sleeping in the main cabin with Johnny. Before going to bed, Johnny had brought in a couple of shuck pallets he kept for wayfarers and an armload of quilts and buffalo robes. Deborah slept soundly on this couch once she lay down, but first she and Sara, heedless of the cold, sat for a long time on Sara's bed and held each other.

Sometimes they wept softly, sometimes they sobbed, sometimes their hands locked in rebellious protest, but they used no words. They mourned the same man, brother of one, sweetheart of the other.

As Deborah, who'd earlier believed all her tears were gone, finally kissed Sara and went to her own bed, it seemed there was only sadness and loss. She wondered if life would ever seem bright again, and she felt that even if it did, it would be a disloyalty to the dead.

Fortunately, there was work. Deborah and Sara awoke before the faintest gray. It was torment to lie wakeful with their memories, so they dressed quickly and left Judith sleeping.

"I need to bake today," Sara said. "Might as well get the bread rising before breakfast."

"You must have quite a washing piled up after the bad weather," Deborah said. "Let's do that, too." She wanted to keep busy, exhaust herself physically so she could sleep that night. Sara and Judith must feel the same way.

Early as it was, Johnny was up and had fires going in the fireplace and cookstove. A smell of coffee filled the air. Deborah made biscuits and cooked mush and fried side meat while Sara got the bread dough ready and set it for its first rising, covered with a clean cloth, over by the hearth. Informed that this was wash day, Johnny set the tub on the stove, pressed against the skillet and mush pan, and filled it half-full of water he fetched in from the well.

"Don't know why you women have to wash in the middle of winter," he grumbled, fetching in the rinse tubs. "If it were me, I'd let everything pile up from first snow to last one."

"A good thing it's not you," returned Sara. "Now be sure you've brought in all your drawers and undershirts and socks. I want that shirt, too; you've been wearing it a week!"

"A week!" cried Johnny. "Why, I used to wear the same clothes from frost to thaw!"

"And you had to burn them!" Sara scolded. She went to the passageway and shouted down it. "Laddie, you gather up all your clothes and bring them when you come to breakfast!"

Maccabee got the same instructions when he came in

from milking. Judith had come in and set the table. By the time they pulled up chairs and benches for breakfast, heaps of washing lay in different-colored heaps, and the yeasty smell of dough mingled with that of biscuits, pork, and coffee.

Right after breakfast Laddie set off for Friedental, admonished to stay overnight if he didn't get started back by early afternoon. Maccabee and Johnny put the tubs on benches, including the one containing soft soap and white things which had been boiling on the stove.

Sara poked and stirred these vigorously with a stick, then set to kneading the bread dough. Deborah and Judith did the dishes and then all three gathered at the tub, rubbing and scrubbing each sheet, towel, or garment till it could go into the first rinse after being wrung as thoroughly as possible.

After the whites were out of the soapy water, coloreds went to soak, and each woman took a tub, though when a sheet or heavy trousers had to be wrung out, two of them did it.

Sara had a real clothesline and pins Maccabee had carved. The sun was bright in spite of a razor-edged wind that numbed fingers and made them clumsy on the washing, which froze almost as quickly as it was pinned up. By the time Maccabee and Johnny came in for dinner, the heaps of laundry were transformed into stiff shards hanging from the line, and the smell of baking bread filled the main cabin.

The men dumped the wash water and turned the tubs upside down behind the well-house, except for the cleanest rinse, which would be used to scrub the floor. As soon as the bread had cooled enough to cut, a golden, crusty loaf was placed on a board on the table beside a crock of butter and Johnny sliced off generous hunks with his Bowie while Sara served big bowls of leftover stew.

Tired but with a sense of having worked well, Deborah was glad to sit down and felt hungry for the first time since she'd eaten here last, right before she left to discover the ruins of her home.

All three friends had wept that morning, tears spilling into the wash tubs or freezing as they hung out washing. Work had been a relief, a way to use up some of their feelings. They hadn't talked, except about their chores, the brightness of the sun, the piercing breeze.

Speaking brought a choking lump to the throat. Deborah

was glad that Johnny and Maccabee talked at the meal and filled the silence with their comfortingly deep male voices, discussing the news brought by a traveler who'd stopped to get his horse shod.

John Brown had come out of Missouri with eleven slaves, some fine horses, and other valuables. One slave-owner had been killed, and the governor of Missouri had called for Brown's punishment both to President Buchanan and Governor Denver of Kansas Territory.

The Governor of Missouri offered a three-thousand-dollar reward for Brown. President Buchanan offered two hundred fifty dollars. "Got to hand it to old Brown for nerve," said Johnny. "He's put out handbills advertisin' a twenty-five-cent reward for Buchanan, and he's headed north in an ox wagon with the slaves he rescued."

"While gangs of Missourians hunt around for him in Kansas," said Deborah bitterly. "I think he'd like to stir up a war!"

"He'd sacrifice anyone, includin' himself, to put an end to slavery," Johnny said. "And now Kansans are as riled up as Missourians were about the Brown raid. Dr. John Doy—him who came with Dan Anthony and the first bunch of New England Emigrant Aid Society folks—he was back into Kansas with thirteen slaves when Missourians captured the whole 'train.' They took the whole shebang across the line into Missouri, put the blacks back in slavery, and jailed Doy and his men for trial. They'll be sentenced sure as shootin'."

"Bet somebody tries to break 'em out of jail," rumbled Maccabee. "Them Missouri fellers comin' on Kansas soil to arrest Kansans and take 'em to Missouri—people don' like that."

No more than Missourians liked for Brown and Doy to cross the line to steal out slaves. That looked different to those who believed slavery was wrong, but to slave-holders it was plain robbery. It didn't lessen her grief and anger, but Deborah knew that Thos had been killed by men who considered him as guilty of theft as if he'd been stealing horses or cattle. And, of course, John Brown would sell the stolen horses and plunder to pay for the escaped slaves' passage north.

She believed in Brown's cause but not in his methods. "I wish he'd get himself martyred since that's what he seems to want!" she breathed. "He got my parents and

Thos killed, he's murdered helpless men himself, but nothing happens to him!"

Judith gave Deborah a long, level look. "Brown be God's man, Deborah. Slavers cain't touch him 'cause his hour not yet come. But God has a time for him. When it comes, it'll be God's sword waved in the sky. Everbody'll see it. Brown will die, but not what he's done. Your family's dead, but not what they believed in."

Shaking her head wordlessly, Deborah turned away from her friends. She would think her tears were used up, but then they'd collect and force themselves out again. She was glad that Johnny went on to tell what he'd heard about the legislature's meeting in Lawrence. Not only had they repealed the "bogus" laws, but they'd collected all the copies they could find and made a bonfire of them on Massachusetts Street.

"And someone sent a copy by express to the Missouri officials at Jefferson City. Wrote on the parcel, 'Returned with thanks.' Don't that beat all?"

Deborah managed to nod, though her throat ached to remember how eager Josiah had been to report on that triumphant legislative session.

After the men went to work, the women did the dishes. Sara put a ham in the oven and poured more water in the beans, which had been cooking since morning.

"Dried apple pie or peach pie?" she asked. "Let's make two of each."

They did. Then they scrubbed the splintery floor, put clean sheets on the beds, and brought in the frozen laundry, draping it around to finish drying. As winter twilight darkened the cabin, Sara lit two iron Phoebe lamps Johnny had made, hung them by chains on their handles to hooks above the table, and went to gaze out the window.

"I hope Laddie comes tonight," she said. "I wouldn't mind his staying the night if we could be sure he was at Friedental, but—"

She didn't need to finish. It was hard to feel sure about anything after what had happened. However, Johnny and Maccabee had just come in and were washing when hooves sounded. Johnny pulled on his horsehide jacket and hurried out. His booming voice carried back, plus Laddie's treble, and a strange, deep one. Sara, relieved, hurried to put on another plate. Deborah put the cornbread and beans in the warming oven and wondered who the third voice belonged to. Maccabee slipped his jacket around Judith and took her to the door of the passage to the women's cabin.

"Better wait till we know who's come in," he advised.

Judith nodded. He closed the door. It didn't take long to see to the horses. Laddie came in first, wriggling out of his sheepskin and eluding Sara, who tried to hug him. "Mr. Lander came back with me!" he cried, black eyes shining. "He doesn't think Proosian boys could ride so far in a day. His sister's real pretty, and she gave me *three* pieces of cake, big ones! Not stingy little slivers like you cut, Sara! Wait'll you see Mr. Lander's horse! He let me ride him for a while. Those Proosians talk funny, but they're nice and—"

"They're certainly patient, to put up with the likes of you!" Sara steered her brother to the washstand. "Use soap on your hands now; that's what it's for."

Reminded of when Thos had been in the hate-to-wash years, Deborah smiled, then winced. The door opened. She looked into eyes as deeply blue as a lake under summer skies.

So tall he had to bend to enter, Conrad Lander bowed in courtly fashion to all of the women, but his gaze was fixed on Deborah.

"I hope it does not incommode that I stay the night," he said in his careful English. "But it seemed to me wise, Miss Whitlaw, to escort you to Friedental as soon as possible. My sister sends greetings and is most eager to welcome you."

Deborah murmured something while Sara took his gray hat and caped coat, hanging them on a peg. "We're glad to have you," she said. "It was kind of you, Mr. Lander, to come for Deborah."

"I wanted to," he said simply.

Once more those clear eyes rested on Deborah. His features were so patrician that they might have been chisled in marble, a knight's face, or a saint's, and his light yellow hair was almost silver, but his smile was warm.

"Wash up," urged Johnny. "Have a seat! Sara always sets a good table, but with friends to help, she's outdone herself tonight. Judith hidin'? Tell her there's no need. Come on, folks, I could eat a buffalo—and without it bein' skinned!"

Maccabee called Judith. She was introduced to Conrad Lander, who bowed as courteously to her as he had to the other women. Soon they were all at the table, Sara ladling beans from the pot while Johnny sliced off ample portions of ham.

"Glad to have a chance to talk to you, Conrad," said Johnny when he'd apparently satisfied his sharpest hunger. "I'm sure Sara's letter put it plain, but bein' new to the Territory, you might not understand perfectly what's goin' on."

A smile touched Lander's eyes. "We founded Friedental three years ago," he said. "It was my agent's report on the struggle for freedom in Kansas that decided my sister and me to settle here. While our colony stays aloof from politics, we oppose slavery. We believed we could succeed so well at farming that it would show free men produce more than slaves. In our own way, though we bear no arms, we wished to take a stand in our new country."

Johnny's glance touched the scar across the young man's cheekbone. Touching it, the guest smiled. "I wasn't always of my present bent. I bear more saber cuts than this from my student days, and as a young officer I helped put down street fighting in Berlin in the 1848 revolution. But I left my pistols and sword in Brandenburg. There's not a weapon in Friedental."

Johnny stared, transfixed. "Conrad, you're more than a mite crazy! Let me make you some good Bowies!"

"My people won't use them." Conrad's smile deepened. "Mennonites are forbidden violence."

"Even to defend themselves?"

Conrad nodded. "The tenet's been strengthened by three centuries of persecution. I'm not a Mennonite, but I can assure you none of them came here to abandon their beliefs."

"I never heard the like!" Frowning, Johnny carved more ham. "What're you goin' to do if someone steals your fine oxen?"

"Pray for the thief and pull the plow ourselves."

Johnny scanned his guest's attire, which, though plain, was of good cut and material. "You?"

"I."

"And if they trample your grain?"

"Plant again."

Johnny didn't push further, perhaps deciding that mention of fire and murder was cruel to the bereaved women. He looked Conrad in the eye and said grimly, "I'll nowise let Deborah bide with you unless you promise to protect her."

"I've told you I'm not a Mennonite," Conrad said gently, but his tone held an edge of hauteur. An aristocrat might renounce his privileges but would never quite cast off his rearing, the manner bred into him from the cradle. "I will wrap my life around her like a shield. But Friedental is rightly named. We have peace. Indians have stopped there several times, armed warriors, but we gave them food and they left as friends."

"They knew you were crazy," Johnny growled. "And Indians think it's bad luck to bother the insane!"

Conrad laughed at that, unruffled. Deborah tore her eyes from him.

He spoke as her parents might have. Look what had happened to them! It was a shock, both brutal and poignant, to listen to him. He behaved as if he had searched out many answers for himself, as if he were at peace with the deepest part of his nature.

But when he watched her, his eyes held a question.

• XV •

Conrad's tall gray stallion was the color of river mists. Beside him, Chica was a small bright cloud. "You ride a high horse," grinned Johnny, seeing them off at dawn next morning. Conrad's straight lips curved in a smile.

"Ah, my friend, I gave up my sword and place in the Herrenhaus, but I couldn't part with Sleipner. I raised him from a colt. Only I have ridden him."

"He's a fine animal." Johnny eyed the horse critically. "Might not fare so well, though, on open prairie with no extra fodder."

"Well," shrugged Conrad easily, "he shall have what he requires through his life. His colts, from your smaller, tougher horses, won't need pampering."

"I'd admire to see them," said Johnny.

"I have a likely two-year-old I'd trade you for blacksmithing if he suits you. I'll bring him next time I come, or you can visit us. All of you," he added, including the rest of the gathered household.

Good-byes had already been said, but as Conrad collected his reins, Sara ran forward and Deborah bent to embrace her, pressing close the body her brother had loved, cherishing the memory of him in Sara, as Sara must know in her his twin flesh.

"Don't be any sadder than you have to," Sara whispered. "Smile when you can."

Deborah couldn't speak but kissed her friend, raised her hand to the others, and rode off beside Conrad, blinded by tears.

The sun climbed, warming the prairie, gilding the withered grass, sparkling where moisture left beads or patches. January. Much winter lay ahead, cruel March winds, but spring *would* come. The wheat she and Thos had planted last fall would sprout and grow, but he wouldn't see or harvest it. Was there no way to escape this circling of thoughts? No matter what she tried to concentrate on, the linkings ran inexorably to Thos or her parents.

"Perhaps it's good if I talk?" suggested Conrad. He'd kept the big gray reined to one side, slightly behind, obviously not wishing to intrude. "I can tell you about Friedental."

Deborah nodded mutely.

It was a fascinating story. Conrad's house descended from one of the Teutonic Knights, an order formed in the thirteenth century to check the surging tide of Slavs that randomly threatened to overwhelm Western Europe. Though the knights in time became pillagers, seizing land from heathen and convert alike, till soundly defeated by the massed strength of Poland and the Lithuanian Empire, which reached from Baltic to Black seas and almost to Moscow, crusading zeal continued strong in Conrad's forebears, though it took an unorthodox streak which made him suspect that some ancestor had sympathized with the Waldenses.

When these heretics were being burned by the hundreds throughout Europe for refusing infant baptism and for following the Scriptures rather than the Roman Church, the count of that day had given them asylum, and a later count had refused to imprison and burn or drown those of his tenants who became Mennonites.

"What do they believe?" Deborah asked.

"You've heard of the Amish in Pennsylvania? They're a branch of Mennonites who came over in the early 1700s from Switzerland, where persecution was terrible to a fairly late date, and from the Palatinate. In the canton of Bern, Mennonites were sold as galley slaves as late as 1750, and full toleration wasn't granted till 1815. You can see why the hope of freedom to worship according to their beliefs brought many Mennonites to your country."

In spite of her aching heart, Deborah couldn't repress a wry laugh. "No, I guess we don't kill people for their religion. In Kansas and Missouri it depends on whether you're Free State or pro-slave."

Conrad sighed. "It's strange! To us in Europe, America seems so free, a land to grow in and believe what you will. But, indeed, I see the Indians pressed back, made sick and corrupt with whisky and vice, and there is this monstrous custom of slavery, fostered in your young country when it had become unthinkable in the civilized world." He added hopefully, "At least you're facing the evil. It belongs to the old, bad days and can't endure."

"But will it take a war?" cried Deborah. "Will what's happened along this border have to spread through the whole land?"

"Pray that it won't," said Conrad somberly. His gaze touched her like a physical comforting. "But countries survive wars. I'd weary you with telling, even if I could remember them all, the battles that have wasted what we call Prussia. Out of all that's ruined and wasted, some people survive, some seed buried in trampled ground brings forth grain. The martyr's agony buys freedom for those who follow."

"You still haven't told me what Mennonites are."

"The best farmers in the world." He laughed at her incredulous look. "I didn't bring them here only because I had sympathy with their faith. Since they were repeatedly driven from good land to bad, Mennonites have reclaimed boggy land in Holland, Prussia, and Poland, and they established rich farms in drought-plagued regions of the Ukraine, where they were especially invited by Catherine the Great."

That name conjured up the vague impression of a bejeweled, plump despot with an appetite for handsome, strong young guardsmen. "Why ever did *she* want Mennonites?" Deborah asked.

"Not for her personal entertainment," Conrad chuckled. "But she was German-born and knew the Mennonites to be resourceful farmers and the most law-abiding of people so long as their religion wasn't tampered with. After Russia took the Crimea from Turkey, Catherine wanted the region settled. Her envoy, in 1786, offered Prussian Mennonites free transport, one hundred seventy-five acres of land per family, self-government, and their own schools—and, most importantly, exemption from military duty and complete religious freedom so long as they didn't try to convert native Russians."

"I'm surprised there were any left to come with you!"

"Especially when Prussia and the Lutheran Church were determined to check the growth of the Mennonites," he agreed. "They were taxed to support the state church, taxed in lieu of military service, and couldn't buy more land without special permission. More than six thousand went to Russia, where they've mostly prospered."

"Why didn't your colonists?"

"Alexander the Second is the fourth czar since Catherine. He doesn't feel bound by her promises, and it seems unlikely that he'll let the Mennonites retain their special privileges. The czar wishes to unify his country, and especially after losing the Crimean War, he is determined to have a strong military."

"Mennonites won't serve in an army?"

"No. Nor swear an oath. But the main reason they've been hounded and persecuted since their beginnings in Switzerland and Holland over three hundred years ago is that they reject infant baptism and claim that sacrament should be given only to adults who understand its seriousness."

"Were they part of the Reformation?"

"Yes. But when reformers like Calvin and Luther had finally been successful in defying Rome and making their beliefs the official creeds of various Protestant countries, Calvinists and Lutherans joined with Catholics to savagely torture and murder those whose only sin was trying to live according to what they found in scripture."

"Like the slaughter of Jews?"

"Very like."

Deborah thought aloud. "You admire them. You chose

them for neighbors when you left your country. Yet you're not of their faith."

Those deep eyes sought hers, probed. "I don't wish to offend or trouble you, Miss Deborah, but I'm not of any faith."

She gasped. "But you must be! To give up your title, your privileges, come here and be a farmer—"

"I should say that having lost faith in God, I'm compelled to have faith in man."

It was so near her own recent thoughts, without the grief and anger, that she stared at him in disbelief. "I—why do you feel like that, Mr. Lander?"

"I suppose it began when I saw boys teasing an idiot, and it has increased with experience, though so long as 'God's will' didn't press on me, I remained philosophical and called myself Christian. But as I learned that hundreds of thousands of innocents have been burned at the stake, drowned, tortured, or beheaded in the name of a loving Christ, my whole nature rebelled."

He stopped and glanced at her frowningly. "I shouldn't say this. If you're comforted by your religion—"

"But I'm not!" Deborah cried, the relief of being able to say what she thought feeling much like the sudden draining of an infected wound. "That's one of the terrible things! My—my parents, they were so *good*. I can't believe a God fit to worship would have let them die like that if He could help it. So either there's no God, or He doesn't concern himself with what happens, which amounts to about the same thing. I've been brought up to pray, but I can't pray now and it hurts! It—hurts!"

"Of course it does."

The odd note in his voice made her look at him. Again he seemed to be gazing into her heart. "It will hurt for a long time," he went on. "But the pain will become a part of you, a blending into other things so that it won't stab as it does now. So much of our poetry, music, and art comes from trying to assuage loss."

"And a lot of regular work, too," Deborah said, moved to a faint smile. "Yesterday we went through about a week's ordinary chores, but it was better than sitting around crying."

"The same impulse drove Shah Jahan to build the Taj Mahal for his favorite wife." Conrad gave a small chuckle. "I've wondered if that made for peace with his remaining ladies."

Deborah laughed, then choked it off, feeling guilty. Fleetingly, Conrad laid his gloved hand over hers. "The dead, if they know anything of what we do, won't grudge you laughter."

Why was it possible to say things to him that she'd have had trouble putting even to Sara? "Sometimes I forget for a few minutes," she pondered. "Then I feel guilty, as if I'd forsaken them—Mother and Father and Thos. It's as if—as if the life they have is in me, my remembering."

"It is. But wouldn't they rather be remembered for the happy things, for the good times? Surely there were enough of those to outweigh the end."

"It's remembering the happiness that makes the rest so awful!"

"Now, yes. But in time, unless you fight to keep the horror, the good will be far stronger."

"How can you be so sure?"

He shrugged. "I call myself a happy man. Yet twice my life was a burden I could scarcely endure. I adored my older brother. When he was killed in the Revolution, I stayed drunk for weeks, tried to still my pain in any wild way I could think of. But time *does* heal."

He was saying this to help her, so Deborah prompted, "And the second time?"

"My wife." Shocked, Deborah raised her hand to protest that he needn't go on, but he did. "She was delicate; I knew that when I married her. Gradually I had to admit that charming, hesitating little cough was changing into seizures that left her exhausted. She grew so weak that she couldn't put her arms around me when I carried her through the gardens. She died like that, eight years ago, in my arms among the roses."

Tears stung Deborah's eyes. She bowed her head. Conrad went on slowly. "But, you know, what lasts for me is not how ill she was, but how she loved roses. I called her Röslein because of that, and because we loved Heine's poem. Röslein had no thorns for me, except the losing of her."

"She sounds—sweet."

"She was. There's an old folksong I learned in my student days and used to sing for her. Would you like to hear it if I can remember? And English it, more or less?"

If he could sing, Deborah could listen. She nodded. He looked ahead, cleared his throat, and brought up the words, at first like something unwinding slowly from a hidden place, then with a rough male tenderness that penetrated even Deborah's numbness.

"Your garden is so lovely, girl.
Please! May I walk there?
Let me see your roses, girl,
Your blossoms so fair—"

He urged the plucking of those flowers. Fall would be too late. It was so much the cry of all lovers, the way she'd felt about Dane, the way Sara and Thos had been, that Deborah smiled through her tears as Conrad's voice trailed off and she told him through the aching in her throat, "That's beautiful!"

The road from the Kaw to Friedental was a dim pair of ruts, scored deeper by the tracks of Laddie's and Conrad's horses. It followed a small stream, bordered by winter-naked hickorys, oaks, and maples. Conrad called one halt to water the horses and walk around to stretch. He had a cup in his pack and brought Deborah a drink, then drank himself.

"I wish it were wine," he told her, blue eyes as warming on her as the sun. "I've thought of you much, Miss Deborah, since we met at the smithy and again on the Fourth of July." His mouth tugged down in quizzical self-deprecation. "In fact, it was the hope of seeing you, not a desire to join in my adopted country's patriotic fervor, that took us to town that day."

His frankness compelled the same from her. "Sir, I should tell you I consider myself engaged."

Straight ash-colored brows drawing together, he said, "Not to Rolf Hunter?"

"No. His brother."

"Where is this brother?"

"He—went to California." Deborah looked away, mouth trembling. Conrad took her hand, drew back the gauntlet cuff, and kissed the pulse of her wrist. "Oh, my dear," he muttered. "Don't let me trouble you! It's just that, if you were plighted to me, I couldn't leave you."

"Dane could." The bitterness escaped before she knew it.

Eyebrows lifting, Conrad said, "But he'll be back, surely?"

"In the spring, he said. But what good will it do? He'll

still want to take me away. That's why we quarreled before."

"You don't wish to go?"

"I won't."

"Perhaps he'll stay."

Deborah shook her head. "No," she said woefully. "He's too stubborn."

Conrad burst out laughing. "Like you," he said. Sobering, his contemplative, almost speculative gaze reminded her that, in spite of his renunciation of it, he was used to command, an older, wiser, more experienced man even than Dane. "Permit me to wonder how, this dilemma appearing unsolvable, you feel betrothed?"

"Because I love him."

The amused expression left Conrad's face. Turning, he brought the horses, then helped her into the saddle. For a moment, his hands closed on horn and cantle, locking her in. "Love, like grief, wears out," he said, then sprang up on his tall gray horse.

Friedental, a safe distance from the stream, presented a curious, extremely neat pattern. A dozen white frame houses ranged on the north side of the road, facing south. Rows of young cottonwoods and other trees were planted between the houses, on either side of the road, and around a church that looked much like the other houses except for its steeple.

Fields and orchards ran in long broad strips on either side of the road and houses, and one lone dwelling sat back in the orchards. There was a sod stable near each house and two large, lofted barns in what appeared to be a common meadow stretching along the stream.

Pausing at a distance to stare, Deborah exclaimed, "I can't believe such a place is really here! It looks like a giant child's toy village!"

"Wait till you see the dolls!" Conrad laughed. "They're inside for dinner now, but you'll meet them later."

Till she saw the village, it hadn't really occurred to Deborah that other people were involved in whatever risk there might be in sheltering her. She reined in Chica.

"Mr. Lander, did Sara tell you in her letter that Rolf Hunter may look for me, that he could be dangerous?"

"Yes. I beg you not to fear. My colonists are dedicated to peace and non-resistance. I'm not."

"I'm not worried for myself, but if he hired some ruffians—I'd never forgive myself if the village were hurt because of me!"

He closed his hand over hers; she felt warmed even through glove and gauntlet. "Chances are slight that anyone would look for you at Friedental. We're off main-traveled ways and have no visitors. But I wouldn't make a decision like this by myself. While Laddie ate and rested, Elder Goerz called a meeting. The unanimous vote was to welcome you. Though you'll stay with Ansjie and me, you're asked to consider yourself an honored guest of the settlement."

"How kind of them, to run risks for a stranger when they themselves are in a strange land."

"Mennonites have so often been fugitives that they feel sympathy for the hunted."

Deborah's jaw clamped shut. "I'm in my own country! I won't hide forever." Her Bowie was gone, but Johnny had promised to make her another, though he advised her not to carry one at Friedental. "Forget all that for now," he'd said. "Let Conrad take care of you this little while."

"Of course you won't stay in hiding," Conrad now said calmly. "I hope you'll think of this as a visit, not an ordeal, and yourself as a blessing to us, not a problem."

"You're very, very kind."

Gravely, he shook his head. "Very, very lucky."

They splashed across the stream, stopped to let the horses drink, then rode past the church and a row of shuttered houses, angling back past the fields to the house in the young orchards. "Since we're not of their religion," he explained, "Ansjie and I thought it best to live a little apart." His teeth flashed. "Also, to be honest, I can do without so much proximity. The trees are young now, but in time they'll make an effective curtain, and I suspect everyone will be pleased when thick green leaves give privacy without the affront of a wall."

"But in winter the trees are bare."

His eyes touched her. "In winter one has the patience of hope and waits for spring."

As they rode up to the stable, where doves cooed about the thatch, a young woman Deborah recognized as his sister hurried from the house, hands outstretched to take Deborah's as Conrad helped her from the saddle.

"Wilkommen!" she greeted, then chided herself. "No, I must my English practice! Welcome, Miss Whitlaw! Come

inside and warm yourself. Hurry, Conrad! I've been keeping dinner warm and I'm hungry!"

"Hungry or sated, it takes the same time to care for horses," said Conrad, taking Chica's reins. "Besides, if I know you, you've been nibbling! Isn't that a *strudel* crumb on your cheek?"

Lifting a guilty hand, Ansjie found nothing and blushed. "*Taugenicht!*" she bubbled. "Good for nothing! For such a tongue, there may be no crumbs left!" She slipped her arm through Deborah's and drew her up the path through trees which, though leafless, were warmly tinged with sun, and neatly trimmed hedges bordering garden plots, raked and awaiting spring.

In a sort of back porch or anteroom, crocks and food stood on shelves and a trapdoor closed off what must be a cellar. Most of the porch was filled with brush, apparently trimmed from the hedges, corn stalks and corncobs, weeds, cow chips, and tightly twisted bundles of long prairie hay. Though the Friedentalers had used wood for their homes, they weren't wasting it as fuel.

Near the inner door was a long, low shelf holding boots and house shoes. Above these were pegs holding coats and cloaks, hats and gloves. "Please?" Ansjie selected a pair of crimson felt slippers. "These will fit you, I believe, and so the floor stays *schön.*" At Deborah's puzzled look, she put her fingers to her rosy lips. "Nice, I should be saying! Beautiful is too much for floors, *nein?*"

"But yours *is* beautiful!" Deborah exclaimed as Ansjie opened the door.

The floor was made of seasoned hardwood, not warped, splintering cottonwood shrunk to leave large cracks—and, of course, on the frontier, anything better than a dirt floor was a luxury. Polished to a sheen, the floor actually reflected the big brick stove, which was almost as long as the women were tall and stood six feet high. It was built in the wall, the cooking surface and oven reaching into the big kitchen, which ran the width of the house.

Carpet stretched beneath a polished table and chairs beside a curtained window. Shelves gleamed with copper and pewter, enamel and blown glass, while a handsome cabinet, carved with leaves and flowers, held crystal and porcelain that reminded Deborah for a heart-stopping moment of Mother's fine china, smashed in the cabin's smoldering ruins. The scoured long table beneath the shelves was fitted with ingenious holders for knives, rolling pin, sieves, and other utensils, and beneath were bins and drawers.

"Praktisch!" declared Ansjie, opening a bin to show flour. "Peter Voth, the carpenter, made it, and the shelves, too."

She gestured at the other side of the room, where two cushioned chairs were positioned to catch warmth from the stove and light from the window. A table held a three-branched candlestick, and there was a large single taper on a graceful writing desk by the window. Again, Deborah's heart skipped in half-painful, half-grateful recognition. Bookshelves filled the walls of the sitting room portion, more books than she had seen anywhere except in libraries. There was a globe on a reading table, another candle, and several opened books.

Following Deborah's feasting glance, Ansjie sighed. "Books we bring here, hundreds! But aways Conrad scolds me not to bring too much—too much clothes, dishes, furniture, bedding! These we can do without, but not his Bücher!"

He laughed from the door. "So abused, because I won't let you transport paintings and gimcracks and elegances that would crowd us into the stable! Besides, Ansjie, I think I'm not wrong in saying you've read most of these books."

"Because you won't talk to me when you thrust your nose in the pages!" his sister retorted. "Wash now—you first, Miss Whitlaw—and I'll see if the goose can still be eaten!"

Deborah washed with castile soap at the stand near the stove and dried her hands on a spotless towel while Conrad went through a doorway on the other side of the oven. He had her pack, which contained the sketch pad, one of the dresses she'd given Judith and which Judith had given back, and Sara's contribution of drawers and chemise.

Not including what she stood in, it was all she had, except for the farm—the farm, with its wrecked house and stable, which she didn't even want to think about right now. But she shrank from charity.

"I hope there'll be something I can do here to pay for my keep."

Ansjie handed her a bowl of steaming dumplings, herself hoisting a platter holding a braised fowl anchored by golden roast potatoes.

"Keep?" She snorted daintly. "Do you speak of yourself like a horse or oxen? Of course there is work and you may

help, but Conrad and I are glad to have your company." She set down the goose and her frown changed to a smile. "Please," she coaxed, "no more foolish words. Conrad will think it's my fault—"

"For what now?" he demanded, striding across the room and laughing as he dropped a kiss on her forehead.

"She's one of your independent women." Ansjie wrinkled her uptilted, somewhat freckled nose. "She wishes to measure her food according to the socks she mends or butter she churns!"

Conrad watched Deborah while Ansjie plunked down side dishes of red cabbage and gravy, then put out a loaf of brown bread. Butter and several kinds of preserves and pickles were already on the table, which was laid with fine china and silver.

Drawing back one of the chairs, he seated Deborah, and then his sister, filled crystal goblets from a decanter of red wine. Deborah had never seen wine served at a meal. It seemed rather wicked, decadently European, and wholly desirable, sparkling with tiny bubbles.

She swallowed her demur along with her first taste of wine, sipped again, cautiously, and decided she might come to like it in time, though it was the appearance and idea that she enjoyed most.

Was Conrad looking slightly amused? Unfolding his linen napkin, he began to carve the goose and pass the plates while Ansjie added generous helpings of the other things. "There's a way you could earn not only your board, but a salary, if you'll accept it."

"Conrad!" remonstrated Ansjie, eyes going wide.

"It's true," he said stoutly. "You know better than anyone, sister mine, how I've labored with this writing! Now here is a lady with English for her native tongue, one accustomed to reading articles and editorials for a newspaper. What could be more providential?"

"Oh." Ansjie relaxed and shrugged. "That!"

"*That* happens to be an important goal of mine," he said good-humoredly. To Deborah, he explained, "An English publisher would like an account of emigrant life on the prairie, and though they could get a translation done, it's a point of pride with me to write it myself with the proper words."

"Your English is very good, and Miss Lander's, too."

"Please call me Ansjie," the young woman implored.

"If you'll call me Deborah."

"May I do that, also, and be Conrad?" he asked.

Having reached the ease of first names, Conrad said that he'd had an English tutor. His father, the count, had much admiration for England, and though Conrad was also required to learn French and some Italian, he and his brothers were expected to use English at every other family meal.

"It was one of Father's amusements. At the start of the meal, he would say, 'We are English,' or, *'Nous sommes français,'* or, *'Siamo italiani'*. Or sometimes he assigned us positions or identities. One of us would be Augustine, another Pelagius, and a third a judge hearing us argue original sin."

"But *you* can't believe in original sin!"

He laughed. "No, but historically, alas, Augustine's unhappy theory has dogged Western civilization to reach its noxious flowering in Calvin."

Deborah nodded. "I've never understood why people should worship a God who was supposed to have condemned practically all of them to eternal fire before they were even born."

"Meanwhile," interpolated Ansjie, "the goose gets cold!"

"It's delicious!" said Deborah. And she disposed of a respectable amount of food before observing, "Your father had unusual ideas, surely. What did your mother think of them?"

"She died at the birth of my younger brother, who is now count. Father took my decision to come here quite philosophically. I think he would've come himself had he lived. Even at seventy-nine he was still avid for new experiences, and, besides, he was very fond of Ansjie. I think she was his favorite child."

"I was a daughter," Ansjie said. "Besides," she added with tolerant affection, "since I was not a *Gräfin*'s child, the *Graf* didn't trouble himself about equipping me for a place in society. He just, praise the good God, let me grow!"

Did that mean . . . ?

Sensing Deborah's confusion, Ansjie said matter-of-factly, "Noblemen have always taken pretty women, but the *Graf* was different. He loved my mother and put her in charge of his household, was faithful to her, and brought me up as a daughter."

"She tended him lovingly in his last years," Conrad said. "But though my brother made it clear that she was welcome to live on in the castle, she preferred to take a house in the village. Last year she married the chief forester and, from all accounts, is happy."

That explained several puzzling things. Though Conrad and Ansjie resembled each other, his features were etched, almost ascetic, while hers were rounded. She exuded an earthy robustness and pride in her home and cooking.

"When Conrad said he would come here," said Ansjie with a fondly indulgent glance at her brother, "Mutti said I must look after him. Besides, there was no one I wished to marry."

Conrad smiled but Deborah guessed that he was worried about the future of this sister, born between classes, fitting neither. "Since it seems you'll never return the longing of Elder Goerz's son or accept Peter Voth since he became a widower, we'll have to put you in the way of meeting some eligibles."

"The Territory's full of bachelors," Deborah said.

"But Friedental isn't." Conrad smiled teasingly. "We have a carpenter and shoemaker, but we need a blacksmith, and it would be good to have a doctor. Which, *kleines,* shall I recruit first?"

"Whichever is strongest, nicest, and best-looking," said Ansjie promptly. "He must be honest, no *dummkopf,* and no drunkard. Also, he must enjoy his food and be sure that there is always plenty." She considered. "These things are more important than his looks, but he must be strong!"

"I'll remember," said Conrad. "No, I simply cannot eat another morsel! If I don't want to become gross, I must find that hungry brother-in-law swiftly!"

"There's *strudel,*" Ansjie said coaxingly. "*Apfel strudel,* Conrad, tender and crunchy, with rich, thick cream."

"Sometimes," he groaned, "I think you're fattening me up like the witch in Hansel and Gretel. A very small piece, then, and after she rests, perhaps we could take Deborah around Friedental."

The *strudel* was the flakiest pastry Deborah had ever eaten. As she helped Ansjie with the dishes, Ansjie explained that the unusual flavoring of the goose was due to being rubbed with caraway seeds, and the red cabbage was cooked with onions, fat, and caraway. When the last pan was stowed away, Ansjie took Deborah into a large bedroom.

Several feet of the brick oven warmed this room, too. Ansjie said that Conrad, knowing there would be a scarcity of wood, had studied the problem and learned of the hay-burning stoves used in Russia. The brick structures were rather expensive, but only needed firing morning and night and heated several rooms, served for cooking, and also the wide chimney was used for smoking meat.

Ansjie's pretty canopied bed was a fluffy mass of blue featherbeds, but the plain bed set up on the other side of a dresser was heaped equally high and looked wonderfully inviting. There was a large carved chest under the window and an armoire which Ansjie opened to reveal many pretty gowns, shoes, hats, and a cleared space.

"We're of a height," Ansjie said. "We must find a few dresses you like and change them to fit." She brushed aside Deborah's objections. "*Please* help me wear them out! Then I can tell Conrad I need some new clothes. He's not stingy, but he's a *man* and understands nothing of such things. I feel wasteful to ask for something different when these are still good, but a woman needs something special now and then, *nicht wahr?*"

Deborah had to smile at the appeal. "If you put it that way, I'll be glad to help you justify a few new dresses."

Ansjie gave her a quick hug. "I'm so glad you've come! It'll be like having a sister! I wanted to come with Conrad, but I didn't realize how homesick I'd get sometimes."

"Are there no young women in the village?"

"All my age are married. Besides, in spite of equal votes on public matters, the people still think of Conrad as the *Graf* and me as his sinfully born sister." Her lower lip jutted petulantly before she giggled. "It's a good thing I don't fancy any of the young men! Their families wouldn't want them to marry out of the faith, and I could never be a Mennonite. I like pretty clothes and jewelry too much!"

Deborah forebore to say that lack of these wasn't confined to those who eschewed them for piety's sake. As Ansjie went out, wishing her a good rest, she was more than ready to slip off her dress and shoes and get into bed, the sketch pad tucked beneath the bottom feather mattress.

Enveloped in down below and above, she thought she'd never felt anything so luxurious. She meant to stay there just a little while, relaxing after the long ride, but comfort, the content and happiness that radiated through the house like Ansjie's distant singing, sent her deeper and deeper, like snuggling into a nest.

She awoke to Ansjie's touch and smiling eyes. "If you

don't rouse now, you might not sleep tonight," she said. "And there are only a few hours of light left. Do you feel like walking?"

Deborah nodded, swinging her legs off the high bed to a padded stool. She dressed quickly, but before they started on their outing Ansjie showed her the toilet, a white frame building behind the stable. It was whitewashed inside, there was even a curtained window, and Deborah laughed at the thought of, for instance, Johnny's probable reaction to such elegance, though she was careful not to betray her mirth to her hostess. As Johnny had predicted, this was indeed a world apart!

• XVI •

Though the Landers had their own well because of their distance from the settlement, the other families relied on a well located near the church beneath several large cottonwoods. This was a place for the children to play while their mothers visited, and here Deborah met the wife of Elder Goerz, a dour woman who regarded Ansjie with suspicion and seemed to feel that Deborah, too, was a sort to bear watching.

"She thinks everyone's after that hulking son of hers," Ansjie whispered as they exchanged polite farewells and moved toward the church. "I hope he finds someone to marry *quick* so she'll stop watching me with eyes like boiled eggs!"

"Your other suitor, Peter Voth, doesn't have a mother," Conrad teased.

"And he's old enough to be my father," Ansjie retorted.

"I'll just have to find Friedental a blacksmith or a doctor," he said with a mock sigh, opening the door to reveal a high pulpit in the front center with a high bench on either side.

"The benches are for deacons," Ansjie said somewhat

airily. "More bench than deacons, but, of course, the village will grow. In the three years since we came, there've been eighteen children born." She pointed out the rail where the *Vorsingers,* or hymn leaders, stood, and Conrad added that the building was also used as a meeting house and that he taught classes here.

"Elder Goerz schools the young ones in Bible and church history," he explained. "Ansjie teaches penmanship, and I do the best I can with English, arithmetic, geography, and what little I've learned about the United States."

"Perhaps I could help with that," Deborah offered. "I'm no scholar, but Father—" Her voice faltered; for a little while, she'd *forgotten,* really forgotten, except for a shadow at the back of her mind. "Father talked a lot about our history and what caused things that're happening now."

"Good." Conrad's voice was warmly pleased. "I must discuss it with the council; I'm sure they'll be glad. Before we left Prussia, it was agreed that though they wished to practice their religion and retain the use of German, they should try to be good Americans, too, and encourage their children to learn English. As the Territory fills up, Friedental will have closer neighbors and must prepare for that."

Next they visited the communal barns, where the village herd was milked. The lofts were filled with hay and there was a partitioned room for separating the milk and letting the cream rise. Each family got as much milk as it needed, and part of the village business was seeing to a fair distribution of dairy-connected chores from haying to churning. Conrad and a committee had searched Missouri and Arkansas for good cows and bought the best they could locate, mostly fawn-colored Jerseys.

"As the herd increases, we'll keep the best and sell or butcher the others," Conrad said. "As new towns spring up, we can sell the extra cheese and butter we should have by then."

They left the barn as the cows were coming in to be milked. Conrad introduced Deborah to the bearded men who apparently were that night's milkers. The youngest, crimsoning, choked a greeting to Ansjie, who tossed her head and answered grudgingly.

"Poor Dietrich," Conrad said when they were out of earshot. "You're hard on him, Ansjie."

"Not as hard as his mother would be if I let him get any foolish notions," she retorted. "Have I reproached you because every girl over fifteen finds excuses to come to our house or drop by school when you're teaching?"

She stalked down the lane ahead of them for a few minutes, but she slowed as Deborah admired the pigs. These were very clean, pink skin showing through coarse white or spotted hair. Their sod sties were neatly thatched and a hedge formed a large enclosure for them with a small stream from the creak running through it.

"Pigs are tidy," Ansjie said. "People make them dirty by putting them in little pens where all becomes muck." She gazed pridefully at the animals that had trotted over, squealing. "These get lots of skim milk and all the scraps of the village. In the fall, enough are butchered for everyone and the meat is divided up. We eat well at Friedental."

"Don't coyotes ever get piglets or chickens and geese?" asked Deborah, for every house had a chicken coop and hedged pen.

"The men take turns patrolling on summer nights, and in winter all the creatures are shut up before dark. We loose a few geese and chickens; not many."

They walked back through the orchards, Conrad pointing out apples, cherries, peaches, pears, apricots, and plums. He touched the reddish bark of one young cherry tree. "I hope they will bear fruit this year." His eyes met Deborah's through the bare, dead-seeming branches. "But one must have patience. The leaves will be beautiful."

Ansjie sniffed. "One can't eat leaves."

He was still watching Deborah. "No. But one can see them and be glad."

"Not unless the stomach is filled with something else! Which reminds me that it's time for *Abendbrot!* As soon as the chickens and geese have theirs!"

Supper was delicious smoked sausage, rye bread and butter, cheese-thickened cauliflower soup, and tea flavored with spice. Conrad worked at accounts till the women had done the dishes, then moved his desk chair over by the cushioned ones near the stove. Ansjie lit the three tall candles and settled in the chair beside a knitting basket.

"Won't you sit with us?" Conrad invited, indicating what was obviously his accustomed place. "We read and talk in the evenings."

"*You* read and talk," said Ansjie. "*I* knit or mend."

"I'd enjoy listening," Deborah said. "But I'd like to have

my hands busy. Is there something I could knit or mend, Ansjie?"

"Socks!" exclaimed Ansjie. "There are always needed socks! Several of the women have so much to do that they can't keep their children's feet covered, and so the rest of us help. We also knit for Peter Voth, who's a widower."

"But doing his best, poor fellow, to win a bride," put in Conrad roguishly.

Disdaining to answer, Ansjie produced a pair of bone needles and a ball of gray wool yarn. "You could do socks that would fit you for the middle children of Lorenz Schroeder, the shoemaker," she suggested.

Deborah set to work. Conrad opened the book. "This is one of your poets," he said. "I like him very much. Walt Whitman—"

The needles dropped from Deborah's fingers. "Oh, no! We—my family read, too. We were reading *Leaves of Grass* just the night before—"

Ansjie came and held her, stroking her hair. "There, there, *mein kind!*" she soothed. "Maybe it's better we don't read for a while, Conrad. You could sing instead or play your violin."

"Whatever Deborah wishes," he nodded.

Using the handkerchief Ansjie offered, Deborah managed a shaky smile. "I'm glad you read. It does make me remember, but it's a good memory. Only I—I can't hear Whitman yet."

Conrad rose and went over to his desk. "I've been Englishing some of Friedrich Rückert, my favorite modern poet. I haven't tried for rhyme, but to my mind he says some things better than anyone else has. Shall I read from him?"

"He's sad," objected Ansjie.

"I don't mind sad," assured Deborah. "Just not Whitman."

Conrad brought back a slender leather-bound book. Slipping out a loose page, he read in a conversational tone, as if speaking to the subject of the poem:

"I have told all the bushes,
And mourned to all the trees,
And every greening plant,
And every brilliant bloom.

And still I mourn afresh,
And always anew I cry it,
And always have you meanwhile
My grief forgotten.

You are forgotten in this place
By flower and plant, bush and tree,
Only not from my heart, child,
My pain and my delight."

Just so, thought Deborah. *Just so does one cry out to earth and sky and all in between, but they move on their round. The human heart aches without an echo, except from other mortals, yet they are so often the source of grief.*

Conrad read other translations then, including Rückert's paraphrase of a mystic Persian Sufi named Rumi who had written of God in the passionate way of a lover.

The last poem was again spoken to a lost loved one, gone to earth, sun, wind, and water, joining the spirit of each, manifested in flowers, sunlight, breath, and rushing torrents, but living also in the bereaved heart, celebrated by love.

Though Deborah's heart stirred painfully, there was relief in hearing the poet's words, listening to what she felt spoken by Conrad's deeply masculine but gentle voice.

"The poems are beautiful," she said, in spite of the swelling pulse that blocked her throat.

"Rückert's are. My renderings are clumsy, but I did them after Röslein. I wrote them out quickly, also, in French and Italian, anything to busy the mind."

He understood. He was telling her, too, that she'd survive. Ansjie made a clucking sound. "That's enough sadness! Play something happy on your violin!"

Deborah nodded eagerly as he glanced her a question. Getting down a case from a shelf on the warmed central wall, he took out an instrument of gleaming, mellow wood, tuned it carefully, then set it under his chin.

He drew from the strings gay, lilting, laughing tunes, trills that made the foot tap, and then, pulling a face at Ansjie, he made weird sounds like an owl hooting, punctuated with the calls of many birds.

"You played that for me when I was little!" Ansjie laughed, clapping her hands.

"Alle Vögel sind shon da,
Alle Vögel, alle!"

"All the birds are back again,
All the birds, all!"

He made the strings squeal like a pig, squeak like a mouse, give a howl like a dog's, tricks with which, judging from his sister's laughter, he'd beguiled her when she was a child. Then he drifted into sweet music, tender and dreaming.

Ansjie sang softly in German, then, as he played the last tune again, changed the words to English.

"Sleep, my child, sleep.
In heaven move the sheep.
Little stars are like little lambs,
The moon's a little shepherd boy.
Sleep, my child, sleep."

"And it's time we did." Conrad made a last sweep of the bow, smiling at Deborah. "Have a good night. We're glad to have you here."

"Indeed, we are," said Ansjie.

She rose on tiptoes to give her brother a kiss. He returned it, then inclined his silver-blond head to Deborah, who impulsively put out her hand. "You've been so kind! I can't thank you!"

"You do by being here," he said, calm blue eyes darker by candlelight. As blood mounted to her face, he put away the violin and then made ready to fire up the stove.

That was the first night she slept well and soundly since her parents' death, though she awoke early with the now familiar sense of loss flooding her consciousness before she remembered why, or even who she was. But after the memory, a welling up of sorrow, she remembered where she was.

The comforting warmth and softness of lavender-scented down bedding was so airy light that it felt the way clouds look. She savored this a moment, then swung her legs down, encountering first the padded stool, then the sheepskin rug.

In the dim light, Ansjie appeared to still inhabit the fluffy mound atop her bed. Quietly, Deborah carried her clothes to a bench near the stove bricks and dressed in rare luxury, not having to race to get her clothes on before her fingers went too numb to manage buttons.

There was no sound from the other room, so she took some time combing her hair, working out snarls she'd been too rushed to worry about.

Carefully opening and closing the door, she was startled to be greeted by the aroma of coffee. Conrad was already at work. As he rose from his desk, the candlelight emphasized the angles of his face, turning it gaunt, though his smile softened that impression.

"You're up early."

"So are you," she countered. "Or didn't you go to bed?"

"I did. And dreamed."

Silence hung between them while she tried desperately to think of something light to say. It was he who broke the awkwardness, moving to the stove, getting two cups from the shelf. "Will you have coffee?"

"Please."

He poured out the steaming brew, creamed and sugared it, then put it in her hands. "Will you come to school today?" he asked. "Or would you like a while to settle?"

"With no more than I had, that didn't take long! I'd like to hear you teach and get an idea of the children before I start a class, though."

"Do it in whatever way is comfortable." He followed her gaze to the pen and paper on the desk and gave a diffident laugh. "That's my story of this settlement, full of blots and scribbled additions. I must copy it over before I ask you to look at it."

Deborah laughed. "If you could see the rough draft of Father's editorials!" Of which no more, now, would be written. But the pang faded into the warmth of remembering.

Conrad said, "That glow will come without pain after a time. Instead of aching loss, you'll have an awareness in your spirit of those you loved. It can be a blessing, not grief."

"Can it?" The cry was wrung from her. "That might be so if it weren't for the *way* they died! How can I make peace with that?"

He ached with her. From the look in his eyes, Deborah knew that, and it helped. But, just then, he didn't answer her in words. Stepping out on the closed porch, he came back with a knee-length dark green cape with a hood, helped her into it, and put on his own gray cloak.

"I want to show you something."

Leading her out into the dawning, after they changed into outdoor shoes on the porch, he brought her to stand among the leafless trees on the frost-covered ground, kept his arm around her outside the cape as streaks of red widened in the east, gripped the dull sky and thrust higher, casting rosy brightness on the sparkling frost, flushing the naked winter branches.

Deborah caught her breath, thrilling. In spite of herself, the familiar words sounded in her mind. *"The heavens declare the glory of God and the firmament sheweth His handiwork."*

"Beautiful!" she whispered.

"Yes. The eternal enduring best answer to pain, to horror. Why is it? What causes it? The sky is there, whatever the sins beneath it, the sun and moon, the mountains and earth, this vast prairie. When spring comes, these bare limbs will burst into flower, then fruit. Why? Who can know it?"

"It's another question, not an answer."

"A question is an answer that makes you find your own." Turning, he kept his hand beneath her arm as they walked back to the house, feet crunching on the frozen earth crust. "But there are more human answers, too, my Deborah. Moments of joy—and you will have them again. Love in its many forms. Kindness. Faith and hope. These are as real as sickness, cruelty, hate, and despair."

"Yes, but—"

"A man named Jacob Boehme, from whom I'll read to you some evening, put it this way: 'Man is a hinge between light and darkness; to whichever it gives itself up, in that same does it burn.' "

Inside the porch, he helped her off with the cape. "This shepherd's cloak is for you," he said, unfastening the horn buttons. "It's made from long fleece, is very warm, and turns rain. Ansjie has another she prefers."

"Oh, I can't—"

"You can." He chuckled. "You'll find it very easy when you get used to being snug."

They changed into house shoes and entered the warm kitchen.

"Why don't we surprise Ansjie and fix breakfast?" Deborah asked. "I can cook if you'll show me where things are."

"Sausage, ham, or bacon?" he asked. "Things like that

are stored on the porch. So are eggs and milk, unless it gets cold enough to freeze them."

They decided on eggs scrambled with sausage. Deborah cooked these while Conrad cooked millet, a white grain she hadn't seen before, flavoring it with dried plums and currants, and he set the table, a task he was obviously used to.

Ansjie emerged, sniffing rapturously. "I thought I was dreaming! Getting up early to make breakfast is one thing I can't like, though Conrad helps much by having coffee ready."

"Then let me do it," suggested Deborah. "I'd like to help wherever you most prefer."

Ansjie sank into her chair, hungrily eyeing the golden eggs and crisp bits of sausage. "You've found my weakness! I like running my own house, it's much cosier, but I do like to wake up and find breakfast."

"Gnädige Fräulein, here's your coffee," said Conrad, louting low, and they began their meal with merriment.

That first day set a pattern for most that followed. After household tasks were done, the three went to the church and worked with different ages of children after Elder Goerz had drilled them on Bible and church history. Since Deborah had no German, either Ansjie or Conrad helped with her class, translating words the children wouldn't know and helping to answer their questions.

The twenty-five children ranged from five or six to fourteen or fifteen. Mennonites felt everyone needed enough education to handle business affairs, read the Bible, and appreciate their religious heritage. Beyond that, learning was suspect, a temptation to frivolity and vanity. But when she met the villagers around the well or school, they all, even gruff Elder Goerz and his sour wife, thanked Deborah in halting English for teaching the children about their new country.

"Perhaps it goes better here," said Lorenz Schroeder, a thin man with hair like wisps of old rope, stooped from working at his last. "No state church supported by taxes. Many churches, none strong enough to use the government. It may be we will at last be left in peace. It is good our children learn the story of this land."

"I must tell them about slavery. I must tell them how the Indians have been driven farther west."

Schroeder nodded. His watery green eyes were sad and

hopeful at once. "Yes, they must know that. But to us it is a very large thing, that religion and government do not join to rule." He smiled shyly. "Believe in your country, *Fräulein*. Before we voted to come here, the *Graf*—no, he is Herr Lander now—read to us your Bill of Rights and your Constitution. A country with written law like that must try to fulfill it."

Touched and shamed by his simplicity, Deborah returned to her teaching with a new perspective, trying to imagine what it would be like to live where the church preached obedience to the government, however corrupt, and the government reinforced the church, where common people had little to say about their laws, judges, or governing bodies.

Viewed like that, the problem in Kansas was one of too much freedom, not enough law and control. At least the Border Ruffians and, on the other side, Lane and Montgomery and John Brown's men, weren't raiding for the government, with its approval. Law would come to the frontier, and surely, someday, so would justice and peace.

Because these children would be growing up while the slavery question was decided, Deborah took special pains to explain to them the Missouri Compromise and the effects of its repeal, the importance of Kansas as a battleground between Free Soil and pro-slave forces. But she couldn't resist slipping in at least one story of which pacifist parents wouldn't have approved: Jim Bowie at the Alamo with Travis and Crockett.

Blue eyes fixed on her breathlessly as she told how the men of Gonzalez marched into the Alamo, coming to certain death; how none of the men left, though Travis would have let them; and how Mexican bugles played the *Degüello,* or "Throat-cutting," an old call from Spain, which meant no quarter.

"The knife, Miss?" queried the biggest Goerz boy in a voice that was just starting to crack. "Bowie's knife?"

"It was burned with him, Hansi." At first, apart from size and sex, the children had looked disconcertingly alike, watching her with intent variations of blue, gray, and hazel eyes peering from beneath yellow or flaxen thatches or tightly pulled-back braids. After a few days, though, she'd begun to sort them out, and by the end of the week, she knew the names of all twenty-five. "I hope," she added, smiling at the gangling boy whose older brother was enamored of Ansjie, "that someday you meet Mr. Chaudoin.

He learned blacksmithing from the man who made Jim Bowie's knife."

Hansi's eyes grew wider. "Truly, Miss?"

"Truly true," she answered, then went on to explain how Texas remained a republic for almost ten years before joining the United States.

"Kansas is not a—a republic?" asked Cobie Balzer, a wiry, tanned girl whose mother was always calling her in from playing with the boys.

That led to a discussion of the differences between states and territories, which took up the rest of the class. Then, between Conrad and Ansjie, Deborah walked home and helped get dinner ready.

The Landers' laundry was done by the village women as a thank-you for their teaching, so there was no really tiring work. Deborah helped with the baking, cooking, and cleaning, plus gathering the eggs and feeding the chickens.

During the first week, at Ansjie's insistence, they altered to fit Deborah a dark green cashmere and a rust-brown poplin which, ironically, made her better dressed than she'd been since childhood.

Usually the three of them took a walk in the afternoon, and several times Conrad took Deborah riding, a thing Ansjie did not enjoy since she was afraid of horses.

Beginning in February, they caught glimpses of prairie chicken males displaying themselves on a booming ground north of the village. Through fall and winter the flocks had moved together, but now the sexes separated while the males vied for the interest of the hens by finding a spot on the booming ground, probably used for centuries, striking the ground, blowing out the bright orange air sacs on the sides of their throats, raising orange eyebrows, erecting neck crests, and spreading out tails like fans. They then boomed—a strange, hollow vibrating sound like blowing across an open bottle.

Sometimes cocks battled much like barnyard roosters, but seldom tore more than feathers.

"They're so much showier than the females," Deborah complained. "It doesn't seem fair."

"Why not?" Conrad laughed. "The poor males have to go through all this to attract females—who don't have to do anything but choose!" She had no answer to that, and they rode on.

When the weather was bad or there was no housework,

Deborah read Conrad's account of Friedental and found it fascinating.

"I'm sure the publisher will want it," she told him. "You really don't need my advice, though there are a few places where I can smooth out the language."

"What you suggest makes it much better," he assured her. His eyes twinkled. "Besides, I want you to read it."

"I'd want to do that, anyway," she laughed.

After the evening meal and dishes, he usually read aloud, pausing for discussion, but sometimes he played the violin and sometimes he sang, turning the words to English.

"Oh, when will you come back again, dear
love of mine?
When it snows red roses, girl, and when
it rains white wine."

But what he sang most was the one he'd sung on the way to Friedental the day that seemed so long ago, but which was only a few weeks past.

"Oh, child, fair maiden, so lonely, forlorn,
Who taught your sad heart to treat me with scorn?
Who says that I may not your sweet roses see,
And pluck them to pleasure your dear self and me?"

Deborah felt an inner melting as his voice, so tenderly, deeply male, caressed her. She dared not look at him, knowing that his eyes would catch and hold hers. It would be easy to accept his courtship, easy to be loved and protected. She was safer, happier in this house than she would have believed possible the day she rode here with Conrad almost six weeks ago.

Though vitally masculine and handsome, he was kind, wise, and patient. Having loved and lost those loves, he understood how she felt; he couldn't demand her whole heart at once. At such moments it was hard not to lift her eyes to him, give silent assent, but she resisted the urgency till it quieted.

It wouldn't be fair to take what he offered for what, just now, she could give. Foolish or not, she still loved Dane, longed for his arms and hard, sweet mouth.

Though he'd been far away when she needed him most, she still wore his medallion of Saint Rita, that saint who interceded for hopeless causes, and his sketch pad was the only thing she'd saved from the wreck of her home, except the Bible, which was buried with her parents. One night when Conrad's singing had shaken her, she rose quickly, asking if he and Ansjie wouldn't like to see the sketches Dane had made along the Santa Fe Trail.

Ansjie responded eagerly. Conrad's straight mouth quirked down; he knew what Deborah was doing. "By all means," he said gravely. "It'll be a privilege to meet, through his work, the man who has such a hold on you." The twinkle was unmistakable. "Perhaps I can learn something."

Blushing, she fled to the bedroom. That was the disconcerting thing about Conrad, what made her feel so young and, in a way, pitted in a struggle he'd win because he knew how to wait.

If Dane had possessed some of that humor and tolerance — She sighed, picking up the pad, holding it to her breasts. He wouldn't have been Dane, then. Besides, Conrad was thirty-five, as much older than Dane as Dane was than Rolf.

Rolf. Her thoughts veered away, as always, like a hand touching white-hot iron, but this time the nagging question persisted. Where was he? Had he carried out his terrible promise—killed the men who'd murdered her family? What had he done when he came back to find her gone?

If he lived, he should be back by now. He'd surely look for her at Johnny's. No news from the outside world had reached Friedental. At first that insulation had been welcome, but she needed to be sure that her friends at the smithy hadn't been bothered on her account.

And if Rolf presented no threat, it might be best if she left this comfortable refuge. It wasn't fair to accept Conrad's cherishing when she didn't return his love.

Taking the sketch pad into the other room, she put it on the table between brother and sister and watched as Ansjie turned the pages, exclaiming here and there.

Buffalo, horses, birds, plants, Indians, Bent's abandoned fort, Santa Fe. A journey portrayed in deft, decisive strokes, each one intended, achieving that aim.

"What a talent!" Ansjie said as they looked at the last sketch, the cathedral. "And he paints, also?"

Deborah nodded, glad of a chance to speak of Dane, though she didn't want to overdo it in front of Conrad. "I haven't seen his painting, but it must be good. He traded portraits to Fall Leaf for Chica."

"Practical, as well as artistic," Conrad observed. He turned back to the picture of the Cheyenne girl, the mantilla-graced lady of Santa Fe, then glanced up at Deborah. He spoke softly, in a tone between gladness and regret. "This man loves you. When he draws a woman, the face is yours."

The next day at breakfast, Deborah said that perhaps it was time she returned to the smithy, and that she was anxious to know how her friends were.

"Oh!" pleaded Ansjie, looking quite stricken. "Stay till summer, at least!" She appealed to her brother: "You won't let her go, will you? We should miss her sorely!"

He smiled. "I'm not a robber baron who holds fair maids to ransom, tempted though I may be. I'll hope that a visit to the smithy will reassure Deborah about her friends, and that Johnny Chaudoin can help convince her that she'd better stay a few more months with us."

"You needn't take me," Deborah protested. "I can't lose the road."

"Unless there's a blizzard." He gave a short laugh and looked at her in a way that made her glance away. "Do you think I'd let you ride that distance alone?"

"But—"

"No but's," he said sternly. "If the weather's good, we'll go tomorrow."

"Tomorrow?" Ansjie wailed.

He said serenely, helping himself to more preserves, "The sooner we go, the sooner we'll be back." He didn't think it necessary to accent the *we'll*.

As if summoned by her thoughts, Johnny rode in late that afternoon, but even if he'd arrived during school hours, he was in no mood to tell big-eyed youngsters about Bowie and his legendary knife.

As soon as he'd greeted Conrad and Ansjie, he'd squinted closely at Deborah, making her feel like a heifer or filly being examined for sale, and told her that Rolf had indeed come hunting her, and though he might not have believed Johnny or the others, he had to accept the word of two travelers—people who'd had to stay four days at the smithy while Johnny fixed their broken wagon—that no such young woman had been there.

"So he went back swearing to wring that Melissa Eden's neck if she connived at letting you out after he'd paid her a small fortune to guard you." Johnny shrugged. "Ought to teach her to be more careful of her boarders, providin' he don't take her hair like he did those Missourians'."

"Hair?" echoed Deborah.

"Scalps."

Ansjie gave a shriek and covered her mouth. Several times, with fascinated horror, she'd asked Deborah about this custom, which seemed to be widely publicized in Europe. Deborah felt a sickness rising in her stomach.

"Did he—do that?"

Johnny nodded. "He hired a half-breed Shawnee who knows the country around Westport. Between them, they brought back eleven scalps. Don't look like that, gal! Them devils had it coming."

So. Her family was avenged. Blood covered the blood of her twin, her mother, and her father.

"It doesn't help," she said in a kind of dull wonder. "It doesn't help at all."

Johnny shifted from one moccasined foot to the other. "Won't bring back your folks, honey. 'Course not. But *that* bunch won't cross the border to kill more people in their own stableyard."

"This Rolf," said Conrad. "You don't know where he is?"

"It was about two weeks ago he came foggin' to the smithy." Johnny rubbed his sideburns pensively. "Took off for Lawrence when he finally believed Deborah wasn't with us. Ain't heard anything about him since, so I'd reckon he didn't do much damage to Miz Eden."

Ansjie had recovered enough to remember hospitality. "Supper will be ready soon, Mr. Chaudoin. But you'll have coffee now and a few honeycakes?"

"Well—" Whatever was bothering Johnny eased enough to let him grin at this plump, pretty girl of whom he clearly approved. "That sounds prime, ma'am, if it's no trouble."

"A pleasure," she assured him. And she bustled to set out a plate of cakes and a cup of the coffee to which Conrad was so addicted that there was always a pot ready.

Johnny passed on the latest news he'd heard from travelers. Eli Thayer, founder of the Emigrant Aid Society and now a Massachusetts Representative to Congress, had said late in February, "I would rather see a state free for the worst reasons than see it slave for the best reasons." And he had gone on to scoff at the Southerners who'd hoped to gain Kansas by repealing the Missouri Compromise. He'd said that New Englanders could hold a town meeting, vote to emigrate, and be on their way in two weeks, as compared to the great length of time it took a slave-owner to sell his land and move with his slaves, and he had crowed that pro-slavers had insisted on a game at which they were bound to be beaten.

Doy, with his son, was still jailed in Missouri awaiting trial, and even Kansans who had no love for abolitionists were still incensed that the arrests had taken place on Kansas soil. John Brown had vanished north with the slaves he'd freed or stolen, depending on one's view. Republicans were planning to organize in Kansas, taking advantage of resentment at the Democrats' mishandling of the Territory's problems. The election of 1860 would be crucial; no matter which party or factions triumphed, the conflict between North and South was coming to a head. It would be a miracle if the nation escaped war.

"Not but what we haven't had it here for the last five years," Johnny finished grimly. He looked at Conrad. "Tucked away where you are, I hope you folks can stay clear of the mess."

"So do I." Conrad frowned. "I brought these people here because I'm sure Prussia will become increasingly militaristic, and Mennonites will be forced into the army or have to pay even higher rates for exemption. They'll have no cause to thank me if I've trapped them in the middle of a civil war."

"Oh, I don't reckon much will happen back here," Johnny comforted. "Probably the chousin' back and forth across the border will get worse, but the fightin's goin' to be where there's lots of people and supplies. Not too much'll take place out west."

Though he complimented Ansjie on the cakes and coffee, Johnny was upset about something, and it certainly wasn't Rolf's scalped raiders. "Has Judith gone north?" Deborah asked. "And how is Sara?"

"Judith may just stay with us." A fleeting grin loosened Johnny's features before his jaws clamped audibly. "Sara—well, I need to talk to you about her."

Conrad rose. "Ansjie and I will leave you for a bit."

"Much obliged," grunted Johnny. "This is sort of private." As Conrad ushered out his sister, the blacksmith's gaze followed them warmly. "Good people. No need to ask how they've treated you."

"They've been wonderful. Now, what's this about Sara?"

Johnny stared at the floor. The knuckles of his clenched hands showed white. "Sara— I don't know how to say this. Hell, what can I say? She's goin' to have a baby."

• xvii •

Deborah's brain whirred. "A baby? But—" Swallowing, she fought back a flood of questions and simply asked, "Thos?"

Johnny nodded. So Thos and Sara had loved, delighted in each other, and there would be a baby of that joy, a living part of the father. One part of Deborah rejoiced in this while another part was shocked for her friend.

Ironic that Thos hadn't thought it fair to marry Sara when he might leave her a widow! Trying to spare her that, he'd left her a child with no name. They must have been carried away, past reason and waiting. And how it must grieve Johnny, who'd loved his ward enough to stand aside for her young lover.

"How is Sara taking it?" Deborah asked. *And you?*

"She's glad there'll be a child." Johnny's tone was gruff. "So'm I. Who could grudge that pair their lovin'?" His massive shoulders slumped forward. "Trouble is, Sara won't marry me. Says it wouldn't be fair. Real proud, that *wastewin!* No matter what I say, she think's I'm just sorry for her!"

"You've told her you love her? As a man, not a guardian?"

"Hell, that made her worse!"

"Why?"

"Oh, she took on about how blind and heartless she'd been and how I need a wife who won't always love a dead man!"

Deborah winced. Johnny passed a big hand over his eyes. "Sorry, but I'm at my wit's end. I won't have people sniggerin', sayin' I got the baby on her, or someone else who didn't care enough to marry her."

"But you'll take care of her! It doesn't matter what people say—"

"Hell, it don't! I'll carve up anyone looks at her sideways, but think about the kid! He's your nephew—well, niece, maybe. No fun bein' a bastard. But Sara's not thinkin' straight."

Watching his struggle, Deborah understood and was shaken at the depths of this formidable man's adoration. Sara might be able to proudly carry and bear Thos's child, rear him with her love for a shield and pride for armor, but Johnny couldn't endure that she'd be gossiped about, speculated on by the men who stopped at the smithy. If that explosive situation developed, he'd kill anyone who insulted Sara; and if she persisted, there'd be insults.

Head bowed, Johnny cleared his throat. "I'm older than Sara, ugly and rough. I wouldn't expect her to share my bed. If she meets up with a man who'll do right by her and the kid, she can divorce me."

"Oh, Johnny, she'd never use you like that!"

"Whatever she does is fine," he said stubbornly, "providing it doesn't hurt *her.*"

"You told her all this?"

"Tried. Made a botch." His smoke-dark eyes lifted to her hopefully. "Figgered maybe— You're Thos's sister. You might do better."

"I'll try."

Deborah was quiet a moment, absorbing the news. Thos's baby! He wouldn't, after all, completely vanish. There might even be a little boy who'd look like him. Oh, Sara mustn't make it a harsh and bitter thing, to bear the child of Thomas Whitlaw, the grandson or granddaughter of Leticia and Josiah!

"Good!" breathed Johnny. "Can you come with me in the mornin'?"

"That's when we were going," said Deborah. "I thought it was time I stopped imposing on the Landers, and, most of all, I wanted to know how all of you were getting along."

Johnny looked at her keenly. "Conrad's not givin' you trouble?"

"No!" The sharpness of her cry startled her.

"Loves you, don't he?"

Deborah nodded mutely.

Johnny sighed. "And you're still longin' after Dane

Hunter! Beats all, don't it, the way people get so mixed around?" His gentle growl was soothing. "But listen, honey, don't you feel bad about Conrad. It's when a person's got no one to love that they're to be pitied." He grinned at her attempted protest. *"Hin!* Don't you reckon I know?"

She had to smile at that. Johnny chuckled, too, before he went on. "You best stay here till that Rolf's gone for good. We'll keep you out of sight of strangers while you're visitin', but I sure don't want that wild young feller learnin' where you are."

He shook his head. "Never quite liked him, though I took to his brother the minute I laid eyes on him. Rolf's sort of crazy. He may have gone after those raiders because he cared about your folks, but he wound up enjoyin' what he was doin'. Said Dane can't call him a youngster now. Said he didn't kill from a distance, but up close, and has the scalps to prove it."

Deborah shuddered. "That's going to be awful for Dane! What'll he do?"

"What can he do?" Johnny spread his snarled, blackened hands. "Rolf was a handful, I guess, even in England." He added hopefully, "Maybe he'll join the gold rush and get *his* hair lifted! My brothers-in-law always admired that gold shade of hair."

He said it with such wistful reminiscence that Deborah wondered if he'd possessed a scalp or two. She didn't ask.

The next morning, early, they bid Ansjie good-bye. "Hurry back!" she told Deborah with a warm hug. "I wouldn't let you go, except that Mr. Chaudoin's promised you'll come again."

"You'll be tired of me by spring." Deborah laughed. "But after I move back to the smithy, you'll have to come and visit. Maybe we can find you that doctor or handsome blacksmith—one who's no *dummkopf,* enjoys his food, and is strong!"

"We'll find a doctor," Johnny declared. "I don't want any *handsome* competition!"

"Who could compete with you, Mr. Chaudoin?" dimpled Ansjie.

She waved them on their way as they rode out of the village across the frost-glittering, crunching prairie grass. Following was Sleipner's two-year-old colt, the one Conrad had promised to Johnny. "Fine figure of a woman, your sister," said Johnny to Conrad. "You'll lose a grand housekeeper when she marries."

"For her sake, I hope that's soon," returned Conrad. "Ansjie's twenty-three. From the way she looks at children, I know she wants some of her own, but there's no one for her in Friedental. I'm serious about finding a doctor and blacksmith for the village, though, and you may be sure I'll view prospects through the eyes of a possible relative."

"Well, if that don't work, she's mightily welcome to stay at the smithy for a while," Johnny said. "All kinds of people stop, and come spring, the gold rush to Pike's Peak'll be on full blast." He winked. "Maybe she better catch some feller on the way back when he's got gold in his pockets, not just on his head!"

"Ansjie has enough to marry poor." Conrad smiled slightly. "I was glad to let my younger brother become *Graf* and lord of the castle, but I made sure of sufficient funds for Ansjie and myself."

The sun turned the high brown grass rosy-gold as the frost melted. Chica pranced coquettishly between Johnny's Appaloosa and Sleipner, named, so Conrad had explained, for the eight-legged steed of Odin. The colt often ran ahead and kept a respectful distance from his elders. There was no wind and the air was bright, crystalline, bracing.

At noon they watered their horses and shared the generous lunch Ansjie had packed: sausage, cheese, rye bread, boiled eggs, pickles, gingerbread, and dried fruit.

"Enough here for supper and all day tomorrow!" Johnny said. "Whoever gets your Ansjie sure won't waste away!"

"No," agreed Conrad. "And he'll win much more than good food. Ansjie has heart to give, cheerfulness and hope."

Do I? thought Deborah. *What can I give Dane, except my love?* That, just now, seemed a despairing, battered thing. She knew she could be a good friend, but she had no confidence in her gifts as a lover. They hadn't been enough to hold him before. Perhaps the only thing to say for her love was that it had lasted.

They rode with an eye for other travelers, having agreed that Deborah would muffle her face with scarf and hood in the unlikely case of their meeting anyone, but the trip was uneventful. Squirrels, woodchucks, and prairie dogs were burrowed away for their winter sleep, but a sleek, coffee-brown mink was fishing in the creek and cottontails frequently bounded out of their way, one pursued by a coyote. Prairie chickens whirred and a hawk, wheeling in the sky, plummeted to seize one that left the cover of the grass.

Maccabee and Laddie were still at work, so they only waved and shouted greetings, but Sara and Judith ran out, enfolding Deborah in their arms before she was well out of the saddle. Swept inside while the men saw to the horses, Deborah laughed and cried, said she was fine, and cut off the flow of questions to catch Sara's hands and say, "Oh, Sara, it's wonderful about the baby!"

To her shock, Sara gave her a searching look. "You mean that?"

"Well, of course I do! It was awful, Thos dying that young—there was so much he never got to do! But at least you loved each other. And the baby will keep him alive. What could it be but wonderful?"

Sara looked as though some rigidity had melted. "That makes me happy. I thought you might not want an Indian to have your brother's child."

Stunned, Deborah couldn't speak for a minute. Then she caught Sara's shoulders and gave her a fiercely gentle little shake. "Don't let me hear such foolishness again!"

"But—"

"Anyway, I'm stuck with you for a sister-in-law," said Deborah with mischief. "Thos didn't love anyone else!"

"Just what I been tellin' her," approved Judith.

"I'm glad, too," Sara murmured. "But I—I told Johnny before anyone could see so that if he were angry, I could go away and no one would say bad things."

"But since he wasn't angry, you'll let him take the blame?" thrust Deborah.

"No! I—"

"People *will* blame him." Ruthless because of her two loved friends, her dead brother, and the unborn child, Deborah pressed on, though she ached for the slender girl, who stared at her in disbelief. "Everyone knows how Johnny's kept men away from you. Some will think the worst. And if Johnny hears you blackguarded, you know what he'll do!"

Sara made fists of her small hands. "It wouldn't be fair to marry him!" she cried. "I still love Thos! I always will!"

"All the more reason to marry someone who understands that and will help you with the child."

"He does it from pity!"

"He does it from love." Sara shook her head blindly.

Deborah persisted. "I've seen for a long time that Johnny worships you. Let him do this thing, *meshema*. It will make him happy. He'll be a strong, kind father. And he asks nothing."

"Look here!" They turned at Judith's brisk tone. She had her hands on her hips and her eyes sparkled. "Wasn't for that pesky pride of yours, Sara, what'd you want to do?"

Sara bit her lip. Judith laughed, slipping an arm around her. "You study on it, you'll see what's right!" she encouraged. "But I hear those men and I bet they're hungry! We better rustle!"

After a hearty meal, they gathered in front of the fireplace. Johnny started humming "Sweet Betsy from Pike" and soon they were all singing. Maccabee led into "Follow the Drinking Gourd," a song of how escaping slaves traveled toward the North Star, marked by the gourd, or dipper, and when they'd learned that, Conrad sang his English version of "The Rose Garden" and then taught them a lusty drinking song, till the men were roaring *"Du, du liegst mir im Herzen . . ."* as stoutly as if they were in some *Hofbrauhaus*. Judith began a song in which Maccabee joined with a tune so sweepingly infectious that the rest of them were soon chorusing.

> "Oh, now, my brother, when the world's on fire
> Don't you want Abraham's bosom to be your
> pillow—"

When they'd clapped and sung through that, Johnny sang in his rusty, oddly touching voice, his gaze on Sara, beautiful in the firelight:

> "I gave my love a chicken that had no bone,
> I gave my love a cherry that had no stone.
> I gave my love a story that had no end,
> I gave my love a baby with no crying."

And when he'd finished the tender riddle, Sara held her shawl almost as if she held a child and sang a Shawnee lullaby. Then she crossed to Johnny and put her hand in his.

"That will be my song for our child," she said. "But you may sing to him in English, or even in Sioux."

He stared at her. Then bafflement dissolved in joy and he sprang up, catching her in a bear hug that he belatedly gentled. "Hey, that calls for the best whisky! We're goin' to have us a weddin'!"

Even Laddie was allowed to drink to that.

Much as Deborah wanted to attend the ceremony, Johnny felt it dangerous for her to be seen in town till Rolf had positively left the region. Judith, as a runaway, couldn't risk appearing, but the next day, when Conrad and Deborah rode back to Friedental, Johnny and Sara started to Lawrence, accompanied by Laddie and Maccabee.

When Sara and Deborah embraced in farewell, Sara gripped her tightly. "You—you think Thos wouldn't mind?" she murmured so no one else could hear.

"If he knows, I'm sure he's glad," Deborah said. "He'd certainly better be!" She sounded so much the stern twin sister that they both burst into shaky laughter.

Taking Deborah aside, Johnny had asked her if she wanted another Bowie. "Not yet," she said. She needed no defense at Friedental. "When I come back, Johnny, then I'll need one."

"Yes," he said. "Then you will. But I'm glad you don't want it yet."

At noon Deborah and Conrad finished the food Ansjie had sent with them, resting by the creek. "Johnny's a good man," said Conrad. "I think they'll do well together."

"Yes. Strange, but it's about the only way Johnny could ever have felt it was all right to ask Sara to marry him." Remembering Thos, the manner in which he and Sara had glowed together, Deborah forced back the lump in her throat. "Johnny is a lot older, of course, but—"

"He's forty-three." Conrad's tone was dry. "Not such a vast age when one's within eight years of it."

"I didn't mean—" Deborah floundered. "I suppose it's his beard and gray hair. Besides, he *did* seem old when we met four years ago because Thos and I were so young."

"Children, in fact," suggested Conrad with a twinkle.

"One does grow up," said Deborah with hauteur.

"Does one?"

Evading that question along with his amused gaze, Deborah grew pensive. "I'm so glad about the baby and gladder that Sara quit being a mule, but it's certainly going to be different when I go back. They'll have each other and they'll both have the child." She chuckled ruefully. "I feel left behind. And I've a strong suspicion that Maccabee and Judith will marry. I think he's cared about her since she first visited the smithy last summer."

"So patience may have it's reward." Conrad shook his head, rising among the leafless oaks. "I hope the man you love comes back to you. But remember, always remember, that I'm a man who loves you."

When she would have spoken, he smiled and raised his hand. "I'm happy in it. I won't speak of it till you've seen him or had word. You owe me nothing. But you can ask me for anything."

She looked at him, distressed. He put out his hand and touched her face. "What I noticed the first time I saw you, and when I came to fetch you from the smithy, is your April face. It changes so quickly from sadness to gaiety, and the other way around. You were meant to be a happy person, Deborah, but you've been fated to endure the struggle of your country. You will, I fear, have to weep often. Laugh, then, when you can."

"When I really think about my family, how they died, then I feel guilty, ashamed that I can eat and sleep and smile."

"But if you're to live, you must. In you, your loved ones survive. You can work for what they believed; your children will have their heritage. You're their link between what was and what will be."

"That's so—heavy!"

"Make it light. You don't dishonor the dead by loving life, by joy."

She knew he thought of Röslein and that idolized elder brother. He helped her into the saddle and they continued on their journey. She felt as if they rode toward home.

Ansjie's welcome increased that feeling. Soon they were back in the familiar pattern, and this time Deborah wasn't worried about her friends. She thought of Thos's and Sara's —and Johnny's—baby with much the same anticipation as she had for Dane's return, except that the birth wouldn't be till September, and Dane should come after the snow melted from the passes, perhaps in June, surely by July.

In late March the Mennonites began working the soil, "plowing the dew under," which meant plowing from dew in the morning till dew at night. They planted wheat, corn, rye, and millet, acres of squash, pumpkin, watermelons, and muskmelons, as well as the large family gardens in the strips behind each house.

"We get enough rain here for spring wheat," Conrad told Deborah and Ansjie during an evening walk through the fresh-smelling fields and budding, leafing orchards. "But there's a hard winter wheat grown by Mennonites in the Crimea that should grow well where there's less rain and more cruel winds. I want to get some and experiment with it."

The villagers shared plows and oxen, but each family took care of its own fields, which were laid out in strips along the valley, divided so that choice and less desirable land was equally shared. There was no doubt that farmers like this would learn the secrets of any earth they settled on and soon bring it to its best fruitfulness.

"They put Americans to shame," grimaced Deborah.

"Remember that for generations their life has been the soil. They're almost as devoted to it as to their religion." He laughed. "Their motto could be the old proverb: 'Pray as if work wouldn't help; work as if prayer wouldn't.'"

Along the creek redbuds sprouted and tentative light green leaves darkened and grew, while orioles and bluejays flashed through them. Blossoms perfumed the orchard. Wild roses and morning glories peeked from the grass while buttercups, daisies, Johnny-jump-ups, and black-eyed Susans brightened the road edges. Crows called from their lookouts, and geese were on their way north again, honking, making their wedges in the sky.

On their rides, Deborah and Conrad saw new-hatched prairie chickens and passed buffalo wallows, some small, some as large as the one where she'd met Dane and Rolf almost a year ago.

It seemed a lifetime.

Sometimes she felt unreal, escorted around Mennonite fields by a former Prussian count, teaching children whose native language wasn't hers. Dane seemed a phantasm, too, someone she had dreamed up. She had a sense of waiting, of being suspended between lives and worlds.

Ansjie had learned that Deborah's birthday was in May, and it was celebrated with a birthday cake at the school and an hour of games and singing on the green near the well. The whole village came for a sort of picnic and the afternoon ended with children gathering around Deborah to sing "Yankee Doodle," trying not to burst into laughter at her surprise.

After supper Ansjie produced a lace shawl of gossamer-connected roses and insisted that Deborah have it. "I've two more," she said. "When will I wear out even one?"

Conrad's gift was a leather-bound handmade book of poetry and selections from authors they'd shared that winter: Marcus Aurelius, Plato, Boehme, Heine, Rückert, Goethe, Morike—Whitman?

Conrad had copied from *Leaves of Grass:*

> "And now it seems to me the beautiful uncut
> hair of graves,
> It may be you are from old people, or from
> offspring taken soon from their mother's laps,
> And here you are the mothers' laps."

She looked at Conrad. "Thank you," she said. "I can read it now."

He nodded. Ansjie, excitedly, had opened the bedroom door. "Come!" she called. "Look at your present from the villagers!"

"The villagers! Why, they didn't need to—"

"They wished, much, to thank you for teaching their children." Ansjie was almost dancing on tiptoes as Deborah stared at the beautiful chest standing on carved legs and worked with vines and flowers, polished to a rich sheen. "Open it!"

"Oh, it's too much! I can't take it!"

"Will you offend Peter Voth, who made it, and the people who paid him their share in produce or labor?" Conrad's voice was stern. "The Friedentalers took great pleasure in planning this. Will you cheat them of their gift?"

Put that way, what could she do?

"Open it!" Ansjie cried again.

Deborah hesitantly lifted the lid. The chest was full: snowy linens, embroidered pillowcases, quilts, down pillows, a blue featherbed that seemed to swell as articles were lifted off it, smelling of rose leaves—lovely, useful things, enough to start housekeeping.

In a way, it held a dream. One she couldn't dream yet. She suspected that the Landers had contributed heavily to the contents but knew it was useless to protest. Smoothing down the bright quilts, she closed the chest, blinking back tears.

"It's a wonderful present—a lifetime present."

"Don't sound as if you had to carry it!" Conrad laughed.

"It'll wait, sweet with roses, till you're ready for it." His eyes touched her till she couldn't look at him. "And one day you will be."

That seemed far away. But possessing some home furnishings again made her strangely happy, even though she had no bed on which to put pillows and quilts, no table for cloths and napkins. Before she went to bed that night, she picked up Dane's sketch pad, placed it on the chest.

Would he someday sleep on those sheets, rest on the soft down? When would the snow melt? When would he come?

It was Johnny who came at the end of May, just as she was deciding that she couldn't stay at Friedental much longer, from hope of Dane or fear of Rolf. The children were working all day now in the gardens and fields, so school was out till after the harvest, and though she helped Ansjie in the garden and house, she wasn't really needed.

If Rolf was still in the Territory, she couldn't hide forever, and surely he realized now that he couldn't force her to marry him.

Friedental had been a saving respite, but her real life lay out where the striving, changing shaping of a free state was taking place. Her family had come for that. She was the only one left.

Johnny's news, given after reporting that Sara and Judith were fine, increased that feeling. Indignation over the Doy "train's" arrest and jailing was still high. Doy had been tried March 24 in St. Joseph, but the jury couldn't agree and he faced a new trial. The Republicans had held a convention at Osawatomie May 18, one day short of the first anniversary of the massacre at Marais des Cygnes, and close enough to the May 21, 1856, sack of Lawrence by pro-slavers and the retaliatory May 25 date of John Brown's bloody work at Pottawatomie to call both to mind. Abraham Lincoln had been invited but couldn't come because of his law practice.

"Had a problem, the bigwigs did." Johnny grinned, accepting Ansjie's second servings of mixed sausages, sauerkraut, tasty salad of potatoes, ham, pickles, eggs, green onions, and sour cream. "Horace Greeley offered to speak and they didn't know what to do with him!"

"The editor of the *New York Tribune?*" breathed Deborah.

"Guess that's it." Except for Josiah Whitlaw and Dan

Anthony of Leavenworth, Johnny considered newspapermen a scurvy lot. "The Republicans wanted to rope in people who weren't necessarily red-eyed about slavery, and they figgered a New York radical was bound to say some things that'd make 'em sound pure-dee abolitionist. On the other hand, they sure didn't want to make Greeley and his eastern friends mad."

"How'd they handle it?" Conrad asked interestedly.

"Pretty slick. Honored him with a big parade. Marchers had *Tribunes* in their hats. Then he was asked to address an open-air meeting. There were a thousand delegates. No room in the boardinghouses, so they slept by their rigs or in the groves. Greeley felt properly honored, but he was kept out of the real organizin' where things got down to brass tacks."

"And what were the brass tacks?" prodded Deborah.

Johnny rubbed his beard, which looked as if it had been pruned considerably. In fact, instead of resembling a grizzled old buffalo, he looked thinner, younger, and if not handsome, distinguished. "Well, you know the Free State party kind of fell apart during the tug of war between Lane and Robinson, especially after Lane killed Jenkins last June. Lane pretty much organized the Osawatomie show, but Free Staters see they have to quit squabblin' and stick together, so even though apportionment of delegates gave Lane's radicals the edge over Robinson's conservatives, about the same number turned up from each side."

Conrad shook his head. "American politics," he murmured, "are—different! The Herrenhaus was never like this!"

"What's that?" demanded Johnny.

"The upper house of the Prussian parliament. Rather like the British House of Lords. Its members represent the large estates, big cities, or are nominated by the king as hereditary members."

"Don't the people elect anybody?"

Conrad shrugged. "The lower house is elected by taxpaying citizens, but it's split into three groups according to the amount of taxes paid by the electors. So those who pay most have the largest voice."

"We sure wouldn't like that here!" bristled Johnny. "My vote's just as good as . . . as . . ."—he tried to think of someone rich, then brightened as he succeeded—". . . as Russell's, Major's, or Waddell's. They've got rich on freightin', but their vote's just like mine!"

"Except when the Missourians came across the line and voted ten or twenty times apiece," Deborah reminded him.

He turned red at that. *"Cesli tatanka!* Well, them days are done! By the way, Russell's joined a Missourian to start an outfit called the Leavenworth and Pike's Peak Express Company. Began service May 17. Should do real well if the gold boom keeps up." He spat. "Seems like every man and his jackass is headin' for Denver!"

Deborah's heart skipped a beat. "Even Rolf Hunter?"

"No, more's the pity. Hear tell he's hangin' out with a wild bunch around Westport." Johnny sighed. "Best you stay here a little longer, honey. He's still lookin' for you. Has come by the smithy twice, and I hear he's offered a reward for anyone who can tell him where you are."

Fear chilled Deborah for a moment, only to be overwhelmed by anger. "I can't hide forever!"

Johnny's eyes narrowed. "No, you can't. But Dane should be back in a month or so. I'd like to give him a chance to handle his brother. If he don't—well, when you come live with us, I'll skin that young varmint if he comes prowlin' around."

As she tardily realized that moving back to the smithy could cause trouble for her friends, that it wasn't just a matter of personal risk, Deborah had no choice but to stifle her protests, though she was determined not to stay in hiding much longer. Swallowing her frustration, she asked what else had happened at the convention.

"Hin!" pondered Johnny. "They allowed as how the Declaration of Independence was the bedrock of proper government, bad-mouthed the Dred Scott decision because it gutted the Missouri Compromise, came out for a railroad clear to the Pacific, free homesteads, better harbors, and they asked the Wyandotte convention, which is supposed to meet July 5, to prohibit slavery in the new state constitution."

"Let's hope this one finally gets us into the Union," Deborah said rather bitterly. "Let's see, now—isn't this the fourth constitution?"

"Free-Staters drew up the Topeka Constitution, but the federal government was pro-slave and said it wasn't legal," mused Johnny, counting fingers. "The Lecompton Constitution that President Buchanan tried to get Kansans to accept was brewed up by slavers. The Leavenworth Constitution provided for a free state, but it wasn't approved by Congress." He blew out his cheeks. "I think they'll approve whatever comes out of Wyandotte, though. Buchanan knows now that Kansas is free-state to the backbone, and there's nothin' he can do about it."

"A long struggle," said Conrad.

"It's been that." Johnny looked at Deborah. "Hadn't been for folks comin' in to make it go free, the Missourians would've seen that it was admitted as a slave state. Now that can't happen."

Deborah hastened to make it clear that most territorial settlers *weren't* New England abolitionists. "You could say the New England Emigrant Aid Society's pioneers kept a foot in the door for Free Staters, but what's really made the difference has been the flood of people from Iowa and Ohio. They came for land, but most were against slavery just because it wasn't part of what they were used to."

Johnny nodded. "What's sure now is that Kansas will go in free. Just in time, I'd reckon, to help fight a war!"

"You think it'll come to that?" frowned Conrad.

"Bound to unless the South is allowed to make up its own rules. All the hotheads aren't goin' west to look for gold, though it seems mighty like it. That's the main reason I rode over."

To the puzzled looks turned toward him, Johnny said, "Goin' to be mobs of gold-hunters passin' the smithy this summer, along with the usual settlers' wagons. Won't be very safe for an underground railroad station till fall, and without the Whitlaws' place, there's no station west of Lawrence till Topeka."

Ansjie's eyes widened. Conrad was impassive. "You think we might help runaways. Ansjie and I would, but this concerns the whole community. I'll go around tonight and explain to each family. Then we can have a meeting and vote tomorrow morning." He smiled. "It'll be a short meeting. The men will want to get to their fields."

It was short. Twenty minutes after the men had assembled in the church, Elder Goerz led them out. They scattered to their work, except for the elder, who accompanied Conrad to where Johnny waited by the village well with Deborah and Ansjie.

Sturdy, sun-browned legs showing below trousers that reached just below the knee, with feet thrust into sandals and a wide-brimmed black hat shading his whiskered face, the Mennonite elder from Prussia looked at the buffalo-hunter-blacksmith from the frontier.

"All have talked with their wives," he said in careful English. "All have prayed. All say yes, it is God's will that we shelter the oppressed."

Johnny gripped his hand so hard that the elder, no weakling himself, flinched. "Thank you, friend! From now on, folks from Friedental get their smithin' at half-charge!"

The elder shook his head. "*Besser* we pay," he said austerely. "We do this for God. He has brought us to a land where we can be free. Shall we not help those who also wish freedom?"

With a word to Ansjie and Deborah, he went to his field. Conrad dropped a hand on Johnny's shoulder. "It took only five minutes to vote." He laughed. "The other fifteen minutes was for praying!"

"*Tatanka wakan!*" gasped Johnny. "Now, wouldn't it be something if our legislators did that?"

June ripened along with wheat and corn. When Conrad went to reap, Deborah asked to be allowed to bind. "But that's such hot, dirty work!" protested Ansjie. "Conrad always hires one or two boys."

"But I'd like to do it." Deborah tried to answer Ansjie's baffled stare. "Last year we had our first wheat. Thos and I were so proud!" She gave a shaky little laugh. "And we were so glad that we'd have wheat flour instead of cornmeal all the time!"

What would cornmeal matter if her family was back? But working in the wheat would be a link with what endured when reapers changed.

"Of course you may bind if you wish," said Conrad. "And it's likely your old wheat field has a new crop, sown from dropped grain. Would you want to go and see?"

Deborah stiffened. She hadn't been back to her home since Rolf took her away that night five months ago. But Thos's child would inherit it, which gave it a future, not just a tragic past, and if there were wheat, sowed from that reaped by her brother, she didn't want it to go to waste.

"Could we take a scythe or cradle?" she asked. "If there's a fair crop, after your share's taken out, it can be threshed with Johnny's, sold if it's not needed, and maybe Johnny could buy the baby a few cows or use the money for expenses."

"That baby's not going to lack for people who care about it." Conrad grinned. "But my share of the reaping will be your satisfaction. Shall we harvest the baby's field first?"

Deborah shook her head. "We know you have a crop." She smiled. "Let's get that in first!"

Ansjie helped, of course, though she grumbled that in Prussia only peasants did such work, or madmen like Conrad. "So?" he chuckled, pausing, white shirt open at the throat. "Are we in Prussia, then?"

He went back to swinging the cradle. Ansjie, sighing, moved her shoulders to ease tired muscles, but she resumed her work. It reminded Deborah inescapably of the harvest last year, how Dane had helped. On the last day of the harvest, they'd ridden to the river—

A year ago. Blinking back tears, she added a bundle of grain to the shock. When was he coming?

Was he?

They harvested the Landers' field in four days. Conrad proposed to leave the next day for the Whitlaws', taking food and bedrolls so they could camp out the three or four nights they'd be gone. Conrad figured to strike due east rather than go the long way around by Johnny's. Cross-country, he thought it was about fifteen miles.

"Fifteen miles?" wailed Ansjie. "On horseback? Never! I'm still sore from bending over!"

"I'm sorry!" said Deborah contritely.

Ansjie shrugged. "I was the fool—no one made me do it! But I'm not fool enough to jog all day over the prairie and then do more of this back-breaking work!"

"But Deborah needs a chaperone," worried Conrad.

"You won't get any of these *hausfrauen* to gallop with you," Ansjie predicted. "But one of the girls might. What about Cobie Balzer?"

Boyish, leggy Cobie was elated at the prospect, and Conrad reluctantly agreed that what he paid her parents would be deducted from the crop. The three would-be harvesters left Friedental at dawn. Conrad's cradle was wrapped with bedding and fastened behind his saddle. Cobie rode Ansjie's neat sorrel mare and kept stroking her mane, crooning to her ecstatically.

"Hansi Goerz's jealous because I got to come instead of him!" she crowed with a toss of her yellow pigtails. "So I'll bind better than he could! You won't be sorry you picked me!"

"I'm sure we won't." Deborah laughed.

Even apart from propriety, she was glad the girl was with them. She had shrunk from visiting her home, though she felt it was time she did, time she accepted it as it was now.

Reaping the wheat would be both farewell and promise to Thos. And having a frolicsome youngster about would exorcise the haunted mood that might otherwise taint the pilgrimage. It was good to return like this, to harvest the fruit of her twin's labor for the child born of his seed.

Yet in the early afternoon when they struck the almost grown-over trail from the smithy and the country grew familiar, Deborah's nerves tautened. A sickness began in the pit of her stomach, then increased till she was shivering in spite of the warm, bright day.

There was the Osage orange hedge she and Thos had planted around the field to keep the horses and poor Venus out. The wheat was high inside, as high almost as if it had been planted.

Unwillingly, her gaze moved to the stable, the walls still standing, though half the roof was gone. There was the well-house.

And the cabin.

Charred logs, the fireplace seeming to wait, puzzled at its exposure to the elements. The debris was gone. She suspected that Johnny had finished burning it and cleaned away the remnants. Climbing down from Chica, she stared at the fireplace.

How many meals had been cooked there! How often the family had sat near the warmth and read or talked. Her eyes stung. She moved blindly toward the stable.

The earth where she'd buried her parents and from which they'd been moved had been carefully smoothed over. They were buried in the cemetery on the slope west of town and someday she'd have to go there, but to her this was their resting place.

I love you! she cried to them through silence and death and time. *Mother, Father, Thos! Please hear me! I love you. I always will!*

No answer. But the wheat waved golden in the sun.

Turning to Conrad and the hushed young girl, she straightened her shoulders. "Let's water the horses," she said. "And then let's start the harvest."

• xviii •

They worked till sundown, Cobie and Deborah following Conrad's steady swings of the cradle that left the grain pointing in one direction for easier binding. After washing off as much dust and chaff as possible the three sat down to feast hungrily on sausage, cheese, crusty fresh bread, nut cake, and molasses cookies, all washed down with water from the well.

Deborah had drawn it up, though she'd had to combat memories of the last time she'd done that, getting rid of strangled chickens before she could wash her parents. Using familiar things was, she felt instinctively, the only way to cleanse them of that last horror. She'd wept sometimes that afternoon, but with a sense of relief, of healing.

Sleipner and Ansjie's mare had been hobbled, but Conrad thought it safe to release them now, especially since Chica seemed to recognize her old pastures. Cobie and Deborah made their beds by the big plum thicket where laundry used to be hung, and Conrad spread his on the other side, out of sight but in hearing range. The late-rising moon, diminished at the top, silvered the prairie with its cool light, and the breeze made it pleasant to lie beneath a thin coverlet, weary body luxuriating in rest. The horses moved gently, crickets chirred, and distant coyotes set up a yipping that blended with other night sounds.

Everything was so much *now,* including the ache of her back and shoulders, that Deborah sighed as the wind teased her hair and snuggled deeper into her pillow, sinking into sleep.

She awoke to the aroma of coffee and the song of meadowlarks, dressed hurriedly, spread her bedding on a plum bush, and joined Cobie and Conrad. As well as the pot of coffee perched on the edge of the dug-out firehole, a skillet of eggs was frying.

"You brought *eggs?*"

Flipping them, Conrad smiled. "Ansjie wrapped them well. She said cold breakfasts are no good for this kind of work."

He set the skillet on a stump, and they made a hearty breakfast. "No dishes!" Cobie laughed. "No housework! I wish I could live like this forever!"

"It'd get very cold in the winter," reminded Deborah, rinsing out the tin cups and setting them to drain.

Cobie cleaned the skillet of egg and butter by rubbing it with a piece of bread, which she then popped in her mouth. "In the winter," she said reflectively, "I might go south. Maybe to Texas. I want to see the Alamo. Or I might go to California."

Oh, dear! thought Deborah. Have I given this child ideas that'll get her into trouble?

"What do your parents think of these ambitions?" Conrad asked with a quizzical lift of his eyebrows.

"I don't tell them," said Cobie flatly. "But Hansi—we talk sometimes. He wants to see it all, too—outside!" And she spread her thin young arms, embracing the horizon.

She danced off to caress the horses. Deborah looked ruefully at Conrad. "Don't blame yourself," he chided. "That one, and Hansi, they've always been curious, restless. Good workers, but it's clear they won't stay in Friedental. Some are born to stay, some to go, and all other people do is perhaps hurry the leaving a trifle."

"But it's so peaceful in Friedental. No drinking or brawls, no stealing or hunger!"

"It also gives few choices for how to live. Mennonites will die for freedom to practice their religion; they'll give up everything and move halfway around the world for this. But as for freedom of the individual to be different, that sounds like vanity and folly to them."

"There certainly are individuals out here," said Deborah rather grimly. "And they tend to be *very* different!"

"So Cobie and Hansi will fit right in, paradoxically." Conrad smiled, rising. He surveyed the wheat. "We may be able to finish by early afternoon tomorrow and get home before dark."

At mid-morning they stopped to drink from the bucket Cobie fetched. It was hot. Conrad's shirt clung wetly to him and Cobie had unbuttoned her dark green dress. Chaff and dust mixed with sweat trickling between Deborah's breasts and between her shoulder blades. She promised herself a good washing that night behind the plum bush.

Cobie called suddenly and pointed. Stopping their work, Deborah and Conrad scanned the moving figure, barely in sight, along the road from town. They relaxed slightly when no other horsemen appeared. Roving Indians, as well as pro-slavers, might hit an isolated farm, and enough had happened at the Whitlaws' to make anyone nervous about riders.

This one seemed alone, though. Sleipner and the other horses whinnied from where they grazed beyond the cabin and loped down to meet the approaching animal, a powerful steel gray.

She had seen that horse before.

A cry lodged in her throat. Dropping the wheat she held, she squeezed through the Osage orange hedge, heedless of the prickles.

Dane! It was Dane!

She ran forward as he brought Lightning to a stop, sprang down, and swept her close.

"Deborah!" His voice broke. He kissed her as if to prove she was real, bruising her mouth, crushing her against him till she had no strength. Then his lips turned sweet, cherishing, caressing, then left hers and moved to her throat.

"Oh, my darling!" he breathed. "No one in town knew where you were!"

"Then how did you—"

He held her back, eyes going over her, as if to make sure she was real. "Melissa thought you'd gone back to New Hampshire. I was going to the smithy, hoping Johnny would know, but something made me stop here."

"It's been so long! Oh, Dane—"

He held her, stroking her hair. "Your parents. Thos. And I wasn't here when you needed me."

"You're here now." She smiled through her tears. "That's what matters."

She really thought so in the joy of that reunion. But it wasn't to be that simple.

Conrad and Cobie came to meet Dane, who treated the former nobleman in a distinctly guarded way even after Deborah had explained the Landers' hospitality and this harvest excursion.

"I must thank you for sheltering my fiancée," Dane

said as he offered his hand. "There's no way to repay all you've done, especially since my brother seems to have made her trouble worse, but if there's any way I could lessen the debt, I'd be happy to do it."

"Deborah's presence has been a joy, not a problem."

Conrad's tone was courteous, but there were white marks at the corners of his mouth. He and Dane were almost the same height, but Dane was slightly broader of shoulder. Each was tanned by wind and sun and their appearance would have astounded the people on their distant estates. Catching Deborah's anxious silent pleading, Conrad relaxed a bit and grinned.

"You might do something for me, though. If you run into a doctor or blacksmith who'd like to settle in a quiet farming valley, we'd make him warmly welcome."

"I'll keep it in mind," Dane promised.

Looking from him to Deborah, Conrad said, "You must have much to talk about. Cobie and I can finish the harvest."

"You've done too much as it is." Dane sounded grim. "I'll help."

And he did, after a search turned up the Whitlaws' cradle, where it lay beneath half-burned straw in the stable. Dane whetted off the rust and soon they were in the field. Following her love, as she had done a year ago, Deborah was happier than she had been since he went away.

They took a longer than usual rest at noon, both because of the heat and because everyone had questions about California and the trip out there.

"Mighty interesting," Dane summarized at last. "As railroads reach California, it's bound to become an important part of the country. But I got so restless waiting for good weather, when I could start back here, that I've had enough of it." He smiled at Deborah. "Unless you'd like to make it a honeymoon trip?"

Blushing, acutely aware that Conrad must be distressed, Deborah said they'd talk about that later and led the way back to the field.

After a supper augmented by dried buffalo meat and pemmican, pounded berries, nuts, and tallow Dane had bought from Indians, Deborah and Cobie took turns rinsing each other off. It didn't take long to dry in the warm air, and even though she had to put the same dress on, Deborah felt much fresher when she rejointed the others.

Dane rose, taking her hand. "If you'll excuse us," he said to Conrad and Cobie, "we've considerable things to talk about!"

"You must," conceded Conrad.

His tone was amicable, but Deborah felt a pang of hurt for him as Dane led her away. This faded quickly, though, in the marvel of actually being with her love again, seeing his strong face outlined against the twilight, thrilling to the warm strength of his fingers beneath her arm, being aware of his breathing, the wonder of his body near her after this long, terrible year.

She hadn't realized how tired she was, how much she needed him. Lovely just to walk like this, share silence together. . . . He stopped abruptly, covered her mouth with his, held her till the heavy beat of his heart seemed rooted deep in her, as if their blood had joined, their breath, their being.

As he stepped back, catching in his breath, Deborah swayed, would have stumbled, except for his steadying hands. "My love!" His voice was harsh. "Oh Deborah, my love! Maybe I should take you, the way I long to, the way I've dreamed of so many times across so many miles. You'd be mine, then. But you've no family. I must protect you—even against myself."

"I—I would have been yours last year, Dane."

"You were too young then. Now you're too vulnerable." He made her sit by the side of the overgrown road, then located himself a resolute distance away. "I've got to track down Rolf and put a stop to this nonsense he's gotten into."

Did Dane know about the scalps? Surely not! He couldn't call that nonsense! "How much did Melissa tell you about Rolf and—and me?" Deborah asked.

"That Rolf brought you to her house when you were suffering from shock, that he took care of the funeral arrangements, and that he tore off after the raiders."

"That's true, but she left out quite a lot. After you left, Rolf often came home for Sunday dinner and began inviting Thos, Sara, and me to go places." Deborah averted her face, even though it was dark out. Why should she feel apologetic about what would never have happened if Dane hadn't left her? "I thought Rolf accepted that I considered myself engaged to you. But he proposed at Christmas, then went off really angry when I refused."

In the darkness, Dane seemed carved from stone. "You couldn't be expected to sit home," he said at last. "It's a bitter dose, though, to know my own brother was squiring you about."

"It wasn't like that!"

"No?" Dane laughed harshly. "If Rolf restrained himself for all those months, he must have been deeply smitten!"

Deborah ignored that. Dear God, were they quarreling, already wounding each other! "Dane," she said carefully, "I think you should know that Rolf fell in with some Missourians. He says he didn't know they were chasing Thos, and I believe him. But the gang split up. The party Rolf rode with killed Thos—Rolf didn't get there till Thos had been shot, and he did break away from the group then and bury Thos. But the other party—" Her voice trembled. "They killed my parents."

"So that's why he had to be the avenger," Dane muttered, dazed. "Crazy young fool!"

"He told people in Lawrence that I was deranged, but that he was going to marry me, anyway, and take me away for treatment." Dane gasped. Deborah rushed on, feeling the truth must be known, but not wanting to go into details. "Melissa locked me in a room with boarded-up windows. I don't know if she truly thought I was out of my mind or just pretended to, but if Judith and Sara hadn't helped me, I think Rolf would've smuggled me off to St. Louis."

"It sounds as if he's the insane one," growled Dane. "But hell, Deborah! Did you think you could keep a hothead like Rolf dangling for months and expect him to take his dismissal gracefully?"

"I—I *told* him!"

"Men—and women—have a way of believing what they wish, my dear."

He blamed her! Stunned past anger, Deborah felt as if she'd run up for a kiss and been brutally slapped. As she sat there in the ruins of her joy, she scarcely understood what Dane's tightly scornful voice was saying till the full impact struck.

"And this Herr Lander! Has he been content to wait, too?"

Then the anger came, the bracing outrage. Rising, Deborah spoke in a cold voice, though she was shaking with hurt and fury. "I think I've been waiting for the wrong person!"

She started down the road.

"Deborah!"

She didn't falter or turn. To dream of him for a year! To believe he'd have helped her bear the loss of her family, be understanding and kind! Instead, having been half a continent away at her time of need, he now accused her of enticing Rolf! Even worse, he'd insulted Conrad's steadfast and patient love. She fought back wrathful sobs, struggled for control as she heard Dane striding after her.

"Sweetheart, I'm sorry!" Catching her by the shoulders, he made her face him. "I feel like such a cur, not being here when you needed me, that I guess I'm hitting out at you." His tone roughened and his hands moved up to the naked flesh of her throat. "Of course men will love you. It's up to me to see they don't trespass."

He tried to kiss her, but she turned her face away. He was still a moment. "Can't you forgive me?"

"You—that was awful, what you said about Conrad! He's sheltered me, he loves me, but he's never expected anything! He hasn't even kissed me!"

"It wasn't for lack of inclination." Dane's voice was dry. "He must be a man of steel—looks it, too, with that dueling scar and bearing."

"He was a count, a *Graf*."

"An earl in England." Dane threw back his head and laughed. "No one can say you've lacked strange suitors! All right, love, I sincerely beg your pardon! What else must I do? Apologize to Herr Lander for what he didn't know I said?"

Almost disarmed, Deborah said, "Of course not! I just want you to know how good he's been!"

"I'm properly chastised." This time she didn't avoid his lips, but though his mouth, urgently compelling, coaxingly sweet, left her tremulous, there was a shield between them, a barrier. She could forgive what he said, but she couldn't forget it.

Dane sighed as he lifted his head, then bent again to kiss the curve of her jaw. "Implacable little thing, aren't you?" His mouth brushed the front of her dress, his breath warming her. "Now sit down and let's decide how we're going to do things."

"What things?" Ridiculous, the way he'd hunkered down out of reach, but she was bemusedly ready to conclude that men often were, to a woman's view, exactly that.

Ridiculous. Stubborn—

He permitted himself to touch her hair. "Our wedding's

the most important matter. But I'd best attend to Rolf first of all—give him a choice of joining the gold-hunters, where he could certainly work off a lot of his energy, or going back to England."

Deborah thought Dane was in for a surprise if he supposed that Rolf was meekly going to follow his advice. Something had happened to that young man.

Between the time he'd angrily told her good-bye at Christmas and when he'd come back from Missouri with scalps at his belt, Rolf had crossed from wildness, reckless high spirits, into evil. But Dane couldn't believe that; to him, Rolf was still an exasperating but loved younger brother.

"You may not be able to find him," she said.

"I'll find him."

"And then?"

"Where shall we be married? Is it important to have your friends, or could we have the ceremony in England?" He chuckled. "That might help Sir Harry adjust to the shock, though I'd reckon he's so anxious to have a bride around the place that he won't care how she gets there!"

Even if she's a commoner from the wilderness? Deborah didn't voice her resentment, though, startled by what he seemed to be taking for granted.

"But I won't be around the place," she pointed out, "at least not for years!"

His hand dropped from her hair. "What do you mean?"

"What I've always meant! I'm not leaving till the fight for Kansas is won, till it enters the Union as a free state."

"My God!"

"I'm not sure God has much to do with it, but my whole family died for freedom. I can't go off and leave them in this ground until I know it's free, that what my family worked for has finally come to pass."

"I can't believe it!" he said.

Taut with dread, the fear of losing him, Deborah made a tremendous effort to keep her voice level. "I don't see why. It's what I told you a year ago."

Under his breath he said something vexed, bewildered, and certainly obscene. "Deborah! Your family's gone! They wanted you safe before, out of this damned place, and they'd want it more than ever now! Your home's burned. Not even you can be crazy enough to try living here alone."

"I can stay with my friends!" she retorted, braced by anger against the sick, desolate feeling once again trying to engulf her.

"Oh, damn your friends!" He gripped her shoulders, fingers biting till she set her lips tight to keep from crying out. "Do you mean you'd rather take their charity than be my wife?"

"You don't understand anything! You're a hateful, conceited, condescending—*Englishman!*"

"And you're a headstrong, priggish, holier-than-thou wildcat!"

She gasped. "If that's what you think, go back to England and marry some pink-and-white Miss who'll think what you tell her to and do exactly as you say! I never will!"

Wresting away from him, she ran along the road. This time he didn't try to overtake her.

Conrad and Cobie were already in their beds. Deborah spread hers far enough away so that they wouldn't hear her crying. She'd been a fool to long for him, a fool to think he might change! Let him go—and the sooner, the better! She still loved him, but she'd get over that!

Of course she would.

She'd expected him to be gone the next morning, but when she awoke he was drinking coffee with Conrad. Dressing, she cooked the rest of the eggs with bits of sausage. She said as she handed Dane a fork, "We'll finish well before noon. You needn't help."

"There's something about harvest that makes a person want to see it through." Dane's tone was coolly polite. But when Conrad and Cobie started to the field, Dane stopped in front of Deborah, barring her way. "I want to talk to you."

"That never does us any good."

"I love you, Deborah."

"I love you." She said it grudgingly, unwilling, because it was true.

He kept his hands rigidly at his sides, but his gray eyes embraced her till her pulse leaped. She felt utterly soft, utterly yielding, his woman, eager, mutilated without him.

"Come with me," he said.

"Stay."

His muscles tightened, cording his neck and jaw. "I'll

take care of Rolf for you before I leave the Territory," he said. Swinging around, he strode toward the field.

Deborah clenched her hands and clamped her teeth tightly together. Why couldn't he have the decency to leave? Now she'd have to see him in front of her, endure his presence for a few more hours, battle against succumbing. Perhaps it was difficult for him, too. She hoped so.

In a few hours, the last bundle was shocked. Dane put the cradle out of sight in the stable, then splashed his face and arms beneath rolled-up sleeves. Deborah unfastened the Saint Rita's medal and tried to give it to him.

"There's no use in my wearing this," she said, aching, hurting, wishing him gone.

He said with an edge of mockery, "My willful darling, as patron of lost causes, she's more appropriate than ever." More softly, he added, "Remember me a while."

"Dane—"

With a smothered sound, he drew her out of earshot of the others. "Deborah, I'm not just being bloody-minded. I thought most of the night about staying, but it comes down to being pushed into the sort of thing I swore I was done with in the Crimea, and worse, seeing you buffeted and suffering."

"But—"

"I don't believe you should be here," he cut in brusquely, "more than ever after what's happened. I want you more than I've wanted anything, but I won't have you by sacrificing my duty to my wife."

When he talked like this, when he tried to make her understand—and she did—Deborah was robbed of the support of anger. Mournfully, she said, "I believe you. Please believe me."

His breath escaped in a shudder. "I do. That's what makes it hard."

He brought her hands to his lips, swore, and swept her against him, kissing her till her arms closed around his neck and she knew only that she couldn't bear to lose him.

"Good-bye, my sweetheart." He put her away from him, his face twisted with pain. "I'll see you again after I've found Rolf and talked some sense into him. Keep wearing that medal. Maybe the lady can work a miracle for us!"

He collected his gear, saddled up, told Cobie she was a good harvester, thanked Conrad again for sheltering Deborah, and said good-bye to her with a crooked smile.

Then he turned his big gray horse and started toward

town. Deborah wrenched her gaze away from him. "We'd better go," she said. "We're all finished here."

June passed with no word from Dane. July 5 came and Deborah wondered what was happening at the constitutional convention in Wyandotte. Judging from the past, it'd take the delegates weeks to accomplish anything, but she told Conrad in a burst of irritation that if someone didn't bring news by the end of the month, she was riding to the smithy. She wanted to see Judith and Sara, anyway, especially Sara.

Strange. Since she'd last seen her friend, Sara had become Johnny's wife, and in a month or so now she would be a mother. All that winter and spring, Thos's baby had grown from a tiny seed toward what would be a separate person, mingling the looks and characteristics of the parents. It was heartbreaking that Thos would never see the child, but at least he'd made one with the woman he loved. and Johnny would care for it as if it'd been his own.

As July passed, Deborah also began to worry about Dane. He'd be searching for Rolf among border riff-raff, men who cut throats on a whim. His accent and manner were enough to brand him as a "Yankee" to belligerents.

If he simply disappeared, she didn't know how to learn what had happened. Johnny could probably ferret it out by hanging around the river towns, but she hated to ask that. As well as being dangerous, it'd take him away from his work and Sara. Deborah wished she could go herself, but it was unthinkable for a lone woman to undertake such a hunt. Even so, as her anxiety grew, the thought began to persist in her mind rather than being immediately dismissed.

A woman couldn't frequent Westport dives, but a boy might.

While she was mulling this over and helping with the busy round of summer work, a small caravan came into view one late afternoon in early August. Deborah and Ansjie stopped picking strawberries, and Deborah, heart thudding, moved into the shelter of the well-house. It didn't seem likely that Rolf would travel with a wagon, but—

"Why, they're black people!" Ansjie cried. *"Richtigen Schwarzer!"*

Deborah, from the door, shielded her eyes. "That's Maccabee! Ansjie, these must be runaways! But that man lying in the wagon, he's white, and he must be sick or hurt."

They caught up their skirts and ran toward the village green, where Elder Goerz and Conrad were already greeting the wayfarers and hearing Maccabee's explanation.

"These five folks here, they crossed over from Missouri with Doc Challoner. He lived in the big middle of a slave-ownin' part and couldn't stand it no more." Maccabee grinned. "Figgered if he was makin' the jaunt to Kansas, he might as well bring out a few of his neighbor's slaves."

"Is he sick?" Ansjie hurried over to the wagon.

"Bad shoulder wound. The slave-catchers would've had him for sure, but Rebe here"—he nodded at the tallest Negro—"found a cave and they holed up till their old masters quit huntin'. Doc had found out about stations from Doy, who's been sentenced to the Missouri pen along with his men. So Doc sent Rebe ahead to the smithy, and Johnny told me to take the wagon for Doc and bring everybody along here."

He beamed.

"Get this poor man into bed!" ruled Ansjie.

"He can have mine," said Conrad. "Now, Elder Goerz, we need to find places for five men."

Deborah and Ansjie climbed on the wagon seat with Maccabee, who said it would be best if the fugitives could hide till autumn lessened the westward teeming of gold- and land-seekers. "Then we'll start them north," he said.

Challoner wasn't a small man, but fever had wasted him. Maccabee carried him easily into Conrad's bedroom and placed him on the downy featherbed, removing his boots.

All this time Challoner hadn't opened his eyes. He had reddish-brown hair and a square, pleasant face. There was something pathetic about the way his blunt, capable fingers lay useless.

"Hot water!" said Ansjie. "Cloths! Soap! And broth!"

Following her, Deborah asked Maccabee if he'd bathe the young man. "Get him into a pair of Conrad's drawers," Ansjie requested, bustling about the kitchen, handing Maccabee a basin of warm water, soap, and towels while Deborah put chicken stock on to heat.

"The poor man!" Ansjie kept repeating as she roved the kitchen and porch, looking for things he might eat. "Starved, he is, on top of his wound! But too much at first we must not give him. Applesauce?"

"That should be good. Maybe wheat cooked in milk?"

Ansjie nodded and started the wheat while Deborah got applesauce from the cellar. "First broth," decided Ansjie. "Then, if he feels like it, the soft wheat. And for the poor shoulder, healing ointment and a clean bandage!"

She was collecting these when Maccabee came out with well-used water and towels. "Doc's ready for you ladies now. I'll go see how Rebe and the others are doin'."

The young doctor's eyes were still closed when the women put down the tray and bandages on the night table. A sheet was drawn up to his chin. His clothes, including a torn and bloody shirt, were folded neatly on a stool beside his boots.

"Doctor?" Ansjie said softly.

He opened his eyes. They were brown—rich, deep brown with hazel sparkles. A smile spread from them to his mouth. "I've died and gone to heaven!"

Ansjie caught in her breath with a little, excited happy laugh. She had on a blue dress that matched her eyes, and something about this man touched off a magic, made her glow.

"Let me hold you up," she said. "You have this good soup. Then we dress your wound, yes? Then you have the wheat. Later, applesauce." Helping him sit up, plumping pillows about him, she forestalled his question. "The five with you are being taken care of. You, you must not worry—you must get well!"

"Yes, ma'am."

His meekness held a twinkle, and he seemed to lean against Ansjie a bit more than was necessary. Or was it that she pressed forward? At any rate, when Conrad joined them, the amused look in his eyes confirmed what Deborah was thinking.

Ansjie's man had come.

Rebe and his friends had been taken into homes that could best accommodate them. They would help with the work, of which there was plenty, and go north when the seasonal swarming west was over. Maccabee ate dinner before starting back and patiently answered Deborah's questions.

No, neither of the Hunters had been around the smithy and there was no news of them. Sara was fine. Looked like *she* might have twins. Maybe Doc Challoner would be hearty again in time to take care of her. Doc wasn't going north; he planned to settle in Kansas, which he admired for its struggle to be a free state.

"Though I don't know about those delegates at Wyandotte," sniffed Maccabee. "They sure ain't gone hog-wild on who can vote! They listened polite to a lady who argued for woman suffrage but turned her down. *Did* give women equal rights to property and young 'uns."

"Did they prohibit slavery?" Conrad pressed.

Maccabee nodded. "Forty-eight to one. Don't mean they love us. Blacks can't vote and they came mighty close to keepin' us out of public schools. Some even wanted to make it against the law for us to come into Kansas after the constitution's 'dopted."

"Oh, how could they?" Deborah cried in wrath.

Careful, careful people, wanting a free state but none of the risks, more concerned with economics than people! No wonder Dan Anthony's sister Susan thought women should vote! They should help make laws, too, and maybe they'd be fairer!

"They didn't get away with it," Maccabee pointed out. He shrugged. "Slow, Miss Deborah, mighty slow, but it's movin'. My people will get the vote one day."

Maccabee went on to say that the delegates had battled over state boundaries and the capital. Some wanted to annex the part of Nebraska south of the Platte. Others feared that would add to Democratic strength or locate the capital farther west.

"So Nebraska keeps its Platte country," concluded Maccabee, "and Kansas don' stretch out to Denver no more."

"What about the capital?" Deborah asked. That would be an important prize for any town, and Lawrence, the Free State citadel from its founding, had high hopes.

"Topeka," said Maccabee. "Only other towns in the runnin' were Atchison and Lawrence. 'Course, they all accused each other of bribery and vote-buyin'."

Conrad shook his head, fascinated at his chosen land's way of government. Chuckling, Maccabee went on to say that naturally none of the delegates had been born in the Territory, but it was interesting where they *had* come from.

England, Scotland, Germany, Ireland, and Virginia had given one delegate each. There were fourteen from Ohio and about the same number from all the New England states. Indiana, Pennsylvania, and Kentucky contributed seven, six, and five, respectively. A real mixed bag.

"Once Indians aren't the only ones who can say they were born here, I'll wager that becomes an important factor," Conrad remarked. "Were most of the delegates lawyers?"

"Eighteen of them to sixteen farmers. Sizable sprinklin' of merchants, a few doctors and manufacturers, and a surveyor, a mechanic, one land agent, and one printer."

"All white," said Deborah. "All men."

The enormity had never struck her this deeply before. But to hear of the framing of a new state's constitution without women having a vote, to know it would be voted on only by men—that galled, especially when she thought of her mother, of Judith, and Sara. The most stupid, bigoted, depraved white man could vote, but no woman and no Negro, and most Indians were members of their tribes, not citizens.

Maccabee's teeth flashed. He said, with ironic enjoyment, "Well, Miss Deborah, once you get us slaves freed, you can think on how to get free yourself!"

She fixed an indignant eye on him. "When you get the vote, Maccabee, you'd better help me get it, or I'll—well, you won't be any better than that crowd in Wyandotte that just refused suffrage to Negroes!"

He raised one shoulder. "Miss Deborah, I don't reckon we'll be much better. But this country got the *dream* of freedom. It keeps movin' that way."

So in October, white males over twenty-one who'd been residents of Kansas for six months and were U.S. citizens, or had announced the intent to become so, would vote on the constitution, which would then go to Congress for approval. Thos's baby would be born in a Territory, but before he could say he was a Kansan, it should be a state. A free one.

Deborah thought of riding back to the smithy with Maccabee and from there deciding how to trace Dane. But for a few days Ansjie was going to be preoccupied with the doctor, and Deborah felt an obligation to see how the runaways settled into Friedental.

They settled well, working hard to repay their hosts. They gathered on the green after supper and sang and talked because most of the day they were working separated. The children of the village started shyly coming to listen till bedtime, which came early since the workday began before dawn.

Rebe proved to be a blacksmith and liked Friedental so much that he asked if he could stay. The council voted to welcome him and to buy or barter the anvil and other tools he'd need.

"Johnny might have some things he could give," suggested Deborah. "Perhaps I could take a message to him. I've been wanting to go to the smithy. In fact," she added slowly, "it's really time I moved back. Sara's baby will come next month, and I want to be there. If Dane couldn't find Rolf in all these weeks, he must have left the Territory."

Ansjie looked distressed, but not nearly as much as she would have before the doctor's advent. Once where he could be comfortable and well-tended, he'd improved rapidly and was sitting up today for the first time, joining the family for supper.

"Why don't you wait," Ansjie suggested, "for your Mr. Hunter to come back?"

"I've waited long enough."

Ansjie sighed. "You'll come stay with us often? You won't forget?"

"I'll never forget," said Deborah warmly. "You more than saved my life—you saved my mind! And of course I'll come when I can."

Challoner flexed his capable hands and his brown eyes were kind. "In a few more weeks I should be able to tend to your friend. If she'll let me know when she's expecting, I could go a week early and be ready when she is."

Ansjie looked less than thrilled at such an absence, but she said admiringly, "Mrs. Chaudoin will be fortunate! I hope when I—" She broke off in confusion, pinker than a rose.

Doc laughed. "I think I can promise that you'll have the best of care! After all, won't you have a doctor in the house?"

"What?" blinked Ansjie.

He put his hand over hers. "I didn't mean to blurt it out like this, Miss Ansjie, but I surely am hoping you'll be my wife! Come on, now! You must know that!"

"I—I—" Her blue eyes glowed. "Oh, Doc! Doc! *Ich liebe dich!*"

Conrad said to Deborah, "Shall we take a walk?"

And so it was that two days later, leaving Ansjie and Challoner betrothed, with Mrs. Balzer moved in as a chaperone, Deborah started off to the smithy, escorted by Conrad. She had her clothes and Conrad's translations, but she'd stored Dane's sketch pad in the carved chest of household things.

It was like storing the past with a future that might never come. But it wasn't possible to shut away her love for Dane.

• xix •

The gardens of Friedental were green because people carried water to them from the well or creek, but away from the life-giving stream and its trees and thickets, the grass was sere and brittle, the wind a dry scourge that cracked lips and made eyes smart. Conrad had insisted that Deborah wear one of his broad-brimmed hats, but she was still dizzy from the heat when they stopped at noon to water and rest the horses.

She drank thirstily, splashed her face and hands, and held her wrists under the water for cooling. The thought of food was repulsive.

Conrad, scanning her sharply, cut off small crisp slices of apple from one of his trees and made her eat them. The tart, sweet juiciness gradually whetted her appetite, and Conrad made her lie back against the packs while he fed her bites of bread, cheese, and smoked ham, himself eating between his ministrations.

"Shall we go on now?" he asked presently. "We could wait a few hours and still be there before dark."

"We might as well travel," she said. "It's too hot to get much relief from it. Conrad, do you realize there hasn't been a rain that wet more than the surface in over two months?"

"I know it very well. The council has talked of little else their past few meetings." How reassuring was that familiar smile of his! "In Germany we think we're in a drought if two weeks pass without rain. Still, our corn is fine and tall this year, and the wheat was good. It won't be a hungry winter.

But what about next? thought Deborah. What if it doesn't rain in time to help the spring crops?

She pushed the fear aside. It *would* rain. There'd be snow to melt and sink into the earth. She sighed as Conrad helped her into the saddle, smoothed Chica's sweating neck, and lifted the reins.

It was still punishingly hot when they reached the smithy in mid-afternoon, but Johnny, Maccabee, and Laddie were heating and hammering away. Johnny roared at them to go on in and make themselves at home. Several wayfarers, gold-seekers from the look of their gear, lounged under the trees, waiting to have their horses shod or other work done.

Sara came out as quickly as she could, burdened so heavily that it seemed she couldn't carry the baby much longer. In spite of her awkwardness, there was a sort of blooming about her that made her eyes shine and her skin glow.

At least she'd had her lover; at least she'd have his baby. And she was loved and protected by a man who'd cherish that child of another man's. Deborah wondered, with a cry of inner despair, if she and Dane would ever have that much.

While the women embraced and Sara drew Deborah inside, Conrad led the horses around to the stable. A safe distance from the door and curious eyes, Judith hugged Deborah, too, and announced that she and Maccabee had been married "proper and fast" by a circuit-riding Methodist preacher who'd stayed the night a few weeks ago. Deborah was glad for her and said so, but the news made her feel more solitary than ever.

Each of her friends had loved and lost a man, then found another. Their lives flowed on while hers seemed stranded on Dane's immovability and her own sworn purpose. But she was going to look for him, try to be sure that at least he was alive. And behind that resolve was the persistent, though rebuked, hope that he might change his mind, might stay with her.

Nothing had been seen or heard of him at the smithy, or of Rolf, either. Deborah learned this before Conrad joined them. There was nothing for it, then, but to borrow some of Laddie's clothes, get another Bowie, and head for Westport. After Conrad was safely gone, of course.

During and after supper they exchanged news. Dr. Challoner's offer to attend Sara was gladly accepted by Johnny, though Sara looked mutinous and said she could manage perfectly well with Judith and Deborah.

"I'd rather you had the doctor," Deborah said so fervently that everyone laughed. "Besides, he might bring Ansjie with him, and you'd like her. They plan to marry."

Her only other friend! Why was it that none of them had to choose between love and responsibility?

Johnny told how Doy had been tried again in June and sentenced to the penitentiary. Free Staters had met at Elwood and crossed into Missouri on Saturday, July 23, getting the lay of the town. That night, during a storm, they came to the jail, pretending to have a horse-thief prisoner. When the jailer let them in, they held a gun on him and made him release Doy. Mingling outside with crowds just getting out of the theater, they managed to get away and escape into Kansas.

Friends met them at the river. They triumphantly took Doy to Lawrence and celebrated his liberation with a big reception.

"Was John Brown in on that?" Deborah asked.

Johnny shook his head. "Don't think he's been in Kansas since he got away with that bunch of slaves. Probably chasin' around up north raisin' money from the abolitionists and cookin' up some prairie fire scheme." He looked thoughtfully from Conrad to Deborah. "So you think it's time to come back, honey?"

She nodded. "I can't hide away forever."

"Wouldn't exactly call it hidin'," Johnny chided. "I bet the way you taught their children had somethin' to do with the Friedentalers voting to be an underground station."

"It did," said Conrad to her surprise. "If Deborah hadn't made the Territory's problems real to them, it would've been easy to decide to keep clear."

With mixed feelings, she pondered that. She was grateful if she'd had anything to do with the decision to shelter runaways, but feeling the weight. If that peaceful valley were ravaged as her home had been— It couldn't happen! Missourians had never raided that far. Besides, Friedental was tucked far away from the main routes, scarcely known about.

But concern for the village had been irrevocably added to her other debts.

Johnny said the village could probably get an anvil from the new foundry in town, but he could swap them about everything else they'd need to set Rebe up. "Glad you've got a smith," he said. "I'm snowed under, what with all these folks goin' west, and about the time we see the last of *them,* everyone'll be bringin' in their butcherin' tools or needin' new ones. And, of course, they'll tote along every dad-burned broken chain, hook, shaft, plowshare, or axe that they've been gettin' by with all summer while they were too busy to bring 'em in." He snorted. "So I'll have to pound on their stuff all winter whilst they lounge between their barn and house just waitin' for spring so they can bust everything up again!"

"But Johnny," remonstrated Sara, smoothing his sideburns, "if people didn't need new things or old ones fixed, you'd have no trade."

He looked astounded. *"Cesli tatanka!* You're a smart *wastewin* on top of bein' pretty!"

"Pretty?" She laughed, ruefully glancing at her ripening belly. "I'm bigger than a buffalo!"

"Hell, you're goin' to have a big strong boy! And it's time you went to bed! You gals're goin' to have plenty of time to catch up on all your chatter."

"First let me be sure Laddie hasn't made the bedroom a pigpen," Sara insisted. As she and Deborah went down the covered passage to the small separate cabin, Sara asked, "You sent Dane Hunter away? Again?"

"I had to. He still wanted me to leave."

"Stiff-necked creatures! Both of you!"

Deborah let that pass. She helped Sara toss Laddie's things to one end of the partitioned room and put fresh sheets on what had been Sara's bed. "I'm worried about Dane, Sara. I want to go look for him."

Straightening in shock, Sara gazed in disbelief. "Look for him? In those rough hangouts where he's hunting his no-good brother?"

"Yes."

"Meshema, you're crazy!"

"I have to know if he's all right."

Starting to argue, Sara frowned, then shrugged. "Wait till Johnny's work lets up. Then he'll go."

"That'll be weeks yet! Besides, you heard him saying tonight there won't be much of an improvement. And the baby's coming. No, Sara, I'm the one who has to know, so it's up to me to find out!"

"If you travel alone and poke into the kind of places where men hang out, you'll be taken for a prostitute."

Deborah laughed. "Not if I borrow some of Laddie's clothes."

Sara sank down on the bed. "Crazy! Plain crazy!" She pointed at Deborah's breasts. "What'll you do about those?"

"Wrap a cloth around to flatten me. And I'll cut my hair."

"Would you like to glue on some of Johnny's beard?"

"It'll work, Sara." She peered in the mirror. "With my hair short, I'll look almost like Thos when he was about fourteen."

"Hah!"

"*Hah* all you want, but I'm going."

"Johnny'll have a fit!"

"Johnny doesn't have to know. You can just say I forgot something and went to look for it. He'll think I'm at Friedental and won't worry if I'm slow coming back."

"That's the same as lying!"

Deborah picked up a relatively clean pair of brown corduroy pants and an old red shirt. "Would you rather bend the truth a little or have Johnny get mixed up in something that's not his problem at all?"

Sara didn't answer for a moment. Then she said, "When do you do this crazy thing?"

"Conrad should leave tomorrow. So I'll start very early the next morning."

"Sneaking off from your friends," reproached Sara.

Deborah held the clothes up against her, nodding approval. "Just so," she said.

Conrad set off after breakfast, saying he'd send someone with a wagon for the smithy tools. After their good-byes, Sara shooed the others away so that Deborah was left looking up at him, heart unbearably heavy at the parting. She loved him, not as she did Dane, but as a friend who'd sustained her through a time when without his special understanding, her inner self might have curled up tight and withered.

Something of a father, something of a brother, something of a lover. Wholly a wise, strong, and gentle man.

"I can never thank you," she said, tears coming to her eyes. "But at least we'll see each other sometimes."

He smiled. "We will. So let's not be sad." His eyes changed. One hand dropped to her shoulder while the other tilted up her face. "Farewells have their sweet parts," he said, and he kissed her.

His mouth was cool and firm, till with an incaught breath, he swept her against him and his lips grew searching, hungry, demanding, rousing sensations in her that she tried to escape by pushing at him, trying to twist away.

He took away his mouth and held her till she was quiet, sobbing. "Oh, my love!" he said, stroking her hair. "Thorny wild rose! Does it distress you so much to think that if you let me, I could make you love me?"

She couldn't answer. He dropped a light kiss on her cheek and swung up on his big gray horse. She felt a terrible sense of loss as he rode away. Turning back to the cabin, she went swiftly to work, and she put him and that shattering kiss determinedly from her mind.

It was necessary for one person to know what she was doing in order to keep the others from looking for her, but Deborah decided not to tell Judith. She'd only argue, perhaps try to come along. Then Maccabee would have to know and there'd be a mess.

Sara had put some food in a bag and told Deborah to take blankets and whatever else she needed, all the while asserting that this was the most hare-brained notion she'd ever heard of.

"I expect so, Deborah soothed. "But there are lots of boys this age looking for work or running away west. No one'll pay any attention to me."

"Cesli tatanka!" Sara replied.

Deborah had her pack ready: food, canteen, bedroll, extra socks and underwear. Sara's shears were hidden under the bed for use first thing next morning. She wished for a change of clothes, but though Laddie probably wouldn't miss one set of garments, he hadn't so many that more could vanish without his noticing.

That day she'd asked Johnny for a plain Bowie and he'd loaned her an old one, promising to make her one as fancy as that which Rolf had taken when work slacked off a trifle. Deborah felt guilty at deceiving him, but she knew he'd never let her go alone. Long after Laddie was breathing heavily beyond the partition, she lay awake, alternately exhilarated and frightened.

She wasn't too nervous about masquerading as a boy. Growing up with Thos made it easy to swagger a bit, whistle, thrust hands in pockets, sprawl when sitting. But would she find Dane? And supposing she met Rolf? Shorn hair and trousers wouldn't fool him.

Still, she never seriously thought of abandoning her scheme. She'd waited long enough. This was the kind of adventure Thos would've loved. She seemed to feel the closeness of his eager, questing spirit.

Ride with me, Thos, she told him. *You understand. And you know about your baby, don't you? He'll be born soon and we'll all love him just as we loved you.* Her brother seemed to smile at her, silently tell her she should seek her love, and she drifted deeper and deeper into sleep.

She kept rousing, though, her senses alerted for the faintest light, and at last, though she didn't know what time it was, she rose, made the bed, and dressed in the dark except for the boots Lorenz Schroeder had made for her.

Getting out the shears, she hesitated, nerving herself as she gripped a handful of hair close beneath the ear. She'd so often detested the trouble of brushing and washing the long curly mane that she should've been glad to be rid of it, but as she took a deep breath and chopped away, it felt like a mutilation. Still, it had to be done. Later, with a mirror, she could even out the jagged edges.

When the cutting was done, she put the long tresses beneath the bed, not quite able to throw them out. Hanging the sheathed Bowie at her side beneath the trousers, she took her equipment and Conrad's hat, then went around to the stable without passing through the main cabin. A wavery gray was showing in the east, but she'd be several miles away before even Johnny stirred.

Nuzzling for a treat, Chica accepted part of the apple that was Deborah's breakfast and made no trouble at being prepared for the road at this unseemly hour. She never puffed up with air, as many horses did, so that the cinch later got loose and let the saddle slip to one side or the other.

"We're going to look for the man who gave you to me," Deborah told her, leading her through the stableyard and mounting only when they were well away from the buildings. Picking up the rutted road along the Kaw, Deborah let Chica pick her own gait but was glad it was a trot.

Even this early it wasn't cool. For weeks the sun had sent down scorching heat as soon as it toiled heavily into the sky. Spurts of powdery dust rose from Chica's hooves, and as the sky lightened, Deborah saw gaping cracks where grass was worn away beside the road and there was nothing to hold the parched earth together.

She wondered how many of the prairie chicks were finding enough food. Most of them, of course, wouldn't have lived this long. They were tasty morsels for skunks, wolves, coyotes, foxes, and birds of prey. But these also ate vast numbers of rodents and rabbits, which, unchecked, would destroy the prairie chickens' food and shelter.

Johnny said that half the prairie birds built nests on the ground and another third selected weeds or small shrubs. If this drought stretched on, every creature from field mouse to man would suffer. No legislating or planning could change that. It *did* seem that with all the natural travail man was heir to, he wouldn't try to create more!

Deborah passed a wagon whose encamped owners were beginning to stir. She spoke and received a cheerfully unsuspicious return. As she rode on, she realized she'd been holding her breath, another tightness added to the binding around her breasts, and she laughed, taking a deep breath and whistling as Thos might have done.

She might be recognized in Lawrence, so, though tempted to inquire there about the Hunters, she decided to pass around Mount Oread. Rather than push Chica to reach Westport late that night, she'd camp in some ravine tonight before it got dark, then enter the Border Ruffians' town tomorrow while she could look around in daylight.

If she learned nothing in Westport, she'd ride to Wyandotte, and if that was fruitless, she'd spend the night at the Shawnee mission. Leavenworth the next day, then probably Independence.

And then?

Oh, surely one of those places would turn up news of him! His English accent was sure to be noticed. But if she learned nothing? Nothing at all?

Her shoulders drooped before she set them straight. If a return through Westport yielded no clues, she'd go to Melissa Eden and ask if she knew Dane's whereabouts. So long as it couldn't interfere with her search, Deborah wasn't going to worry about scandalization over her clothes. If Melissa knew nothing, Deborah could only go back to the smithy and hope Dane was still alive and would be in touch.

Almost as desperately as she wished for that, she hoped she wouldn't meet Rolf.

It was getting hot. The cut ends of her hair prickled and

stuck against her neck. She unbuttoned her shirt as low as possible without showing the binding. Chica had lapsed from a trot into a smooth, graceful single-footing that, though slower, was much easier on Deborah's spine.

They were halfway to Lawrence when Chica nickered and a horseman rode out of the trees in a ravine. The horse was gray. And the rider was Conrad.

Quelling the impulse to whirl Chica and run, Deborah instead took the offensive. "You pretended to go home, but here you are, following me!"

"I didn't follow you, dear girl." His tone was humorous, but there was a light in his eye that told Deborah he wasn't to be blandished. "I went home to send a wagon for Rebe's tools and to tell Dr. Challoner that he'd best take up residence at the smithy as soon as he's mended, but then I cut across country. Far from following, I've been waiting for you for hours."

"Sara told you!"

"She did." The corners of his mouth twitched, though his expression was grave. "But don't blame her too much. I knew you were planning something. When I asked what it was and vowed I'd haunt the region unless she told, she found considerable relief in letting me worry about you, especially since I could do something about it."

Deborah flushed at the rebuke. "I didn't want to worry her, Conrad, but—"

"Someone had to cover up for you," he said equably.

She bit her lip, shamed at troubling Sara—and him—but still determined. "It's no use arguing! I'm going to look for Dane."

He smiled and shook his head, eyes running over her in a swift caress. "Deborah, Deborah, you harrow up the instincts of my robber-baron ancestors! I *could* take you back."

She stared at him, instinctively tensing to spin Chica to the side and onward. "That won't work," he said. "You can't lose me. But I'll go with you."

"You?"

"That's why I came—to help you find your love." He moved Sleipner in beside Chica, swept off Deborah's hat, and exclaimed ruefully. "You've cut your hair! I was going to pass you off as my sister, but now you'll have to be my scraggly young brother. I feel like sealing that relationship by giving you a good thrashing." But from the way his eyes rested on her mouth, she knew that wasn't what he wished most to do.

Her chagrin faded as they traveled on. She hadn't wanted to mix her friends up in her private search, but it was undeniably comforting to have Conrad beside her. Whereas a young boy, orphaned or runaway, might be brushed aside, people would pay attention to Conrad, make some effort to answer his questions. Conrad would have money; that might restore an innkeeper's or saloon owner's faulty memory. Without any conscious decision, Deborah stopped worrying and scheming. Conrad would know what to do and how to do it.

As they came within sight of Lawrence and the familiar slope of Mount Oread, Conrad suggested that after they watered the horses, Deborah should rest and wait while he rode into town and inquired about the Hunters.

"Mrs. Eden might know what a wayfarer stopping at the smithy wouldn't," he said reasonably. "And much as I enjoy being your escort, there are many places I'd rather take you than to brawling border towns."

Deborah assented gratefully. If the quest could end here, so much the better. She thought briefly of visiting her family's graves in the burial ground west of town, then decided against it. That could still unnerve her, and she might need all her strength for hunting Dane. Her family deserved a separate time when she could give them the unhurried tribute of full attention.

So she and Conrad skirted Lawrence on the south and he left her a short distance from the Kaw in a ravine shaded by a large single oak which had somehow escaped prairie fires which had probably kept trees from growing heavily on the south side of the river.

"I suppose I shouldn't help my younger brother from the saddle." Conrad grinned. "But since no one's watching, I'll have that pleasure."

He swung her down, strong hands almost closing around her waist. "I won't be long," he promised. Then he added with a grimace, "If I find your Mr. Hunter, I'll feel more like telling him to leave than bringing him to you!"

His mouth brushed her sheared hair. Then he was back on Sleipner, riding back to town.

Deborah sighed, watching him grow smaller, then disappear in the rolling prairie. Both Sara and Judith had lost the men they loved and married others with whom they seemed happy.

If Dane were dead, Deborah knew she'd have to accept that. After a while she could perhaps open herself to Conrad, let him love her, grow to love him fully. But stupid as it was, she couldn't put Dane from her heart; while they both lived, she was bound to him, just as in a perverted way she was tied to Rolf because he'd given her that first kiss with her own blood on his lips.

She loosened Chica's cinch, rubbed her down with an old handkerchief she'd found deep in one of Laddie's pockets, and rummaged in the pack for the food parcel. It'd be noon by the time Conrad got back. They might as well picnic in the shade before going on. It wasn't hard to find patches of barren ground where small foragers and grasshoppers had eaten grass and plants to the roots. Placing two chunks of limestone where they'd support the coffeepot Sara had provided, Deborah started collecting twigs and tinder to start a fire, using larger pieces to hold it.

Boiling river water would make it safe to drink. Rather than empty her canteen, she went down to the river and was filling the pot when she picked up the sound of hooves.

Conrad? In a few minutes more she knew it couldn't be. The sound was coming from the wrong direction; there were a number of horses.

Heedless of spilling water, she started to run for the ravine and Chica, then controlled herself and walked, instead. The first riders were coming over a rise to the east. Getting on Chica and trying to outdistance them would simply create suspicion.

She'd known she'd have to face people on this mission, but here she was, wanting to scoot like a rabbit! All the same, if the strangers decided to stop a while, she hoped Conrad would return quickly.

Pulling the hat almost over her eyes, she started making a fire. Or trying to. Her fingers shook till one match after another had to be discarded. The horsemen were pulling up.

"Trouble, sonny?" called a rough voice. "Reckon we could get your fire goin' for a cup of coffee."

Deborah glanced up. Her heart turned over, seemed to stop. Next to the burly man who'd spoken, Rolf Hunter sat on his tall bay. She ducked her head and mumbled something, hoping he hadn't seen, that in the flashing glimpse he hadn't recognized her.

He spoke to the men, who fell back a distance. Then she heard the creak of leather, followed by his steps coming toward her. There were spurs on his boots, long-roweled, polished. That was all she saw, keeping her face lowered, praying he didn't know her.

"So here you are," he said after a long moment, when she thought her nerves would break and she'd scream. "Hair cropped, breasts bound, but God! You're beautiful! Stand up, my love. Let me see your face."

She didn't move, trembling inwardly, trapped, trying to think how to save herself, but even more, how to keep Conrad from riding into this troop. Her upper range of vision caught on dangles of hair hanging from his belt, and she thought of the horsehair trimming Johnny's coat.

This wasn't horsehair. Some was yellow, some was black, there was one dingy reddish cluster, and the rest was brown, from sandy to dark, some straight, some curly.

Eight, nine . . . She stopped counting.

Faint with horror, she couldn't move. The Bowie pressed against her leg. But even if she got it out before he could stop her, she couldn't escape that pack of men.

Rolf pulled her to her feet. "I can't handle you gently or the lads would wonder. It's best they think you're what you're dressed as." His tone was conversational, but the ridge behind each nostril showed white, and in the searing noonday sun, his eyes shone brilliant green, with the pupils contracted to tiny points. "Now, what's this masquerade?"

Her brain hummed. Conrad. Any minute he'd ride into this. She had to think of something! Rolf's arm lifted.

Deliberately, he struck her, obviously calculating the force so that though it staggered her, she didn't fall. "I'm not the soft boy you diddled. You'd better know that right from the start. What're you doing dressed up like this?"

She could think of no way to protect Conrad. If she wasn't here when he came back, he'd look for her. "I'm hunting for Dane. Have you seen him?"

"I've done my best not to," Rolf said with a harsh laugh. "I go by another name these days: Charlie Slaughter. Like the ring of it?"

"Do you know where Dane is?"

Rolf slapped her again, casually. It jarred her neck, brought tears to her eyes. "Answer my questions before you ask any. How do you like my name?"

"It seems to fit," she said between her teeth.

He laughed. His eyes played over her, bringing a humiliated flush washing upward to the roots of her hair. "It's acquired quite a luster along the border. We're what you might call specialists at catching runaway slaves and liberating good horseflesh from trashy owners."

He was still strikingly handsome, but in the seven months since she'd seen him, his features had coarsened. He reeked of sweat, horses, tobacco, and whisky. Only his hair, hanging below his shoulders, was the same raw gold.

A dark blue shirt faced with red silk was slit halfway down his chest, and she suspected her Bowie was on the other end of a braided leather thong hung around his sun-darkened throat. The other Bowie and pistol at his scalp-laden belt gave him a look of restraint compared to the bristling armaments of his men: their Bowies, Arkansas toothpicks, braces of pistols, and scabbarded shotguns and rifles. Deborah made a helpless gesture at them as they loafed in their saddles.

A pack they were. Beasts. And Rolf's whistle could bring them down on her.

"Why?" she asked. *"Why?"*

"Why did you break out while I was avenging your family? Why didn't you want me instead of my noble brother, who, I hear, has gone looking for me in St. Louis since his snuffing around here fetched him nothing?" Rolf shrugged. "Let's just say, sweet Deborah, that I've found my *métier*. I've always believed I was a throwback to Vikings. Your border's given me a chance to be myself."

"A plundering killer and night thief?"

This time he knocked her to her knees. The side of her face was numbed, but she felt the slow trickle of blood from her lip. At his feet, in range to touch the dry bedraggled scalps, Deborah thought with lucid remoteness that she still had her thoughts, could say anything she wished, but the price would be a blow. Enough could break her physically no matter how right she was.

As if considering the plight of another person, she tried to see if provoking Rolf to kill her would save Conrad, then saw no way that it could. If she were missing, he'd follow the plain track of the brigands.

"At first I stayed because of you," Rolf said. "Someday I was sure to find you. But your chance at being my pampered wife in St. Louis or London's over. You'll ride at my stirrup, share my pallet, and if you've any sense, you'll keep my hell-hounds from knowing you're a woman." His voice roughened. He took a step forward and stopped.

"Blood on your mouth, Deborah! As it was that first time. I want to kiss it away, but that'll have to wait till dark."

"You can't keep me alive long if I decide to die." From somewhere, bracing for his hand, she found the strength to laugh. "I might show your men I'm a woman, work them up into killing you."

To her shock, he didn't strike her but laughed in delight. "I knew there was fire in you! I'll have it if it roasts me! But you mean to bargain or you wouldn't show your hand. What do you want that I might give you?"

"There's a man, a friend, helping me hunt for Dane."

Rolf's pupils seemed to spread dark over the irises. "A man?"

"Yes. He's in Lawrence trying for leads. If you'll promise not to hurt him when we meet, I'll say—oh, that you know where Dane is and will take me there, that he needn't trouble further."

Rolf slanted her a strange look. "If you weren't waifing after my brother, I'd think you loved this—*friend*." He studied her with narrowed eyes, then finally shrugged. "I suppose it's worth some forebearance to have you pliable. Convince this fellow that you're freely with me and he can depart in peace."

The Bowie pressed against her leg inside Laddie's loose corduroys, a last grace. She wouldn't feel bound by her promise once Conrad was safely gone, but she couldn't guess now whether the blade would be for her or for Rolf. She only prayed that Conrad would accept her story and not insist on seeing her reunited with Dane. He was stubborn enough, certainly, and this gang was pure and undiluted Border Ruffian.

"Get your stuff together and let's ride," Rolf ordered. "I promised the boys a drink in Lawrence if we can find anyone with the guts to sell it after those temperance ladies took to telling men what to do!"

Fresh alarm shot through her. She'd been too dazed, too frightened for Conrad and herself to wonder what the troop was doing this far from the border. There were still back-and-forth raids in the southeastern part of the Territory, but since the Doy affair, this northerly region had been fairly quiet.

"You're not going to cause trouble in Lawrence?" she cried.

"Not unless your Black Republicans and abolitionists ask for it," Rolf drawled. "I had some fine times in that funny little town. Hurry up! The boys are getting restless. I'll go tell them how you're all in a sweat to join up with us."

"And why would I want to do that?"

"Because you're a runaway kid who liked a little authority once he got a taste of it," Rolf taunted. "And if you're smart, you'll stick close to me after you join us. You've somehow flattened your breasts, but your throat and mouth still look damned womanish."

He swung up on Sangre and cantered toward his men. Deborah poured out the coffee water, then hastily bundled up her pack and tightened Chica's cinch. She was mounting, awkward from the length of the Bowie against her thigh, when Conrad and Sleipner came into sight.

Pausing at sight of the gang, Conrad's head turned toward Deborah. She waved and rode to meet him, trailed by Rolf. *Make him believe you,* she told herself. *For his life, he must believe you.*

"Conrad!" She tried to sound happy, but her voice cracked. She swallowed, close enough now to see his frown. "Conrad, such luck! This is Dane's brother, Rolf. He's going to take me to him."

"Is he, indeed?" Scanning Rolf, Conrad nodded, then turned again toward Deborah. He flinched, then made a sound in his throat before his eyes, catching Rolf's, changed to winter ice.

"I can't believe any man would hit Deborah, but some*thing* has. Since you've apparently become a brigand, Mr. Hunter, what do you ask for our lives?"

"Deborah's safe." Rolf stared at the older man, gave a slow nod. "She wants to go with me. Do us all a favor and head back from where you came from." He leaned forward suddenly, spurred by some flickering recollection. "Where *do* you come from, *mein Herr?* Are you the *Graf* of Friedental who's taken to stealing niggers?"

"I've stolen nothing." Conrad's thoughts must have flashed to his sister, Rebe and the runaways, and the villagers, but his face was as impassive as carved stone. "But if you have questions about Friedental, I'm the one to ask."

Rolf laughed venemously. "I don't have any questions, *Graf*. One of the men I pay for information—it's taken some doing to dodge my determined brother—told me all about your nigger nest. We were headed there to get those slaves back and teach the Prussians to stick to their plowing."

Deborah shrank. "But—you said—"

"That we weren't out for blood in Lawrence. We're not. My lads don't know where we are headed, really. I never tell them anything I don't have to a second earlier than I have to. Prevents a lot of misunderstandings."

"So." Conrad was musing aloud. "Your men don't know about Friedental?"

"No. I figured if we ran into something lucky on the way, we could save that for later." Rolf chuckled. "Farmers are sitting ducks. Always there."

"Especially when they're pacifists and forbidden by their religion to fight," thrust Deborah.

Rolf shrugged. "They should've thought of that before they let niggers roost with them." He cocked his head at Conrad. "But you, *Graf*, bear the ritual saber scar. How are you with Bowies?"

"Rolf!" cried Deborah, bringing Chica forward.

"It would be interesting to find out," Conrad mused. "I'll gratify your curiosity if you'll agree, win or lose, to leave Friedental alone."

"You'll lose," said Rolf. "Why should I bargain?"

Conrad smiled. On his tall gray horse, he looked very much the nobleman descended from generations of men used to weapons and command. "I thought that as an Englishman, you might have racial memories of single combat when two men spared their armies."

"Ah! So it comes to chivalry!"

"I've always thought it the only saving grace veiling spurs and swords. Having met your brother, I hoped for it in you."

Rolf stiffened. After a moment he slapped his knee. "Done, then! A tournament with Bowies! I'll tell my men that in the unlikely chance you carve me up, you're to go unharmed and they're to head back to Missouri."

"And Deborah?"

Rolf cast her a tigerish glance of possession. "I won't lose. But if I do, she can go with you. I don't want her to belong to anyone but me, and I'm sure you're too honorable to seduce her. My men would wear her to the backbone in a week." He laughed at the fury in Conrad's face and inclined his head mockingly to Deborah. "Credit that to me," he said, "though tonight I mean to have what I was too soft a fool to take before."

"Rolf!" she pleaded, riding forward. "Fight me! I can use a Bowie!"

"Thanks for reminding me," he said. "But I've another use for you."

He rode toward his men and announced the duel in a swaggering way that made them whoop and form a wide ring, some dismounting, others keeping to their saddles. He walked briskly about, inspecting eagerly proffered knives, then accepted one of cutlass dimensions and continued the search for its match.

Deborah bit back pleas to Conrad not to fight. He was bound to, not only for Friedental, but because he now knew Rolf's intent toward her. Pressing Chica close to him, she said fiercely, "Keep yourself covered! Try for the guts, the soft spots beneath his ribs! For God's sake, kill him if you can!"

"For your sake." Conrad dropped a hand on her shoulder, as if bracing a youngster, but his touch was a lover's. "Don't fear too much, my darling. For sport, we used to spar with daggers."

"If I hadn't come—"

He shook his head. "Then this mob would've struck Friedental. No, Deborah, live or die, as I may, the village is safe this time But you—I have to win because of you."

Rolf raised two blades that flashed blindingly in the sun. They looked eighteen inches long. Deborah knew so well the broad-ribbed blade, that curving point, honed to razor-edge sharpness on both sides.

"I love you." She fought to be steady. "Conrad, I love you."

A light flared in his gray eyes; they searched her, knowing what she meant. "I know you do," he said. "And I love you—with all my heart and strength, with my life and death." He slipped from the saddle. "Will you hold Sleipner for me?"

She dismounted, too, and, leading the horses, followed him.

• XX •

Conrad must have been a peerless swordsman, for years later and with a strange weapon, he moved with grace and decision. Rolf had held the blades together, proving the lengths equal, and offered a choice. There his gallantry ended.

He gave Conrad no time to get the feel or balance of his knife, but pressed his attack at once, slicing for Conrad's torso while defending his own vitals.

Had Conrad not been cool, content to parry, the fight would have ended within seconds. As he sensed his opponent's unshakability, Rolf dropped back, feinting now, trying to draw Conrad's blade.

Conrad kept his knife on guard, but he didn't push. Deborah could guess his mind. The longer he had to accustom himself to the weapon, the better he could use it, the more his old skills would revive. He'd take no chances he didn't have to.

"Get 'im, Charlie!" one of the men yelled. "Quit your fancy dancin'!"

"Let the Proosian have it to the hilt!" another urged. "Spill his guts!"

"Goddamn!" jeered the bearded man who'd first ridden up to Deborah. "If this is how gentlemen fight, I'm glad I'm not one!"

Rolf renewed his assault. Deborah felt Conrad's motions, moving her body with them in an agony of suspense. She'd never dreamed he could last this long. If Rolf would just grow restless, raise his knife, lunge too far—

Parry and cut.

Parry. Cut.

Beautiful. Deadly.

Deborah gasped. Conrad's left arm came up like a shield and caught Rolf's blade. While it was embedded, held by a deliberate twist of Conrad's arm that must have been excruciating, Conrad slashed.

There was the sound of incaught breath from rapt spectators. Releasing his knife, springing clear of Conrad's stroke, Rolf reached over his shoulder and brought out Deborah's Bowie. In the split second before Conrad could recover, Rolf ripped his throat.

Blood gushed, a bright fountain. Conrad sank to his knees, Rolf's other blade jutting from his forearm, then fell heavily, the knife slipping from his loosening hand.

Dropping the reins of the horses, Deborah ran to him, falling on her knees, trying to raise him. His head lolled. Blood spilled over her. His eyes were wide in surprise. Half-decapitated, he was already dead.

Rolf's shadow fell across them. Maddened, Deborah reached for Conrad's knife. Rolf kicked it aside.

"Up!" he said, panting from the battle, wiping off the blade. He caught Deborah's wrist and dragged her to her feet. "Go to the river. Get the blood off you."

Deborah snatched for the knife embedded in Conrad's arm. Rolf spun her away. "Listen!" His eyes were like a great cat's. "Shall I take these lads to Friedental?"

"You—you promised—"

"What's a promise?"

Deborah's head whirled. Her knees wanted to bend. She would have crumpled except for Rolf's brutal hands, shaking her to half-awareness, tossing her into the saddle.

"Behave, and he gets a decent burial." Grudgingly, he added, "A brave man, your *Graf*."

"You'd be dead if you hadn't cheated!"

"One can't cheat in a Bowie fight," Rolf said with a harsh laugh. "And he used a cute little trick of his own."

"At least send his body to town. Let his sister know!"

"You can write her a letter when we're back in Missouri. I admired his spirit, if not his common sense." He detailed several men to dig a grave down in the ravine. "Chunk some stones on it," he ordered.

"Man like that shouldn't git chewed up by varmints," agreed one of the diggers.

Rolf closed Deborah's nerveless fingers over the reins. "Ride!" he commanded. And he called over his shoulder, "Bring the gray along. It's a fine horse."

They passed a few farmhouses, but no one came out. Bands of horsemen too often meant trouble. If they were sighted by any travelers, those prudent souls detoured, leaving them the way along the river, which, at the border would empty into the Missouri. Conrad's blood dried, in places gluing Deborah's clothing to her skin.

She rode as if in a nightmare, numbly thinking this couldn't be real: Conrad's head nearly sliced from his shoulders; Conrad's blood sticky on her hands. She'd wake up.

In a little while, Sara would call her, or Ansjie. She'd be at the smithy or Friedental. Not here. Not slightly behind Rolf, encircled by his unholy crew, still absorbed in discussing the fight they'd just seen.

"That Proosian was a spurred cock!" said one. "Never saw a man trap a knife that way in his arm!"

"Goin' to try it yourself?" hooted a companion.

"Hell, no!" chuckled the first. "Ruther have another Bowie stashed like Charlie did! Slick as a greased razor-back, he is!"

It would be a tale to embroider and marvel over in saloons, to spread back down the Kaw till at last Johnny heard and took the word to Ansjie.

A story, a legend.

Was that all that was left of Conrad, so kind to her, so faithful, except for the body spilled in a hasty grave?

No. There was his colony, Friedental. Deborah's hands tightened on the reins as the first jolt of bitter outrage pierced her grief-drugged sensations. And there was his blood on her! She'd feel it burn till Rolf's cleansed it.

She'd kill him. He'd never kill another good man, never take runaways from Friedental. Dane flashed through her mind, but he was in another world. She was locked in hell with Rolf.

The Bowie pressed her leg in grim promise. She wouldn't try till she had a perfect chance. She didn't care if he or his men killed her so long as she got him.

Tonight, when they were a distance from the others, tonight, when he'd try to have her.

Tonight, tonight, tonight.

They rested once that afternoon. Deborah drank from her canteen and forced down some dried meat Rolf gave her. She must be strong for what was coming. But he misread her.

"That's it," he approved. "I'll send a few of the boys ahead to see if they can shoot a turkey or deer for supper. If they miss those, they can sure get enough prairie chickens." He shook his head fastidiously, said under his breath, "You're getting a soaking in the river tonight! How you can wear those clothes—"

She turned her back on him to caress Sleipner—Sleipner, who must wonder what had happened to his master, had never been ridden by anyone but him. She must try to get him away or let him loose. The thought of Rolf or one of these men using him made her sick.

As the afternoon wore on in merciless heat, she felt as if she were suffocating; she rode gripping the saddlehorn to keep from falling. Through her closed eyelids, everything glowed dull, sullen red. Several times there were distant shots and she roused, hoping for rescue.

"Sounds like supper," said the man leading Sleipner. "Hope it's a deer."

But it was prairie chickens that the hunters had basting on skewers when the main group halted just before sundown. Horses ridden or led to water, saddles thrown off, coffee started, and biscuits set to bake in Dutch ovens while one man made a skillet of gravy from fowl drippings.

Bottles came out, and cards. Several of the brigands looked Sleipner over, examined him minutely, and speculated on how much he'd bring from some rich horse fancier.

In much the same spirit, they eyed Deborah, though they kept a distance. Rolf's treatment of her made it plain that she wasn't an ordinary homeless boy, but she didn't understand what it meant when, after staring at her curiously, one nudged a friend and spoke loud enough for Deborah to hear, though Rolf was out of earshot.

"A real purty boy. But I never figgered Charlie had that bent."

"He kin sure handle ladies," the other said, grinning. "Must crave a change. You ever try that, Hank?"

"Naw." Hank spat neatly at the edge of the fire. "Ain't natural. But Charlie bein' English and all—reckon they have different ways. *I* ain't goin' to twit him, you bet!"

"Me, either. Like my hair right where it is!"

Rolf came back from rummaging in his saddlebags.

"Come on," he said to Deborah, handing her a bar of perfumed soap. "Got other clothes?"

"No."

He patted the bundle under his arm. "Then you can wear these till yours dry."

She would have liked to keep Conrad's blood till it was covered with Rolf's, but argument might lead to forcible disrobing and the discovery of her Bowie. Rising wearily, she followed Rolf to the river. He moved down it till they were out of sight of the camp, hidden by willows and brush. Then he turned on her.

His nostrils were distended. "The first time's going to hurt. It *is* the first time, isn't it, my dear? I know my virtuous brother!"

He began, with trembling hands, to unbutton her shirt.

"Rolf! Please! Wait till night—"

"Not a minute longer!"

He tossed her shirt down, then seized one end of the cloth and revealed her breasts. Already feeling violated, Deborah gave a moaning cry and covered herself, but he forced her hands behind her and bent, grasping her nipples with his teeth, hungrily, savagely stroking her.

Writhing, Deborah slid into oblivious panic, then roused at one penetrating thought: the Bowie. He mustn't find it. And she couldn't use it now. Even if she managed to kill him without noise that would alert the camp, she couldn't get far on foot before they learned the truth and tracked her down. She was ready to die, but not for what would happen then.

"Rolf," she whispered, "let me wash. Please!"

He lifted his head, watching her as his hand caressed her breasts. "All right. Wash—quickly." He walked with her to the water, watched, smiling as she turned to take off the trousers, careful to conceal the knife.

"No call to be modest with me," he called, chuckling. "I'll know every inch of you by morning!"

Keeping her back to him, she waded knee-deep into the coffee-with-blue-john-colored water, then had to stop because of the current. Rolf stood on the bank as she soaped herself and rinsed.

"That's enough," he said in a choked, husky tone. "Come." He had taken off his clothes. She saw for the first time, with shock and dread, what a lusting male was like.

Impossible to hide herself with her hands. After a futile attempt, Deborah let her arms fall, looked him in the face, and walked to the bank. He dragged her the last few steps to where his clothes were spread, forced her down, and fell on her like a storm.

Sheathed, her outcry at his breeching thrust stopped by his hungry mouth, he raised himself up on his elbows. "Look at me."

When she didn't he moved forcefully in her. She stifled a sound and opened her eyes. His face was only inches away. She could see the pores of his skin, the sweat on his forehead.

"You hate me, don't you?" He moved slowly, coaxingly. "But tonight I'll pleasure you. I'll have you beg for this. Only now—" His breathing changed. He gripped her with his hands; she felt he must break her. Then there was a convulsive striving. He groaned, quivered, then collapsed on her.

There was this time when he'd be helpless, she thought in bitter triumph. This time, when, if her knife were close, she could pay him back for Conrad. When he let her up, she went back to the river, washed herself of him, and then scrubbed her clothes, stiff with Conrad's blood, having to keep the Bowie in the trousers.

Fortunately, Rolf was bathing, too. When she put on his garments, she managed to sneak the knife under the trousers. The wet sheath was uncomfortable, but compared to the ache caused by Rolf's entry, it didn't matter. She hung Laddie's things on a bush and started back to camp, moving painfully.

"Sore?" Catching up, Rolf gave her a possessive pat, then laughed in a boasting way that made her hate him with new ferocity. "That won't last. What will is your being my woman!" He sucked in his breath. "God, I want you again already! I'm going to put our packs in that hollow west of camp where we'll have privacy. You go ahead and eat. I don't want you falling apart."

Deborah had no appetite, but if she got away she'd need her strength. She gnawed on what was left of one of the prairie chickens and filled her cup with coffee several times. Chica and Sleipner were hobbled and roved about with the other horses, grazing where they found grass all but cured into hay by the unremitting drought.

There'd be a moon tonight, but would she dare find Chica? She revolted at the thought of leaving Sleipner to be used or sold by these men. If she possibly could, she'd unhobble him, and if he wouldn't follow her, at least he might stay a safe distance from these thieves.

Rolf was back now, joking as he ate, accepting compliments on the duel. "Hey, Charlie!" called a ruffian whose bald head shone in the firelight. "How come we're headed for the border? You promised us a drink in Lawrence!"

"I'll stand you two in Westport," Rolf promised. "And that gray horse's worth twenty regular nags. You boys can split what he brings." He dropped a hand on Deborah's shoulder. "This lad reminds me of my brother. I want to get him settled proper, arrange for his education."

"Want we should help?" guffawed someone from the shadows.

Rolf said pleasantly, "Touch him and you're dead." In the nervous silence, he bent for a whisky jug he'd fetched from his gear, then handed it to the nearest man. "Drink up, boys. I may sleep a little late in the morning. Had a tiring day."

"It's the nights as does a man in," said the man with the bottle. "Sleep tight, Charlie!"

Moving ahead of him, Deborah's cheeks burned. "You—you want them to think something bad!"

"Best for you they do since none of them fancies boys!" They were out of sight and he stopped, bringing her against him backward so his hands could close on her breasts. If he turned her, pressed her close, he'd feel the Bowie.

She managed a breathless laugh. "Rolf! Let me take off my clothes!"

"So eager?" He laughed in flattered surprise. "If I hadn't had your maidenhead, I'd wonder about you!" Catching her by the hair, he pulled her head back and buried his face in her throat. "Be wild for me, Deborah. Use me up. Let me be your man." Releasing her, he began stripping. "Hurry! I've already made our bed."

Shaking, she pulled off the trousers, freed the Bowie in its sheath, and left it near the bedroll, covered by her shirt. Rolf was beside her in an instant.

"Be sweet to me," he whispered. "Oh, Deborah, be sweet and wild! I won't make you live like this; I'll take you away! Why are you trembling, love? Yes, it must scare you, but you can tame it. Here. Touch me, darling. Let me touch you—God, but you're beautiful! Soft!" He groaned. "I can't wait! You drive me crazy!"

She clenched her hands, lay still beneath his onslaught.

When this was over, the panting, the spasms, he'd lie exhausted.

Should she reach for the Bowie then or wait till he slept? But supposing he didn't sleep? Supposing he took her all night long, each time his desire and strength revived?

Working above her, he seemed caught in some mindless grinding compulsion that used him as much as her. He gasped; sweat dripped from him; it was terrifying to hear the laboring of his heart.

He rested, then went on with a strange dogged patience. Would he never finish? She ached and her bones felt as if there were no padding between them and the baked soil.

Involuntarily, she moved. The slight flexing touched him off. He battered at her with short, hard thrusts, then cried and sank into her, twitching in a way that made her remember how Conrad's body, dying, had done the same thing.

Nerved by that thought, she waited till Rolf lay spent upon her like a swimmer battered by a great wave. She spread both arms, sighing, then continued the motion of her right hand to search under the clothing, close on the knife.

Her fingers found the walnut handle. She couldn't reach his throat; the bones of back and shoulder might turn the blade. Her best, surest mark was his side, between ribs and flank. Stab in, rip as hard as she could down and to the front . . . .

Why was it hard to reach?

She thought of Conrad.

Her hand gripped the knife, drove it deep, cutting forward. Rolf's cry bubbled into a gurgling. Had she hit a lung? Rolling from beneath him, eluding his hands, which seemed to clutch more in agony than purpose, Deborah knew she should, to make absolutely sure, cut his throat.

She couldn't. The obscene noises he was making seemed to smother. He stopped thrashing. *I've killed him,* she thought, but she felt nothing.

It was only part of the grotesque dream begun with Conrad's death, and in this dream she groped in his clothes and found her own knife, the one Johnny had given her. Slipping it around her neck, she dressed quickly, then ventured to the slope.

The fire had died low. Most of the men lay in their bedrolls, though a few were still drinking. The horses had scattered. She held her breath till she saw Chica. Sleipner grazed near her.

Creeping forward, she kept an eye on the men at the fire. It should blind them to what was going on in this outer rim of darkness, but the moon was rising and that might betray her.

Blessedly, Sleipner was a calm-tempered animal and knew Deborah. As she undid the rawhide hobbles, he nuzzled her and followed companionably as she unhobbled Chica. The saddles and bridles were down by the camp, unreachable. Deborah didn't want to go back near Rolf to get her pack. She should reach help by morning and could do without food or water till then.

She led Chica along till she found an outcropping high enough to let her scramble onto the mare's back. The best thing to do, she decided, was to ride to Lawrence and alert the town about the Missourians. She suspected the men, leaderless, would drift back across the border, but they might first take it into their heads to do some mischief in the hated Free State stronghold.

Lying low, hands woven in Chica's mane, Deborah urged the little golden mare into a smooth lope. Before daylight, before Rolf was found, she wanted to be in Lawrence. When she tired of bareback riding, she walked, holding Chica's mane. The moonlight silvered rises and gullies.

Conrad was buried down one of them. He must be brought back to Friedental, buried with honor.

Honor?

I've killed a man. Deborah rode and walked, walked and rode, talked to herself and the moon and Conrad, and all the time his big gray horse followed her.

The next few days were as hazy and unreal as that night. Coming into Lawrence at daybreak, greeted by barking dogs, Deborah had gone straight to Reverend Cordley and told him everything—except where she'd spent the winter and her violation. She felt it far best for Friedental to be as little known as possible.

Cordley sent a messenger to Chaudoin's, and Johnny returned, speaking no blame to Deborah, but going with her and the militia to reclaim Conrad's body, wrap it, and seal it into the walnut coffin hauled in a wagon. He'd be taken to Friedental for proper burial, but he was already decomposing, so opening the coffin was unthinkable.

The militia scouted on to the camp but found only trampled ground and a burned-out fire. They might have disguised Rolf's grave or taken the body with them. The best-mounted volunteers followed the gang to the border but never came within sight of them.

Deborah and Johnny spent that night at Cordley's. After supper Melissa Eden came over with the old dress Deborah had left when her friends broke her out of the widow's bedroom last winter.

"I thought you might need this, dear," she said. "It's so romantic to go questing as a boy, but once everyone knows—well, then it's silly, if not scandalous."

Johnny squinted at the woman under bristling eyebrows. "I reckon if there's any scandal, Missus, it mayn't go well for them as spread it."

Handsome, ruffle-capped Mrs. Cordley covered Deborah's hand with her own and Reverend Cordley sighed. "The people of Lawrence owe Deborah every grace after being so quick to believe what *others*"—here he gave Melissa a meaningful look—"said about her sanity last winter. It's no wonder that she's adopted unusual methods."

"Oh, indeed!" agreed Melissa, but her bland smile couldn't disguise the eagerness in her voice as she searched Deborah's face. "Did you find Dane Hunter?"

Find Dane? With shock, Deborah remembered that all this had happened because she'd tried to do that. Conrad's death, her body's plunder, Rolf's blood on her hands. It did no good to tell herself that meeting Rolf's party had probably saved Friedental from pillage and its runaways from being returned to slavery.

Conrad had died on her account, because of her self-will. The thought of Dane now brought revulsion, self-hatred.

Find him? She never wanted to see him again. Her bruised, aching body shrank when she thought of a lover. The rape had sealed her more tightly than any nun's vows.

"No," she said to Melissa, "I didn't find him."

That night she dreamed. Her mother lay in a coffin and a sword was in her hands. Thos, Father, and Conrad stood in the shadows, and though Deborah saw no wounds on them, she knew they were dead. Her mother's coffin was large; there was room enough for her. Deborah longed to lie down beside this woman who'd given her birth, return to her beginnings, but the sword, the eyes of her watching loved ones, rebuked that.

She was dead as a woman, but there was purpose in her life. She must work for what her dead had believed, in a sense they lived through her. Weeping, she knelt to kiss her mother.

"I won't come now," she said. "But I'll do the things you can't. I'll always love you."

And she took the sword.

Elder Goerz led prayers for Conrad before the coffin was placed in its grave on the slope above the valley. Children and women laid flowers on the mound. These withered in the blasting heat. Next spring, though, there'd be the wild roses he'd loved, and if there was an afterlife, he'd be with his Röslein, in whose gentle garden he'd walked and whose blooms he'd savored.

Ansjie sobbed in her doctor's arms. Thank goodness, she had him! Rebe and the escaped slaves stood with their heads bowed, a dusky group among the blond Mennonites. Johnny had closed the smithy and left Laddie in charge. He kept a protective arm around Sara, who'd insisted on coming in spite of her advanced pregnancy. Deborah stood between her and Judith. Maccabee loomed behind them. Instead of the hymn, Deborah heard echoes of Conrad singing:

> "Oh, when will you return again, dear love of mine?
> When it snows red roses, girl, and when it rains
> white wine."

But there was more to do than mourn. If Rolf had learned of the runaways in Friedental, so might other slavers. As the procession moved back to the village, she mentioned this to Johnny.

"Hin!" said Johnny, his brow furrowing. "Well, sure, I guess we better move 'em north, though I'm behind at the forge."

"I can take them," Deborah said. "It's not so far to Topeka, and that's the next station, isn't it?"

"Yes, but sometimes if there's no one to do it, I have to take a train across the Kaw and travel north by east till we hit the Missouri and cross into Iowa." Johnny shook his head. "You can't do that alone."

"I can if you tell me how."

"I'm goin' with you," Judith said.

Maccabee, in rapid succession, looked startled, serious, and reluctantly approving. "They can do it," he told Johnny. "And someone 'sides you'n me needs to know that trail."

And so it was that within an hour of Conrad's burial, the runaways at Friedental, except for Rebe, were preparing for the next part of their journey to freedom.

Well before dawn the next morning they were on their way. Deborah and Judith, dressed as boys, would ride one ahead, one behind, the party, warn them to seek cover if other travelers came within sight. As much as possible, they'd keep off the road and wait till dark to go to the farmhouse "station."

All went smoothly. Covering the twenty miles to Topeka before sundown, the group waited in a ravine thick with cottonwoods till darkness, while Deborah rode in and told the "conductor" that she had eight "passengers" for him. Amos Blakeman, a white-haired, mild-eyed Quaker, couldn't take them north for a week and was much relieved that Deborah and Judith could.

When Deborah returned with her party, Amos and his wife had beds ready in the attic and cellar and a plentiful, hot supper. He'd also arranged with a sympathetic ferryman to take the "train" across before light and curiosity might make problems the next morning.

On the north side of the Kaw, Deborah was in strange country, but Johnny's map was good, and one by one they passed his markers pointing the way to the Missouri, including a farm where they spent the night.

Woods grew densely where there was water, the slopes became small hills, and at last the river brakes came into sight.

Scouting ahead, Deborah located the next station, a mill on the river. The miller's nephew would pole them across the river to Iowa and see them to the next stop, but they were now well out of the reach of Missouri raiders. Deborah and Judith wished them good luck and turned back for the Kaw.

They reached the smithy on September 1 to find Doc Challoner, exhausted from delivering twins, being ministered to by Ansjie while Sara cradled a child against each breast, spent, but so proudly beautiful she lit up the room.

Johnny looked as wrung out as Doc and as delighted as

Sara, hovering over her like a big grizzly with its first cubs—a mother grizzly, of course, since males were notoriously unfond of progeny.

"Ain't that a sight?" he crooned to Deborah and Judith. "Ever in all your born days see anything so purty?"

In truth, the babies were red mites with astonishing amounts of silky fine black hair. But their hands! Perfect, down to the minute fingernails. Deborah's little fingers dwarfed the tiny ones that gripped them, but she was amazed at their strength.

Had she and Thos looked like this? She hoped that somehow he could know. "This one is Thomas," Sara said, dipping her chin toward the slightly smaller infant. "Shall we call the girl Leticia?"

"That would be lovely."

Deborah could scarcely speak and knew that Sara, even more than she, must feel grief that the new twins' father and grandparents couldn't see and marvel at them.

Laddie glanced proprietarily about, folding his arms like a guard of honor. "These babies goin' to belong, sort of, to all you folks, but I'm their only really truly blood uncle! Ain't that right, Sara?"

"That *is* right," she corrected. "So remember that uncles wash their hands before they pick up babies."

"These are the finest I've ever seen," said Doc Challoner from the doorway. He wiped his brow. "But next time, young woman, try to have just one! Twins are the quick way to get a family, but it's hard on your doctor!"

"Come have a drink," invited Johnny, moving forward to put an arm around the doctor. "Let's have several! Wastewin, would you like some *mne wakan?*" The Sioux called whisky holy water.

"I'd rather have cold buttermilk," she said. "And then I want to sleep." Judith and Deborah stayed with her till she did.

During the next weeks, Tom's and Lettie's scarlet hue faded to dark ivory. Both thrived, but Tom seemed given to colics and temper outbursts. "I don't know whether to be glad or sad there's always someone to hold him," Sara grimaced as Johnny picked up the baby at his first howl.

"Be glad," Johnny advised. "Happy babies don't cry, and if they're not happy, somethin' damned well needs to be done!" He often walked about with both. Sometimes each had a firm grasp on his sideburns, but though Johnny might wince and grumble in Lakotah, he plainly adored the children.

Though everyone from Maccabee to Laddie helped with the twins, Sara was kept busy with them. Judith and Deborah took over the cooking, housework, and voluminous laundry. They put up two barrels of cucumber pickles, cut and dried pounds of pumpkin, squash, and rhubarb, and began gathering grapes and nuts down along the river.

There'd still been no rain, but Johnny left off smithing for a day to plow while Maccabee and Laddie sowed wheat. Toward the end of September a traveler left a letter for Deborah addressed to Johnny's care.

She stood holding it, staring at the bold, slanting script. Something stirred deep inside the scarred, tough armor around her heart. Surprised at this, for when she thought of Dane it was with the bitter-sweetness reserved for a dead loved one, she opened the letter with trembling hands.

St. Louis
September 15, 1859

Beloved Deborah,

I regret not coming to tell you good-bye, but perhaps it's best since I doubt either of us has altered our convictions. At least I can assure you that Rolf's border career has ended. After weeks of unsuccessful searching, I found him ten days ago, near death in a Westport hotel. He'd been left there by cronies after some urchin he'd befriended all but murdered him. Rolf apparently managed to drag himself into camp and, for a miracle, his companions got him to Westport without killing him or even robbing his pockets.

The best surgeon in St. Louis has saved his life, though it will be months before he mends completely. This seems a propitious time to take him back to England and put *finis* to his Kansas adventures.

I can't forget you, Deborah. I see you in harvest, golden wheat in your arms, or riding Chica, your hair blown back. But, mostly, I feel you in my arms—which ache, and always will, till I hold you again. I will be back. This time, somehow, let's work things out.

Dane

Faint, disbelieving, Deborah sank down on a bench.
"What is it?" Sara demanded.
Unable to speak, Deborah handed her the letter.
"Why, that no-good Rolf!" Sara cried after a hasty scanning. "If Dane knew—"
Deborah shrugged. "I should have cut Rolf's throat, the way he did Conrad's. But I just couldn't." She'd told Judith and Sara everything, but she didn't want anyone else to know about the rape.
Sometimes she dreamed of it, not so often, though, as she dreamed of Conrad. Rather than feeling disgraced or humiliated by that invasion, she felt numbed in her secret parts, closed and dead.
"Dane says he'll come back," Sara said like a question.
"It'll be no use."
"Why? Don't you love him?"
"I—I don't know. It doesn't matter now."
"Why not?"
She could think of no way, without sounding tragic or silly, to put it into words. "I belong to something else."
Sara frowned. "I don't know what you're talking about, *meshemah,* but I don't like it! If it's because he's Rolf's brother—if it's because you're shamed—"
"That may have a part in it," Deborah said, trying to be honest about the implacable core that had held her together this past month. "But it's more that Conrad died because I was so set on looking for Dane."
"His death saved Friedental, and those runaways!"
"Maybe." Deborah folded the letter. "But I—owe debts. Till they're paid, I can't have my own life."
Judith, who'd been rocking small Lettie, shook her head. "That's a sad thing to say, honey."
"It's a true thing." Deborah put the letter in her apron pocket and poked up the fire to cook supper.
She was a weapon. There could be no softness in her. How she would be wielded, she didn't know; she could only wait and be ready.

Johnny rode into Lawrence to vote for the Wyandotte constitution on October 4. The Territory's voters ratified it almost two to one and now looked forward to the December Territorial elections, when Free-State men, united now as Republicans, should win resoundingly.
It was a far cry from the reign of the Bogus Legislature and Border Ruffians, but John Brown, absent from Kansas

since January, when he spirited through his last "train" of escaped slaves, wasn't ready to leave abolition to gradual change.

The night of October 16, with eighteen men, he moved into Harper's Ferry, Virginia, about sixty miles from Washington, and took the U.S. arsenal and armory. Three others of his men had been left to move supplies and arm the slaves and enthusiasts Brown expected to join his cause. Apparently he hoped to free the slaves of Virginia with his volunteer army.

Instead of being filled with supporting hosts, the armory was attacked the next morning by citizens who forced Brown's men and his prisoners into the engine-house.

Two of Brown's sons were killed, but he didn't harm his prisoners. The siege lasted all day. During the night Colonel Robert E. Lee arrived with government troops and sent J. E. B. Stuart, his aide, to ask Brown to surrender. Brown refused that night and again the next morning.

Amidst firing, the troops battered in the door. A marine lieutenant hacked Brown to the floor and struck him repeatedly across the head with his sword. Brought to trial October 27, Brown claimed throughout the next six days that he intended only to free slaves, not foment rebellion.

Twelve of the men with Brown had helped him in Kansas. Most were young zealots. Though conservative Free-Staters denounced Brown, Jim Lane and Dan Anthony praised him. Money was raised for a Doy-style rescue, but Montgomery, the dour jayhawker, traveled out to Virginia and declared this impossible.

North and South, the press blazed for and against the grim old man. Greeley, in the *New York Herald Tribune,* blamed Brown—and Kansas—on ex-President Franklin Pierce and Senator Douglas for supporting the Kansas-Nebraska Bill.

> John Brown is a natural production, born on the soil of Kansas, out of the germinating heats the great contest on the soil of that Territory engendered. Before the day of Kansas outrages and oppression, no such person as Osawatomie Brown existed. . . . Kansas deeds, Kansas experiences, and Kansas discipline created John Brown as entirely and completely as the French Revolution created Napoleon Bonaparte. He is as much the fruit of Kansas as Washington was the fruit of our own revolution.

"He'll hang tomorrow," Johnny said, returning from voting for the Territorial legislature on December 1. "Won't plead insanity. By dyin' he'll do more to free the slaves than ever he could alive. Old fox knows that."

Except for him, Thos might have been alive. There was that bloody work on Pottawatomie Creek. But the man had stepped across the line that made monsters and martyrs. Judith bowed her head and wept.

"He's the sword of the Lord and of Gideon!" she said when pride in the man triumphed over grief. "His soul can't die. It'll never die!"

Abraham Lincoln, hoping for nomination in 1860, came on a five-day speaking tour of northeastern Kansas. He spoke in pro-slave Atchison, condemning Brown's methods, on December 2, when John Brown was hanged in Virginia.

Brown wasn't accompanied by a minister; he'd said he couldn't pray with Southern preachers who supported slavery. But on the way to the scaffold, he kissed his jailer's child.

• xxi •

January customers at the smithy brought a running account of the overwhelmingly Republican Territorial legislature's refusal to hold session in Lecompton. Meeting there, they moved to adjourn to Lawrence, the governor vetoed their resolution, they passed it over his veto, and they moved to Lawrence.

Governor Medary and his secretary wouldn't go or send necessary records. The legislature passed a resolution to adjourn since the secretary wouldn't provide these documents. Governor Medary immediately issued a proclamation for them to meet the next day at Lecompton. The legislature did so, again resolved to go to Lawrence, were again vetoed by the governor, and again passed the resolution over his veto.

At that point the governor gave up, though he did veto their February 11 abolition of slavery within the Territory. They overrode his veto and went on to pass Kansas's first fencing legislation, ordering that when the property of two claimants adjoined, each must build half the dividing fence.

"Hate to see fences," rumbled Johnny. "Plumb ruins the country!" He grinned reminiscently. "Sometimes I think that Shoshoni, Washakie, was right about what he told the agent who wanted him to farm. 'God damn a potato!,' he said."

"That's wicked talk," Sara reproved. "The buffalo are gone, from here, anyway, and we need potatoes and gardens to eat."

Johnny sobered. "We sure need rain. Precious little snow this year. But it's bound to rain in the spring."

But it didn't. A severe late freeze added to the misery. There was a ripple of excitement in April when Russell, Majors, and Waddell started the Pony Express mail run from St. Joseph to California, but as that pitiless summer wore on, Kansans thought of little but the weather.

Johnny's wheat shot up but quickly withered, and the wheat sowed that spring didn't come up at all, though corn down by the river produced about two-thirds of the usual crop. The members of the household at the smithy were lucky to be near the Kaw. By hauling water from the river, they kept the garden alive, but settlers at a distance from water saw all their food die in scorching blasts from the south.

Great cracks split the earth. Ponds, wells, creeks, and streams dried up. Thirty thousand settlers, about one-third of the Territory's population, begged or borrowed their way back east or farther west. Of those remaining, half would have gone had they been able. The others, like those at Chaudoin's, managed to raise enough food for their own use and shared what they had.

The creek by Friedental never went completely dry, nor did the deep wells. Several times that summer Deborah took fugitive slaves to Friedental to let them rest from their flight; then Challoner would take them on to Topeka and Amos Blakeman. Each time she visited Conrad's grave on the hill and watered the wild roses that Ansjie ordinarily tended. It seemed impossible that he'd been dead almost a year. In her heart, she still heard his voice.

"God has given us the grace of water," Elder Goerz told Deborah during one of her visits. "The council has voted to give all the food we can spare to those in need. Will you see to the distribution, Fräulein Whitlaw?"

So with Ansjie and Challoner, Deborah visited parched farms. Often what they brought was the only food in the house except for a little corn. Doc, a big, gruff but incredibly gentle man, delivered babies, set broken legs and arms, and did whatever else he could.

"But there's not enough food," he said, looking gaunt and drawn himself. "These malnourished children and frail women—men whose hurts won't heal because they're run down! Food's the medicine they need, and there's just not enough of the right kind."

He and Ansjie, like the people at the smithy, ate abstemiously in order to share with the virtually starving.

Prairie chickens, usually so plentiful, were scarce, and even when one could be shot, it was tough and leathery. Where grass had once grown waist-high, it reached only a few stunted inches, except along the river and creeks.

In Washington the debate on admitting Kansas was fiery on both sides. Senator Wigfall of Texas railed against Massachusetts for "subverting" the Territory through the New England Emigrant Aid Society. He charged they had filled it up with "vagabondism of the North; not only the vagabondism of the North, but that of Europe also has been drained in order to get emigrants to send into that country." And he went on to say: "The inhabitants of that so-called state are outlaws and land pirates . . . a set of Black Republicans, and traitors, and murderers, and thieves."

To which Eli Thayer, founder of the Society, blamed Southerners for the Kansas-Nebraska Bill, recounted the terrorism of the Border Ruffians, and said the Free-Staters had quite rightly resisted a fraudulent legislature.

As fall came without rain, Johnny closed down the smithy and, with Challoner, Maccabee, and Laddie, took a wagon several days' journey west till they found buffalo, gaunt from the drought but still good. Killing a dozen, they butchered and jerked the meat, and again Deborah and the Challoners made the far-scattered rounds of the hardest-pressed settlers.

The twins, now rapid crawlers and slow walkers, cut their first teeth on that jerky. Lettie's hair had stayed silky black, but Tom's was turning red. Both had warm brown eyes. It was a shock to realize on their first birthday that they'd never seen rain.

People would certainly have starved that fall and winter if easterners hadn't contributed, through a relief committee set up by Samuel Pomeroy, steamers and freight caravans of food and other supplies. Pomeroy became known as "Baked Beans" because New Englanders sent so many of them to Kansas. Illinois shared its corn.

Rain fell in November, but it wasn't till the snows of January that people began to dare hope the drought was broken.

Meanwhile, border troubles had heated up. A newcomer, Charles Jennison, stole so many horses that people said any good horse was "out of Missouri by Jennison." Down at Fort Scott, pro-slave Judge Williams fled to Missouri, and without even his loaded justice, pro-slave men hanged two Free-Staters, and Free-Staters returned the compliment.

While the Missouri militia was called to the southwest part of the state to defend its borders, there was a peculiar raid on the rich plantation of Morgan Walker, seven miles from Independence. Walker was warned ahead of time by a man calling himself Charlie Hart. Hart said he'd be with the raiders but was betraying them because jayhawkers had killed his brother.

Actually, the raiders were Quakers, dedicated abolitionists, whom Hart had recruited by claiming Walker's thirty slaves were thirsting to be set free.

When the Kansans knocked on Walker's door on the night of December 10, he invited them in. They told him they'd come for the slaves. Walker gave them directions to the quarters and the Kansans started out, except for Hart, who stayed in the house. Walker's hiding neighbors cut loose with shotguns. One man was killed and a wounded one was dragged off by a companion to be tracked down and killed a few days later.

The double-dealer was a young hanger-about Lawrence who had boarded for a time at the Whitney House and been nursed through a long illness by the Stones, who owned that hotel. He'd taught school briefly and followed the wagons to Pike's Peak. In Missouri he was pro-slave, in Kansas a Free-Stater. He had blue-gray eyes and pale gold hair.

His real name was William Clarke Quantrill. The Walker

raid was the beginning of his known depredations, though from then on he would prey on Kansans and Unionists.

In January 1861 the last Territorial Legislature met at Lecompton, and, as usual, adjourned to Lawrence, where they waited for news of Kansas's admission to the Union.

Because President Buchanan and his party opposed Kansas's entry as a free state, admission had been stalled in the Senate till the 1860 elections were over and Kansas could have no part in them. As the Senate debated admission, six senators from seceding states left Washington for their homes.

Late on January 29, Dan Anthony strode into the Eldridge House after a hard ride from Leavenworth and told the legislators that Buchanan had that day signed the bill making Kansas the thirty-fourth state.

In spite of windy cold and snow, people poured to the hotel and public places to celebrate. "Old Sacramento," the cannon captured from pro-slavers back in Lawrence's besieged summer of 1856, was hauled out and fired.

If Father could have been there! Deborah thought as she listened to Johnny, tears springing to her eyes. She blinked them back and picked up little Tom, waltzing him in wide circles as his moccasined feet braced sturdily on her hip and he squealed with delight, red curls dancing.

"You're a citizen of the United States!" she told him, then plunked him down and gave Lettie a twirl. "As for you, honey, I may not see it, but the day's coming when you can vote! Why, you might even be a senator!"

"Cesli Tatanka!" roared Johnny. "Her Indian blood should give her better sense than that!" But he got out a jug of wine and even the women got slightly tipsy that night.

After seven years and eight months, six governments and five governors, shifting the seat of government from Leavenworth to Shawnee Mission, to Lecompton, to Pawnee, back to Shawnee Mission, then to Minneola, and at last Topeka, the strife-born Territory was at last a state.

It entered a Union from which southern states were rapidly seceding. Lincoln was inaugurated in March and on April 12 Confederate troops opened fire on Fort Sumter.

Jim Lane and "Baked Beans" Pomeroy had been elected as Kansas's senators late in March. At news of Fort Sumter, Lane hastily organized a Frontier Guard which bivouacked in the East Room of the Executive Mansion with Sharps rifles and cutlasses.

"Lane's back here raising a Kansas Brigade," Johnny reported one noon. "Just shod a horse for one of his recruits. If I know Lane, it'll be a gang of thievin' jayhawkers who'll make Missourians wish they *had* seceded!"

Missouri had voted to stay in the Union, but loyalties were bitterly divided, and the raidings of Lane, Jennison, and Montgomery had done nothing to soothe those Missourians who lived near the border.

"But Lane's a senator!" Deborah objected. "How can he be getting up an army?"

"*Hin!* He and Governor Robinson, who've always hated each other's guts, are sort of arguin' that point. Robinson wants to appoint a replacement. Lane says he'll resign when he gets the brigadier general's commission he's been promised." Johnny cleared his throat. His smoky eyes rested on Sara till she glanced up at him in alarm. "No doubt, though, that Kansas needs to muster every soldier she can, fast. Missouri could easily fall to the Confederates. If she does, Kansas is easy pickings."

Almost-two-year-old Lettie was snuggled in Deborah's arms. With a rush of fear, Deborah held her closer so that the child's soft black hair brushed her cheek. "I thought Missouri wanted to be neutral!"

"That was what Claib Jackson, the governor, tried to bring off. Made an agreement with General Harney in May, but Lincoln booted Harney out and General Lyon—" Johnny chuckled. "*Tatanka wakan!* Lyon was stationed at Fort Riley during the worst Border Ruffian days. Hates slavery, claims to be infidel, and has been known to make a man who was beating a dog kneel down and beg the dog's pardon. Well, Lyon replaced Harney. He listened for about an hour to Jackson, General Price, and other big guns carry on about states' rights and Missouri's right to be neutral."

"And then?" prodded Deborah.

"Lyon got up, spurs jinglin', and told them that before he'd let Missouri dictate to *his* government on anything, he'd see all of *them,* and every man, woman, and child in the state, dead and buried. So they took off for the capital."

"Jefferson City?"

Johnny nodded. "Lyon is calling for men. He's got to keep Jackson from handing Missouri over to the South."

"And you think you've got to help him!" Sara cried.
"Wastewin, I know I do."

She sat as if frozen. Tom, clambering onto her lap, patted her cheeks. "Mama? Mama?"

For once, she put him down. After a moment's pout, he ran to Judith's inviting arms. The twins were usually absorbed in their own world, but when they came to the grown-ups they were used to being indulged.

As Sara reached for Johnny's rough, powerful hand, Deborah couldn't keep from a flash of wondering how they were with each other as husband and wife. Was Sara merely grateful to Johnny, or had he become her man? If that hadn't been so before, it certainly happened now.

Sara pressed Johnny's hand to her cheek and then released it. "When will you leave?" she said.

Maccabee wanted to go, but Johnny persuaded him to stay. "No use in your goin' along to do camp chores, but you could keep the smithy runnin' and look after the women."

"*We'll* look after him," said Judith saucily.

"Fine." Johnny grinned. "Just so you're all here when I get back. Maccabee, I'm thinkin' maybe you and Rebe can work together at Friendental for a spell and then here, takin' care of the work at both places. His striker's not much account."

Maccabee considered a moment. "No one could say we wasn't real *black* smiths, could they?" he chuckled. "But if I get a chance to do some real fightin', Laddie may have to take over."

Laddie looked rebellious. At fifteen, he was as tall as Johnny, but he still had a child's smooth face. "I want to go with you, Johnny!"

"Your turn's liable to come," said Johnny in the tone that meant he wasn't open for argument. "Don't rush it, son. One man at a time's enough from our outfit."

But Johnny didn't go alone. Doc Challoner came by on his way to join up. He'd wanted to ask Deborah to visit Ansjie sometimes. "She says men are fools to blow holes in each other." He grinned. "And she's right. But it's still my job to patch 'em up."

He spent the night. The next morning he and Johnny rode east, Johnny on Sleipner's colt, given to him by Conrad, and Doc on Sleipner.

Sara didn't cry then, but later that morning Deborah

found her hugging Johnny's old horsehide coat and weeping as if her heart would break. Thos had been her joy, but Johnny had made her happiness.

Slaves began to come—not through the underground railroad, but like leaves before the wind. Many slaveowners in Missouri and Arkansas were afraid of losing their "property" and were selling their people south, a fate blacks dreaded. To escape this, or simply taking advantage of the confusion caused by war, hundreds of slaves flocked into Kansas, often bound for Lawrence, which was to them a sort of Jerusalem.

According to the refugees, Lawrence people had been kind, feeding and sheltering slaves who wanted to settle there, helping them find work and even running a night school. But the town was overcrowded and not recovered from the drought of the year before. So singly or in groups, these wayfarers stopped at the smithy.

Though the Fugitive Slave Act was still in effect, the war made it unlikely to be enforced in Kansas or the North. After their guests were rested and fed, Deborah, Sara, or Judith talked with them to see what they wanted to do. Deborah took those who wished to go north on to Topeka and white-haired Amos Blakeman. The problem was what to do about those who wanted to stay in Kansas.

Penniless, with no tools or supplies, all they had was the ability to work. Brooding on this, things suddenly clicked in Deborah's head.

"Johnny and Doc aren't the only men who went off to war," she said, glancing around the supper table and at the three refugees who'd come that day, having trudged barefoot from central Missouri.

Sam and Jewel were husband and wife. Jace was Jewel's younger brother. They all looked to be in their twenties, and their elation at reaching freedom had been considerably dampened by realities.

"Marse Hugh couldn't find anyone to buy us together, so he was fixin' to sell us separate," Sam had explained. "So we took off for where we heard the Union army was. We thought they'd take care of us, but the cap'n, he say we still Marse Hugh's, and Marse Hugh a Union man, so if he come huntin' us, we have to be handed back. Cap'n say we better scoot for Kansas."

"Glad we cain't be sold no more," said Jace. "But we

don' know what to do, and no one else seem to know, either!"

Now, swept up in the simplicity of her idea, Deborah clapped her hands together. "You need a place to live and work," she said. "And there are lots of farms where the men have gone off to fight. Do you want to farm?"

"All we know." Sam shrugged. "But how we goin' to do that?" He shot her a suspicious look. "We don' come here to be slaves again, and we sure cain't own land, no more'n a mule."

"Well, that's bound to change," reasoned Maccabee. "Unless the South wins the war, the slaves are goin' to be freed. Then they'll own land 'stead of bein' owned by it!"

The fugitives looked skeptical. "Maccabee, I'm sure you're right," said Deborah. "But for right now, I'll bet we can find places for lots of folks who want to stay." She turned to the young blacks. "My family's place was—burned down, but the soddy we lived in till we built a cabin is in fair shape. There's a good well and we've kept planting the fields, so there's wheat and corn this year. If you want, you could take it over for a while."

"For sure?" asked Sam between hope and doubt.

Deborah shrugged. "With Johnny gone, it'll be hard for us to take care of it. It'll belong to the twins someday, but long before they need it you'll probably have land of your own."

"Land of our own!" echoed Jace.

Tears glittered in Jewel's eyes and Deborah felt a lump swell in her own throat as she comprehended something of what it must mean to people who'd been chattels, possessed like horses, to think of being owners themselves, holding land and the fruit of their labor.

It must be scary, too, making decisions after a lifetime of being told what to do and when, having to supply one's own necessities instead of having them provided, however inadequate.

Freedom was choice, and choice was scary. Deborah had a treacherous moment of wondering whether most people, providing they could consider themselves free, wouldn't rather be relieved of choice, the struggle to support a decision.

"We saved a few tools from the place," said Maccabee. "You want to loan Belshazzar, Deborah? There's a plowshare I can weld a new point on. Yeah, I figger we can get you off to a purty good start. Damned lucky you come this year 'stead of last! Wouldn't have been a crop."

Judith nodded. "You got time to get food for winter. We'll give you seeds for melon, squash, and pumpkins."

"Maybe we can build a new cabin," Jewel dreamed.

Deborah felt a pang. Other people living where her family had, sitting by the fireplace. . . . But the stab of pain eased into thankfulness. If her parents knew, they'd be happy. What better way was there for their home to come alive again?

"But before we start," said Sam with new, quiet authority, "I notice your wheat's high enough for harvest. We help you."

"Obliged," said Maccabee. "I've been tryin' to get away from the forge, but everyone seems to need somethin' fixed yesterday, or teams go lame 'cause they need shoes."

So Deborah, Judith, and Jewel bound as Jace and Sam swung the cradles. "When my back aches," said Judith as they paused beside a shock to wipe itching sweat from their faces and necks, "I just remember last year, when there wasn't any wheat!"

Deborah laughed and nodded. "It was like the first years, when all we had was cornmeal."

As she bound the ripe grain, she thought back to all her harvests: Thos reaping that first June, with Dane joining them; the second strange harvest, with Conrad and Cobie, and again Dane had helped.

Strange, considering his absences, that he'd taken part in both reapings. Last year, there'd been none, only drought. Drought in her, as well.

Thos was dead, and Conrad. In spite of the heat, a chill ran down her spine as she bent to her work, hoping that no one's life would be exacted for this crop. Roused memories, usually forced beneath her consciousness because of their pain, took possession, compelled to think of Dane as a living man, not an impossible, rejected dream.

She had heard from him twice since that letter saying he was taking Rolf to England. Rolf! Another sealed poison burst loose. Her body felt again that tearing, that assault, and she clenched her hands, staring unseeingly at the reaped grain before her. He still owed for Conrad's death. He would pay, if he came back!

And Dane?

His letters had said that he loved her but that Sir Harry

was enfeebled from a stroke and clung to him like a child. Dane felt he couldn't leave him.

If Deborah would come to England, though, Dane would joyfully arrange her passage and Sir Harry would bless their marriage. He didn't mention Rolf.

Deborah hadn't answered. She loved Dane in a despairing, muted way, but there could be nothing between them till the war ended and Rolf was dead.

Almost two years had passed since they parted. How much nearer was she to fulfilling her debt to her family and what they'd believed in?

She'd helped scores of slaves get away to the North. Kansas had entered the Union a free state. She must help raise food and keep things together while this war went on, and for a while it would be a big task to help refugees get settled.

None of this was militant or glorious, but it had to be done. The one who sowed might not reap, but there'd always be hungry people.

She pushed away the dread of what would happen if the Confederates weren't checked in Missouri, if instead they surged into Kansas. She couldn't leave this land while it was disputed or in danger.

Ironically, she could only leave if it became safe and easy to stay. Dane would never understand that, or, rather, he couldn't accept it for the woman he loved. Not that it mattered, she thought bitterly. He was in England. By now, since she'd never responded to his letters, he might be married to a lady who'd please Sir Harry and dutifully reflect Dane's opinions. Deborah could only hope it'd bore him to distraction.

Dumping her bundle on the shock, she stretched her tired muscles, saw movement on the horizon, and shaded her eyes. Jewel peered, too.

"Rider comin', Sam! You don' think Marse Hugh—"

"He got more to do than chase us, what with both armies in his yard!" In spite of his words, Sam looked nervous. Then he threw back his shoulders and laughed. "Whoever that be, it's just one man, and one man ain't takin' us back, huh, Jace?"

"That's the plain truth." Jace grinned. "So whyn't we get on with our reapin'?"

They all went back to work, but Deborah kept glancing toward the figure, which increased in size till she could tell it was a dark gray horse and make out the rhythmic swing of the horseman's body.

She gave a little cry. It couldn't be!

But Judith, squeezing her, called out with joy. "Dane Hunter! Bless God, Deborah! Here comes your man!" She added sternly, "And this time let's not have nonsense about it from either one of you!"

For the third harvest, Dane insisted on helping, and for the third time, with the reaping finished and supper over, he asked Deborah to come with him for a talk. All that afternoon, watching him swing a scythe or bind, she'd been anticipating and dreading this moment till her nerves were stretched to screaming tautness.

When he'd swung down from Lightning, his gaze had taken Deborah in a swift embrace. He'd strode through the stubble to bring her hands to his lips. What she'd thought dead within her quivered and trembled.

He was her man, always would be, whatever had happened, whatever might. When he straightened up she saw his face was leaner, the lines were deeper-etched, but his gray eyes were the one's she'd dreamed of and which reached now to her center.

"We have a lot to say," he told Deborah after he'd greeted Judith and met the others. "But I'd like to swing a scythe again. Let me take care of Lightning and then I'll join you."

Now, in twilight, he seemed as much at a loss for words as Deborah, though his reasons must be different. What had loomed threateningly for her that afternoon was Rolf.

How could she tell Dane? How could she not? And he had to know Rolf had killed Conrad and how; he had to know that Deborah couldn't forgive that.

The only way she could keep from going into all these wretched details would be to refuse to marry Dane—if he intended to ask her again.

Her heart skipped a beat. Dear God! Supposing he were married? Or had he felt it the required, gentlemanly thing to tell her in person that he no longer loved her?

"What are you thinking?" he asked, taking her hand.

Sweet fire ran up her arm from his strong, warm fingers. It was the first time a man had touched her as a woman since Rolf—

"I—wonder why you've come."

"You do?" He laughed harshly. "Why would I come,

Deborah, except that I love you, can't get you out of myself? I would have come before, but Sir Harry's had a long, hard time of recovering."

"How is he now?"

"As well as he's likely to get. Resigned to dropping what's too much for him, except for his port, which he says he'll die sooner than give up." Dane laughed a little. "He wants me to bring you over as soon as possible."

"Dane . . ."

His fingers across her lips silenced her. "He's relieved that I want to marry and accepts that I may spend most of my time in 'the colonies,' as he still dubs your country. He's got an eager brother to take over the estate in case Rolf doesn't. But he wouldn't understand why I stopped at Fort Leavenworth on my way here and joined Major Sturgis's command."

"What?" faltered Deborah, unable to believe.

"I'm a captain in one of the volunteer regiments. Maybe you haven't heard that General Lyon has occupied Jefferson City, chased Jackson and Price's forces down to Boonville, and whipped them there. The Confederates are massing again. Lyon's collecting all the men he can—German volunteers from St. Louis, volunteers from Iowa and Kansas, regulars from Fort Riley and Leavenworth. He hopes to crush Price's army, save Missouri for the Union, and put a quick end to the war in this part of the country."

Deborah's head swam. "But you—why should you fight?"

"For my woman. For her home."

"You don't believe in war!"

"Who does except for mad dogs and profiteers?" He took her face in his hands and tilted it up. "It was one thing when you insisted on staying in the midst of turmoil, but quite another when war grips a whole country. I booked passage the day war was declared. Pretty much guessing how things would go in Missouri, I had to defend my woman." His lips were very close to hers. "Didn't I?"

"You could have tried to take me to England."

"You wouldn't have gone."

"No."

"So why try?" His voice was rough, husky. The pounding of his heart seemed to fill her so that she lost all strength. "Hell, Deborah, of course I'd rather have you out of this! But you are what you are; that must be part of why I love you."

His mouth claimed hers, achingly sweet, urging, seeking.

She melted against him, joying in the hard strength of his body, unable to get close enough.

At last, drawing back, he said with a small choking laugh, "Will you marry me now, before I join Sturgis? Or do I first have to whip the Confederate army?"

Marriage? Stiffening, happiness turning to ash, Deborah knew she couldn't refuse him without a reason. She didn't want him swearing vengeance on his brother, the vengeance she felt bound to exact if ever she had the chance. She hated to tell him the truth about Rolf, and yet she must, for he stood between them. She would kill him if she could, so how could she marry his brother?

"Rolf killed Conrad, Dane. And it was trickery—Rolf pulled a second knife! I—I was that boy who almost killed Rolf."

"They were fighting over you!"

She shook her head. "There were runaways at Friedental. Rolf and his gang were after them. He promised not to capture the slaves if Conrad fought him."

"Ah. Single combat. And to the victor went the spoils? You?"

"It wasn't like that! I—" She broke off. How could she tell him how Rolf had used her without provoking brother-murder? And in spite of everything, Dane loved Rolf.

"I can guess how it was," Dane said with a weariness worse than fury. "I can even see that it's my fault for leaving you when I knew Rolf was crazy for you."

Dane drew away from her. She'd never felt so naked and exposed, even when Rolf had plundered her. "I suppose I should apologize for carrying your lover back to England," Dane said at last. "This is why he's been eager to return, though, on my advice, Father packed him off on the Grand Tour as soon as he could travel." Deborah wasn't prepared for Dane's next words. "Do you want to marry him?"

"I'd rather die!"

A long sighing breath escaped the man looming above her in the night. "Marry me, then."

"Not when you sound as if you're asking for a prison sentence!"

His hands gripped her shoulders. "Shall I caper with joy that my betrothed gave what was promised me to my brother?"

"He forced me!" She drove the words through her teeth.

"Forced you?" Dane's hands dropped from her. He

seemed to freeze. His voice broke hoarsely. "Raped? Not just rough wooing?"

She laughed in bitter anger at the thought, and suppressed rage and humiliation came flooding back. "He killed Conrad, made me wash his blood off me, and had me by the river. He took me again that night. That's when I hoped I'd killed him." She shook her head wearily. "But I couldn't cut his throat to make sure. I'll kill him if he comes back."

Dane took her hands. "Deborah, Deborah, what can I say? Must I kill my brother?"

"I don't want you to." Moved at the anguish in his tone, she softened her own. "But you must surely see that I can't forget what happened."

"Neither can I. If I hadn't already joined a command, I'd track Rolf down. Now I can only hope someone else takes his life before I must."

Shaken at his implacable words, Deborah caught his arm. "You mustn't, Dane! That would be horrible!"

"What Rolf did was horrible. I hope our father never has to know, but if he did, though it would break his heart, he'd agree Rolf shouldn't live."

Shaken from her own grief by pity for Dane's cruel position, Deborah bowed her head. She couldn't steel herself to resist as Dane drew her close.

"Shall we be married in Lawrence?"

Her heart leaped and a frozen dead part of her seemed to warm, but then she remembered Rolf and Conrad's blood. "It's not possible, Dane—not while what Rolf did is between us."

"But that's all the more reason! My brother wronged you. If I can make some restitution, take care of you—"

How hard to close herself against the pleading of his voice, the compelling strength of his arms! Deborah longed to go limp and yield to his tenderness, marry him, have what they could. He might die in a war he'd come to for her sake. Rolf might well be killed in some European duel with a gallant as hotheaded as himself. Who knew how fate would weave the strands?

Yet she knew that if Dane had to kill his brother, or if she did, it would be a poison at the roots of their love. It might bind them together in guilt, but it couldn't be a happy union for them or for their children, not to mention the poor old frail father in England who loved both sons.

No. While Rolf lived, she must not marry Dane. But

they had waited for each other so long. . . . Shaking her head, she said slowly, "I can't marry you now, Dane. I won't! But—"

She didn't know how to say it. Taking his long, hard fingers, she moved them to her breasts. Shock passed from him to her. His fingers moved convulsively before he snatched them away.

"No! Not till you marry me!"

"But I'm no virgin. Dane, please! Let's have this, at least!"

Silence grew between them, assuming solidity. Deborah ached to reach out to him, at least touch his hand. She knew he was as tormented as she, forbore to weep or press him further. In this thing, they must respect each other's integrity. At last he shrugged with a heaviness that made the set of his head and shoulders seem suddenly old.

"I can't take you, darling, though I'd give my soul for it. A man's urge to make love before battle is nature's trick to be sure there's always someone to fight the next war. Sweet as a night with you would be, I can't risk giving you a child I might not be around to father."

"Dane—"

Gently enough, he laid his fingers on her lips. "Deborah, let's not talk about it while all we'll do is hurt each other. In spite of my pathetic words about a fatherless child, I'll use all my old cavalryman's tricks to stay alive. I'll be back." He laughed savagely. "You'd marry me, I'll bet, if I lost an arm or leg! Or had my manhood blown away!"

"Don't!"

"My God, Deborah!" Struggling with himself, he said huskily, "I'm sorry . . . sorry for both of us!"

Taking her hand, he drew her firmly along the path. "I won't lose a hair of my head more than I have to. You'll just have to take me as I am."

"And that's how you must take me."

The lights of the house shone mellow as they passed the forge, its fire banked till morning. "Truce!" said Dane. He paused in the shadows. "I've taken your kisses tonight, Deborah. Will you give me one?"

She drew his head down and kissed him with all her love and grief, longing and hope. It was he at last who put her away, turned her toward the house as if he dared not be alone with her another moment.

Jewel, Sam, and Jace had gone to bed, but the others had waited up. Even the twins were awake, and they stared a long time at Dane, and then each appropriated a knee and arm, thin, red-headed Tom watching this big stranger with wide, soft brown eyes, Lettie snuggling against him, closing a dimpled, honey-brown hand around his thumb. Though Maccabee and Laddie played with them, they missed Johnny, a father-man.

Deborah poured coffee, wryly conscious of her friends' perplexity. Instead of the wedding announcement they'd expected, they were regaled with how Alexander II had abolished serfdom and arranged for the peasants to be allotted land through communes which would repay the government over forty-nine years.

"It might work for slaves here," Dane finished. Then he went on to laugh about Sir Harry's outrage over Darwin's evolutionary theories. "In 1650 the Archbishop of Armagh calculated all the 'begats' back to 4004 B.C., and John Lightfoot of Cambridge later fixed the time of man's creation precisely at nine A.M., October 23. Father agrees with the good wife of the Bishop of Worcester. At the notion of being descended from apes, she cried, 'Let us hope it is not true, but if it is, let us pray that it will not become generally known!' "

Sara shot him a look of such mystification that Deborah announced he was joining Sturgis at Leavenworth for the push into Missouri to reinforce Lyon. After a flurry of surprised appreciation, Sara remarked wistfully, "Maybe you'll see Johnny."

"And Doc Challoner," added Judith.

They then had to explain who Doc was, and they passed a while longer in talking about the tide of black refugees pouring into a Kansas that was only slowly recovering from the terrible drought.

"When I heard Kansas had been made a state, I drank a toast to you all," said Dane. Rising, he gave Sara the now-sleeping Tom, then handed Lettie's sweet chubbiness to Deborah. "Well, ladies, you'll come through the war just as you did through Border Ruffians, freezes, and the drought."

Judith snorted. "I could do with some plain old monotonous bein' happy!"

"That'll come, too," said Dane.

His eyes met Deborah's over the child's black hair. "Good night," he said. He touched the side of both their cheeks before he turned away.

"Good night," echoed Judith, following as Deborah carried Lettie to Sara's room. "What's that mean?"

"Exactly that!" Deborah snapped. "He—I—we're not going to talk about marriage for a while."

"For sure not, him goin' off to fight them Missouri Secesh," agreed Judith. "Something's wrong here, Deborah! Man don' come back from England and join up for a war unless he's mighty interested in a woman!"

Sara tucked in the twins, then put her hand on Deborah's. "Don't pester her, Judith! It's that Rolf: trouble when he's here, and trouble when he isn't!"

Judith, with a malevolent grumble, went off to her bed, as did Deborah. But it was a long time before she slept, miserable over what she'd done, but not able to see what other course she might have taken.

She didn't know whether she should be glad or sorry that Dane meant to return to her. What could lie ahead for them but trouble?

But with all her heart she prayed he would come back.

• *xxii* •

Dane left the next morning after an early breakfast. He was waved off by the entire household. He bent from the saddle to pull Deborah up against him and give her a last kiss. He touched the chain around her neck. "Keep wearing it," he said. "I love you."

"And I love you." That, at least, could be said.

He looked at her ruefully. "If you mean that— Hell, there's a war to fight! Good-bye, Deborah." His mouth jerked crookedly. "Stay as safe as you can."

When he was lost from sight, Deborah turned back to the others. Had she been a fool, to refuse the happiness they might snatch now? But she could never, if they all lived to be a hundred, forgive Rolf for killing Conrad with that hidden knife.

That blood debt must be settled before she could live with Dane. Only now, concern for his safety overrode future worries.

Pressing her hand to the little medallion, she willed him to be protected, before she said to Jewel, Sam, and Jace, "Are you ready to move to your new home?"

Belshazzar pulled the wagon loaded with equipment, such bedding as Sara could scavenge, half a dozen chickens, and a pig. A cow, one of Venus's offspring that'd been traded to Johnny, walked behind the wagon. She was coming fresh in a few weeks and would supply milk, butter, and soft cheese.

"Pity we got no children for all that milk," Jewel said to Deborah, who was riding alongside on Chica. "If folks turn up with a baby or two and need a place, reckon we could take 'em in."

"I'll remember," said Deborah gratefully. It was beginning to look as if every available shelter was going to be needed for refugees who wanted to stay in Kansas.

Jewel wasn't dismayed at the soddy-stable's dilapidation. "Won't be hard to fix the roof. And that chicken coop in good shape." She gazed about, her face glowing. "Dandy well-house! And look at that wheat and corn all hedged in with Osage orange! Miz Deborah, we sure goin' to get this place fixed up good. You won' be sorry when you ready to take it back."

"By that time you'll have a good farm of your own," Deborah said. "There's unclaimed land on two sides of us."

Sam was standing near the fireplace, surveying the ruins of the cabin. "Some of these logs are solid," he mused, thumping them. "Fireplace jus' need a little daubin'. Be all right with you, Miz Deborah, if we build back the cabin on this same spot?"

In spite of a stab of grief for her parents, Deborah was able to say truthfully and with a smile, "That'd be one of the nicest things I can think of!"

On her way to the smithy, she detoured past Friedental to see Ansjie and ask if the village could take in more people. Ansjie, sadly missing her doctor, looking thinner and older, said she'd be glad to house a couple or several women and children, and nearly every family in the settlement agreed to house one or two fugitives. But the really important plan was the council's proposal to help those who wanted to settle permanently build homes and get started at farming.

Because of irrigating through the drought and their thrifty habit of storing food, the Friedentalers were rich compared to most Kansans who'd survived. Though they'd lived here the five years necessary for naturalized citizenship, none had taken that step because taking an oath was against their religion, so it was unlikely they'd be forced into the army even if conscription became necessary.

Such service was absolutely against their faith, and since even Prussia had let them pay a tax instead, it seemed sure that the U.S. government would provide an alternative. This meant that while most able-bodied men were going off to war and their work was either abandoned or managed as well as possible by women and children, Friedental would keep its skillful, tremendously productive farmers.

"There can be a village on the other side of the well and church," Elder Goerz explained, gesturing with calloused hands. "The *Graf* all that land bought, though used it we haven't."

"How many people could come?"

He puffed out his ruddy, bearded cheeks. "Maybe a hundred. Between twenty and thirty families, say. If it goes well—" He spread his hands, gray eyes sober. "One thing, Fräulein Whitlaw—they Mennonites need not be, though they're welcome in our church. They can have their own council and rules. But they must respect our faith."

Deborah nodded, resolving to screen candidates carefully. She never wanted the villagers to regret their offer.

She and Ansjie visited Conrad's grave together, then sat quietly for a while among the wild roses. A warm wind stirred the grass. "I seem to feel his smile here," said Ansjie.

Deborah nodded. She, too, sensed that peace. Two years had dulled the sharp edge of her guilt and loss; just as Conrad had truly predicted she'd do with her parents, she remembered their happy times more frequently than the appalling end. Still, though Conrad's gentle ghost didn't require it of her, she would never forgive Rolf.

After spending the night in Friedental, she found eight new refugees at the smithy, including three young children. After they were rested and there'd been time to talk with them and observe, Deborah took the mother with children to join Sam, Jewel, and Jace.

That left a couple and two single men who were eager

to start at Friedental. Judith escorted them to the village, but no more than three or four days ever passed before more homeless, barefoot wanderers trudged to the smithy.

One gnarled old man called Tiberius had smithing skills and stayed on, but since the smithy had to temporarily shelter whomever turned up, as soon as possible Deborah or Judith would take the people to Friedental or Topeka, where Amos Blakeman was finding homes and work for those who decided not to run farther north.

When she could be spared, Deborah, protected at least in part by her boy's clothes and Bowie, began searching for places where refugees could stay.

A number of farms, abandoned during the drought, now had water again and could produce some food between now and frost, while wheat planted this fall would yield next summer.

If the escaping slaves couldn't speedily be put in the way of feeding themselves, this could be a cruel winter that would find them wishing they'd stayed where they at least had food and a roof over their heads.

Many times she rode up to an isolated farm in time to help a woman or child struggling with a task too difficult for one, or find a woman heavy with child, or with several small ones, wondering how she could plow and get in the seed that meant food next year. These women were ready, out of desperation, if not generosity, to feed and shelter someone who could take over the heavy work and give them some sense of security and protection.

To such farms, Deborah brought a couple, sometimes with children. Other women preferred to move in with friends or go east to their families, provided someone trustworthy would keep the farm going. Two couples or three or four single people could be situated at such places, and Deborah made sure that there was a responsible leader for each caretaker group.

Deborah kept no count, but through that summer she and Judith must have settled two hundred people, including those at Friedental. And, of course, there was fodder to pull and food to preserve or dry, all the usual work of a large household.

There'd been no word from Johnny, Doc, or Dane, but from runaways and travelers they heard of the Union blockade of the Confederate coastline, shutting off munitions and supplies from abroad, and of July's Battle of Bull Run in Virginia, where Confederate General Thomas J.

Jackson's refusal to retreat gave him the name of "Stonewall," and which brought a Southern victory.

Over in Missouri, Price, with reinforcements from Arkansas, had swung ten thousand men against Lyon's six thousand and defeated them after a struggle that locked Missourian against Missourian; Texans, Louisianans, and Arkansans against Kansans, Iowans, and St. Louis Germans. Lyon, wounded several times, kept rallying his outnumbered forces till he was shot through the heart.

"If Lyon hadn't been killed, the Union would've won," growled a man whose pistols and Bowie hinted that he'd done some jayhawking. "But Sturgis from Leavenworth, he was left in command and was scared his men couldn't stand up to another charge. They'd been fightin' without anything to eat since the night before. So he ordered a retreat."

Sturgis! He was the commander Dane was with, and probably Johnny and Doc, too. How long did it take to learn if someone was killed?

Sara and Ansjie, being wives, would surely hear in time, but Deborah realized that Dane might die and she'd never know. She resolved to send him several letters in the hope that one might reach him, and ask him to be sure that she was informed if he were hurt or killed.

Sara's voice was trembling as she asked the beweaponed traveler if there'd been many men lost.

"Why, ma'am," he said, spitting at the side of the forge, "a quarter of the men were killed or wounded. Rebs lost over twelve hundred and did for over thirteen hundred of our'n. The First Kansas lost two hundred eighty-four men out of six hundred forty-four, with Company E havin' only twenty-six left out of seventy-six." He spat again. "Price and his Secesh are fixin' to take Missouri while General Frémont's bound to stop him. Both sides are recruitin' and restin' up."

"Are you going back?" Deborah asked.

One of the whiskered man's eyelids drooped in a slow wink. "Soon's I can round up a few of the boys, we're throwin' in with Jim Lane. He's gettin' his brigade together at Fort Scott. Goin' to teach them Rebs a lesson, you bet!"

When his horse's thrown shoe was nailed back on, he jogged on his way, carrying a letter to Dane that he'd promised to mail in Lawrence.

Judith stared after him, lips pursed. "Look like this war

goin' to be an excuse for lots of plain robbin' and wickedness," she said.

No one could argue. Missouri Border Ruffians might have begun the violence, but jayhawkers like Lane, Jennison, and Montgomery were just as bad. Deborah felt shame and anger that such plunderers dirtied the cause her family had died for.

Early in September a thick letter was brought to the smithy by a former volunteer of the First Kansas who'd been wounded severely enough for mustering out. Pale and hobbling, he was going home to Topeka. The women insisted that he stay overnight and rest. His shattered condition brought home the reality of Wilson's Creek. Sara and Deborah waited on him in the same fashion they hoped some woman might tend their own men.

Dane had written to Deborah and taken down Johnny's message to Sara, since Johnny couldn't write, and could read only with great difficulty. Both men were with the First Regiment but hadn't been wounded, nor had Challoner, also with the First. After Wilson's Creek they'd been sent by train to St. Louis, and now the battered command had been ordered to crush out guerrillas along the Hannibal–St. Joseph Railroad.

Dane wrote:

> General Frémont's declared Missouri under martial law. Anyone bearing arms without authority's to be court-martialed, and slaves belonging to those disloyal to the Union are to be freed. Strong medicine.
>
> Johnny surely saved my life. Lightning was shot out from under me. When I came to my senses, Johnny was standing over me fighting off a horde of Missourians. . . .

Johnny's letter, in a postscript added by Challoner, said:

> The captain don't want me sayin' so, but I got knocked endwise by this Reb swingin' his musket like a club. Would've been trampled sure's you're born, but the captain toted me off on his back.

To Deborah's relief Dane added that in addition to Johnny and Doc, who'd let her know if he had "bad luck," he'd given her address to Major Sturgis. She and Sara looked at each other across their letters.

"At least they're together," Sara murmured.

Deborah delivered Ansjie's letter the next day and listened to as much of a doctor's view of a battlefield as Challoner had felt able to share with his wife. Then she crossed the village green to the neat houses occupied by people who three and four months ago had been homeless.

Rebe had his smithy between the two settlements and left his forge to greet Deborah. "Most ever'body had a good garden this year," he reported. "Picked berries, killed lots of prairie chickens, and dried the breasts. And we've had a mighty good wheat crop and lots of corn and rye."

"Yes." Elder Goerz nodded, beaming with understandable pride. "We can feed all in the valley and send you grain for those others who need it. Also apples and vegetables. Dietrich can drive a wagon tomorrow to the smithy with these things."

In spite of her joy at Doc's letter, Ansjie was depressed at being without either of her men. When Deborah suggested that she stay for a while at the smithy, she eagerly accepted and left her chickens and house in charge of the refugees who'd been living with her. The next day the two women escorted Dietrich with a supply laden wagon back to Chaudoin's. It seemed rather hard on Dietrich, who had pined after Ansjie for so long, though he'd married Cobie Balzer's elder sister and seemed busily content. He still watched Ansjie with a certain wistfulness.

Ansjie settled in happily, taking over much of the cooking and quickly becoming a favorite of the twins because, unlike the rest of the adults, she always had time for them and liked nothing better than to cuddle one or both and sing them songs in German, or play counting rhymes and riddles which made them scream ecstatically.

"Don' know what you children mean, now that you're mixin' German with Sioux and Shawnee!" grumbled Judith as Tom was beseeching her to give him and Lettie "*ein bisschen*" of the corn fritters she was frying.

"You know!" Tom cried confidently, his big brown eyes shining. He looked so much like Thos that it was hard to be stern with him even when he needed it.

"Reckon I do." Judith grinned and gave them each a crisp bit of fritter.

The twins felt the vast importance of being two years old and "helped" till it was a constant problem not to step on them, but they brought laughter and warmth to a household beset with anxiety for its men and aiding the flow of men, women, and children who kept trudging in.

Often after supper the twins made it seem a fine idea to make molasses candy, pop corn, tell stories, or sing. Morning and its labors came too early for such evenings to be long, but they were a blessed respite.

Having settled refugees on all available places within fifteen miles, Deborah proposed one morning to venture nearer the border.

"We may not find farms that'd be safe for refugees," she agreed when her friends objected, "but such places aren't safe for lone women, either. There must be lots of them having to choose between giving up everything they've got or being easy pickings for jayhawkers or Missouri bandits, whichever comes first."

"That's surely true." Sara caught the twins in boisterous flight and cuddled them a moment. "But what can you do about it?"

"I don't know. No one thought the war would last long. Lots of men volunteered for only three months, but it begins to look as if three years will be more like it. They didn't make arrangements for their families to get along without them, and if a woman's tied down with chores and children, it's hard for her to find a better way to manage."

"Maybe some families could move in together?" asked Judith.

"Maybe. If three, four, or even two women got together, they could share childcare and get a lot more done. And where there's no one able to plow, refugee men could go around and do it in return for part of the crop. There are workers and there's land. If they're put together, maybe we can have food instead of famine." Deborah got to her feet. "Anyway, I'm going southeast for a few days. Don't worry about me. No one's interested in a scrawny red-haired boy."

Maccabee snorted. "*That* I believe, but plenty no-goods have an eye for your Chica mare!"

He was right. Deborah weighed the advantages of Chica's companionship and speed against the safety of a mount no one would covet. "I'll outrun them," she said airily, then turned.

"Hold on!" Judith planted herself firmly in the way. "You ain't gettin' close to the border by yourself alone! I'm goin'!"

"Maccabee!" Deborah appealed.

He shrugged. "This place runs to headstrong women. Judith's my wife, not my slave."

Sara turned to Ansjie. "Could you look after the children for a few days?"

Ansjie beamed. Having the twins to spoil to her heart's content would please her like nothing else except the return of her handsome doctor. "*Ja,* but—"

"We'll do the washing today," ruled Sara. "We'll bake, roast a turkey, and leave everything so that Ansjie can manage while we're away."

Deborah stared. "You can't! The twins—"

"The twins have been weaned for six months," Sara returned tartly. "Hasn't it entered your head, *meshema,* that I get tired of staying home while you and Judith gallop around the countryside?"

Now everyone stared, including the wide-eyed twins. "Let's get busy," Sara said firmly. "Laddie, before you go to the forge, bring me your dirty clothes—all of them! I hope I can still get into your trousers!"

It was still warm enough to wash outside, so boiling, scrubbing, rinsing, and wringing out went on in the backyard, while the main cabin filled with tempting smells, first of rising, then of baking bread, including Ansjie's delicious rye. Apple struddles and rhubarb pies, fragrant with steaming juices, joined the crusty loaves, and by mid-afternoon the kitchen could have passed for a bake shop.

Before supper, clean sheets were on all the beds, clean clothes were folded away, and the pantry was stocked with baking. "I have nothing to do but with the twins play!" protested Ansjie.

"By the time you feed them and three men and wayfarers, you may not play much," Sara warned. "But when we come back, we'll give you a vacation."

"Better it is to be needed!" Ansjie said with a vehemence that made Deborah realize how lost the young woman had felt without Conrad or Doc to "do" for.

Armed with Bowies and carrying enough food for five or six days, the three friends left early the next morning, rigged out in a motley assortment of masculine clothes and broad-brimmed hats.

"If you ain't enough to set dogs howlin'!" chortled Maccabee, while Tiberius, more polite, sputtered on his boiled wheat. "Lordy! Them ladies you wantin' to help may say howdy with loaded shotguns!"

"We don' all have to ride up at once," Judith pointed out coldly.

Ansjie's blue eyes were worried. "You'll careful be?"

"We'll careful be!" promised Sara, giving the twins a last hug, the daughter, so like her, cuddled close with the son, so like his father.

Stopping that noon at a farm near Lawrence where Deborah had settled refugees to help the widowed owner, they learned that Lincoln had canceled Frémont's emancipation proclamation and that Price's overwhelmingly large Confederate army was besieging a smaller federal force at Lexington, headquarters of Russell, Majors, and Waddell's freighting business, which had gone bankrupt over its Pony Express.

Sturgis's command was supposed to succor Lexington, and so was Jim Lane, but his brigade, making its way north from Fort Scott, instead of attacking Price's rear or flank, was more intent on following Lane's exhortation to clean out "everything disloyal—from a Shanghai rooster to a Durham cow."

As Lane's men stole, foraged, and burned their way north, Missouri guerrillas sacked and burned Humboldt, forty miles west of Fort Scott. The border wars were on again, more savagely than ever.

"Bad times," said the widow, juggling a baby on her hip. She was a drawn, frail woman whom Deborah remembered as dancing and gay at the Fourth of July celebration three years ago. "If guerrillas could get as far as Humboldt, they might try for Lawrence." She laughed bitterly. "My man thought our troubles were over when the drought broke and Kansas got into the Union. Now he's dead at Wilson's Creek, and what's to become of us, God only knows!"

"Gotta hang on, Missus," encouraged Jerry, the man of the couple staying with her. "We put in five acres of wheat, and there's corn for this winter and plenty of melons and squash."

"I couldn't have done it without you," the widow said. She looked at Jerry and his wife and smiled reluctantly. "All right. Maybe all of us together can pull through. For my baby's sake, I'll stick it out as long as I can." She frowned at Deborah's, Judith's, and Sara's boyish garb. "I sure hope you don't run into jayhawkers or Missouri guerrillas. One named Quantrill was fighting in Price's army, but they say it didn't suit his style and he's cut loose to rob and murder."

Quantrill again, formerly known sometimes as Charlie Hart. As the women rode southeast, stopping at farms and an occasional settlement, they heard his name often, though he couldn't have been at all the places he was rumored to be, and he was undoubtedly getting blamed for the deeds of unknown brigands, just as Lane, in Missouri, was cursed for every strayed mule or chicken.

"Don' think there be an able-bodied white man over sixteen left in this part of Kansas," observed Judith as they rode past another abandoned farm. "Wonder if it was drought or war that got this one."

They asked, as they'd been doing about unused places, at the nearest occupied farm and learned from the woman there that it had been her eldest son's before he volunteered. Widowed before she came to Kansas, she, with ten- and twelve-year-old sons, was managing her own land, but she welcomed the idea of neighbors who'd help with plowing and farm her soldier son's acres on shares.

By nightfall of the next day the friends had a list of six available farms, providing refugees were willing to live near the border. And they had matched up two households that, between them, could manage what neither could alone. There were also three women who wanted to join their parents in Ohio and Iowa if trustworthy farmers could take charge till the men came home.

"We'll go as far south as we can tomorrow," said Deborah, "and then start back. It's already been worth the trip."

Sara nodded. "It's like trying to keep things rooted in a high wind. The more you can keep the soil held down, the faster it'll heal when the storm ends."

Gazing across one forlorn deserted field with a few straggling stalks of corn, Judith shifted in her saddle. "Cain't help wonderin' how many of these men are with Lane, ruinin' folks's little farms in Missouri while the men from those farms are burnin' and robbin' here. Be a sight better if they all stayed home and tended to their plowin'."

Deborah had had the same thought. The "real" war was, for a lot of Missouri and Kansas men, a continuation of their old vendettas. "Maybe this'll thin out the hotheads and get things settled so people can get on with their lives," she said. "Shall we spend the night outside or try to find a house?"

"It's not cold," Sara said. "We can go on a ways, and if we don't find a roof, we've got the stars."

"Better'n jammin' in with a houseful like we did last night," muttered Judith. Because their hostess had been pitifully eager for them to stay, they'd shared a one-room cabin with her and her five children.

Sara giggled. "Maybe before we call out, we'd better try to look through the windows and see what we'd be spending the night with!"

An acrid odor struck Deborah's nostrils. Sniffing, she peered in the breeze's direction and saw a plume of gray-black smoke waver and swell against the scarlet sunset.

"Horses!" cried Sara.

She rode for a wooded ravine. Deborah and Judith followed, ducking low as their horses found a way through the brush and scrub oak. Reining in, they peered through the leaves as the dull thunder of hooves rolled down the slope.

Four—five—six riders, whooping and shouting. They led two horses and several of them had limp-necked chickens strung across their saddlebows. Besides pistols and knives, each had a shotgun or rifle. One flourished what looked like a woman's nightgown.

Quieting their restless horses, the women stared after the gang till they vanished over a rise, then looked at each other. Without a word, they followed the ravine as far as they could in the direction of the smoke, then glanced to see if the men had doubled back.

No sign of them. The friends rode out of the trees and down the slope, putting the horses to a lope when they reached the level ground. At the end of a long, wide valley, smoke and flames rose from a cabin.

Deborah choked down a scream, her mind flashing back to another burning cabin. A body lay by this one, too, but as they sped up and sprang from their horses, the sprawled figure stirred, shrieked, then tried to crawl away.

"We won't hurt you!" Deborah cried. "We're friends!"

"My baby," moaned the young blonde woman, dragging at her torn clothes. "Where's my baby?"

Could it be in the cabin? Sara gasped and ran for the blazing house, with Judith and Deborah beside her. It was too late to put out the fire, but if a child were inside, they'd have to get it out.

Deborah almost tripped over a small body. Sara screamed and fell to her knees.

"Good God!" gasped Judith. "Dear, good God!"

The little boy was about Tom's age. His blue eyes stared at the twilight and his neck was fixed at an angle like a broken doll's. There were livid marks on his face, as if a large hand had been clambed over it. He looked as if he'd been literally broken and then thrown away.

"She'll have to see him." Sara was trembling. "I'll carry him."

"I'll get some water," Judith said, "We can get the poor girl washed up, anyway."

Deborah ran to where the dazed woman was trying to get to her feet. Her ripped garments and marks that would later be bruises told plainer than words what had happened.

"All of them!" she mumbled through bleeding lips. "All of them . . . ! My baby! Where is he?"

She saw him in Sara's arms, then sprang to take him in her arms. "Billy!" His head jounced as she shook him. "Billy, don't be naughty!" She gazed down at his open eyes. "Billy?" she whimpered, sinking down, cradling him. "Billy!"

They let her cry and then they washed her and wrapped her in one of their blankets. Holding her dead child, now and then wracked with weeping, she told how the raiders had come while she was fixing dinner.

The leader, now a Missouri guerrilla, had quarreled with her husband over this farm five years ago, insisting he'd filed on it first. Apparently he'd nursed the grudge and had come to pay it off.

When he'd learned his old enemy was in the army, the Missourian had said he was going to make sure he had nothing to come home to.

"Billy kept screaming. They were holding him. Then I couldn't hear him anymore . . . couldn't hear anything. . . ." She rocked her child and wept.

In the flickering light of the burning cabin, the three friends looked at each other. "Let's move away from this" —Deborah motioned at the ruin—"and get her to eat and sleep." They did, helping Esther, as she said her name was, up on Chica and moving back to the sheltered ravine where they'd hidden.

Esther begged not to bury her child that night. "Let me hold him," she pleaded. "Just this last time." After she'd had some soup made from jerky and a handful of dried apples, she huddled in the bedroll they'd put together, Billy pressed close against her, their fair hair intermixed.

Deborah got to her feet. "I'm going to follow that bunch," she said. "If I'm not back by morning, take Esther on home."

"There's six of them!" cried Judith.

"I'll be careful."

"What you goin' to do?"

"Kill them if I can."

"I'm coming, too." Sara stood up and sheathed the Bowie she'd used for shredding jerky.

"No, you got the twins!" said Judith. "I'll go. Someone got to take care of Esther."

"I suppose so." Sara gave in. "But, Deborah, *must* you?"

"Yes. But I don't want either of you coming along. You've both got family."

"Well, you're *our* family!" said Judith positively.

"We may have to follow them into Missouri."

"They can't see me in the dark." Judith shrugged. "And if they get hold of us, won't matter what color we are!"

Deborah had resolved on vengeance the moment she saw the dead child. It meant desperate risk. She was ready to die, but she hadn't wanted to imperil her friends.

Still, setting out with Judith, she knew there was a better chance of coming back, and it was good not to be alone. "They got an hour-and-a-half start," speculated Judith. "Reckon we can spot their campfire?"

"That's what I hope. They'll probably cook those chickens they stole, and the smoke ought to hang in the air even after they turn in."

Judith sighed. "We sure want to wait till they're asleep."

"Yes." This wasn't going to be like the time she hadn't been able to make sure of Rolf. "Judith, can you do this?"

"I've stuck many a pig that never harmed a soul." Judith's voice was grim. "If we don' kill these devils, they're goin' to rape more women, kill more little children."

They rode in silence after that, going west, following the easiest route, as the horsemen had presumably done. Stars glittered and the night was almost balmy. Deborah ached from hours in the saddle; she shifted wearily.

The guerrillas might have made for some haven in Missouri, riding through the night. If they were stopping for supper, surely they couldn't be far off, though they might have turned in some other direction. Turning into another valley, letting the horses pick the way, Deborah stiffened.

Smoke. Of course, it might not be the raiders.

Judith touched her arm and pointed. A gleam came faintly from up ahead on their left. Riding toward it, Deborah's heart pounded and her mouth felt dry.

Six men.

Esther and Billy.

She hoped that if she and Judith were caught, they'd be killed before the raiders learned they were women. "We'd better leave the horses here," she said softly. "They might whinny. But let's tie them loose enough so that they can get away if we don't come back."

"You think of everythin'!" grunted Judith unappreciatively.

They tethered the horses and continued toward the light. Soon they could hear voices and could presently see that the raiders had camped among some trees, with their hobbled horses straying about.

Taking off their moccasins, Judith and Deborah worked up behind a thicket. One of the men, a black-bearded skinny fellow, held the white nightgown up to him and did a little shuffle.

"Guess I'll be tuckin' in, gentlemen."

Another laughed coarsely. "You ain't got the right form for it, Jim. Maybe we shoulda kept that little gal for a while. She had purty yella hair."

"She'd only been trouble, weepin' and wailin'," a huge blond man said and yawned, stretching. "We got our use outa her."

"You shouldn't of killed that kid," said Jim tossing the gown in the fire, where it smoldered, then burst into flames.

"Hell, I didn't mean to," growled the big blond man. "But he bit my hand and I jerked him harder'n I intended."

Jim retired to his bedding. So did the others, first stepping off into the bushes to relieve themselves. One came within a few feet of the two women, who scarcely breathed till he went back to the fire.

Deborah watched where each man lay down. She was glad that none were close together, and several went off among the trees. The large yellow-haired man kicked dirt over the fire and spread his blankets where the sullenly glowing coals outlined his bulky figure.

Almost at once, snoring came from several directions. They'd been drinking and should sleep heavily. Deborah was glad there were no boys in the gang. She was just afraid there'd be noise and that she and Judith would be stopped before they finished.

Getting the two men in the trees might crack twigs. They could be last. Minutes crawled. Several men shifted positions. The snoring was heavier.

Were they all asleep? An hour must have passed. Embers cast a dim glow, both a blessing and a curse. It would make it easier not to trip into someone, but if a sleeper awakened and saw them . . .

Judith touched her questioningly. Deborah pressed her hand and gave it a slight tug, unsheathing her Bowie, pointing her toward the nearest man while she moved stealthily toward the next.

He was snoring, arms flung back, mouth open. Deborah raised the Bowie as she bent low. It had a razor-sharp edge. On the whole, the light of the coals was fortunate; she could never do it fast enough in the dark to prevent an alarm.

He's asleep, she thought, *asleep, and he'll never wake up.* Then she thought of Esther and thrust the blade down and across.

Gurglings, thrashing feet. But as the women moved around the circle, no one stirred. It didn't seem real. After the second man, Deborah had to wipe her knife's bloody handle so it wouldn't slip in her fingers.

Judith had finished one. That left two in the trees and the big man near the fire. Judith started for the ones beyond the circle. Deborah moved toward the dull sheen of yellow hair.

He was lying face down, arms cradling his head. His throat was somewhat protected. He was a bull of a man. If he weren't killed at once, he could be a problem.

Blankets made it hard to aim for his side and carve forward. She drew a slow, silent breath and sent the blade into the side of his neck, thrusting forward. He grappled upward, choking, one arm knocking her sideways, though she lunged up with all her strength.

He collapsed on her, blood pumping as his arms and legs writhed. As she struggled free, gasping, there was a muffled sound in the trees.

"What—" a man yelled.

Deborah ran forward. Judith was battling one prostrate man. The other had jumped up and held a knife. Deborah remembered Johnny's teaching in her muscles and bones.

She waited for the man's attack, then turned it with the brass guard. He slashed wildly, baring his middle. Deborah thrust in and yanked the blade down and to the side. He shrieked, clutching at his belly, and took a step toward her before he fell.

"Mine's done, too," panted Judith, getting to her feet. They leaned upon each other for a moment, shuddering. "My God, Deborah! We done a terrible thing!"

"Yes. But could we let them go?"

There was no way to really bury the men, but the women dragged their bodies to a slight defile and covered them with leaves, limbs, dirt, and the bloodiest blankets.

Need in the country was too great to shrink from using what belonged to the dead raiders. Quickly bundling up clothing and weapons in usable blankets, the women unhobbled the horses, selected the best two for leading, saddled and loaded them, and let the others go. Recovering their own mounts, they rode back the way they'd come, leading the extra horses.

Sara had kept the fire going. It guided them in. They were too spent, too isolated with the horror of what they had done, to talk beyond bare facts. Sara helped them unsaddle and hobble the horses and spread out their bedding.

Esther slept with Billy. Their bright hair reminded Deborah of that of the big man. He wouldn't see the sun in the morning.

Nor would Billy. And would Esther ever be more than a trembling husk? Sara put out the fire and they all lay down. But as exhausted as she was, Deborah could, for a long time, sink no deeper than thin nightmare skimmings of sleep.

She had killed. She would do it again, under the same circumstances, yet she felt covered with blood, indelibly branded.

Was this the kind of thing Dane had feared for her, why he'd wanted to take her away? She wept but found no ease in it. She couldn't say she'd kill no more. This was the bitter cup of her time and place. How could she beg to be spared from it?

Dawn was graying when she finally slept, and she awoke at a cry from Sara.

"Esther! She's gone!"

Scrambling up, they looked about the camp but found

no sign of the woman or child. "Maybe she went back to the cabin to see if anything was left," Sara suggested,

They dressed hurriedly and almost ran the half-mile down the valley. Esther lay at the door of her charred home with Billy in her arms. They lay in blood that had streamed from her wrists, hacked by a butcher knife that lay beside them.

Sometime in the early morning she had crept here and made sure she wouldn't be separated from her child.

The friends buried them beneath an oak and made rough markers carved with their Bowies. If the father and husband came home, he might never know what had happened to his family, but that was probably best.

This was not a place where Deborah meant to send anyone.

• *xxiii* •

By silent agreement they turned toward home, leading the extra horses, which they left at farms where they were most needed, along with weapons and blankets.

"Let's keep three of the rifles," Sara urged. "I can teach you to shoot, and if we're going to make more trips like this, we'd better have them."

Trips like this?

Deborah shuddered. But Sara was right. Each kept one of the new Spencers, which had probably been "liberated" from Union regulars. Maccabee whistled when he saw them.

"That's the kind you load on Sunday and shoot all week!" He grinned, examining the tubular magazine in the butt stock that held seven of the plump, copper-cased cartridges, while another could go in the chamber. "Mi-i-ighty nice!"

That wasn't how Deborah felt about it. Though she learned to shoot competently, she hated the roar. Still, it was reassuring to have the Spencers thrust in saddle scabbards when they journeyed toward the border.

Before the first freeze the women had found places for dozens of refugees and helped a number of households combine to mutual benefit. Several times, with their rifles, they ran off scavenging guerrillas who had no taste for real fighting.

They also collected women and children who'd been burned out by raiders and found places for them to live, but never again did they come upon a raped woman or murdered child.

Generally, Southern guerrillas professed a code of chivalry and prided themselves on sparing women, though boys past childhood and old men were fair game. Nor did they worry about how the women and children would live without the food and livestock robbed from them.

During September Lexington had fallen to Price, while Lane, instead of aiding that beleaguered command, had burned Osceola, court-martialed and shot nine citizens, and captured tons of lead, kegs of powder, cartridge paper, camp equipment, and food intended for the Confederates.

In addition to military supplies, Lane plundered four hundred head of cattle, three hundred fifty horses and mules, and freed two hundred slaves. He also stole an expensive carriage, which he sent to his home in Lawrence. Three hundred of Lane's Brigade got so drunk on looted brandy that they had to be hauled out of town in wagons.

Reprimanded by his superiors for looting, Lane scolded his men for their worst excesses, but he insisted that his method was the only way to protect the border, and he began calling on President Lincoln to create a Department of Kansas and put him in command.

Union forces pursued Price and won a battle at Springfield "on the anniversary of the charge of the Light Brigade at Balaclava, October 25," wrote Dane sardonically. "We can take Price if we thrust south now, but General Hunter, replacing Frémont, has ordered us to retreat."

With the Union forces went refugees who'd been burned out by the Confederates. Hundreds of slaves joined Lane's Brigade and added to the destitute pouring into Kansas. At the end of November, Lane went back to Washington for the opening of Congress and renewed his pleas to be given command of an army with which to scourge Confederates in Missouri, Arkansas, and Indian Territory. Lincoln created this department in mid-November, but reports of

Lane's brigandage led the President to make General David Hunter the commander. In a tantrum, Lane abandoned his military career and resumed his seat in the Senate.

In January of 1862, General Ulysses Grant moved, along with a gunboat flotilla, against Confederate garrisons on the Mississippi, Cumberland, and Tennessee rivers. That winter and spring, Kansas men were in the fierce battles that raged through Kentucky, Tennessee, and Mississippi, culminating at Shiloh in April.

Later that month, Flag Officer Farragut bombarded New Orleans, which was then occupied by General Benjamin Butler, who'd later be known as "Beast" because of his treatment of Southern women sympathizers. It was Butler who declared blacks "contraband of war" and let them work on fortifications and otherwise aid the Union.

In March, the Confederate ironclad, *Virginia,* formerly the *Merrimac,* battled the Union ironclad *Monitor* for five hours, the first battle between those armored crafts. The *Virginia* had to go to Norfolk for repairs, and when that town fell early in May, Confederates burned the ironclad to keep it from being captured by the Union.

As Federals and Confederates skirmished in Missouri through that bitter winter, guerrillas terrorized the border. By spring Quantrill's name was being coupled with that of Charlie Slaughter.

Handsome, English, deadly with gun or Bowie.

Deborah's heart skipped a beat when she heard about it, then hammered till the pound of blood in her ears brought on a violent headache. It must be Rolf. The scent of blood had drawn him back.

She watched for him on her relief missions to the border, but though several times the three women forted up at threatened farms and drove off guerrillas, she saw none with that raw gold hair.

Refugee Indians from the Indian Nations added to the flow of homeless, despairing people seeking help in Kansas. Friedental built a large house and sheltered and fed blacks, Indians, and whites dispossessed till they could be squeezed in somewhere else. And all the time crops had to be planted till the harvest.

Lane finally persuaded Lincoln to let him recruit Negro troops, and by mid-August, Maccabee and Rebe had joined the Zouaves d'Afrique. Each smith's striker would now advance to smith, choosing for his striker the best of several men and boys who had been helping at the forges.

Laddie, thus promoted, argued strenuously that he should be allowed to join the army, but Sara managed to coax him into staying till he was seventeen, at least.

When he grumbled that the war would be over by then, everyone chorused, "I hope so!"

"You're goin' to look like a circus in red pantaloons," Judith grumbled to her husband.

Maccabee chortled, "You're just jealous 'cause I'm gettin' to wear real French clothes!" he teased. Though he'd be greatly missed at the smithy, no one tried to dissuade him. It was clear how much it meant to him and Rebe to fight as equals, not trail along as cooks and ostlers.

After the crushing Confederate defeat at Pea Ridge near the Arkansas-Missouri border in March of '62, in which Confederate Cherokees, Creeks, and Choctaws had taken scalps, bushwacking tactics generally replaced conventional military operations for the Confederacy, and as all available Federals were called to fight at Vicksburg, the charge of defending Kansas, Arkansas, Missouri, and the Indian Nations fell more and more on Negroes and Indians.

Dane wrote that summer that he was transferring to the newly forming Eleventh Kansas. Most of the present forces were being sent to the raging battles in Tennessee, Mississippi, and Alabama, "but I became a soldier again to protect your region," he wrote. "Deborah, *can* you remember me? It seems forever."

Johnny's letter told of the same transfer for him and Doc, of being so thirsty after one battle that men fought over water used to wash wounds, of lips and tongues so swollen and bleeding that saltpeter in the powder stung each time they bit a cartridge.

In August Lee defeated Pope at Second Bull Run and invaded Maryland in the hope of isolating Washington, but after Antietam in mid-September, Lee withdrew to Virginia. The battle had been a draw, but the French and British, who had seemed on the brink of recognizing the Confederacy and forcing mediation, now reconsidered. In November the British rejected the French proposal for intervention. This left the South without hope of foreign help.

It was also after Antietam that Lincoln issued his preliminary Emancipation which would, on January 1, 1863, free all slaves in states still in rebellion.

The Eleventh spent that winter and the spring of '63 marching, fighting, and countermarching through the muddy, when not freezing, rutted roads of northern Arkansas and southern Missouri. The women at the smithy shared letters from their men, and when they had a chance to send letters back by someone who was going through Lawrence, Ansjie, Judith, Sara, and Deborah all sat writing at the big table. Judith needed some help, but she'd learned to write in a large, clear hand and was tremendously proud of being able to "talk" to her husband.

Deborah wrote of every day life, filling up a few pages with talk of the twins, travelers, and the settlers at Friedental. She didn't mention her certainty that Rolf was back on the border and riding with Quantrill, but her heart stopped when Dane wrote that he'd heard from Sir Harry how Rolf had come back from the continent so restless that he'd almost immediately left for the United States. "He told Sir Harry he was going to Oregon," Dane's letter ran. "I can only hope he does—and that I never see him again, for if I do, I'll have to kill him."

Still praying that Dane could be spared that, Deborah never told even Sara and Judith that Charlie Slaughter, of rising infamy, was indeed Rolf.

Johnny and Doc came home in March on furlough, but Dane was near Fort Scott recovering from pneumonia. Johnny still limped from a thigh wound and needed to recuperate while he told the twins stories and marveled at how they'd grown.

Doc and Ansjie, though, insisted on driving Deborah down to Fort Scott and spent their time together while Deborah sat with Dane, reading to him and writing to Sir Harry. She was grateful to be with him but ached at his gauntness, skin stretched over bone. There was gray in his hair. She knew she had changed, too.

Her hands were calloused, her skin weathered. Her spirit felt hardened, too, tough and dry. It had been a long time since she felt like a woman. Yet she loved this man with a depth that made her earlier longing seem childish and shallow.

One day, when he seemed to be sleeping, tears slid from her eyes to the hand she was holding. He looked up at her, gently wiping away the tears with his long fingers. "Our time will come, love. As I've seen men die around me, things that were important aren't anymore. I'd hoped that on this furlough—" He gave a little shrug. "But I don't fancy being an invalid bridegroom!"

Neither of them mentioned Rolf. Also, it was firm in

Deborah's mind that before she could marry Dane, if that time ever came, she must tell him she'd killed men. But not now. Not now. Let them have this little time together. They were gentle, grateful, after separation, just to be with each other, to touch hands and smile.

When Johnny rejoined the Eleventh, Laddie was with him. "Bound and determined," Johnny explained, rubbing his stiff thigh. "Said if he couldn't come with me, he'd run off and enlist." He blew out his cheeks. "Sara cried her eyes out, but *Cesli tatanka!* The boy's seventeen!"

"Be careful!" Deborah pleaded, kissing Laddie on his smooth brown cheek in spite of his squirming. He had become a very handsome young man. *Almost as old as Thos had been when he was killed.*

"Careful!" Laddie scorned, thrusting back his dark hair. "I'm tired of bein' careful!" He grinned and was for a moment the boy she remembered. "Think I want my nephew askin' what I did in the war? Got to get some stories to tell him!" There was a swagger in his gait as he went off to mix with the veterans.

When the Eleventh left Fort Scott to join the First Division of the Army of the Frontier under the command of General Ewing, Dane kept his saddle more from willpower than strength. As he waved back at Deborah and the column faded toward the border, her tears seemed to fall inside her heart and freeze.

An echo of Conrad's voice and Boehme sounded in her. *"It can only be likened to the resurrection of the dead. There will the Love Fire rise up again in us and rekindle again our astringent, bitter and cold, dark and dead, powers and embrace us most courteously and friendly. . . ."*

She was astringent and bitter, felt cold and dead. But she must endure. And in a tiny hidden part of her deepest self, she still believed in the Love Fire.

Quantrill was back on the border, disappointed that he'd wangled only a colonel's commission during his trip to Richmond to visit President Jefferson Davis. His chief lieutenants, Bloody Bill Anderson, George Todd, and William Gregg, had managed without him during several pitched battles at Prairie Grove, Cane Hill, and Springfield, and according to rumor, they weren't particularly pleased to see him.

As battles raged that July of '63 at Gettysburg and Vicksburg and the whole length of the Mississippi fell to the Federals, Confederates in the southwest were cut off from Richmond, left to survive as best they could. Cherokees, mostly full-bloods, and Negroes fought Stand Watie's Confederate, mostly mixed-blood Cherokee, and Jo Shelby's "Iron Brigade" was serenaded to the tune of "Maryland, My Maryland":

"Jo Shelby's at your stable door;
Where's your mule,
Oh, where's your mule?"

Guerrilla ravages surged to a peak as the war shifted inexorably against the South.

Lawrence, hated as the old Free-State citadel and refuge for blacks, as well as for being the home of Jim Lane and other jayhawkers, had for months been swept with rumors that guerrillas planned to attack. General George Collamore had been elected mayor that spring and he was very anxious for his town.

He organized military companies and wangled from the military discarded Springfield muskets which were kept locked in a vacant storeroom on Massachusetts Street. For part of the summer, a squad of Federals was sent to guard Lawrence, but in August it was ordered to reinforce the border. Most Lawrence people believed that if the commanders in Kansas City felt the border in that region was sufficiently protected, then it must be.

Deborah knew from Dane's letters that Ewing was doing his best to protect the north-central border below Kansas City with troops, stationed at intervals, that patrolled back and forth. Dane had also added details about the collapse of a makeshift, a prison run by Federals in that city.

Late in June a number of women had been arrested as spies, among them three sisters of Bloody Bill Anderson and a cousin of Cole Younger's. To be separated from male prisoners, the women were housed in an old brick building and treated with all possible consideration.

"But whether a tunnel was being dug to free the prisoners or whether hogs rooting about had weakened the foundation, the walls fell in and four women were killed. Naturally, southern sympathizers are blaming the Federals, some even accusing Union soldiers of undermining the building. However that is, Bill Anderson and other guerrillas will take vengeance for their women. Be very careful, love, on your journeys near the border."

A wagonload of food was ready for distribution, and

Deborah meant to take it to a refugee farm community ten miles southeast of Lawrence, where she hadn't been since getting the people settled. She decided to stop at Lawrence for news and to buy the twins' first book as a present for their fourth birthdays next month, so she didn't wear her boy's clothes, though she tucked them under the seat along with her loaded Spencer and Bowie.

Would the war ever end? Would there ever be a time when everyone had food and shelter, their own place in which to work and live? When one could travel unarmed and not take fright when more than two or three horsemen came into view?

Sighing, Deborah got into the wagon and started the team. She was going alone. Judith was heavy with a child conceived during one of Maccabee's leaves. Sara was in her fifth month. Johnny's March furlough was going to give the twins a brother or sister. Sara had offered to come, but Deborah hadn't wanted her to risk miscarriage from jolting. Ansjie was terrified of what dangers might be on the roads, so Deborah had refused her brave, if faltering, offer.

Much of the wheat in the fields she passed as she neared Lawrence had been harvested that year by the Kirby Patent Harvester that one enterprising farmer had bought. By starting before the grain was quite ripe, he'd been able to cut most of the community's supply.

The driver sat over the bull wheel while a man with a rake pulled the grain off the platform, where it'd been dumped by the reel, and tossed it to the ground in bunches to be bound up by five to eight men scattered across the field. At day's end, the cutting stopped and the whole crew piled the wheat into shocks.

It made possible much larger crops and was certainly faster. Probably a binder would be invented next, even a shocking machine. But Deborah was glad she'd bound after a reaping man, much as harvesters had done since biblical times. Changes seemed to be coming with dizzying rapidity. She wondered if it was good for human beings to be so pressured by the speed of their inventions.

Two years ago the first daily overland coach had gone from Sacramento to St. Joseph, Missouri, in seventeen days. The transcontinental telegraph had been completed that same year, and the year before that the first oil well west of the Mississippi had been dug at Paola, in eastern Kansas, only a year after the first American well was drilled at Titusville, Pennsylvania.

Railroad building in Kansas had been stopped by the war, but it would be only a matter of time before trains thundered to all parts of the nation. The Homestead Act had gone into effect that January, giving title to settlers who stayed on their one hundred sixty acres for five years. Again, once the war ended, a flood of homeseekers was bound to cover the prairies.

She wondered how many would be Negroes, and she wondered when they'd be given the vote. January 1, the same day that the Homestead Act became law, so had the Emancipation Proclamation, declaring all slaves in rebelling states "forever free."

Slavery wasn't yet abolished, but that was bound to come. It just took so long—and so much blood, so much grief. Her whole family was dead, and every man she felt close to, from Dane to Laddie, might not come back from the army.

Usually she had no time for introspection, but the slow pace of the team going this way she'd first traveled eight years ago brought memories crowding. How much had happened since that twelve-year-old had come to the Territory! It seemed a hundred years ago; in fact, it seemed a century since she and Thos and Sara had enjoyed Rolf's Fourth of July celebration, or that last Christmas with her parents. . . .

Most of the time, as Conrad, himself now one of her gentle shades, had predicted, she was aware of her twin and parents as comforting, loving presences deep within her. She often thought of them without having to confront the horror of their deaths. But sometimes, with a stabbing wrench left throbbing with exposed pain, it all flooded back. Blinking at tears, she led her thoughts, as she had trained herself to do, from the occasion of grief to something she could do now.

On their last Christmas, her family had read *A Christmas Carol.* Would the twins be old enough for it this year? Probably, if Marley's chains were rattled with sufficient drama. If Wilmarth's had a copy, she'd ask them to save her one, but for their birthdays she'd buy them something else.

Mount Oread loomed ahead. The legislature had that year voted to locate the state university there if Lawrence would give forty acres and fifteen thousand dollars to the state. Amos Lawrence of Boston, for whom the town was named, had in 1856 donated ten thousand dollars in notes and stocks for a university, and this, with accrued interest, had secured the school, though the war was sure to delay its building. Governor Robinson's house and stone barn presently dominated the hill.

Though there hadn't been much new building, Lawrence had done better during these war years than the few preceding drought-stricken ones. Deborah drove past spacious, rubble-laid limestone, frame-and-brick dwellings between Indiana and Tennessee streets. New houses were under construction all over town, and churches were starting new buildings or improving old ones.

As she hitched the team off Massachusetts Street, she again admired Colonel Eldridge's brick mansion on Rhode Island.

He'd built the Eldridge House on the ruins of the Free-State Hotel, destroyed by Sheriff Jones in the days when Border Ruffians ran the legislature and wreaked their will on the Territory. The Eldridge House was more than a fine hotel; it was the informal capital of the state, even if Topeka was the legal one, and the whole town was full of bustle.

It had a Chamber of Commerce, a Scientific and Historical Society, and, more practically, a foundry and machine works, a saddle and harness emporium, a carriage and wagon maker, and a plant nursery. Massachusetts Street was lined with impressive two- and three-story buildings, and she couldn't resist a peek at Dalton's latest shipment of ladies' clothes before turning into the City Drug, in Babcock and Lykins' brown brick bank building.

She looked wistfully at the array of magazines, especially *Harper's* and *Knickerbocker,* but she stuck to buying a few pencils, some gargling medicine for Tiberius, who had a persistent sore throat, and some gumdrops.

At the grocer's, she bought salt and matches and remarked to Mr. Ridenour that the bridge replacing the ferry at the end of the street seemed to be nearing completion.

"Won't be long," he agreed. "If you're in town overnight, Miss Whitlaw, you ought to come to the concert. The band's going to perform with their new silver instruments on a platform down by the bridge."

"I'd like to," said Deborah, "but I've got to leave as soon as I do my trading."

She gave him one of the greenbacks Lincoln had issued

the year before. It was the first legal U.S. paper money, but Tiberius never liked accepting it for smith work and always besought that it be spent as quickly as possible "befo' the guvmint change its min'."

Collecting her change, Deborah proceeded to Wilmarth's. She would've enjoyed the band. Its members had been among the earliest Lawrence settlers, and when the Whitlaws' group arrived, she remembered singing the "Pioneer Hymn" to the band's stirring music, and how the band had played at the Fourth of July gala. Splendid that they'd finally gotten new instruments. The Kansas Conference of Methodists had been held in Lawrence that March, and the band had performed so well that Governor Robinson had headed a subscription list to buy some really fine instruments.

In Wilmarth's, she resolutely kept from examining Elizabeth Barrett Browning's *Last Poems,* Ruskin's latest essays, and Christina Rosetti's *Goblin Market,* concentrating instead on the children's books. Dickens, Tennyson, Scott, and Kingsley were too mature for them, except for *A Christmas Carol,* which she asked to be held for her till nearer Christmas.

Longfellow? Washington Irving? Alphabet books or Mother Goose? She narrowed her choice to Lear's *Book of Nonsense,* which she and Thos had roared over, and Hawthorne's *Tanglewood Tales.*

"For the twins, Miss Whitlaw?" asked the owner with a twinkle. "Well, then, buy one and I'll throw in the other."

"Oh, but—"

"But me no buts, young lady! It's a good investment, to start customers young."

He'd been a friend of her father's and clearly wanted to make the gift, so Deborah thanked him, paid for the higher-priced volume, and went out in a glow of happiness. Now the twins would have a book apiece instead of squabbling over one.

It was only when it came to wanting things for them that she was sorry most of the smithy's profits went to helping refugees and the destitute.

She followed the California trail east for a way and forked off south, then stopped under a lone hickory. She gave the horses corn to munch while she hungrily demolished bread and butter, half a jug of buttermilk, and two apples. She finished with two gumdrops, changed into her boy's clothes, slung the Bowie under her arm, and resumed her journey.

It was sunset when she drove gratefully into the stable-yard shared by the two cabins. No one came out to meet her, which was a surprise. Several pigs grunted in their pen and a few hens pecked about, but there was no other sign of life.

Then she noticed horses were in the cornfield out beyond the shocked wheat, eating the shucked heads. Seven—nine—twelve horses. When she'd last seen them, the three Negro families living here hadn't possessed even a single horse!

She gripped the lines, controlling a wave of fear. Better get the team and wagon to a safe spot, then reconnoiter on foot. She was turning the team when a black-bearded man stepped out of the stable, cradling a rifle.

"What's the hurry, sonny?"

Deborah slapped the lines against the horses. They swung with a jerk. Holding the lines with one hand, she reached for the Spencer. Two other men ran out and grabbed the horses. As she brought up the Spencer, the man's rifle blasted.

Exploding force streaked against her, spinning her around, felling her. White-hot pain seared the top of her head, but one part of her brain told her to get her knife. She reached for it.

Rough hands caught her and yanked the knife from its scabbard. "Tough little devil!" grunted her captor. Her hat had been knocked off by the gunshot, which must have glanced across her skull. Blood trickled down the side of her face and neck.

Foul breath from rotted tooth stumps added to her nausea from the wound as the black-whiskered man set his hand in her hair, dragging it upward so that she nearly fainted from pain.

"Hey, Cap!" The brigand punctuated his shout with a tug that made a headache burst out in Deborah's head. "Want this purty hair for your collection?"

The sound of steps grinding into the earth throbbed in her ears. She seemed to be floating back and forth on a rising, then receding, pulse tide of dark blood.

Was she dying? Bright hurts dimmed in the strangely restful ebb and flow. She was sinking beneath it. Deeper, deeper . . .

"So, my dear!" The familiar voice lanced through the comfortable darkness. "Still masquerading?"

She opened her eyes to look into Rolf's dark green ones. His mouth quirked downward in his tanned face. The slit of his silk-faced blue guerrilla shirt ended in a large gold satin rosette, exposing his brown chest.

With his long raw-gold hair, he looked indeed like a Viking—who didn't seem so heroic or romantic once one remembered that most Viking raids had been similar to those of border guerrillas, a plundering of unprepared, unarmed people.

Rolf waved his henchman aside, parted her hair, and explored around the wound with his fingers. "Creased, the way they sometimes do wild horses," he decided. "Whisky, on it and in you, should help."

He swung her into his arms. Her head seemed to shatter, but she pushed blindly at him, trying to writhe out of his grasp. He crushed her against him till she couldn't move her arms. Arching forward, she set her teeth into his neck.

He swore, then cuffed her so hard that her eyes watered and her head snapped back. Through a daze she heard him say softly, "You can make it as cruel or as pleasant for yourself as you choose, Deborah. But this time you're not getting away."

Mute, she lay in his arms like a trapped, hurt animal. "Bring me some rags and water," he ordered as his boots sounded on hard-packed ground and he lowered her to a shuck mattress that rustled as her weight pressed it down.

"That a purty boy, or a gal in boy's britches?" ogled the scrawny redhead, who slopped a kettle of water beside the bed and ripped up what looked to be someone's best white shirt.

"Whichever, I'm keeping it. Go help the boys unload the wagon, keep anything we can use, and dump the rest."

"What about the horses?"

"Turn 'em loose unless someone fancies horse steak for supper. Can't fool with livestock this trip, but we'll make up for it with jewelry, money, and such."

"Pretty rich are they, them nigger-thieves in Lawrence?"

Deborah sat up with a gasp. Rolf forced her down, holding her with one arm and hand while he washed her with the other. "There'll be a nice lot of light, valuable plunder," he promised. "Set the whisky over here, Jeff, and you all just keep busy outside a while."

His arm had worked her shirt down, baring her breast.

Returning with the jug, the redhead gaped and swallowed, pale eyes bulging. "Hey, Charlie, that *is* a gal!"

"Not for shares. Anyone got more of a load than he can handle, he can spill it in one of the nigger wenches in that other cabin."

"Like somethin'—different," muttered Jeff. His tongue slipped hungrily across his lips.

Rolf looked up at him. "I can fix you so the prettiest woman in the world could tease on you all night and you wouldn't care."

Grumbling, but instinctively clutching at himself, Jeff went out.

"Lawrence?" Deborah asked. "You're going there?"

"Not just us, dear heart." Enjoying the dread in her eyes, he mockingly enumerated, "When we rendezvoused on the Blackwater the night before last, there were two hundred ninety-four of us. Yesterday we picked up Captain Holt south of the Little Blue. He had one hundred four men. This morning, at the head of the Grand, fifty more joined." He laughed. "Four hundred forty-eight. Tidy little army! And since I came on with a few scouts, Quantrill may have gathered more."

Stunned by the enormity of the force, Deborah couldn't speak for a moment. "How did you get through the Union cordons?"

"After we crossed the border, we headed south, as if for Fort Scott. Anyway, you think an outpost commander with maybe a hundred men's going to chase almost four hundred fifty?"

"If you want a fight, why don't you attack Kansas City, where the army is?"

"We want revenge."

"You?" she blurted out incredulously.

"I use the word collectively, my sweet."

"But you had friends there! You—"

He shrugged. "That belongs to the time when I was so smitten with you that I tried to become an ordinary human. The border gave me back my true nature."

She shuddered at the savage glow of his eyes in the twilight. "What will you do in Lawrence?"

"Burn it. Kill every male."

"You can't! A patrol's bound to have seen you and sent for the troops."

"Maybe. But Lawrence will be ashes by the time my noble brother and his cohorts gallop in from Kansas City."

The failing light revealed the white gleam of his teeth. "Oh, yes, I know about Dane's quixotism. It seems that neither of us can escape his fate."

Tossing down the rags with which he'd cleaned her scalp and face, he tilted the whisky, washing the graze so that she flinched and gritted her teeth.

"You'll always have an extra part in your hair," he said. "An inch lower and you wouldn't be worried about Lawrence. You're lucky! Ray usually kills what he aims at."

Pulling her up, he forced several swallows of the strong whisky down her. Deborah choked and strangled. Her throat and stomach felt heated by fire.

"The—the people here! Did you hurt them?"

"Just the buck who came for us with an axe. He won't chop any more wood. The rest are in the other cabin. We told them they'll be fine if they behave, but we'll roast 'em alive if they try anything."

He pulled the shirt all the way off her shoulders, holding her in a steel grip as he nipped softly at her breasts and flicked them with his tongue. "Still beautiful," he grudged. "That hasn't changed."

"Rolf—"

He laughed in her face. "You can't bargain. When you carved up my guts, it cured the last of my romanticism. I don't want your love. Your body will do." He stripped off her shirt, dragged off her trousers and drawers, caressing her body with devouring roughness.

Deborah moaned, dizzy from her wound and the raw, stinging liquor. She tried to twist away. Rolf brought her under him, pinioning her hands with one of his, exploring her with the other, laughing excitedly, deep in his throat, at her struggles.

"I always meant to have you again," he said heavily. "Figured I'd wait till I'd had all the border fun I could, then take you off to Oregon or California. But since you're here—well, I'll just call it Providence!"

She wrenched her thighs away from his probing fingers, but he clamped a leg over her, then toyed till she was weeping with rage and shame.

"You're ungrateful," he chided. "I don't want to tear you. My God, you feel tight as a virgin!" His hateful laughter crashed in her ears. "I'll bet that fool Dane hasn't had you yet!"

Dragging her legs apart, he raised her, then thrust deep.

She felt his throbbing hardness seek and delve before he began to rut.

This time there was no knife.

He took her twice more before he slept. She was so bruised and swollen that it was agony. She chewed her lips to keep from crying out, holding onto the hope that when he drowsed, she might have a chance to get away and warn the town, twelve miles away.

Right now they'd be having that concert, cheering the band's new silver instruments. Deborah thought of the friendly, busy streets she'd walked that noon, of Reverend Cordley, Mr. Ridenour at the grocer's, and the generous owner of Wilmarth's. Trusting in the Union patrols on the border, they'd all attend the concert and go happily to bed, prouder than ever of their town, which had endured so much, yet, in spite of the war, was prospering.

Rolf had told her that the main force should be along in the night, Quantrill planned to hit the town before people were awake.

Before having her the last time, Rolf had ordered one of his men to bring food and coffee. Distraught as she was, Deborah forced herself to chew the roasted chicken and cold cornbread. She had to be as strong as possible when her chance came.

He meant to see that it didn't. After his last use of her, he tied a rope around her ankle and let her relieve herself in the dark a little way from the house, but as soon as they were inside, he tossed her on the mattress and tied her feet and hands, securing the bonds to the rawhide frame beneath the mattress.

"You can't get up without moving the whole bed," he taunted. "So you better sleep. Quantrill will have to be here by two if he aims to catch Lawrence snoring."

She shrank from his careless pat. He only laughed and lay down beside her, making the shucks whisper. "Our first night together, Deborah, but not the last. I don't love you, but you've set a fire that only you can quench."

Hating him, she tried to keep from touching him. He spread his arm over her in a claiming gesture and was almost immediately asleep.

Quantrill! *Kill every male!*

Deborah shifted her bonds, found them unyielding, chafing her wrists and ankles if she moved. Even bound,

he might have been able to do something if he hadn't tied
er to the bed!

Desperately, she tried to think of some way to get loose. Smother Rolf? Even if she could lie across his face, he'd vake up. Chew through his throat? Impossible.

She was sweaty, smeared with Rolf's odor. The coarse heet prickled her bare skin, she ached and burned from is assaults, and the top of her skull felt as if the hammer-ng blood must burst through.

Losing consciousness more from exhaustion than from lropping off to sleep, she roused at a stifled gurgling, the straining up of Rolf's body, a meaty thud, and his convul-sive collapse. His arms flung out, his legs thrashed, and he was still.

• xxiv •

A hand reached and found her, roughly reassuring. "It all right, Miz Deborah!" She couldn't identify the whisperer but thought it was Titus, the younger of the two refugees who lived here. Feeling her bonds, he sucked in his breath.

"Lordy, you do be tied! Lemme cut you loose from the bed and then I can get at them knots better."

Rolf didn't stir. As Titus worked on her ropes, a slow, muted sound began. It took her a moment to realize Rolf's blood had soaked through the mattress and was dripping on the floor. She felt a vast relief that neither she nor Dane would have to kill him.

"The others?" she asked Titus.

" 'Spect they dead by now, Miz Deborah."

The ropes fell from her wrists. She flexed and rubbed them, wincing at the quickened circulation. Then she groped at the foot of the bed for something to cover herself with, though it was too dark to see anything.

She pulled on her shirt while Titus alternately hacked

and unknotted the ropes on her ankles, still whispering. "Jes' in case they ain't quite finished out there!"

He explained that after the camp slept, two of the guerrillas had come in to have their fun with his wife and the widow of the slain man, while another stood guard over Titus, who was shoved outside.

No one paid any attention to Titus's aged grandmother, toothless and apparently senile, rocking herself in a corner.

"An' that was their plumb fatal mistake!" chuckled Titus. "They done took the butcher knives an' such, but Gran, she recollect a cleaver hung back behind the cupboard. She wait till them men busy humpin', one in the kitchen, one in the lean-to, and she plumb cave in their heads! My guard, he hear a yip like a hurt cur an' turn 'round. Gran chop off the han' with the pistol and I throttles 'im. We takes those devils' Bowies. The moon almost down. Them other six sleepin' like hogs, drunk theyselves blind last night. Gran take her cleaver an' my woman and Elzie get Bowies. They allow they can take care of that trash 'lyin' 'round where they roast our chickens, so I comes to take care of their boss and see if you alive. Thank the Lord you be!"

"Thank *you!*" Deborah bent to rub her numbed feet. "Will you see if the women are all right? We've got to get word to Lawrence! And no one better be here when Quantrill comes through."

Which could be any minute. Titus went out. Deborah found her other clothing and pulled it on.

The dripping of blood from the mattress was slower now, hesitating longer before each *plash.* Man was a fragile thing; it took so little to change him from life to inert matter.

She felt around on the floor till she located his weapons. By touch, she knew her Bowie, which Rolf must have appropriated. And here was the first beautiful one Johnny had made for her! Her heart thrilled as she ran her fingers over the designs in blade and handle. Fastening both around her waist, she drank a gourdful of water and stepped outside.

The moon was down, but it was lighter than the cabin. As she carefully approached the camp, Titus loomed. Three slighter figures materialized beside him. Deborah put out her hands to the women.

She had done what they just had, been brutalized like them. But they lived and because of a despised old black woman, ten guerrillas were dead and Lawrence might be rescued.

"I take a horse an' ride for Lawrence," Titus offered.

"We both should go," Deborah said. "Quantrill may have more scouts out. If one of us gets caught, the other may get through." She said to the women, "Better take everything you can gather up fast and get as far away from here as you can. Quantrill will be in too much of a hurry to hunt for you long."

"Bet he take time to burn our cabins," moaned Titus's wife.

"Cabins kin be built again," snorted Gran. "No way to stuff life back in your hide!"

She led the way to the cabins. Titus had already started for the horses. Deborah dragged two saddles from where they were piled near the camp, avoiding the silent bulks around the dead fire, which still had an occasional ember glow as the breeze stirred it.

As she and Titus saddled their mounts, they agreed that he'd swing to the west and she to the east, wished each other good luck, and started to warn the slumbering town.

A nightmare ride. Though she put as much weight as possible on her feet in the stirrups to ease the pressure against where Rolf had bruised her, the jolting trot, which was as fast as she dared go in the darkness, wracked her from pelvis to throbbing head. The graze wasn't serious but movement sent pain crashing through her skull.

Her gorge kept rising till she finally vomited and felt better in her stomach. Still, misery of body faded in the dread clutching at her as she strained her ears for sounds that might herald the guerrillas.

They couldn't be far behind. Even if she and Titus roused the town, its men were far outnumbered by Quantrill's. The old muskets locked in the warehouse would be pitifully outmatched by the guerrillas' arsenal. They'd have several pistols apiece, rifles, and shotguns, as well as Bowies.

It would still be a slaughter. But at least the guerrillas wouldn't have it all their own way, and if defenders had time to mass in strategic places, they might repulse Quantrill, save at least some of their lives and buildings.

She kept dozing in sheer fatigue, then was roused to a

distant rumbling in the earth. It seemed to reverberate. Dear God! Could she have let the horse lose the direction?

Thoroughly awake, she gazed about. She must have been riding for several hours. She could make out an occasional bush or tree-filled gully.

"We can go faster now," she told the horse, nudging him with her heels.

The flood of pain from her battered female parts and the head wound almost made her faint, but she bent low to the horse and urged him on.

Darkness gradually lifted. Stars began to vanish. Her ears, her heart, her whole body seemed full of that increasing, menacing thunder of many hooves.

Mists hung heavy above the Kaw. Against them, she could make out the proud march of buildings on Massachusetts Street, the Unitarian and Plymouth Congregational churches. There was no sign of Titus.

Urging her mount to top speed, she shouted as she rode past the scattered houses on the outskirts: "Quantrill! Raiders! Quantrill!"

Tossing her horse's reins over the post at the Eldridge House, she ran inside, alerted the night clerk, and ran to the kitchen to call a warning to the cook, mostly colored help, and an astounded guest descending the stairs.

"Tell everyone!" she pleaded. "Quantrill's coming! Hide or get weapons!" The night clerk was sounding a gong as she sprang to her saddle and shouted till Massachusetts Street echoed: "Quantrill! Quantrill!"

Who had the arsenal keys?

Mayor Collamore would know. She swung her horse toward his house just as two men in guerrilla shirts trotted down the street.

She tried to get out of sight behind the hotel. These must be scouts. They wouldn't want to shoot and alarm the town.

They didn't. Turning the corner, they rushed her, seizing her bridle reins. One clubbed his rifle, which smashed across her head. The world melted in a river of fiery blackness and she fell into it.

Through rising and receding flame-shot mists, she thought she heard Dane's voice, thought he held her in his arms. She tried to touch him, tried to speak, but was again enveloped in darkness.

Next time her eyes opened, she blinked, then stared at a

wallpapered ceiling she'd seen before. And she had been in this bed.

Melissa Eden's back room. Only then did Deborah remember Quantrill. Trying to sit up, she lapsed from consciousness, then revived to find Melissa bending over her.

"So you're coming around." Melissa's yellow hair was carefully coiffed, but her blue gown was smudged with soot, dirt, and blood, and her face was drawn, suddenly aged. "Here, drink some water. There's soup if you can manage it."

"Quantrill?" Deborah asked. Her voice sounded far away.

Melissa's shrug was weary. "They've burned the town, killed every man they could find, and left with all the plunder they could carry on a pack-horse apiece."

Bits of char drifted through the open window. The smell of smoke was acrid, and more than buildings burned, that was the odor of flesh—

"Horses," explained Melissa. "And lots of bodies burned in the stores and houses." She shuddered. "They tied two wounded men hand and foot and threw them in a fire. A Negro baby suffocated. They killed a father holding his small child and shot men in their wives' arms. They killed Uncle Frank, that crippled ninety-year-old Negro, and several Negro preachers. They killed—"

An explosion shook the room. "Fire getting to another supply of powder in some store," Melissa said. "That's been going on all morning."

"How—how many were killed?"

"Dozens. Scores. It'll be days before they find all the bodies. But I think we've got the wounded to shelter." Her mouth twisted. "The guerrillas didn't leave many of those. They put a dozen shots in plenty of their victims, and the thirty or so who're still living were left for dead. I have four of them here to see to, so if you want that soup—"

"Was Dane here?"

"He carried you in. One of the people you'd warned at the Eldridge House saw you in the street and dragged you into that rank growth of jimson weed north of Winthrop Street. If any raiders saw you, they must have believed you dead. Dane was with an advance squad that left Kansas City as soon as the dispatch arrived saying that Quantrill had been sighted crossing into Kansas. Dane almost rode over you."

"The army's after Quantrill?"

Again that listless shrug. "As many men as could be gotten together. Captain Coleman at Little Santa Fe got the warning almost four hours before Kansas City did, and he got together all the men he could to follow Quantrill. He and Major Plumb's force from Kansas City—oh, yes!; and Jim Lane, with about fifty farmers and men from around here—are all after Quantrill. Maybe they'll catch him. But it won't bring the dead back to life." Her voice lifted hysterically. "Why didn't Captain Pike, who saw Quantrill, at least send one of those dispatches to us? If we'd had just an hour, even half an hour! But they came while nearly everyone was asleep and had spread over the whole town before anyone realized what was happening."

"General Lane—didn't he fight?"

"He hid. And Governor Robinson stayed in his big barn. The guerrillas didn't get close to anything that looked like danger, like the ravine in the middle of town or that big cornfield out west where lots of men hid."

"Didn't *anyone* fight?"

"Those who did were killed, except for a couple of soldiers home on leave who stood off their attackers."

Deborah closed her eyes, gripped with horror. But there was no way she could shut her nostrils to the stench, or her ears to occasional screams and a steady, softer ongoing sound of weeping and mourning.

"Is there anything I can do?" she asked when, after a time, Melissa returned with a bowl of thin soup.

"Get over that knock on the head," Melissa advised, feeding her. "You could have a cracked skull and it'll be no help to anyone if you pitch over and hurt yourself."

When Deborah looked amazed at this solicitude, ungracious as it was, Melissa smiled faintly for the first time. "Dane made me promise to look after you, and I can use the pretty sum he promised quite handily, for though I saved my house by pleading impoverished widowhood, they took my jewelry, cash, clothes, and everything else of value. At least they didn't burn my furniture, which they did at most houses."

Melissa could wheedle any man who could be wheedled. It was a major part of the way she'd survived. Her smile grew ironic. "I suppose you wonder if I still want Dane. Of course I do. I always will. But I'm a realist. It's you he loves."

Deborah stared at her one-time rival. "This—is so different from when you nursed me before."

"Isn't it?" Melissa shrugged. "I hoped Rolf would smuggle you away. That might have given me a chance with Dane. But I've never wished you ill, Deborah. I envied you Dane's love, thought you a prude and prig! But I'd take care of you now even if I weren't being paid." Pausing in the doorway, she grimaced. "That helps, of course!"

"Is Reverend Cordley safe?"

"Yes. He's helping with the wounded." Melissa absently tried to rub a bloodstain from her skirt. "They're putting as many of the dead as they can in the Methodist Church, tagging them with names when they can and numbers when they can't, which is often. Most of them are so charred it's hard to guess they were ever even human."

Deborah tried to sit up but was felled by a sledging headache. "Just keep quiet," Melissa ordered. "There'll still be plenty to do when you're stronger."

That afternoon passed for Deborah between nightmare and fitful sleep. When late sunlight gilded the wall, she finally managed to sit up for the first time and grip the edge of the bed till the crashing thunder in her head subsided to a bearable level.

Shakily, she made her way to the window and leaned on the sill. Black smoke shrouded the town. Sooty fragments filled the air. All the houses beyond Melissa's had been burned, and their blackened, uneven walls stood like snagged teeth.

A woman sat in a trampled garden. She held a burned skull in her hands, talked to it, caressed and kissed it. Other women were digging in the cellar of the next house, placing charred bones in a sack.

Deborah slid to her knees, unable to stand. Melissa found her that way, scoldingly hustled her back to bed, and helped her eat a thick, tasty stew.

"Farmers have been bringing in loads of food and any clothes and bedding they can spare," Melissa said. "A good thing. Most of the food in town was destroyed."

"Is there any word about Quantrill?"

"He was burning his way south on the Fort Scott road, but when he saw the dust of the pursuing horses, he evidently started moving as fast as he could." Melissa surveyed Deborah critically. "I don't have an extra dress, but if you'll take off those awful clothes, I'll get the worst stains out so you can have them tomorrow."

With Melissa's neutral, efficient aid, Deborah took off the

dirty garments and washed herself with a small pan of water Melissa fetched.

Strange. Rolf's odor was still on her, though he'd never enter another woman. She rid herself of his smell and then, holding the thought of Dane, trying to remember the feel of him carrying her, she slept heavily till morning.

Next day the town echoed to the sound of hammering. The carpenters who hadn't been killed were making plain boxes from what lumber was left and nails salvaged from the ruins of hardware stores. There weren't enough of these boxes to go around. Fifty-three men were buried in one long trench in the burial ground west of town where Deborah's family was, and others were buried in private yards, to be moved later.

Deborah moved about in the oppressive heat, taking care of children whose mothers were distraught, or helping people search in ruins and cellars, the ravine and cornfield, for their dead.

Only three buildings still stood on Massachusetts Street. The proudly rebuilt Eldridge House was only ragged, blackened walls. Deep in some of the cellars, coals still gleamed. Over a hundred houses and buildings had been destroyed and many more were partially burned.

"I kept putting out the fires they'd start," one woman told Deborah as they searched the ravine for her husband's body. "I'd get the blaze stopped and then another bunch would ride up and set fires again. They burned all my furniture, but the house is mostly sound." Her voice broke. "Enos was real pleased we'd got it finished before winter. Oh, God, why can't we find him? Can't I even know what happened to him, have something left to bury?"

They didn't find Enos. There were several other missing ones who were never located, but as the dead were found and named, or numbered when identification was impossible, Reverend Cordley and the other ministers held burial service after service.

Loads of food, clothing, and other supplies flowed in from Leavenworth, Topeka, Wyandotte, and the farms. Elder Goerz and Dietrich brought wagons of food and bedding, and Tiberius came twice with everything from bread to tools.

He urged Deborah to come home, but she told him she had to stay till the worst part of the burying was over. He was to tell Judith and Sara that she was all right and would get back to the smithy as soon as she could. The second time he came, he brought Chica. Deborah put her face against the mare and caressed her for a long time.

Deborah didn't know if Titus had reached Lawrence, escaped, been killed, or what. There had been no word of Quantrill, either, that Sunday when survivors gathered in the Congregational Church. After the service, Deborah intended to take Chica and look for Titus and the wagon Rolf's men had captured from her. The food had probably been wasted, but she might find the twins' books.

The church filled silently with women and children, a few men. Most were dressed in whatever they'd hastily put on the morning of the raid. The women covered their heads with sun bonnets, shawls, or handkerchiefs. Deborah wore a discarded dress of Melissa's that had been found in the ragbag.

Though all the slain were not yet found, the raid had made widows of eighty women and had left two hundred fifty children fatherless. Some of the thirty wounded would almost certainly die of their injuries, and the death count was already one hundred forty, including seventeen unarmed recruits for the Fourteenth Regiment.

Lawrence's dead were not Redlegs or jayhawkers. Ironically, the two men most venomously hated by the guerrillas, Jim Lane and Governor Robinson, were both in town, but they escaped because the guerrillas were afraid to charge any place that looked as if it might conceal an ambush.

Reverend Cordley and Reverend G. C. Morse of Emporia conducted the service. Morse was the brother-in-law of young, amiable Judge Carpenter, married less than a year, who'd been shot repeatedly by the raiders and finally murdered by a shot fired into him as his wife tried to shield him with her body.

The psalm read was the seventy-ninth. In Deborah's ears, the voice was that of her father: *"Oh, God, the heathen are come into thine inheritance. They have laid Jerusalem in heaps. The dead bodies of Thy servants have they given to be meat unto the fowls of the heaven, and the flesh of Thy saints unto the beasts of the earth. Their blood have they shed like water round about Jesusalem, and there was none to bury them."*

There was no sermon, only the psalm and a prayer. Everyone was weeping. Deborah felt, rather than saw, a tall presence standing next to her. As the prayer ended, she turned to look up at Dane.

He took her hands and led her out.

Quantrill had gotten away. Federals, pursuing him in several groups, and Lane's militia, had harried him to the border. He set up a rear guard to cover his retreat, avoided an ambush on Ottawa Creek, and, once into Missouri, his force splintered and made into the brush by twos and threes and dozens.

"Some of our horses died under us," Dane muttered, burying his face in her hands. "They'd been pushed sixty-five miles without a rest. And men fell from sunstroke. But I still can't believe that devil got away!"

Charlie Slaughter hadn't. She had to tell Dane he need no longer dread meeting his brother and that her own need for justice was fulfilled, but first she let Dane tell her how, when the chase after Quantrill had to be abandoned, he'd received permission to "attend to urgent personal matters" before reporting back to Kansas City.

"And the most urgent is making you my wife," he said, the severity of his haggard face relaxing. "Deborah, let's forget what's happened and what may happen! Let's think about now!"

That was when she told him how Rolf had died, hating to watch his face. Dane was quiet for a long tme. "Poor Sir Harry!" he said at last. "He keeps wondering where Rolf is. I don't think I'll tell him Rolf's dead till you and I can go over and be there to comfort him."

"There—there's more," Deborah said, "more you have to know before you can decide if you'll marry me."

She told him of the six men, about Esther and Billy. When she finished, he took her in his arms and held her while she wept for all the deaths, and all the years, the struggle and the pain.

"Oh, my love," he murmured. "Oh, my love! That you've had to bear all this! I loved you when you were a girl playing with Bowies, but it was nothing compared to the way I love you now. Please, will you marry me?"

She couldn't speak, but she nodded and pressed his strong fingers. He swept her back into the church. As soon as Reverend Cordley was free, Dane shook his hand and said, "Sir, after this sad work, can you perform a wedding?"

A smile lit the minister's worn face. "Nothing would make me happier."

So they were married, there, then, in the church where Deborah's family had worshipped, amid the ruins of Lawrence.

Dane hired a fresh horse for himself and they searched for Titus that afternoon. They found his decomposing body knifed to death in a field north of the Fort Scott road. Quantrill's scouts must have caught him.

His family and the widow of the man killed by Rolf's squad had hidden out while Quantrill passed, pausing long enough to set fire to the cabins in a rage over his murdered advance patrol.

He'd been in a hurry, though, and the women had been able to beat out the flames before much damage was done. They had food in the cellar, had rounded up their pigs, the raiders' and Deborah's horses.

Dane had wrapped Titus in a blanket and helped the family bury him. His wife was too grief-stricken to think about the future, but his indomitable old grandmother, she of the cleaver, clutched Deborah's arm and whispered, "Send us a couple o' likely men. We have food for winter, but crops got to go in."

Deborah promised.

Her wagon had been found—the books and gumdrops and Tiberius's medicine were still wedged under the seat—so she and Dane drove it back to Lawrence, with the rented horse and Chica tethered behind.

In Lawrence, already the talk was of rebuilding. Large sums had been sent from St. Louis and other sympathetic communities.

"We're going to build back every house, every store," said Mr. Ridenour, the grocer, pausing to greet Deborah and Dane. The wheelbarrow he was pushing from his cellar still had embers glowing in the ashes, and his partner, Baker, had been so badly shot in the raid that it was doubtful that he'd live. "We'll make our town better than it ever was. When Quantrill's dead in some ditch, our churches will be full and our streets busy."

The raiders hadn't been able to demolish or open the banking Simpson brothers' safe, and with what was in it, they had reopened their bank in a flung-together wooden structure within their burned walls. Other businessmen were stocking temporary locations.

Meanwhile, those with roofs shared with the homeless. Those with extra clothes or food gave to those with none. Grief and devastation had brought together people who'd scarcely known each other before.

Restoring and holding the town had become almost a religious obligation. And Dane was able to assure the people that a permanent garrison would be stationed at Lawrence for the rest of the war. He and Johnny had already asked for and received permission to be assigned there.

As Dane and Deborah drove out of town for the smithy, she asked him to stop by her family's graves, now surrounded by the new covered trench and many separate mounds.

"I hope they can know," she said, slipping her hand into his. "Dane, when the war's over, do you want to live in England?"

He shook his head. "I've fought for this country. It's mine now. I want to know and love it in peace, Deborah, just as I want to have you. But when the war's over, won't you come to meet my father and stay with him a while?"

"Oh, gladly! Perhaps sometimes he'll visit us, see his grandchildren!"

Dane kissed her. They left the graves and drove across the prairie to where her friends waited, where the twins could have their birthday, and where new babies would be born.

"Dane," she said softly, "I hope we'll have twins, too!"

He maneuvered the team into a ravine, then stopped them under some oak trees. Springing down, he gathered her in his arms. "Well, Mrs. Hunter," he said huskily, "shall we start on that right now?"

Her lips gave him his answer.

Epilogue

By winter, Lawrence resembled a town again. Most homeowners and businessmen built larger and better structures to replace the burned ones, and Lawrence flourishes today, a shady, small city of many historic sites and homes. The state university looks down on the streets where Quantrill's raiders spread terror that August day in 1863.

Quantrill had never worked well with his lieutenants, and his power steadily declined after the Lawrence raid. He was shot May 10, 1865, in a skirmish with Federals in Kentucky and died of his wounds. Some of his gang, notably Frank and Jesse James and Cole Younger, continued as outlaws after the Civil War. Jim Lane, surprisingly, was a moderate on Reconstruction. His influence faded and he shot himself in the head in July, 1866, dying ten days later.

Great suffering came to the people of Missouri border counties through Ewing's Order Number 11, issued two days after the raid on Lawrence. All rural people, whether Union or Confederate sympathizers, had to leave their homes within fifteen days. "Loyal" residents could move to any other Missouri district or to Kansas, except for the eastern border. They would also be credited for hay and grain confiscated by the military, but the crops of Confederate sympathizers were seized or destroyed.

The motive behind this extreme measure was to erode the guerrillas' supply base and destroy their places of refuge and information. Order Number 11 accomplished this to some degree, but the suffering of the dispossessed noncombatants probably had much to do with the lawlessness that characterized that region for years after the war.

Chronology

820, March 3 — THE MISSOURI COMPROMISE. Missouri was to be admitted without restrictions on slavery, but all remaining parts of the Louisiana Purchase north of 36°30′ were to have no slavery.

1841 — Preëmption Act. The head of a family, widow, or single man over twenty-one could file a claim for 160 acres of public land and buy it at the minimum appraised price, usually $1.25 per acre. The claimant had to erect a dwelling and make proof of his settlement at the land office by swearing that: he'd never preëmpted before; didn't own 320 acres in any state or territory; hadn't settled on the land with the intent to sell it; and had made no agreement to turn the land over to anyone else. This Act wasn't superseded by the Homestead Act of 1862, at which time a settler could obtain land under both Acts.

1847 — Mormons started their trek to Utah.

1848 — Gold was discovered in California; westward rush. Butterfield stage route from St. Louis to San Francisco by way of El Paso. Alexander Majors started his first caravan over Santa Fe Trail; William Becknell had taken first wagons in 1821.

1854, May 30 — KANSAS-NEBRASKA ACT. Repealed Missouri Compromise and opened the

	Nebraska country to settlement und "squatter" or popular sovereignty Kansas and Nebraska. This led to scramble for control between pro-slaver and Free-Soil advocates.
1854	Lawrence was founded in July.
	Fall elections were stolen by "Bord Ruffians" from Missouri.
1855, June	Free-Soilers held a convention at Law rence, repudiate "Bogus" pro-slave legisl ture.
October-November	Free-Soilers held Topeka convention an drew up constitution prohibiting slaver after July 4, 1857.
	Topeka Free-State government functione in opposition to pro-slave "Bogus" gover ment based at Shawnee Mission.
1856, January	Election for state officers held unde Topeka constitution; Robinson electe governor.
1856	Increasing strife; in May, Governor Robi son and other prominent Free-Staters wer indicted for treason and arrested. Sheri Jones burned newspaper offices and th Free-State Hotel May 21.
May 24	John Brown and seven others killed fiv unarmed pro-slavery men at Pottawatomi Creek.
	Throughout the summer general war be tween factions and Territory declared i open rebellion.
	Newly elected Democratic President Jame Buchanan denounced Topeka governmen and supported Pro-slavery party.

857, July-August	Free-Staters met at Topeka and reaffirmed support of Topeka Constitution.
October-November	Pro-slavery men framed Lecompton constitution, protecting slavery in the Territory.
December	Lecompton constitution up before voters; Free-Staters refused to vote.
858, January	Lecompton constitution rejected overwhelmingly. Pro-slavery faction refused to vote.
May 19	Massacre of five unarmed Free-Staters at Marais des Cygnes.
May 21	Pike's Peak Expedition left Lawrence.
August 2	Modified Lecompton constitution was rejected.
December 20	John Brown and helpers raided Missouri and brought out fourteen slaves which were taken north and freed.
1859, May	Republicans held a convention at Osawatomie.
July	Constitutional convention at Wyandotte prepared constitution prohibiting slavery (ratified by voters in October).
	John Doy was broken out of a Missouri jail.
October	John Brown and men took Harper's Ferry, were captured.
December 2	John Brown was executed while Lincoln toured Kansas.
1860, February	Legislature abolished slavery in Kansas; Wyandotte constitution laid before Congress.

	April	Pony Express was established.
	Summer	Prolonged drought made crops almost a total failure; 30,000 settlers left Kansas and the rest were in dire want.
	December	Charlie Hart (Quantrill) enticed abolitionists into ambush at Morgan Walker's home and from then on started his career of brigandage in earnest.
1861		Last Territorial Legislature at Lawrence.
	January 29	Kansas was admitted under Wyandotte constitution; Southern states began seceding from the Union.
	April 12	Fort Sumter was bombarded by the Confederacy; April 15 Lincoln called for 75,000 volunteers.
	June	Kansas volunteers were mustered into service.
	August	Kansas troops were in the Battle of Wilson's Creek, which kept Missouri in the Union, though loss of the battle may have been a major cause of the continuing struggle in Missouri for the rest of the war.
1863		Abolition was proclaimed in all rebellious states.
	August 21	Lawrence was sacked by Quantrill.
	August 23	Ewing's Order No. 11 drove settlers out of Missouri border counties.